Vivien Brown lives in Uxbridge, on the outskirts of London, with her husband and two cats. After a career in banking and accountancy and the birth of her twin daughters, she gave up working with numbers to move into working with words and has never looked back.

🐦 @VivBrownAuthor
vivienbrownauthor.wordpress.com

No Sister of Mine

Vivien Brown

OneMoreChapter

One More Chapter
a division of HarperCollins*Publishers*
The News Building
1 London Bridge Street
London SE1 9GF

www.harpercollins.co.uk

This paperback edition 2020

First published in Great Britain in ebook format by
HarperCollins*Publishers* 2020

A catalogue record for this book
is available from the British Library

ISBN: 9780008374150

Set in Birka by Palimpsest Book Production Ltd, Falkirk
Stirlingshire

Printed and bound in Great Britain by
CPI Group (UK) Ltd, Croydon CR0 4YY

To Olivia, the latest and littlest in a long line of sisters

Prologue

EVE

I stood well back and watched my sister Sarah, standing in the rain in the enclosed courtyard at the crematorium, clutching a soggy tissue and dabbing at her eyes, pretending to cry.

She was wearing what was obviously a brand-new coat, in a thick black fabric with a fur collar. Somehow it looked out of place among the over-bright colours of the flowers which the undertakers had laid out in long regimented rows while we had been inside listening to the service. Their little white cards were all still attached, and the perfectly arranged carnations and open-mouthed lilies were bending under the weight of trapped rainwater and spilling over the sides of the baskets, while the condensation was already forming in misty layers inside the cellophane-wrapped bouquets.

I didn't approach her, preferring to stand apart and keep my distance. I don't think she noticed me anyway or, if she did, she chose to ignore me. Too busy talking in whispers and accepting kisses, the raindrops no doubt blurring her vision the same way they were blurring mine.

All the usual suspects were there, of course. Dad, head bowed, walking a pace behind Sarah all the way, his steadying hand ever present on her back. Sarah's teenaged daughter, Janey, ramrod straight and stony-faced, desperately trying to be brave, the tiny beginnings of a pregnancy bump just starting to push the buttons of her tight-fitting jacket apart. Josh's parents, leaning into each other as if they were holding each other up, which they probably were, the devastation mapped into lines across their cold grey faces, the sudden loss of their only son something they would probably never come to terms with, let alone understand.

Josh's work colleagues had turned out too. They stuck together, a good dozen or more, the women young and teary and hugging each other; the men, easy to spot in their typical bankers' suits, mumbling quietly and shaking their heads, and more than likely waiting for the moment when they could move on to the beer and buffet Sarah had laid on for after. I couldn't help but wonder who was manning the tills at the bank, or if they'd somehow managed to close it for the afternoon. Or which one of them was *her*.

For the last half an hour, I'd sat at the back of the chapel, listening to the priest and the readings and the music, my gaze fixed on the polished wood of the coffin, trying not to think of him lying there inside it in the dark. Mouthing my way silently through the hymns, turning the single white rose over and over between my fingers until a crushed petal detached itself and fluttered to the floor. It looked a bit like a feather lying down there in the dust, surrounded by the shuffling of all those shiny black shoes. Isn't that what they say happens when someone dies? A little white feather turns up, like a reminder, a gift from an angel. But Josh was no angel, was he? He was just a man, an ordinary man. A man who should have been mine ... only now he never would be.

Josh was hers – my sister, Sarah's. In life, and in death. Next of kin, wife, executor, widow, mother of his child ... you name it, and she was it. Legally, anyway. She would be the one opening the cards, reading the messages, sorting through his papers, his bank account, his clothes. Little bits of him would live on in her home, lingering in the photos on the shelf above the fireplace, ingrained in the furniture they chose together, remembered in the mug he had used, echoed in the features of that tiny future grandchild he would never meet. I wished I could have had those things, but I couldn't. Not then. Not now. Not ever.

But there was no point in being jealous of Sarah. They had shared a house, a bed, but that part of their lives was already over. She had let him go. She didn't love him. He wasn't etched in her heart, the way he was in mine, and still is, embedded so deeply I don't think the bleeding will ever stop.

She didn't make him happy. I might have been able to accept the way things were if she had made him happy. But now it was too late. He was gone. Ashes to ashes, dust to dust. There was no changing things now, no going back. And, for that, I didn't think I could ever forgive her.

SARAH

Eve was skulking in the shadows, too ashamed to step forward and show her face.

I'd seen that dress before, of course, at our mother's funeral. I assumed it had been shoved away in the back of her wardrobe after that and now it had been dragged out again for the occasion, just like Dad's old black tie. It wasn't as if the dress was new in the first place. I remember being with her when she bought it, in a charity shop. A fiver well spent, she'd said. Black will always come in handy. Handy! Couldn't she make more effort? Had she no respect? But then, what did I expect from someone like her? Would-be home wreckers aren't interested in finding something new, are they? They're more than happy to take what isn't theirs, pick it up, use it from time to time and drop it back down again when they've finished with it. Unable to make up their minds what it is they want. Dresses. Husbands. To the Eves of the world, what's the difference?

I wanted to forgive her, be the better woman, show her there were no hard feelings. But how was I ever meant to manage that? Josh was my husband, my life, and she had sullied that, wrecked us beyond repair. Didn't she know how what she had done – what *they* had done – would alter things, that nothing could ever be quite the same after that?

The rain was tipping down on the day of the funeral, sliding down into my collar, seeping through my shoes. It seemed fitting somehow, a cloud of gloom hanging over the proceedings, and nothing to lift the misery. And there she was, my big sister, an onlooker hovering on the edges, as if she didn't really belong. Like the policeman in crime stories on TV who turns up uninvited at the church looking for clues, watching the mourners come and go, hoping the murderer is suddenly going to show himself and everything will be solved.

I didn't know why she'd come, or what she wanted. Nobody leapt forward to greet her. Not even Dad. Half the people there probably didn't even realise who she was. Nothing was solved, or resolved, by her presence. I turned away, kept close to Janey, concentrated on staying strong for her, and tried not to cry again, in case I wasn't able to stop.

There was a wisp of smoke rising from the chimney behind us. Someone else, from an earlier ceremony, enclosed in a wooden box, being fed to the flames. I closed my eyes, saw the car again, felt that intense overwhelming heat and clenched my fists, my hands still blistered and sore inside my thick black gloves, as I fought back the panic. It was over. The accident. The fire. The fear. I had to remind myself of that. There was nothing I could do to change things now. I was still here. I had survived. And Josh was gone.

I couldn't bring myself to look at Eve, or to speak to her. Perhaps if she had made the first move ... but she didn't, and by the time we all climbed back into the waiting cars she had disappeared. No card, no condolences, no apologies. She hadn't even brought flowers.

Chapter 1

EVE

Twenty years earlier

Sarah didn't want me to go. She stood between our parents on the station platform at Paddington, white-faced and silent, as I hauled my case up onto the train, and just stared at me, as if she needed to memorise my face because she might never see it again.

'I'll be back at Christmas,' I said, as nonchalantly as a scared eighteen-year-old can. 'Time will fly, you'll see.'

By the time Mum had leaned in through the open window and wrapped her arms so tightly around my neck that I thought for a minute she might actually strangle me, and Dad had patted me on the head like a puppy and slipped a twenty-pound note into my hand, the train was starting to move and Sarah and I never did get a proper goodbye.

I stayed there at the window for as long as I could, watching my family waving as they got smaller and smaller, and then suddenly they were gone. All I could see was the arc of the carriages following on behind, and other faces at other windows, all slowly retreating back inside the train.

It must have been the trickle of wind blowing into my face that made my eyes water; nothing else. This was the day I had been dreaming of, and the last thing I was about to do was cry. I was a big girl now, an adult at last, heading towards university miles away from home, my first grown-up adventure … and I could hardly wait!

I bumped my way along the aisle, half carrying and half dragging my battered old case behind me, until I found an empty seat that took my fancy, in the middle of a carriage and next to a window. Forward-facing, obviously. If there was one thing this journey symbolised for me, it was moving on, pushing forward, not looking back.

It had been a difficult summer. No, difficult was not a strong enough word. It had been horrible, traumatic, frightening. There had been a boy. Arnie O'Connor, his name was. Nothing special to look at, with his skinny legs and black-rimmed glasses, and a spattering of angry spots, but he was filled with self-assurance and a level of confidence totally at odds with all of that. He knew what he wanted, and what he wanted had turned out to be me.

We'd come out of a party, quite late, a gang of us, full of the joys of no more school, a whole summer ahead of us with no homework, no revision, no having to get up early, and I was tottering a bit, not quite used to so much wine.

'Come on, Eve, I'll look after you,' he'd said, oozing caring and charm and concern, his voice almost as slurred as mine.

He let me hold on to his arm as the cold night air hit me and all our friends slowly disappeared off in different directions into the night. I think I was giggling, but I have no idea what about. We stopped somewhere in the shadow of a big overhanging hedge, and I let him kiss me, properly kiss me, with tongues and beery breath and all ...

As the train rumbled and rocked along, I couldn't stop the pictures from forming, the memories sweeping over me until I felt like I might be sick. The kiss I had thought I wanted turning into something else. Arnie turned into something else. Something dark and cruel and nasty. Something I didn't want at all. He must have heard my protests, but he chose not to listen. His mouth locked over mine, hard, wet, stopping me from saying no, from crying out. His hands, pressing, pushing, squeezing. His body, heavy, insistent, forcing me down, further into the shadows ...

My eyes flew open, my brain struggling to push it all away and focus on the here and now. I took a few big deep breaths, and unclenched my fists, where my nails were making painful indents into my palms. No, I was not going to be sick, in public, on a train. I was not going to cry, or panic, or let this thing beat me.

Perhaps I should have told someone. Had I done the right thing by keeping it all to myself? I might have felt better if I had reported him, shown the world what he was. But reported him for what? Because I had managed to fight him off, hadn't I? His fingers had forced their way inside me, but nothing else had. So, it wasn't rape. Attempted, maybe. Or assault. But not the real, life-changing full-on rape it could so easily have turned into. It had stopped short of that, thank God, although only just ...

Still, I couldn't help that nagging feeling, somewhere at the back of my mind, that it was probably my own fault. I had drunk too much, and I'd let him kiss me. Kissed him back. How would that look, or sound, once the police got hold of it, or the courts? That I had wanted it, that I had led him on?

My friend Lucy was the only person I told. Sex, especially shameful drunken sex, whether I had instigated it or not, just wasn't the sort of thing I could ever talk to my parents about, so I had kept my head down, hidden away in my room the next day, cried in silence, pretended to sleep. But Lucy was different. We talked about things. Everything. Always had, since primary school. She had taken one look at me and knew something was wrong, pestering at me like a dog with a bone, until she wheedled it out of me. And then she had tried to convince me that it had just been a boy trying it on. A boy too full of himself, and too full of booze, with a stupid sense of entitlement, and not knowing when to stop. It was her way of trying to make me feel better, but she hadn't been there, hadn't experienced what I had. The fear, the panic, the sheer unexpected violence I had been so powerless to prevent. And she was wrong. It wasn't that he didn't know when to stop. It was that he'd had no intention of stopping at all ...

'They're not all like that,' she'd said, really not understanding at all, her eyes taking on a sort of dreamy glow as she pushed my ordeal aside and returned to her favourite subject. 'Take my Robert, for instance.'

To be honest, I'd rather not. She was welcome to him. Talk about boring.

I didn't show her the bruises. Despite all her supposedly wise words, men were still just as much a mystery to her as they were to me. Her Robert hadn't even got to second base yet. If he even knew where it was. But Arnie ...

No! No more Arnie. I was getting away, to a different town, a different country, and putting some much-needed distance between my old life and the new. Arnie was gone, and every mile I travelled took me further away from him. With luck, I would never have to see him again.

University was to be my fresh start, and I was looking forward to it, albeit in a slightly wobbly, nervous sort of way. I would miss Sarah though. She could be annoying at times but, as younger sisters went, she wasn't so bad really. I could imagine her now, wiping her sleeve across her nose the way she always did when she was upset, while at the same time rooting around for any make-up I might have left behind and rearranging the bedroom that, apart from on my occasional visits home, she would no longer have to share. I smiled to myself, knowing she would soon settle into a new routine and make the most of things the way they were, just as I would. And, as I'd told her at the station, it wouldn't be long until we'd be together again at Christmas.

The train wasn't full. Nobody had come to sit beside me, or opposite, so I had four seats and a table all to myself. I slipped out of my shoes and stretched my legs out in front of me, put my book down on the empty seat beside me and threw my coat across the two in front. Nestling back into the contours of the seat, I watched the buildings slip past, warehouses and tower blocks giving way to rows of back gardens, then to smaller villages with cottages and churches and occasional barns, and finally to acres and acres of green tree-lined fields. The further from London I went, the more cocooned and surprisingly calm I started to feel, as if I was encased in a little see-through bubble where nothing, and nobody, could touch me.

Time slipped by, just like the landscape, and I started to feel hungry. Mum had packed me a lunch. I could smell the egg in the sandwiches as soon as I pulled them from my shoulder bag and opened up the foil-wrapped package. I spread it out flat across the table to reveal the contents, shining up the big fat tomato by rubbing it on my sleeve, pulling the slices of bread apart then sprinkling the contents with the tiny packet of salt she'd obviously kept back from one of those shake-your-own crisp packets.

There was something a bit sad about this being the last meal Mum would be preparing for me for quite a while. Who knew what I would be eating once I had to take care of cooking for myself? And I realised that she had probably eaten a whole bag of tasteless plain crisps just so she could save the salt for me. I rubbed my fingers over my eyes to wipe away the beginnings of a tear, forgetting about the salt and making them sting even more.

I was just eating the last mouthful and folding up the foil to keep, in case I might need it again, when the train started to slow down. Several passengers were getting up and grabbing for their bags, bending to peer out to see if it might be raining outside before deciding whether to wear or carry their coats, and starting to make their way towards the exits. The train slid into a station and jolted to a halt, and I turned my attention to the platform that teemed with busyness outside the window.

The girl who climbed on board and made a beeline for one of the seats in front of me was about my age, small and slim, her hair as fair as mine was dark. 'Do you mind?' she said, edging my coat aside and plonking her stuff down anyway.

I shook my head. 'It's a free country,' I said.

'Is it?' She laughed. 'Tell that to the rail company. The price I've just had to pay for my ticket! Anyone would think us students were made of money.'

'You're a student?' I asked as the train moved off again and a pile of heavy reference books slid out of the open bag she'd balanced on her lap, and landed on the floor with a thud.

'Yeah, second year at Brydon,' she said, bending to retrieve them. 'Just heading back after the hols. Lectures don't kick off for another week, but I want to get settled back in, make sure nobody's taken over my room or nicked my boyfriend while I've been away. You?'

'I'm going there too. Starting my first year.'

'A fresher, eh? What are you studying?'

'English.'

'Yuck! All that Shakespeare and stuff. I'm more of a science girl myself. Never happier than when I've got a test tube in my hand. Well, that's not strictly true, of course. A vodka and orange is probably top of the list. Or a man! Anyway, if you're anything like I was this time last year, you'll feel a bit like a fish out of water for a while. It's a big campus, lots going on, but you'll soon get your bearings. God, what is that awful pong?'

'Oh, sorry. Probably my egg sandwiches. But I've eaten them now, don't worry. Maybe we could open the window a bit, let some fresh air in?'

'No, you're all right. It's chilly out there, and wet! So, what's your name? I'm Beth, by the way. Beth Carter. Well, Elizabeth really, but no one calls me that anymore except my mum and dad. And that's usually only when I'm in the doghouse for something!'

'And I'm Eve.' I laughed. 'Eve Peters. Which can't really be shortened to anything much.'

'Eve! I don't suppose you've got an apple in that bag of yours, have you?'

I'd heard it all before, of course. The silly Adam and Eve jokes about serpents, and walking around the garden naked, and having kids trying to count my ribs. But I laughed anyway.

'I did, but I've eaten it.'

'Shame. I'm bloody starving! Anyway, you can stick with me if you like, when we get off the train. Share a taxi, keep the costs down, unless you were planning on getting the bus. It's cheaper but I wouldn't recommend it. Takes ages, and you still have a bit of a trek at the other end. If we arrive together I can show you the ropes maybe. Well, where to report in and all that. Might make it seem a bit less daunting.'

'I'd like that. Thanks. Do you live on campus?'

'No. House share, not far away, but you won't be putting

me out, if that's what's bothering you. I was heading straight to uni anyway, to meet up with friends and see what my Lenny's been getting up to without me.'

'Lenny?'

'Boyfriend. A local lad. Works in the uni shop, part time, in between helping out on his dad's farm. He did come and visit me at home a while back, but I haven't seen him for a few weeks now. Long summer break, and all that. Not that I keep him on a lead, but you know ...'

I nodded and tried to make out that I did indeed know, but obviously I didn't. Leads were just for dogs where I came from, and boys were very definitely off the agenda, as far as I was concerned.

We settled into an easy silence. I picked up my book and Beth disappeared behind the pages of a glossy magazine. Bristol came and went, and with it more passengers, but none of them tried to join us.

'Not long now,' Beth said after a while, putting her magazine down, squeezing around the table to sit in the empty seat beside me and pointing vaguely out of the window. 'Rain's stopped. Tunnel ahead. Time to say goodbye to good old England, Evie Peevie. You'll soon be entering the land of the dragons. And sheep. Passports at the ready!' She giggled. 'Oh, and I do hope you like leeks, and lots of cheese on toast, because the Welsh hardly eat anything else, you know!'

Chapter 2

SARAH

It felt strange that first night, lying in the dark and not hearing her breathe. For as long as I could remember I had shared a room with my big sister Eve and, despite my initial excitement at having all that extra space to myself, to be honest I would rather have had her still there. I missed her clothes, both clean and dirty, dropped haphazardly in messy piles all over the carpet, the smell of her body lotions and sprays hanging in the air, and knowing there was always a secret stash of vodka tucked in behind her T-shirts in the wardrobe which, if she wanted me to keep quiet, I would be allowed to sip from time to time.

Mum had been in a tidying and cleaning frenzy all afternoon. I'd sat on my bed, half reading a book, half watching her as she flicked a duster around in places she had been unable to access for months, and shoved the long hose attachment of the hoover into all the nooks and crannies under both our beds, dragging out a mucky plate and a couple of odd socks and dislodging an enormous spider in the process.

I think she just needed something to do. Like me, she was going to find Eve's absence a bit odd at first. She even inadvertently laid four places at the table for dinner that night and Dad had to eat a double portion of pie, while I no longer had anyone to share clearing-away or washing-up duties with and had to do it all myself. Being a family of three was something we were all going to have to adjust to – until Christmas anyway.

It had taken me a long time to get to sleep that first night, and yet I woke up earlier than ever. I could hear the birds chirping away in the tree outside the window, and later the rattle of the letterbox that signalled the arrival of Dad's newspaper, courtesy of Jenny Harper, a girl from my class at school, who had bagged herself a paper round when she was thirteen and was still doing it every morning, whatever the weather, two years later. Rather her than me.

Eve's big fluffy red dressing gown was still hanging on the left-hand hook on the back of the bedroom door. Too big and bulky to lug all the way to Wales, that had been the general consensus, and it wasn't as if she'd have to cover up and go wandering about the corridors at night anyway, because she'd told me she had a small shower and toilet of her own in a little cubicle in the corner of her university room. I peered at the gown hanging beside my slightly smaller pink one, and decided, then and there, to swap them over. Why shouldn't I have the left-hand peg for a change? These things didn't have to be written in stone. The room was mine now. I could put my things wherever I chose. I climbed out of bed and did it, feeling strangely rebellious, but somehow they didn't look right that way round. I lay back against my pillow and stared at them, the two dressing gowns, mine on the left and hers on the right, all back to front, and knew that was exactly how my life was starting to feel. Changed. Back to front. And I didn't like it, not one little bit.

'You getting up, Love?' Mum called from the bottom of the stairs. 'Only, I think Buster could do with a bit of a walk before school, don't you?'

That was another thing. Buster, who, despite Mum's obviously rhetorical question, we all knew needed a walk *every* morning. It had always been something Eve and I took turns over, or did together sometimes if we were both up and about and fancied a chat. But although we all loved him and he was as much a part of the family as any of us, he was Eve's dog really. She was the one who had begged and pleaded to get a puppy, and he'd arrived on her eleventh birthday, with a big bow around his neck and so excited he'd promptly made a puddle on the carpet at her feet. Now she'd gone I supposed the walking duties, just like the kitchen ones, were going to revert very definitely to me alone.

'Coming!'

I got up and pulled on my old jogging bottoms and a pair of trainers, leaving my pyjama top on to save dirtying up a T-shirt, and after a quick visit to the loo, ran down to grab my coat and Buster's lead. 'Come on, you little tinker,' I said, rubbing the old mongrel's wiry neck. 'Your lamp post awaits.'

Buster wasn't as quick on his feet as he used to be, and tended to amble along the pavements sniffing into corners, as if he had all the time in the world, rather than run about chasing anything that moved, the way he once had. He was seven and a bit. Was that old, for a dog? I didn't think it was, but Buster clearly had other ideas, and would not be hurried, no matter how late for school I might be, or how heavy the rain. Luckily, I wasn't late that day, and the sun was out and looking like it was there to stay, so I let him have his way, the lead hanging slackly between us as we did our usual once round the block, stopping at all seventeen trees and all twelve lamp posts. A creature of habit, our Buster!

I couldn't help my mind wandering as we walked, wondering where Eve was now and what she might be doing. Still asleep, knowing her, although a small unfamiliar bed and the uncertainties of life in a totally new place, surrounded by strangers, would have kept me awake, I was sure. But then Eve, at two and a half years older than me, was always more confident and more adaptable than I would ever be, or at least that was the way it seemed from where I was standing. She had absolutely shone in the end-of-term sixth-form production of *Romeo and Juliet*, her poetry was all over the library walls, and her exam results had won her one of the silver cups the school gave out at the end of every year. And yet, university would be the making of her. I'd heard Dad say that, with pride brimming over in his voice. As if she wasn't pretty much perfectly made already. A flicker of jealousy had run through me when I'd heard that, knowing that she was his blue-eyed girl, the one destined to go far, and that, for now anyway, with another year at school, or maybe as many as three, to negotiate, I was still a kid. Just predictable, plod-along Sarah, washer-upper and dog walker extraordinaire, with dubious potential and not a poetic bone in my body.

'Come on, Boy.' Buster looked up in surprise as I tugged at his lead and tried to head for home. His big brown eyes gave me one of his *not yet* looks as he lifted his leg at a ridiculously high angle and peed, long and strong, against a tree. One final sniff, his nose twitching with interest at his own urine as it ran, stream-like, towards the road, and we were off.

'Weetabix or cornflakes?' Mum said, pulling the milk bottle from the fridge as we came back in through the back door. 'I can't do you any toast this morning, I'm afraid. We've run out of bread. I used the last of it doing your sister's sandwiches for the train. And there's only one egg left, which your father's bound to want.'

'I don't even like Weetabix,' I mumbled, letting the dog off his lead and running upstairs to get my uniform on. Last on the list again, I thought, as I slipped out of my pyjama top, grabbed a clean blouse and stepped into the pleated navy school skirt that had once been Eve's. Only offered what scraps were left when everybody else had had first pick.

'Cornflakes it will have to be then,' Mum said, as if there had been no gap in our conversation, and throwing the last of Friday's cold sausages to Buster, as I arrived back at the table. 'Either that or starve ...'

Faced with a choice like that, there was only one thing I could do, I suppose, so I ate up, making sure I sprinkled the tasteless little own-brand flakes with enough sugar to power me with energy for the day, or at least to set my teeth on the fast track towards my next filling, and quickly left for school.

I hated wearing a tie. Well, what self-respecting teenager

wants to dress like an office worker? And a male one, at that? I hitched my skirt up a few inches higher and rolled the waistband under, pulled a lip gloss and mirror from my blazer pocket and tried to make my lips look at least half kissable. Paul Jacobs might be on the bus today. He'd only joined our class at the start of term, having just moved to the area, and all the girls had their sights set on him.

Paul was tall and dark and quiet, in an appealingly mysterious sort of way, and I was determined to get him to notice me. I just hadn't expected to do it in quite such a spectacular way. The step must have been slippery, that's all I can say. From someone spilling a drink, probably. Either that or one of the other girls had deliberately stuck out a foot or a bag or something. Why else would I have tripped and ended up on my face on the floor of the bus with what felt like a hundred eyes looking down at me and the sound of the sniggers ringing in my embarrassingly red ears? Even Tilly, who lived next door and was supposed to be my best friend, was laughing.

The hand that reached out and helped me up was warm, its fingers firm as they gripped and tugged me to my feet. In the fleeting moment before I regained my balance and looked up into the eyes that went with it, I hoped beyond all hope that the hand might belong to Paul Jacobs, and that he would guide me to a seat and fuss over me and sit next to me all the way to school. It didn't. The hand was Colin Grant's, a fat kid from a year below me and, as unlikely rescuing heroes went, he looked just as awkward and red in the face as I must have done.

'You okay?' he muttered.

'Think so,' I muttered back.

And then we moved down the bus quickly, heading for separate seats, aware of the queue forming behind us in the aisle, and I spent the rest of the journey nursing a sore knee and refusing to look up at all, even to talk to Tilly who had plonked herself down next to me, just in case Paul was there somewhere on the bus and laughing at me. It would take more than a bit of lip gloss to help me recover from a setback like that, I realised. In fact, I might as well just give up right there and then and let one of the other girls have him. And it was double English first thing. The day could hardly get any worse!

Chapter 3

EVE

That first Christmas seemed to take forever to arrive. Settling into university was a weird experience, a mixture of excitement and boredom and, at times, sheer terror.

My home for the next year, maybe longer if I decided not to move off-campus as so many second years seemed to do, was to be a room at the far end of a short hallway, on the top floor of a concrete block called Perseus, but known to students only as P. It was tucked away at the edge of the campus with a view, partially blocked by a line of tall spindly trees, over open fields. I would be sharing a very plain and functional kitchen and a small white-tiled bathroom, for those times when a shower just wasn't enough, with five other girls. We'd tentatively introduced ourselves as each arrived, plonking cases down, unopened, in our rooms and then congregating in the kitchen, where we unloaded assorted mugs and new sets of cheap cutlery and favourite plates from home, and emptied carrier bags that clattered with tins of soup and beans.

'Hi, I'm Eve.'

'Jodie.' Jodie was tall and thin, with long hair that could have done with a brush, and slightly crooked teeth.

Ruth came next. She was small and mouse-like but was wearing very high, very red shoes that pointed out beneath a pair of ordinary holey-kneed jeans. Odd.

'And I'm Fran.' Fran had darker skin than the others and shiny, almost black, hair, utterly unlike her rather pale, balding father who was dropping her off and insisted on coming right inside to check us all out. Fran had a touch of Spanish blood, I decided, with no evidence at all to back up my totally unsubstantiated theory. I was sure I'd find out soon enough, and sure enough I did when her Portuguese mother and two younger sisters turned up in a car the next day delivering enormous boxes of kitchen equipment which they seemed convinced their Francesca would not be able to live without.

The next girl to arrive that first day was Lauren, who tripped as she came through the door, but didn't laugh it off the way I probably would have done. She just looked scared, and pale. She reminded me of my sister, the way I'd last seen her, looking all forlorn at the station and in need of some serious mothering, and I couldn't quite decide if that was a good thing or not.

'Sorry, am I last to the party?' A big ungainly girl – horsey, as Mum would undoubtedly have described her – strode in as it started to get dark outside and pumped everyone's hands up and down as if she was expecting water to come running out down our arms. 'I'm Suzanne. Stupid name. Just call me Annie.'

There was much smiling and nodding, a few basic questions about home towns and family, most of the answers to which I was sure I would forget, and the awkward unfamiliarity of half-hearted hugs with strangers. Fran's father beat a hasty retreat and we all propped our doors open so we could stay connected and carry on talking, or shouting more like, as we unpacked. From my room I could hear Annie's feet thump across the hall as she went to help Fran open a tricky lock on one of her bags, and Ruth making coffee and unwrapping a cake her mum had made and asking if anyone would like a slice.

Within a day or two the initial wariness had worn off and we had become friends of a sort, despite probably having very little in common beyond finding ourselves at the same place at the same time, and all of us feeling more than a little out of our depth.

It didn't take long to sort out who would have use of each shelf in the cupboards and how to divide up space in the two enormous fridge freezers, and where the washing machines were, once Fran had found them in another building a good five minutes' walk away. We'd meet up in the kitchen sometimes and have a chat, maybe share a packet of biscuits but, beyond that, I spent a lot of time alone, lying on the narrow bed in my own room, listening to music, poring over leaflets for way too many clubs and societies I knew I would never join, and trying to make sense of the map of the campus and the notes I'd made during the first introductory lectures.

Sarah wrote to me often in those early weeks, providing a much-needed lifeline to home. She told me about Buster catching a frog and not knowing what to do with it, and about Dad winning a ten-pound cheque from a crossword he'd sent in to the local paper and treating them all to fish and chips, and about some boy at school called Colin who seemed to have developed a crush on her and wouldn't stop following her about.

That unnerved me a bit, the thing about Colin. What if he took things too far, got carried away and wouldn't take no for an answer, like Arnie O'Connor? What if he put my little sister in danger, tried to touch her, scared the life out of her? I thought about writing to warn her, or calling her from the communal phone in the hall, but what could I say? Arnie was still my big secret, one I was desperate to forget, and I knew it wouldn't be right to judge every boy either of us ever met by his nasty drunken standards. And besides, I didn't want to tell her. Didn't want to tell anybody. So I pushed all thoughts of him aside, just as I'd planned all along, decided that Sarah would just have to look after herself, and threw myself into university life.

My course was fantastic. We were studying the novels of the nineteenth century that first term, and reading the Romantic poets. I lost myself for hours on end in the fascinatingly provincial world of George Eliot's *Middlemarch* that reminded me, in so many ways, of my own home town, and luxuriated in the lilting words of Wordsworth and Lord Byron. It felt as if I had truly arrived in heaven, not forced to take lessons or exams in subjects I had no interest in, and no silly school rules or assemblies to tolerate. The study of English, its beautiful language and its centuries of richly engrossing literature, was all I had to concentrate on. It was what I increasingly believed I had been born for, and already I knew I wanted to make a career of teaching it to others.

'Head in a book again, Eve?' Jodie said, one Friday evening, as she and Lauren were getting ready to dash to the station and pay their families a weekend visit. 'Make sure you have some fun while we're gone, won't you? All work and no play, and all that ...'

I nodded, peering over my dog-eared copy of *Wuthering Heights*, my head still lost somewhere on the moors with Cathy Earnshaw. 'Course I will. There's a party over in Block K. Some of the English group. I'll probably go to that.'

'Well, don't do anything we wouldn't do!' The two of them giggled as they linked arms and left. I couldn't help noticing how close they'd become, and how quickly. Still, I had no reason to feel jealous. I had my books, and my own visit home to look forward to. It would soon be Christmas.

The party was in full swing by the time I reluctantly closed my book several chapters before the end and made my way across to Block K, my head still full of windswept landscapes and long-lost loves. The kitchen on the ground floor, identical in size and shape to ours, was packed with people, most of them holding beer cans, talking way too loudly, and looking and sounding decidedly pissed. I hovered at the edges for a while, suddenly realising I should have brought some booze. Maybe I could just make my way to the sink and pour myself a glass of water. Everyone would assume I was drinking vodka, if they even bothered to look at my glass, or me, at all.

'Can't come in empty handed!' Harry, one of the boys from

my course, said, wagging a finger at me and slurring his words. ''Snot allowed.'

I giggled, suddenly imagining something slimy emerging from his nose. 'Right. I'll go and get something then, shall I?'

'Thassa girl.' He merged back into the throng as I hovered again, undecided about whether I even wanted to stay, let alone drink. Well, maybe just for an hour or so, and just for one drink, to be sociable. The shop would still be open. It always was, on Friday and Saturday evenings, when a high demand for alcohol seemed to be the norm. I'd get a cheap bottle of wine, and some cream crackers or something to help soak it up. It didn't look as if there was much in the way of food laid out and I got the general idea that this was very much a bring-your-own sort of a party.

Despite the well-lit paths, there was something a bit desolate about the outer reaches of Brydon's sprawling campus at night, so I was glad to reach the central plaza and the shop with its lights on, the door open and a bustle of customers coming and going.

'Hi, Evie Peevie!' Beth's boyfriend Lenny, who seemed to have picked up on the nickname she had given me on the train, greeted me from behind the counter with a wide smile. 'A ready meal for one, is it? Like every other bugger in here tonight. Or can I get you the latest copy of *The New Scientist*? Oh, don't worry, I'm only teasing. I know science isn't your thing. English, right? Beth says you write awesome poetry. I've been having a go myself, actually. What do you think of this one? *There was a young lady from Wales, who at uni went right off the rails. She dropped her drawers, on too many floors …*

Sorry, I haven't got any further than that yet. Not quite Poet Laureate material, I know. Couldn't help me out with a last line, could you?'

'Afraid not, Lenny,' I laughed. 'You really should be a comedian, you know. You're wasted in this shop.'

'In other words, don't give up the day job, eh? I know sarcasm when I hear it! Right, what can I get you, my lovely?'

I picked out a bottle of wine, a packet of Ritz and a small block of cheddar, and put them on the counter.

'Cor, you really know how to live, don't you? I hope this isn't your evening meal.'

'Party food. I don't expect to be staying there long. I'll probably get some chips on my way back later, if I'm hungry.'

'No hot date tonight then?'

'I wish!' I paid for my things, which Lenny had dropped into a carrier, and gave him a wave as I went back out into the dark. I had no idea why I'd said that. Just one of those things people say. Did I really wish I had a date, a boyfriend? No, probably not.

The last time I had been with a boy at a party ... it had been Arnie. And I had kissed him. Why had I done that? It had been more out of curiosity than anything else, I suppose, because I didn't actually fancy him at all, but I'd wanted to find out how it felt, to be kissed like that.

Sweet and deep, and packed with longing. I knew I was a bit of a late starter, my head still full of wild romantic notions fuelled by weepy films and all the dreamy lovey-dovey books I borrowed from the library and read avidly under the bedcovers. Arnie was just someone to practise on, as far as I was concerned, ready for when 'The One' came along. Nothing more. If only he had known that. Or maybe he did, but ignored it anyway. For him, that awkward first kiss had worked like a green light. Full speed ahead to probing fingers and crushed breasts, and a frenzied attempt at getting his hands underneath my skirt.

He hadn't taken it well when I said no, and kept saying no. Told me I was frigid. Told me that I was just teasing, that I wanted it – and him – but was playing hard to get. Sucked hard at my neck. Hurt my arm. Kept on pushing and probing, his fingers forcing onwards, tugging at the edges of my under-wear, jabbing roughly into my flesh ...

I know I had a lucky escape. Well, the knee I jerked up hard and fast between his legs made sure of that. And then I ran, tripping and gasping, all the way home, and he didn't follow me, so I suppose I should be grateful for small mercies.

It hit me hard though, the fear that came after, and the realisation of my own vulnerability. I stopped drinking so much and stopped going out after dark on my own. I couldn't risk seeing him, couldn't take the chance that it might happen again, or that he would tell people, twist things, say I was a tease, make out it was all somehow my fault ...

I shook the memories away. This was different. I was safe here. Safe, because this was my new life and I was in control now, and that felt good. Empowering. There was no way I was going to get drunk, or let myself get into a situation like that, with anyone, ever again. I wasn't going to kiss any more frogs and hope they turned out to be princes. And, as for 'The One' ... I doubted now that such a person existed.

As I re-joined the crowded party, the carrier bag was scooped from my hands almost as soon as I was through the door, and I was left standing alone in a sea of semi-strangers. I didn't much like being at places like this on my own. I knew that a boyfriend wasn't the answer, but it would have been good to have someone to arrive with, and walk back with afterwards. The girls I shared with were friendly enough but they were all off doing their own thing. I'd met up with Beth for lunch or a coffee a few times, and I wasn't short of people to talk to when I went to lectures, but right at that moment I missed Sarah. My sister was like my other half, the one person I had always felt totally comfortable with, building secret dens out of blankets, curled up in our pyjamas on the sofa, whispering in the dark when we were meant to be asleep. Maybe I'd call her later, before she went to bed.

I followed my carrier bag across the room, anxious not to let it out of my sight or the hungry hordes snaffle all my cheese before I got any for myself. The boy who had taken it turned and smiled as he emptied the contents onto the draining board. 'Want some?' he said, pulling the packet of crackers open and ripping at the plastic wrapper on the cheese with his teeth.

I nodded, quickly reaching for my bottle of wine as an arm appeared from behind us and tried to grab it. 'It should be me asking you that really, shouldn't it?' I said, clutching the bottle to my chest. 'Seeing as it was me who brought it.'

'Oh, we don't worry about any of that nonsense here,' he said, his accent one I couldn't immediately place, but was clearly northern. 'Share and share alike.' He dug his thumb in and pulled a ragged chunk of cheese from the corner of the block, holding it out to me as he put the rest of it down. He rummaged about in the sink for a used glass and quickly swilled it under the tap. 'I'm Josh, by the way. I've seen you around but I don't ...'

'Eve.' I took the cheese and chewed at it, preventing me from having to say anything else, at least for a while.

'English, right? The course you're on, not your nationality!' He laughed at his own joke. 'Like most of the others here.'

I nodded, taking the chance to study his face, his deep-brown eyes looking slightly glazed over. He had obviously had a few drinks already this evening. I swallowed. 'You?'

'Oh, boring stuff. Business Studies, and Maths. Into my final year already and it doesn't get any better. I'm more or less destined to become an accountant or a banker or something equally dreary.'

'Why do it if you don't want to?'

'I didn't say I don't want to. Just that it's boring. But then, most things are, aren't they?'

'Are they? I'm not sure that's true.'

He tilted his head to one side and stared at me, for just a little too long. 'Tell me something that isn't. Go on, I dare you to think of something you find truly exciting. That stays exciting, and doesn't end up boring you rigid in the end.' He took the bottle from me and twisted its top off, then poured some wine into the grimy glass and thrust it into my hand, tipping the rest to his mouth and taking a big swig straight from the bottle.

I watched him wipe his sleeve over his chin to catch the

drips and could instantly imagine what my parents would have said if I'd ever done anything like that in public, or even at home for that matter. 'You don't care much, do you?' I said, trying to sound disapproving but ending up sounding just like my own mother.

'About what?'

'About anything. Your course, your future, what other people might think of you ...'

'That's about it, I reckon. You've summed me up pretty well there, Eve. Careless, carefree, call it what you like. Doesn't stop me *wanting* to care though, does it?'

I sipped slowly at my wine. I'd had very little to drink since that night with Arnie, and I could feel a small alarm bell starting to ring in my head. Josh was looking at me very intensely, and the last thing I wanted was to give him the wrong idea. It was time to seek my escape, while I still could.

'Well, it was nice to meet you, Josh, but I see someone over there I really want to talk to, so ...'

'Yeah, okay. I get it. A better offer on the table, eh?'

'For your information, I am not on offer, to anyone.' I picked up my food and slid it back into its bag. 'And certainly not on the table! As I said, nice to meet you. Keep the rest of the wine. You sound like you might need it more than I do.'

Chapter 4

SARAH

Mum had decided to stay at home and cook, and probably run the vacuum around our room yet again while she was at it, so it was just Dad and me waiting on the platform that Friday afternoon when Eve's train pulled in.

There was still more than a week to go until Christmas but winter had definitely arrived. Dad worked at a local insurance company. He had asked if he could leave early, so he could be there to meet her, and was still wearing his suit and tie, his battered old overcoat pulled over the top. There was an icy wind blowing, so even Dad, usually as tough as old boots, was muttering about how he should have brought gloves. A few shrivelled brown leaves skittered haphazardly about our feet as we stamped them to keep warm.

Eve looked different somehow as she climbed down from the train, turning to lug her case down the step behind her. The coat, the scuffed boots, the hairstyle, or what I could see of it sticking out under her woolly hat, were all just the same as they had been before she left, but Eve wasn't. I suppose if

I had to try to explain it I would say that she looked like an adult now, as she stood absolutely still and scanned the platform, lifting her arm to wave as she spotted us and started to wheel the case slowly and steadily towards us.

'Hi, Dad.' She went to him first, lifting her cheek to be pecked, and handing the case over into his care before turning to me. 'Sprout!' She pulled me to her, crushing my face against the rough wool of her coat. 'Oh, it's so good to see you!'

Sprout! She hadn't called me that in years, not since the days when she had been a good six inches taller than me and anxious to affirm her superior big-sister status. Still, it sounded good, hearing her say it. Like we were kids again, and her only role in life was to be bigger than me, and to protect me. I sank into her chest, felt her arms squashing me in tight, and clung on like a limpet. We pulled apart eventually, running to catch up as Dad strode off towards the Underground, Eve's case bouncing noisily along behind him.

By the time we reached the house, a dour-looking semi tucked away in the older part of Ealing, dusk was falling. Mum had pulled all the curtains closed and lit the gas fire, making the living room feel extra warm and cosy. Our old artificial Christmas tree and the tatty cardboard box of decorations we had used for as long as I could remember were ready and waiting in the corner. We had never left it so late before, but decorating the tree was a task she had decided could not be undertaken until we were all together again, just like old times. She'd made it sound as if Eve had been gone for years. Still, it gave us something practical to do while Dad changed out of his office clothes and settled down in his armchair with his crossword and Mum busied herself in the kitchen, from where occasional snatches of Christmas carols, or her attempts at them, sung slightly out of tune, reached us through the open door.

'So, what's it like?' I asked Eve, sitting cross-legged on the carpet and passing various baubles and bells to her one at a time while she stood above me and pondered where to hang them. 'Living on your own, and having to cook and everything? Do you have to clean your own room as well? What are the other girls like? Met any boys yet?'

Eve laughed. 'Slow down, Sprout. Too many questions all at once!' She reached up high, biting her lip in concentration as she tried to secure a wonky robin to the end of a branch, finally standing back to admire him as she took another ornament from my hand. 'Okay. Cooking's all right. There's a shop on campus, with all the basics. Bread, milk, eggs, tins, and piles of apples and bananas – students seem to eat a lot of those, or someone's trying to make sure we do! And there's a bus that goes to the big supermarket, so one or two of us from the flat will go there sometimes and get supplies in for the lot of us. There's a fair bit of sharing goes on, if someone makes a pan of mince or something, but it's tempting to just eat in the cafeteria or grab something from the chip shop. And I've probably eaten more late-night bowls of cereal than ever before.'

'Very healthy, I'm sure!'

'It is, actually, and much better than all that chocolate you stash under your pillow for midnight snacks. I bet you do that even more now I'm not around to keep an eye on you.'

39

I glanced at Dad to make sure he wasn't listening, but he seemed to have nodded off to sleep. 'Says the girl who used to slurp vodka as soon as the lights went out.' I lowered my voice, just in case I was wrong and he was simply resting his eyes.

She looked down at her feet. 'Not often, and I don't do it anymore. Can't afford to, apart from anything else. And where's the fun in doing something you probably shouldn't when your parents aren't there to lie to or hide it from? I'm an adult now, Sarah. Drinking's allowed. And that takes all the fun out of it somehow.'

'God, you sound boring. I thought uni was going to be all about wild parties and not remembering how you got home!'

'Well, for me it's not. To be honest, I'd rather talk about my course and all the wonderful books we're studying, but I know you'll probably glaze over at the very idea of that, so if you want the nitty gritty ... No, I don't go to wild parties and I haven't met any boys. Not in the way you mean, anyway. Which brings me to the one you told me about. Still bothering you, is he?'

'What? Colin, you mean?' I could feel myself redden just at the sound of his name. 'I never said he was bothering me, Eve. Just that he sort of, well, likes me.'

She pulled the pouffe across from beside the sofa and climbed up onto it to put the fairy on top of the tree. 'There we are. The finishing touch. I made that fairy, do you remember? In primary school. Time we got a new one really. Her wings are getting a bit tatty.'

'I suppose. Be a shame to change things though, wouldn't it? She's a part of our lives, our childhood ...'

'Things change, Sarah. Not much we can do about that. I mean, look at you, all grown up. I swear you're at least two inches taller than when I left.' She sat down beside me on the carpet and linked her arm through mine. 'So, how do you feel about him, this Colin? You said he was younger than you. And a bit on the chubby side? He's not really boyfriend material, is he? And you are still a bit young ...'

'Just forget I ever mentioned him, all right?' I squirmed away from her and stood up. She was just going to mock me, wasn't she? Silly little Sarah, too young to be interested in boys, or for any boy to be showing an interest back. It was typical of Eve, playing the seemingly protective, but-really-I-know-best, big-sister card. But things do change, she was right about that. I had no intention of being Little Sarah, forever in her shadow, any longer. Or of settling for Colin Grant who, let's face it, was only fourteen, and probably still wore Superman pyjamas and took a hot water bottle to bed. There were girls in my year at school who were already on the pill. Dating sixth formers. Wearing C-cup bras and blagging their way into nightclubs. I looked down at my still disappointingly flat chest and horribly skinny knees. Okay, so I didn't quite look the part yet, but it wouldn't be long ...

'I'm going to see if Mum needs any help in the kitchen,' I said, getting to my feet. 'You can walk Buster for a change. After all these weeks of me having to do it on my own, it's definitely your turn.'

'Where is he anyway? I haven't seen him since we got back.'

'Upstairs on your bed, probably. He's taken to sleeping there quite a bit since you've been gone. Your quilt's got a bit hairy, but never mind, eh?'

'Yuck!' She pulled a face and headed for the stairs, taking her suitcase with her, and muttering under her breath, 'I just hope he hasn't got fleas.'

Mum was making shepherd's pie for tea. It was one of Eve's favourites, and I knew full well that the next couple of weeks were going to be all about Eve. By the time I joined Mum in the kitchen she had already peeled the potatoes and they were bubbling away in a pan on the stove.

'Anything I can do?'

'No, Love. You go and make the most of having your sister home. Have a girly chat, swap make-up, play some music in your room, whatever you girls like to do. I know how much you've missed her.'

'Actually, I think she's about to walk the dog. And it's cold out there. I'd rather stay at home. Plenty of time to catch up later.'

'Homework then? I'm sure they must have given you some to do over the holidays, and you don't want to leave it to the last minute, do you?'

Given the choice of dog walking or homework, I knew which I preferred. It may have been cold outside, but not *that* cold. I grabbed Buster's lead from behind the back door and went to find my coat, and my sister, in the hall.

Buster's route around the block was as good as set in stone. I sometimes thought we could have opened the front door and sent him off out by himself and he'd have trundled from tree to lamp post and back again without even realising there was no lead attached to his collar and no human attached to the other end. Still, I never dared try it. Much as I might moan about Buster and the need to take him out in all weathers, I loved that old dog and couldn't bear the thought of anything bad happening to him.

'So, what have you been up to then, while I've been away?' Eve and I fell into step and trailed along, slowly, behind the dog.

'Not a lot.'

'How's school?'

'I hate school. You know that.'

'Well, you won't get to uni by hating school. You've got to knuckle down for your exams next summer, and get the grades, or you won't even get to do the A levels you want. Which subjects do you fancy, by the way?'

'Can't say I fancy any of them, actually. Now, Paul Jacobs ... I do fancy him!'

Eve laughed. 'Boys aren't the be all and end all, you know. Look at me. Still young, free and single, and I don't ever feel there's a gaping great hole in my life.'

'You're different. You're clever and sensible, and you love studying, and books. You'll probably marry some nerdy swot when you're thirty-five and go off to live in a library, and end up with a row of little kids who all wear glasses. Going to uni is all you ever dreamed of. I haven't got a hope in hell of doing as well in my exams as you did, and then Dad'll be on my back about throwing my future away, and Mum'll be trying to get me onto some typing course, and I'll end up being some no-hope office junior for ever.'

'God, Sarah, you sound like you've given up already. There must be something you want to do, something you're good enough at that you could build a career around. And you said you wanted to know all about uni, so you must at least like the idea of going there yourself.'

'Yeah, to get away from home, meet people, party ...'

'We do have to study as well, you know. It's not all fun and games. And some of it is just like the school you say you hate so much. Lectures, and assignments, and deadlines. Don't put yourself through all that just to be allowed to stay up late and drink yourself stupid. You can do that anywhere.'

'Try telling Mum and Dad that!'

'Well, I don't mean now, obviously. Not while you're still only fifteen.'

'Sixteen next month.'

'Yes, okay. Not yet, is all I meant. But later on, when you're earning, when you can get your own place ...'

'Which, without an education and a decent job, I will never be able to afford. It's like some nasty evil masterplan, isn't it? The only way you have any hope of getting what you really want is to have to do the very thing you don't want to do at all.'

'Like work hard, you mean? Pass exams? Get a career? That's how the world works. It doesn't just land in your lap.'

'You do know you sound just like Mum, don't you? But there's always the other way, isn't there? Meet someone rich, have babies, never have to work at all ...'

'And how often does that happen? Prince Edward isn't about to pop up at the corner shop, is he?'

44

'Prince Edward? For heaven's sake, Eve, credit me with some taste. He may be royal and all that, but he's ancient.'

'So you want rich *and* young, do you? And with film-star looks too, I suppose?'

'Of course. I was thinking someone more like Ronan Keating or Robbie Williams ...'

'Dream on, Kid! Besides, Ronan's just got married, hasn't he? You've missed the boat there. But if there's one thing that really is good about uni it's the number of available boys. You'd be spoilt for choice.'

'All poor though, living on student grants and baked beans.'

'Maybe. But with prospects, at least.'

'So, where's yours then? Your boy with prospects? Because I can't see him anywhere.'

'That's because he doesn't exist. Because I'm not looking for him. But that's not to say I couldn't find him if I was.'

'Oh, yeah? Go on then. Prove it.'

'I don't want to.' She turned to face me, her expression suddenly serious. 'It's all about priorities, isn't it? Concentrating on my course instead of going on some kind of frantic manhunt is my choice. Just like whether to try for uni or not is yours. I'm not going to tell you what to do, even if Mum and Dad might try to.'

We stood in silence, watching Buster as he snuffled out a big stick from the base of a tree. Eve bent down to pull it out of his mouth. She threw it up high, trying to start a game, and we watched as it landed on the pavement a few yards away, but clearly Buster didn't want it enough to make the effort to run and retrieve it. Somehow, I knew exactly how he felt.

Chapter 5

EVE

There was a strange noise coming from Fran's room. I had come in from my last lecture of the day, tired and cold and fancying a quick slice of toast before working out what to eat for my dinner, but I had forgotten I didn't have any butter left. I really couldn't face the walk back to the shop, so I took a peek on the other girls' shelves in the big communal fridges, which were looking badly in need of a good wipe down although I felt no great urge to tackle the job myself. I was just about to pinch a scrape of Annie's margarine and a sneaky spoon of Ruth's strawberry jam, when I heard what sounded very much like someone trying to suppress a scream.

I froze. What on earth was that? I tiptoed out into the hall and waited. There it was again, and it was coming from Fran's room, right opposite the kitchen. A kind of gasping sound I had never heard her make before. Was she ill? Hurt? I felt my heart start to race and was about to rap on her door to see if she was all right when I distinctly heard her laugh. Well, I suppose it was more of a giggle really. And then a male voice, deep and low, saying something I couldn't quite make out – in fact it was almost definitely in a foreign language – followed a few seconds later by a slow rhythmic banging, like something hitting hard against the wall, that just seemed to get louder and faster, and more and more blindingly obvious, the longer I stood there, my feet inexplicably glued to the floor.

Fran had a man in there, and they were ... well, I was pretty sure they were having sex.

Another gasp filtered through the wall. It was no good. I didn't want to listen. I might be tired and hungry, but I just wanted to get out of there so I didn't have to hear any more. Flicking the toaster switch off, with the slice of bread still inside, I grabbed my coat and bag from where I'd left them on the back of a chair and ran for the stairs.

It was a chilly January evening, already dark, and I had no real plan, so I just put my head down to keep the wind out of my face and headed towards the centre of campus, and the shop. I might as well buy that butter I needed so I wouldn't have to pinch any more from the others. I can't say I was too keen on that awful margarine that Annie used anyway. And maybe I could run to a bottle of wine, just a cheap one. Suddenly, I felt like I really needed a drink. And a pair of ear plugs, but I doubted they sold them.

Lenny was in his usual spot behind the counter.

'Hello, Evie Peevie. What can we get you today, my lovely?'

'Hi, Lenny. I'll just grab a basket and have a browse, I think. See what takes my fancy.'

'You do know I'm spoken for, don't you?' he said, giving

me an exaggerated wink. 'And you'd need a considerably bigger basket ...'

'I didn't mean you! As well you know.' I laughed, giving him a friendly punch on the arm, and made my way down the booze aisle which was, I suppose unsurprisingly considering the shopping priorities of the average student, almost as big as all the food ones put together.

'What're you up to later?' Lenny had followed me to the wine shelves and was hovering at my side, pushing his floppy hair back out of his eyes. Oh God, I hoped he had only been joking and he wasn't about to ask me out or something.

'Not a lot. I've got a book I'm supposed to have read and haven't. And my dinner to sort out.'

'Come out with us. Beth and me. Have a few drinks, get a burger ...'

'You sure she wouldn't mind?' The idea certainly appealed, but I hesitated. 'I really don't want to be some sort of gooseberry, elbowing in on your date.'

'Course not! She'd love to see you. It's not as if we were planning some romantic twosome. I'm sure there'll be others about. It usually turns into a bit of a group thing on a Friday night. Beth's science crowd mostly. And I think there's a band on, in the bar. Not exactly Take That, but it's a chance to have a dance, a bit of a laugh, you know ...'

Since getting back after Christmas, I hadn't been out much. Too cold, too busy. I was in danger of becoming a hermit, and I knew it. I didn't have a lot else to do that night which didn't involve either studying or being an unwilling witness to someone else's love life, so why not?

'Okay. When were you thinking of meeting up? And where?'

'Look, my shift ends in about ten minutes, so why not hang around now? Keep me company, and then we can walk to Beth's place together. Unless you wanted to go back and get changed or anything?'

I looked down at myself. Clean jeans, a T-shirt and baggy cardi. My warm coat, and a pair of trainers, not too scuffed. I was presentable enough. Not quite nightclub wear, but this was uni, and everyone dressed pretty much the same way, whatever the occasion. And I always carried a toothbrush and a basic make-up kit in my bag. I'd do.

I put my empty basket down. The last thing I'd want if I was staying out for the evening was to drag a slab of butter about with me. I could already imagine it getting warm in the heat of the bar and squashed to a pulp at the bottom of my bag. An excuse not to go back to the flat, and to whatever was going on in Fran's room, was just what I needed.

'No, that's okay. I'll come now.'

'Great. As soon as my replacement turns up, we'll go. Burgers first, yeah? Plenty of chunky chips. Can't beat 'em. I never can face a night of drinking on an empty stomach.'

'Absolutely!'

Within a quarter of an hour we were walking side by side along one of the narrow pathways that spread out, spider-like, towards the outer reaches of the campus, and out through the gates. Lenny's big boots scrunched hard on the pavement, his breath billowing out in long airy puffs as he spoke.

'Bloody cold tonight. I wouldn't be surprised if we get some snow.'

'Really?'

'It's expected, so they say. Means my dad'll have to get out to the sheep if we do.'

'Oh, yeah. I forgot you're from a farming family. Must be tough, having to worry about the animals. We've only got a dog, and taking him out in the snow's bad enough, but sheep ...'

'Well, they do tend to look after themselves, most of the time. Woolly coats and all that. It's just making sure they have food. But right now, it's feeding myself that's top of the list. I hope Beth's ready. I could eat a horse!'

'You wouldn't though, would you? Eat a horse, I mean.'

'Don't see why not. Cows, sheep, pigs, what's the difference? If they're bred for meat. You surely don't think we farmers give them all names and treat them as pets?'

'Of course not.' Suddenly I felt a bit stupid. The city girl, with no idea about country life at all.

'Don't go turning vegetarian on me, Evie, or you and me will be seriously falling out! Can put us out of business, an attitude like that ...'

'Veggie? Me? No way.' I linked my arm through his, to show we were still mates. 'Bring on the burgers!'

***

The bar was crowded that night, and we were lucky to get seats. Beth was drinking at least two vodkas to every one of my glasses of wine and I could see her getting slowly more and more giggly, even though, above all the noise, I could hardly hear a word she said.

The band were okay. Not exactly hit-record prospects, but they managed to keep the place buzzing, with plenty of bodies bopping about on the dancefloor. There were the usual puddles of spilt drink to negotiate as I picked my way through the semi-darkness to the toilets, where the sudden bright light glaring above the mirror and the weird silence when I closed the door behind me brought on an almost instant headache. Or maybe that was the booze, which my body was no longer accustomed to in such quantities. I stood for a while, splashing cold water over my over-heated face, then leaned on the sink, letting my mind clear a bit before going back in. Perhaps it was time to call it a night, especially if I was going to have to get myself back to the flat. Any more to drink and I would have trouble walking in a straight line.

Beth and Lenny were nowhere to be seen and my seat at the small table in the corner had already been occupied by someone else when I returned. 'Sorry,' I said, hoping to make myself heard, as I tried to ease my coat off the back of the chair. 'Could I just ...?'

It was only when he turned around that I saw who it was sitting in my seat.

'Oh, I know you, don't I?' he said. 'The girl with the cheese ...'

'Well, I've been called worse, I suppose. You're Josh, aren't you? Mr Can't Be Bothered. From that party ...'

'Is that really the impression I gave? Can't be bothered? And there's me thinking it was my charm and stunning good looks that the ladies remember me by!'

'I'm sorry. I can hardly hear a word you're saying. Something about good books?'

'Oh, trust you! I remember now. Eve, studying English, right? Bit of a bookworm ...'

I bent closer, and a whiff of the most delicious aftershave hit me. 'Sorry, Josh, if I could just grab my coat, I was about to leave.'

'By yourself?'

'Yep. Time to get home to bed.'

I saw his eyes light up, shining with mischief. 'Mmm, now there's an offer I don't get every day.'

'I didn't mean *that*! About bed. Well, not together ...' God, he was maddening. How did he manage to make me feel so flustered?

'Of course you didn't. How about a dance though? Before you go. We're getting into the slow ones now, and I'd look a right prat dancing on my own. I'll walk you back after, eh? Don't like to think of a lady out alone at night.'

'I don't know about that.'

'About the dance, or the walking back? Because they're not mutually exclusive, you know. You can pick one with no obligation to take the other.'

I couldn't help but smile. Talking like that, he was either extremely sober, or extremely drunk, and I had no way of knowing which.

'A dance then.' I dropped my coat back down and took the hand he was offering. Solid, warm, strong. 'Just one dance. And then I'm going. On my own.'

But it didn't happen that way.

That was the night it started, I suppose. Losing my sensible head. The whiff of romance. Letting myself get near to a boy again without running a mile. The start of my growing obsession with Josh Cavendish. Although obsession is probably too strong a word. Shall we just say my interest, my attraction? My sudden determination to make him be bothered. About me, anyway. Because there was just something about the way he looked at me, the way his hand curled around my back as we danced, the feel of his chest, soft and damp against my chin, and the warm citrusy smell of him ... I was drawn to him, as if I'd been pulled unexpectedly towards a magnet, and was stuck there, unable to drag myself away, even if I'd tried.

Of course I didn't leave. We stayed on the dancefloor, pressed together, swaying along with the music, surrounded by others doing exactly the same. We soon gave up trying to talk, knowing it would be impossible to hold any sort of meaningful conversation, our bodies moulding into each other's curves and echoing each other's movements, his heart next to my ear, pounding out a rhythm that seemed to match the one throbbing through the floor, and I didn't want it to stop. Any of it. But it did. Of course it did. The shutters came down over the bar, the music died away, the DJ said goodnight, the last stragglers edged towards the doors, rummaging about for lost coats, and the lights came on.

Lenny had been right about the snow. Tiny flakes were fluttering down like a scene from a lacy Christmas card. It was shockingly cold, and I staggered a bit, the wine I'd drunk earlier still having an unbalancing effect. I managed to do up my coat at the second attempt, fingers fumbling with the buttons, and felt around in my pockets for my gloves, but Josh grabbed for my hand. His fingers tightened around mine, warmer than any glove, and I just shoved the other hand deeper into my pocket and left it there. He asked me where my room was, which block, and we started to walk back towards it together. Other late-nighters passed us, laughing, shouting, hugging goodnight, and gradually dispersing in different directions, until we were alone in the dark, with just the crunchy sound of our footsteps and the magic of the snow.

'Well, Eve,' he said, turning me to face him when we reached the foot of the exterior concrete staircase that led up to my flat, his hands resting on my shoulders. 'This has been ... nice. Can I say that word?'

'Nice is okay.'

'It just seems a bit inadequate somehow, but words aren't my strong point. Just a regular, spontaneous kind of a guy, me! Say what comes into my head. I don't really do deep and meaningful. But with you being into literature and everything, you'd probably prefer me to say something a bit more profound, wouldn't you? Poetic, even. Like something from ... I don't know ... Keats or Shelley?'

'Do you know any Keats or Shelley?' I laughed, suspecting the drink was making him ramble such utter nonsense.

'No.'

'Then nice is fine.'

'Good.' He was bending forward, his face just inches from mine, our cold noses almost touching. He was going to kiss me. I was sure of it. I closed my eyes in anticipation, felt his cold hand come up and gently cup my cheek, and then the other struggling with a button, angling to find a way inside my coat.

Arnie! Suddenly all I could think about, all I could feel, all I could see was Arnie. The two of us, alone in the dark, in the silence. Nobody else to hear me, to save me, to believe me. His face close to mine. His alcohol breath, hot and sweet on my face. And his hands. Touching me, probing me, forcing me ...

I pushed the hands, the arms, the body away roughly, forcefully, my heart now beating so loudly I swear I could hear it through the silence. My eyes flew open as Josh staggered back, gasping, his hands reaching to steady himself, to grab at me again, a voice asking me what was wrong, what had he done? But it was what he was about to do that mattered. Like Arnie, trying to have his way. Trying to take control. To take me ...

It was happening again. And I couldn't let it. All I could do was run. Get away from him as fast as I could, up those concrete stairs, my breath puffing out of me in short sharp frozen clouds, finding my key quickly, stabbing at the lock, flinging the door open and slamming it hard behind me.

Chapter 6

SARAH

Is sixteen too young to lose your virginity? I knew what the law said, of course, but I also knew exactly what Mum and Dad would have said – not that I had any intention of asking them. When you're ready, you're ready, it's as simple as that, and it made a lot of sense to get that first awkward clumsy go at it out of the way as soon as possible, ready for the better times to come. Or that's what I told myself at the time.

'Make sure you're home by eleven,' Dad had said as I walked down the garden path to where my friend Tilly from next door was waiting at the gate. 'And no coming back on your own. You girls stick together, and call me if you need a lift. There are some bad people out there ...'

We giggled as we strode off down the road, arm in arm, young and cocky and utterly invincible. Anyone would think the big bad wolf was out there, hiding behind a lamp post or a dustbin, just waiting to pounce on us. Dad could be such a worrier sometimes. And so horribly embarrassing.

The party was to celebrate our friend Frankie's birthday.

She was sixteen, like us, but an only child and given pretty much whatever she wanted, her parents being posher and a lot richer than ours. They had promised to go out for the evening, leaving their big detached house to the temporary mercy of a horde of teenagers, something neither mine nor Tilly's would ever have contemplated, so, despite the slight pangs of jealousy, expectations and excitement levels were definitely high. According to Frankie, everyone who was anyone had been invited, from our school year and the one above, and I felt certain that 'everyone' would be bound to include the gorgeous Paul Jacobs.

Tilly had brought a big shopping bag with her, her own parents being far less curious than mine and unlikely to enquire about its contents. Inside it were our new shimmery super-short dresses, bought with many weeks' saved-up pocket money. We had vodka too, the last of the cheap stuff I'd pilfered from Eve's apparently forgotten secret stash and now hidden in an innocent-looking plastic bottle so it looked like water. And a whole host of make-up, two pairs of ridiculously high-heeled shoes we'd found in a charity shop weeks earlier, and some brand-new underwear. Well, you never knew when there might be someone who'd get to see it, and the shapeless white cotton pants we wore for school just wouldn't do.

There was one of those big public toilet cubicles on the corner outside the library, and we'd already earmarked it as our changing room. It was a bit damp and smelly, and someone had left a ball of screwed-up toilet paper on the floor, but there was room for two, standing side by side to apply our make-up, peering into the mucky mirror over the sink. Then

Tilly held the bag and passed out the items I needed, while I balanced on one leg, pulling on lacy knickers and trying to squeeze my feet into shoes that were not entirely the right size, before we changed places and I did the same for her. By the time we emerged, the transformation was complete and even our own families would have had trouble recognising us.

The front door was open when we arrived at the party ten minutes later, tottering on our unfamiliar heels, our legs bare and cold and covered in goose bumps. Music and people spilled out onto the street. Tilly took out the vodka and pushed it into her handbag, and we hid the shopping bag, our T-shirts and jeans, rolled-up socks and crumpled undies rammed inside it, under a bush in a dark corner of the front garden, hoping it would still be there for the return trip but with absolutely no back-up plan if it wasn't. *Live for the moment.* That was our motto back then. And the moment stretched invitingly before us, promising a whole evening of proper grown-up partying.

'Coats upstairs,' someone said, pointing us up towards a small bedroom where a pile of discarded coats covered the bed. We sniggered as the pile moved, two heads emerging from under it and telling us to bugger off, but we dumped our coats on top anyway, touched up our make-up in the bathroom, and then went downstairs, pushing our way through the crowds to the kitchen at the back of the house.

I took a couple of disposable plastic cups from a stack on the sink, not sure if they were new or already used and not caring much either way.

'We'll hang on to the vodka for later,' Tilly said, spotting a queue of people jostling each other to get at a box of wine. 'Might as well have what's on offer first.'

'I can't believe Frankie's mum and dad have let her have booze! You know, out in the open like this. I thought it would all be secret bottles in coat pockets, and pretending we were drinking lemonade.'

'How the other half lives, eh?' Tilly had made it to the front and turned the plastic tap on the box, catching a cup and a half of the slowly trickling red liquid before it ran dry. With a bit of careful pouring she managed to divide it fairly between us and we headed back into the hall.

'Hello, Sarah.'

I could feel the blush rush into my cheeks before I even turned around. I'd have known that voice anywhere. Paul Jacobs was standing right next to me, an open can of beer in one hand and a sausage roll in the other. The hallway was quite dark, the lights off, a few people sitting chatting on the lower stairs, so I hoped he wouldn't be able to see my face, in all its sudden pink glory, too clearly.

'You look nice,' Paul said, his eyes cast downwards and staring perhaps a bit too hard at my legs.

'Do I?' I stammered. I could feel Tilly nudging me from the other side, as if to say: talk to him, you idiot. 'Oh, I mean thanks ...'

'Pretty dress.'

I had never been chatted up before, never received a proper compliment from a boy, and I didn't quite know how to handle it. 'Yes, it's from that little shop opposite the baker's. Liberty

Jane, I think it's called. I bought it specially. You don't think it's too short?'

He smirked. What was I thinking? Boys had no interest in dress shops. But he did seem to have an interest, all of a sudden, in me.

'Definitely not too short,' he said, his gaze rolling over me, his speech a bit slurred. 'Suits you ...'

I turned to Tilly for support but she had slipped away, leaving us to it. She'd probably gone into the living room where, through the open door, I could see the dusky shapes of too many squashed-together bodies all moving to the way-too-loud music that was making the floor vibrate under my feet.

'Wanna dance?' he said, ramming the last of his sausage roll into his mouth and using his now empty hand to grab mine, the beer can still clasped in the other.

'Umm. Yeah, okay.' I drained the last of my wine, dumped the cup on the edge of the stairs and followed him into the room, where I found myself instantly pressed against him – and just about everybody else – as arms and legs and bodies battled for space in the dark. I could feel a trickle from the beer can slide down the back of my neck as Paul's hand moved up to pull my head closer to his. His breath smelled of alcohol and pastry, and his eyes, up close, looked decidedly glazed.

And so we danced. If it could be called dancing. More a shuffle of feet and a swaying of shoulders and a chance for the boys to get close enough to nuzzle the girls' necks and feel the unfamiliar pressure of breasts pushing against their sweaty shirts. After a while the can disappeared. I don't know if he had finished the last drops of beer somewhere over my head and chucked the empty can off to the side of the room or if it had just slipped from his fingers and was making soggy stains on Frankie's mum's carpet, but Paul now had two free hands and seemed intent on making the most of them.

'Wannanother drink?' he said after a while, his words all melding into each other close to my ear, as one hand twisted its way into my hair and the other clutched at my bum.

I nodded, glad to escape for some air and some much-needed thinking time – things were moving quite excitingly fast – and we made our way back through the hall and into the over-bright whiteness of the kitchen.

'Sarah!' Tilly was already there, pushing forward to whisper into my ear as Paul went looking for more drinks. 'You've got a love bite!'

'Have I?' My hand went to my neck. 'How did that happen?'

'Don't you know? Don't you remember? Although I'd be more worried about how to hide it from your mum and dad if I was you.'

'Oh, yeah. A big scarf maybe? Or a roll-neck pullover. I think there's one in Eve's wardrobe I could borrow.' I giggled. Only one cup of wine, not even a full one, and I could feel its effects.

'What? For school? I don't think so.'

'Make-up then. How bad is it?'

Tilly rummaged in her bag for a mirror and held it up in front of my face. I turned my head and looked. It was bad.

'Here.' Paul was back. 'Couldn't find any girl drinks, except

62

lemonade, so will this do?' He was holding out a small can of Guinness, and sipping from another just like it.

'Yeah, okay,' I said, having never tasted the stuff in my life before.

'Wanna find somewhere a bit quieter?' He had turned his back to Tilly and was looking out through the back door towards the garden where little lights twinkled along the path and I could see what looked like a fish pond in the middle of the grass and a greenhouse tucked away by the fence at the side.

'Yeah, that'd be good.'

Tilly raised her eyes as we went and mouthed a 'Be careful' at me, but Paul had hold of my hand now and we were soon outside and making our way down the garden, which was much longer than it had appeared from the kitchen, and away from the lights and music. Right at the end there was a little paved patio area, with tubs around its edges, the fat tips of new plants just starting to poke their way through the earth. There was a wooden bench in the corner, sheltered by an arch covered in something unseasonably leafy and green, making it feel very private and secluded despite the nearness of the party.

I shivered, the thin silver dress being no match for a cold March evening.

'Come here.' Paul took the can out of my hand and placed it, alongside his own, on the ground at our feet as we sat down, then pulled me closer and draped an arm over my shoulders, his hand just skimming the top of my breast through the cloth. 'I'll keep you warm.'

63

It felt good, and very grown-up, being alone together out there in the dark. I lay back as his lips finally closed over mine, his tongue pushing forward and into my mouth. It was warm and wet and tasted bitter and boozy from the drink. I opened my eyes, wanting to see him, to watch what he was doing at close range. Stars shone in the blackness of the sky above his head, giving us just enough light, and I could see the little pores in his skin, his eyelashes fluttering as he rolled his head around and concentrated on his task.

His fingers, as cold as mine, found their way through the armhole of my dress and wriggled towards my nipple. The thought that someone might come outside and discover us at any moment sent a thrill through me. I felt my nipple harden, as if by magic, in his hand.

'Paul ...'

'Don't talk, Sarah.' He pulled his face back, away from me, and looked right into my eyes. 'You know I've always fancied you ...'

'Have you?'

'Ever since I first saw you.' He started kissing me again, picking up my hand from where it lay in my lap and placing it, palm first, against the lump in his trousers. 'See. Can't you feel how much I fancy you, Sarah? How much I want you?'

'I ... fancy you too,' I murmured. A ripple of excitement ran through me. But I was scared too. 'But I've never ...'

'Shhh. Me neither.' He pulled back and looked me right in the eyes. Smiled. 'But there has to be a first time, doesn't there?' Then he nuzzled at my neck again, his fingers still trapped inside my dress, rubbing and rolling at my nipple until I thought I was going to burst. 'And I'd like mine to be with you.'

How could I resist that? I was special to him, just as he was to me.

'Have you got any, you know, condoms?' I felt wicked even saying the word out loud for the first time.

His hand slithered out from my dress and reached into his pocket, bringing out a small square packet. 'Yeah. Do you want to put it on for me?' He was unzipping his trousers, pushing me right back on the bench, moving his body over mine so the stars all disappeared.

'No. You do it. I'm not sure I ...'

'Okay.' There was the sound of ripping, the fumbling of fingers, a quiet gasp as his own hand found what had been lurking in his trousers and released it.

'Are you sure?' he mumbled, already slipping my under-wear down my legs. The new lacy ones I had bought just in case someone might get to see them. But he wasn't looking at them at all. Just at my face, my eyes. 'Sure you want me to do this?'

I nodded and he pushed himself at me, haphazardly, thumping against my thighs, my skin, my bones, as if trying to find his way. He felt hard and wet, his movements becoming more urgent.

'Open your legs wider,' he ordered, his voice suddenly sharper, more desperate, as he pulled my knees apart, shoving hard at me and finally finding his way inside me, groaning loudly. Three pushes and he was done.

We lay there, stuck together, my dress crumpled around

my waist, my white knees bent upwards, the wooden slats of the bench cutting into my naked bottom.

Was that it? Was that what all the fuss was about? It hadn't hurt the way I'd expected it to, hadn't sent any special feelings rushing through me, hadn't done anything much to me at all. I felt disappointed, exposed, and suddenly a bit embarrassed. I didn't say anything as he pulled away from me and sat up, adjusting his clothing and giving me time to adjust mine as I felt about on the ground for my lost knickers, found them in one of the plant pots and shook the earth out of them before awkwardly pulling them back on.

He didn't speak either. Just picked up the two cans of Guinness and handed one of them to me. 'I think I need this,' he said, laying his arms along the back of the bench and tipping his head back, gazing at the sky.

I took a swig. It was thick, strong, nasty, and I pulled a face, but I drank it anyway.

'It'll be better next time,' he said, talking about the sex, I assumed, and not the drink. It was good to know that there would be a next time, that this wasn't just one of those spur-of-the-moment drunken lunges that happen at parties. Somehow that made it all right. It was all about learning, wasn't it? Trying out new things. And at least we had tried it, done it, together.

'Yes, I expect it will.'

We sat there a bit longer, thighs touching, until the cold started to seep into our bones, and the liquid he had squirted inside me started to trickle out down my legs.

And then, I don't know why, but I started to laugh and, a

few seconds later, so did he. A release of tension, I suppose. And knowing that, despite the uncomfortable let-down it had all turned out to be, neither of us was a virgin anymore. Another tick on the way to adulthood. And freedom.

I wished I could tell Eve about it, the way I had always told her everything, but I also knew that this time I couldn't, and that I probably never would.

Chapter 7

EVE

I had successfully avoided Josh for almost two weeks, taking care not to walk anywhere near his block, staying away from the bar, keeping one eye open for him whenever I was in any of the places he might suddenly appear. But I couldn't hide forever. Fate finally caught up with me in the library. Josh was standing right in front of me as I looked up, a pile of books tucked under his arm and a stupid smile on his face.

'Eve.' He didn't say any more than that. Didn't move away either.

'Oh. Hello.' At least in the library there would be no shouting, no arguing. I kept my voice low. And my eyes.

'I haven't seen you around for a while. Not since ...'

'No. Sorry,' I interrupted. 'I've been busy.'

'Too busy for a coffee? Could we, do you think? Only, I'd like to try to ...'

'Umm ...' I hesitated. I knew only too well what he wanted to try to do. Interrogate me. Push me for answers. What had he done wrong? Why had I run off like that? Was I okay? I just wished I could give him some sort of answers that made sense, but I didn't know where to start.

'Come on, Eve. Just for half an hour. A coffee. A bun. My treat.'

I looked up at him, felt my insides lurch. The attraction was still there. But so was the fear.

'Please.'

'Okay then.' I took a deep breath. Time to get it over with, then I could stop hiding. 'Just for half an hour, then I really do have some work to do. An assignment due in.'

'I won't get in the way of your assignment, I promise. I can see your course is important to you. Poetry before people, right?'

'I wouldn't say that exactly.' I gathered my papers into my bag, watched him check out his books, and followed him out through the big glass doors. The weather was improving, clumps of bright-yellow daffodils dancing about in the borders and a few leaves starting to reappear on the trees. I saw his hand reach out for mine but chose to ignore it, switching my bag from hand to hand instead, making sure it hung there between us, like a barrier.

The coffee shop was busy but we found a table in a corner and Josh went up to the counter, returning a few minutes later with two coffees and three cakes on a tray.

'Three?' I said, nodding towards the cakes. 'Are we expecting someone else, or do you just have a big appetite?'

'Wasn't sure what you'd like. Best to offer a girl a choice,' he said, picking up his cardboard cup of coffee and blowing across the surface.

A choice? Like whether or not to be kissed, to be touched, to have sex? Was that what he was hinting at, or was it just my imagination stuck on a topic I really didn't want to explore?

'I'll have the doughnut then, if that's okay?'

'Of course it's okay.' He was studying my face, his own unusually serious. 'Eve ...'

'Yes, I know, all right? I ran away that night, I left you standing there, I overreacted. I know it must have seemed odd, a bit mad ... and I'm sorry.'

'I'm not looking for an apology. Just trying to understand, that's all.'

'If I understood it myself I might be able to explain, but I don't. Not really. It was just ... I felt a bit rushed, pressured, no way out, you know. Like I had no ...'

'Choice?' Josh smiled and lifted his hand, making a big show of hovering over the two remaining cakes.

'Sorry.'

'Stop saying you're sorry. It sounds like it's me who should be apologising, if I made you feel that way. It was just ... well, I thought we both wanted the same thing. And it was a kiss, Eve. Only a kiss.'

'With your hand shoving its way into my clothes?'

'Was it? It was bloody cold that night, Eve. Surely a hand ... well, it was only inside your coat, wasn't it? Not on bare flesh or anything.'

'I suppose.'

'Look, could we start again, do you think? I like you, and I thought you liked me. Okay, so we have absolutely nothing in common.' His eyes twinkled in amusement. 'Beauty and the Beast. With me as the beast, obviously! Maths and English. Numbers and words. Yin and yang. But opposites attract, right? How about we go for a drink later? Hands in my pockets at all times, I promise. Except to get my wallet out, or to go for a pee ...'

I couldn't help but laugh. And I did like him. I really did.

'Okay, yes.' I took a bite of the doughnut and licked the sugar from my fingers.

'You'll come?'

'Yes, if I can get this assignment finished first. How about nine o'clock? Is that too late?'

'Course not. But, just one thing ...'

'What?'

He leant forwards and lifted his hand closer to my face as if he was going to touch me, then stopped himself and pulled away. 'Sorry. Promised to keep my hands to myself, but you might want to know you've got sugar on the end of your nose.'

I wiped blindly at my face, hoping the sugar was all gone, suddenly realising how much the way I looked – to Josh anyway – mattered to me.

'I've missed you, Kid,' he said, his head turned very slightly at the sort of angle that reminded me of a puppy, gazing upwards and appealing for a tickle.

'Not so much of the kid. I'm only ... what? Two years younger than you?'

'Term of endearment, I can assure you. No offence intended. Now, or the other night.'

'I know. And I'm—'

'Don't you dare say you're sorry again. No more, okay? I'm imposing a fifty-pence fine for every time you do. Deal?'

'Deal.'

'Carry on like today and I'll be rich within a week,' he muttered, laughing and almost choking on the huge chunk of iced bun he had just crammed into his mouth.

'D'you know, I think maybe I was wrong about you.'

'Really? About what in particular? Because if you had me down as some kind of sex-mad Casanova, I'm really not. I'm more of your James Bond type actually. Smart, sexy, incredibly charismatic ...'

'Modest?'

'Yeah, that too! And I always know how to treat a lady.'

'By buying her a doughnut, you mean?'

'And why not? What the lady wants, the lady shall have.'

'Prat!' I giggled and flicked at his arm. 'No, I meant I was wrong about my first impressions of you, at that party. What I said about you not caring about anything much. I was a bit harsh. Because I think you do, don't you? Care?'

'About some things, yeah. If it's people, then yes, I care. Definitely. I was raised a Catholic, had it drummed into me how important family is, and looking after others. There's a lot of pain, sadness, hopelessness in the world, you know. My mum does a lot for a baby charity because she couldn't have any more of her own, and the thing about never having any brothers or sisters is that friends come to mean a lot. I don't go out of my way to hurt people on purpose. About my course, my boring financial future, maybe I don't care so much. But, to be fair, you didn't know me at all then, did you? Eyes across a crowded room and all that. Easy to make snap judgements. I probably came across as utterly shallow, and still do a lot of the time, but I'm hoping we can change that. Get to know each other better, I mean. Starting from tonight. How does that sound?'

'Good.' I smiled up at him, felt that warm glow creeping back over me. God, I hoped he wasn't just spinning me a line. I so wanted him to be genuine, a nice guy, maybe *my* nice guy ...

'Right. Half hour's up, and you did say you had things to do, places to be ...' He pushed his chair back, making an awful scraping sound on the tiled floor.

'Yeah, I do. Sorry.'

'Aha! That's fifty pence you owe me.'

'That's not fair!'

'Oh, yes. A bet's a bet. All's fair in love and war.' He picked up the plate with the third cake on it and held it out to me. 'Want this?'

'No. You take it.' I gathered up my coat and bag and walked towards the door, Josh a pace or two behind me. Knowing he could not see my face, I didn't have to try to hide the smile that just seemed to creep up on me. And in that moment I felt special, as if someone had just offered me their very last Rolo.

***

We took our time getting to know each other. Drinks in the bar, sitting together in the library, a coffee between tutorials. I didn't tell him about Arnie. I didn't want to, and I didn't know how. But with the air cleared and the past shoved away behind us, we resolved to start again, to take things slowly this time. To try being boyfriend and girlfriend, but not lovers, not yet, and to see what happened.

'About time you two got together,' Beth said, when I told her. We were sitting on a wall in the sunshine, outside the shop, sharing a packet of chocolate buttons. 'It's been pretty obvious he fancies the pants off you for weeks.'

'My pants are still very firmly in place, thank you very much.'

'Oh, you know what I mean. And who'd judge you if they weren't? Certainly not me. It's not as if Lenny and me have kept ours on!' She laughed, giving me a nudge in the ribs. 'So, if you need any advice about ... well, the pill or anything, then just ask. It's easy enough to get from the campus doc. No questions asked.'

'Thanks, Beth, but I'm all right.'

'Already taken care of, eh?' She picked out the last two buttons from the bottom of the bag, held one out to me and swallowed the other. 'Good girl. Best to be sensible.'

I felt myself blush. Sex wasn't something I was used to talking about, not to friends, and especially not to some strange doctor, and as far as I was concerned being sensible still meant not doing it in the first place, not taking the risk. Josh understood that. Or at least, I hoped he did. And, for the time being, just learning about each other, slowly discovering the joys of kissing, proper kissing with the feel of lips and placement of tongues, the warmth of our faces pressed closely together, was enough. For me, anyway.

Oh, I knew Josh was no virgin. He'd confessed to brief flings with at least two girls back home while he was still at school, and one or two one-night stands at uni, but nothing that had lasted, nothing that really meant anything. I suppose, deep down, I had hopes that I might be the one to change that, the one worth waiting for.

'So, when's the next date then? Only, Lenny's mate Steve is having a party on Saturday. Off campus, but easy enough to find. We could share a taxi maybe? Save hanging about for buses. I know he wouldn't mind the two of you tagging along. As long as you bring beer, obviously.'

'I'll ask.'

'Eve, you really haven't got the hang of this dating lark yet, have you? Time you got him trained. For starters, you don't ask, you tell! Seven thirty, okay? We'll call and collect you. No need to dress up. It'll be pretty casual. And if it goes on late, Steve won't mind us crashing out on the floor.'

Spending the night on someone's mucky carpet, surrounded by people I didn't know who would more than likely be drunk, didn't appeal to me at all, but I nodded anyway. 'Yeah, maybe, but we'll probably get a taxi back. I think I'd rather sleep in my own bed.'

'Up to you, and certainly more private, if you're planning on …'

'I'm not. *We're* not.'

'So you say. Right, I'll see you Saturday then? Time I got to interrogate this man of yours about his intentions, I think.'

'Don't you dare! You sound like my dad.'

'Only joking. And don't forget the booze. I bet that's something you wouldn't hear your dad say.'

I watched her go, hips swinging with a confidence in her own sexuality I didn't think I would ever have. But then, we were different. Very different. Her approach to life, to men, was nothing like mine. She and Lenny seemed happy enough, but I never saw them gaze into each other's eyes, link fingers, nuzzle each other's necks. It was more of a bum slap and a snog and sharing a bottle of lager whenever I saw them together. Sex just seemed to be a natural part of life to Beth, like brushing her teeth. It was something she had done before and would do again, without worrying about it, being frightened of it, analysing it. With Lenny, or whoever came along next. All part of the process.

I wanted more than that. I wanted the real thing. Before I gave myself to anyone. I didn't want to just do it anyway, in the vain hope that the feelings might follow later. I wanted the feelings first. The feelings in my head and heart, not the ones that fizzed away between my legs. I didn't want to be pushed or persuaded. It had to be my choice. I wanted love.

***

We didn't stay long at the party, in the end. The host, Steve, was nice enough but a few years older than us and, according to Lenny, he worked as an auditor at the Town Hall. Somehow that didn't surprise me, as the rather dull décor and choice of music were so clearly suited to the shirt-and-tie thirty-plus group to which the majority of the guests belonged.

It didn't bother Beth and Lenny though. Wedged together in a corner of the sofa, with a bottle of wine stuffed behind the cushions and Lenny's hand stuffed inside Beth's shirt, they looked very much as if they were settled for the long haul and, apart from a vague nod as we grabbed our coats and headed for the door, I'm not sure they even registered that we had gone.

It had started to rain by the time we got outside, headlights shining on the puddles as the cars swooshed past, a bus pulling up at the kerb and sending up a spray of mucky water that just missed hitting our legs. Unfortunately the bus was going in the wrong direction or we probably would have jumped on and headed straight back to uni.

'What do you want to do now?' Josh said, putting a hand on my back and guiding me safely across the road. 'Wait for one heading the other way? Grab a taxi? Or we could walk into town. We're not that far away. Find a pub or a pizza or something? Those nibbles barely touched the sides and I'm bloody starving.'

'Yeah, let's do that. I don't know about you but I get a bit sick of the sight of the campus day in and day out. Last time I went out anywhere was to Tesco's!'

'Wow, you really know how to live, don't you?' Josh teased.

'I quite enjoyed it actually. Except for lugging all the stuff back. I bought more than I'd intended and I hadn't really thought about how heavy it was all going to be while it was piling up in the trolley.'

'You mean you didn't stick to your list?'

'List? Where's the fun in that? Shopping needs to be a

spontaneous thing. From the heart. Like going out for bread and coming back with shoes.'

'Now, that's your poet's brain, you see. Head in the clouds. Ask a mathematician to go shopping and he'll have it all worked out before he starts. He'll have a proper list of what he's shopping for and he'll stick to it, so he knows how much he's likely to spend, how many bags he'll need and what to put in each for even weight distribution. No deviating from the task in hand. Like an equation. A science.'

'Oh, stop being so smug. And so boring! Let's just walk and see where we end up, shall we? A magical mystery tour. No plan, no pre-arranged list. Let's just see where life takes us for a change. Or where this road takes us, anyway.'

'Oh, there is a rebel in there somewhere! Suits me though.' He took hold of my hand and I felt his fingers close tightly around mine. 'Although I must point out I've only got about twenty pounds in my wallet, so it'll have to be a mystery tour with budgetary limitations.'

'Fine. I've got a tenner, so we should be all right. Chinese, Indian, fish and chips ... whatever we come to first we'll eat. It'll be an adventure, a surprise. Doesn't matter what the place looks like, or whether it's take-away or sit-down. Deal?'

'Deal.'

It was a burger bar, as it turned out. One with misted-up windows and slightly greasy tables, and a menu where fruit and vegetables, unless you counted a few limp-looking lettuce leaves and a pile of tomato-ketchup sachets, were non-existent and everything came with chips.

'You sure you want to eat here? It's a bit ... basic,' Josh whispered as we waited in the queue to place our order.

'Not romantic enough for you? And you say I'm the one with my head in the clouds!'

'I just feel a bit mean, bringing you somewhere like this, when we're supposed to be on a date. Like we should be somewhere a bit more ...'

'Clean?'

'I was going to say special, but now you come to mention it ...'

'It is a bit dodgy, isn't it?' I eyed the man behind the counter, sweat dripping down his face and onto a torn blue-and-white striped apron as he shovelled sliced gherkins from a jar onto a burnt bun. A hunched little man in a dirty mac stood in front of us, watching the construction of his burger and rummaging through a handful of loose change, while sniffing loudly without the benefit of a hankie. 'Shall we leave while we still can?' I whispered, tugging at Josh's sleeve.

He laughed. 'Changed your mind then? How about our deal?'

'Deal's off.' I pulled him out into the street and the door slammed shut behind us. A trickle of rainwater poured from a broken gutter up above and bounced onto the shoulder of Josh's coat. 'I just wanted to test you out, to see if you'd go along with it, but I really don't think I can eat that stuff in there. Sorry!'

'Aha. That'll be fifty pence please,' he announced, grinning. 'No sorrys allowed, remember? Now, come on, let's find somewhere decent and get ourselves some dinner. I've actually got twenty pounds fifty to spend now, so we can really push the boat out.'

'I think we might need an actual boat if this rain gets any heavier!'

I dug in my purse and found a fifty-pence piece and pushed it into Josh's cold hand. 'Don't say I never pay my debts,' I said. 'But believe me, I will get it back, if only by ordering extra mushrooms!' And then we hurried away, arm in arm, laughing and dripping wet, in search of the pizza Josh had suggested in the first place.

Chapter 8

SARAH

It was one of those days when the weather can't quite make up its mind. It had been warm when I'd taken Buster for his morning walk, the sky more or less cloudless, so I'd headed off to school in just a T-shirt, a pair of jeans and sandals, making the most of the no-uniform policy that applied now that lessons for year elevens were over for the summer and we were turning up only when we had an exam to sit or needed to use the library to revise.

By the time I came out of the stuffy, silent hall at lunchtime, the History paper behind me and a monumental fail almost inevitable, it was raining. Still, at least I'd never have to think about the Industrial Revolution ever again, so there was certainly a bright side.

'You going straight home?' Tilly said, running to catch up with me as I crossed the playground, only just dodging a ball that came flying straight at us, closely followed by a couple of year-seven boys who just laughed as they retrieved it and ran off. Neither of us mentioned the exam we'd just sat through.

'I suppose. Why? You got something else in mind?'

'Shops maybe?'

'I don't have any money. Well, only what Mum gave me for some lunch. You?'

'Not a lot. We could just go and look in the windows though, couldn't we? Dream a bit! It's not long until the end-of-year disco, and we're going to need ideas, if nothing else. Has your mum said anything about buying you something new to wear? Or how much you can spend?'

'Not really. I think she still has some mad idea about making me what she calls a posh dress, but I'm hoping if I say nothing she'll forget and by the time I remind her it'll be too late. I'd be much happier just getting a shiny top or something from Dorothy Perkins.'

'God. They have no idea, do they? Parents?'

'None at all!'

'I wish we had proms like they do in America. Then we could turn up in one of those long white limousines.'

'Can't see this school ever doing anything like that.'

'And I think you're meant to have a date when you go to a prom. You know, a boy to turn up with, or else you just look like some sad no-mates kind of a person. What a load of rubbish.'

'Well, I'd be all right though, wouldn't I? I've got Paul.'

'Have you? Really? I mean, is he actually your boyfriend or what?'

'Course he is.' The rain was getting heavier and we'd only made it as far as the school gate. A bus was coming towards us and suddenly jumping on it seemed like a very good idea.

'Look, I am going home after all. I don't fancy getting soaked. You go to the shops if you like, and once I've grabbed a coat and seen if I can squeeze some money out of my dad if he's home then I'll come and find you. Meet you outside Debenhams, okay? One o'clock.'

I flashed my pass at the driver, walked along the aisle of the almost empty bus and sat right at the back. Why did Tilly always have to ask such awkward questions? Probably because she didn't have a boyfriend of her own. Of course Paul was my boyfriend. Well, it wasn't as if we'd been out to the pictures or anything like that, and we certainly hadn't made any earth-shattering announcement about us being together, but we'd ... Well, he'd said that he liked me, and we'd done the deed, hadn't we? Three times now, and that had to mean something.

'How did you get on?' Dad said, coming into the hallway as I dashed into the house, slamming the door behind me and dripping raindrops all over the carpet. 'Oh, I see you forgot your coat.' He stepped forward and gave me a hug anyway, laughing as my wet hair made a soggy mark on the front of his shirt.

'Don't ask.'

'Ah, but I just did! That bad, eh? Never mind, Love, we can't all be brilliant at everything, and History's not as important as some of the others. Learning all those dates ... Unless you want to teach it, I've never really seen that it's a lot of use in life. And you've got Maths next, right? You like Maths.'

'Do I?'

'Oh, Sarah, Love, don't look so downhearted. It'll be fine. And once these exams are over, you can start looking around for a job. There must be loads of places that would jump at the chance of employing a clever girl like you. Local offices, shops, maybe even something at the Council.'

I knew he meant well, but if he really thought I was as clever as all that he would be talking about me going on to A levels and researching university places, not looking for jobs.

'Yeah, maybe. But Dad?'

'Yes, Love?'

'Do you think that, as I've been revising so hard, you might give me ... well, a reward of some kind? Some of the other girls' parents are taking them on holidays or giving them some money for, you know, doing well in their exams.'

'Shouldn't we wait until we see the results before we think about rewards, Sarah? I mean, revising is one thing but actually passing is something else entirely. When your sister did so well ...'

'Yes, I know. You bought her a watch, and lovely it was too, but Eve's a brainbox, isn't she? There was never any doubt she'd pass the lot. I'm not in her league.'

'You'll do the best you can, I'm sure. And your mother and I have already got our eyes on a very nice watch for you, every bit as pretty as your sister's.'

'And what if I don't want a watch? Or a job in an office?'

He looked puzzled for a moment. 'What do you want then?'

'I don't know, Dad. I wish I did, but I'm not Eve. We're not the same. We never have been.'

'Of course not. I know that. Each beautiful in your own way. And we're equally proud of both of you. I hope you know that. Now, I only popped home for a quick lunch and to see how you got on, but I really have to get back to the office now. Will you be okay? Your mum will be home soon if you're staying in. Or I can give you a few pounds to treat yourself to some lunch out if you like. Might help cheer you up. Exam time can feel pretty rotten, I remember.'

'Lunch on my own?'

'Oh, no. That would never do! Why not ask little Tilly if she'd like to join you?' He took his wallet from his trouser pocket and opened it, checking the contents carefully. 'Will five pounds be enough?'

I gave him one of those not-quite-sure looks which seemed to entice another fiver out into his hand.

'Chin up, Sarah,' he said, putting two fingers under my chin and tilting my face up towards him. 'It'll all look a lot better when the exams are over, and we can give some serious thought to your future.'

I thanked him for the cash and waved him off at the door. Buster had wandered out from his basket in the kitchen and stood beside me, sniffing at the rain, and I bent down to pat his wiry head. Once Dad had driven away, I followed the old dog as he plodded back towards the kitchen. Think about my future? Right then it stretched only as far as the school disco, and making sure Paul Jacobs would only have eyes for me. And hands. Because I couldn't lose him now. Couldn't let him drift away into some other girl's arms, some other girl's body. I had let him have sex with me, and that had to count for something. It had to count for a lot. Otherwise, what was the point? In any of it.

I made a quick sandwich and opened a bag of crisps. At

least then I could spend the whole ten pounds Dad had given me, and the fiver I'd got from Mum earlier, on clothes. Tilly would have to take care of her own lunch.

***

Paul's breath smelt of chewing gum. As we left the exam hall side by side, he spat the shapeless plug of white goo out into his hand and slipped it down the back of the nearest radiator. 'All right?' he said, nodding back towards the hall. 'That wasn't too bad, was it? Question three was a bit tricky, but the rest of it was easy enough, all stuff we covered in the mocks.'

I nodded, not entirely sure I agreed with him about any of it being easy. It was Maths, after all.

'Paul. Can we ...?'

He sidestepped the main throng of people streaming out into the corridor and pulled me with him against the wall. 'Can we what? You're looking very serious all of a sudden. What is it, Sarah? Only, I haven't got long. I have to get some lunch and then I'm meeting someone at three.'

'A girl?'

'Now, where did that come from? Of course it's not a girl.' He raised his eyebrows and laughed. 'You're my girl, aren't you?'

'I don't know. I hope so. Am I?' I could feel my face go red. This wasn't the kind of conversation I was used to having, and I didn't want to sound too clingy, or get the whole thing wrong.

'Sarah, I don't know what this is about, but chill out a bit, okay? So, we've had a bit of fun a couple of times, but we're not exactly joined at the hip. It's not as if we're engaged or something. I can meet whoever I like without having to tell you about it.'

'Yeah, I know. Of course. I just thought it might be nice to spend some time together. And it's ages until three.'

He looked at his watch and nodded. 'Smart, isn't it?' he said, seeing where my gaze had fallen. 'A present from my mum and dad.'

'For doing the exams?' What was it with parents and watches? Were there no other gifts available?

'Birthday, but first time I've worn it to school. Thought it might bring me luck. No, I'm getting a car when the exams are over. Well, if I pass with decent grades anyway. Which I will.'

'A car? But you're not even old enough to drive.'

'Almost. And there's nothing to stop me learning, as long as I stay off the roads. My granddad's got a farm, plenty of fields to practise in. It won't be a new car. Just a second-hand Mini probably. And my dad's going to show me some stuff about engines, help me do it up a bit before I take my test. That's where I'm off to at three, meeting my dad outside where he works and we're going to look at some cars. So, I've got a couple of hours, I suppose. What did you fancy doing? Getting something to eat?'

'How about your mum? Is she at home?'

'Nope. She's gone to see her sister, my aunt Denise. She's just had a baby. Mum's been knitting like crazy, so it'll be all bootees and shawls and stuff all afternoon. Almost makes me glad I had an exam so I didn't have to go with her.'

'So there's nobody at home then? At your house?'

'Sarah Peters! Are you suggesting what I think you are?'

'Not if you don't want to.' I turned away, my embarrassment obvious in my face. 'I'll just go home, shall I? And be boring. Maybe get my knitting needles out?'

'Don't you dare!' I felt him come up close behind me, one hand sliding sneakily down over my bottom behind the cover of the jacket he was holding over his arm, and the other pushing me gently forward. 'Go on, grab your bags and stuff and I'll see you outside,' he said, hardly louder than a whisper. 'Wait round the corner by the post box. I'll be five minutes, okay?'

I had never been to Paul's house before. It was only a ten-minute walk away, which probably explained why I so rarely saw him on the bus. But it was a walk we took quickly, staying a foot or two apart all the while, with neither of us saying very much. The house, when we got to it, was a fairly standard-looking semi, similar in size to ours, with a blue front door and bright geraniums in pots to either side. Paul found his key and hurried me in, looking up and down the road as if we were about to be caught and exposed as some kind of intruders.

'Phew!' he said, leaning against the inside of the front door and smiling. 'We made it in without Mrs Burton from two doors down seeing us. Or I hope we did, anyway. I swear that woman is a witch. Eyes in the back of her head, that one. There'll be a full written report handed in to my mum before we've even made it upstairs if that one catches us.'

'And who says we're going upstairs?' I said, smiling back at him. 'I thought we might watch telly and have a glass of squash and a biscuit. That's what I usually do when friends come round to our house.'

'And is that what you want to do now, Sarah?' He dropped his bag and jacket on the floor and put his hands on my shoulders. The chewing-gum smell had worn off and in its place there was just the warm sweet taste of his mouth as he leaned forward and placed his lips on mine. 'Because I'm sure I can find you some lemon barley and a bourbon, if that's what you really fancy.'

'No, I'm not hungry.' I shivered, despite it being June and the sun shining in through the patterned glass in the front door, throwing rose pictures onto the carpet at our feet.

'Then what do you fancy? Or who?' His voice had gone all husky and sexy and I could feel myself melt inside.

'You know the answer to that.'

'Hello,' he shouted, stopping totally still at the foot of the stairs and listening for any sound of a reply. 'Just checking,' he said after a moment's silence, when all I could hear was my own heart pounding away in my chest. 'And it looks like no one's at home, except us. Come on.' He grabbed my hand, led me up the narrow staircase and opened a door on the landing that led into what was obviously his bedroom. Football posters on the wall, revision books scattered all over a small desk, an unmade bed piled with rumpled pillows and discarded clothes and what just might have been a cuddly toy. One swipe of his arm landed most of that on the floor and he pulled me down, roughly, on top of him, his hand

91

already up inside my top and feeling for the fastenings at the back of my bra.

'First time in a bed,' he said, nuzzling into my neck. 'Makes a change from doing it outside. Those park benches are way too uncomfortable. And it's not dark this time, which means I can look at you properly.' He was pulling my arms up, easing my top over my head, scooping at my bra as its straps fell down over my bare shoulders, somehow managing to kick off his shoes and wriggle his way out of his trousers at the same time.

It only took a few moments until we were both completely naked and I saw everything clearly for the first time, in daylight. His penis, long and stiff, the curls of dark hair around it, his chest flat and pale, the determined look on his face as he sat up and rummaged about at the back of his bedside drawer, throwing out various boxes and bits of paper until he came to the hidden stash of condoms disguised in an old toothpaste packet at the back.

'You put it on for me this time,' he instructed, ripping the packet open with his teeth and passing me a small, rolled-up pink thing that felt slimy in my hand. 'But hurry up ...'

I wasn't at all sure what I was doing, but it was fun finding out, gliding the condom back over his skin, seeing it expand to fit him, leaving just a little floppy empty bit dangling at the end. 'What's that for?' I asked, my curiosity way ahead of any feelings of lust.

'To catch the sperm,' he said. 'Stop it from going where it shouldn't. We don't want you getting pregnant, do we?'

'No.'

And then we were rolling together, his body coming down on top of me, flattening me and pinning me to the bed.

'Do you think we could slow down a bit this time? Do it like they do in films? You know, more kissing, less pushing?'

'For God's sake, Sarah. Can't you see I'm nearly there already? Wait much longer and it'll be squirting out before I even get inside you.'

'But I'd like to see what it feels like ...'

'Just lie back and let me get on with it. It'll feel good, I promise you.'

But it didn't. It was over in seconds, just like before, and I lay there with his head between my breasts, his hot breath slowing against my skin. I felt his penis flop out of me and onto the bed beside me, its rubber casing already slipping off where I obviously hadn't quite put it on properly, leaving a puddle on the sheet.

I reached for his hand and put it between my legs. I was supposed to feel something, wasn't I? I'd read about orgasms in magazines, read that most women didn't get them from being entered, that a man could do amazing things just with the carefully placed rhythm of his fingers. But Paul wasn't a man. He was a kid, just like I was. His hand didn't move in mysterious ways. He just shoved a finger straight up inside me and prodded me, jabbing like someone digging wax out of their ears. And then he went to sleep.

And as I lay there feeling disappointed, it was pretty obvious he was just a *Car Mechanics* and *Football Monthly* kind of person. Like it probably was for most boys of his age, sex was a selfish thing. Intense, frantic, quick. He'd had what he wanted, and given me what he thought I wanted too. One thing was for sure: he certainly hadn't read any of the same magazines I had.

***

'Where's Paul then?' Tilly nudged me and looked quizzically around the school hall as we stood together in the doorway. The big heavy curtains were closed, so the room was already quite dark, with just some brightly coloured disco lights flashing randomly overhead, and the thump of the music making the floor throb. 'Only, if you're intending on running straight over to him and staying glued to his side all evening, I'd rather know now.'

'Don't be daft.' I pulled at my tight top, making sure it hung a little lower, and smoothed out any creases my skirt might have suffered during the drive here in Tilly's dad's car. 'I haven't made any plans to meet up with Paul at all.'

'You mean he didn't ask you!'

She was right, of course. Things had certainly cooled since that lunchtime in his room and, as we weren't studying a lot of the same subjects, our exam timetables rarely coincided and we had hardly seen each other at school.

'I've been busy revising. There are some things that are more important than boys ...'

Tilly laughed. 'If anyone else had said that I just might have believed them, but since when have you worried about putting school work first? And besides, the exams are over now so he's got no excuse.'

'He doesn't need an excuse. If he wants to see me he knows where I am, and if not then I'm really not bothered. Plenty more fish in the sea.'

'Well, you've changed your tune. I thought he was Mr Wonderful. The perfect man.'

'Oh, that's enough about Paul Jacobs. There's no such thing as perfect. Come on, let's get inside and find a drink. It's free, after all.'

'Yeah, if all you want is fruit juice or Coke!'

'Can't see them providing alcohol, can you? As far as they're concerned, we're all just kids. But I know as well as you do that there's a little bottle of vodka hidden at the bottom of your bag.'

'That's just where you're wrong,' Tilly giggled. 'It's gin! But you're not getting any of it if you abandon me for Paul ... or any of those other fishes in the sea.'

'No chance. All I want to do tonight is dance and drink and have fun, knowing I will never ever have to sit another exam again.'

'Definitely not staying on for A levels then?'

'I'm not sure there's much point. Unless the unimaginable happens and I suddenly get a load of A grades. Fat chance of that! Even my mum and dad have given up on me, and I'm never going to match up to my sister, so I may as well get out there and start earning some money. If only work didn't look so horribly boring.'

'It doesn't have to be.' We picked up two paper cups of lemon squash and found ourselves a corner from where we could watch what was happening on the dancefloor but still just about see who came in through the door.

'You're definitely coming back in September then?'

'Yeah. If I want to be a dentist ...'

'A dentist? That's the first I've heard about that.'

'Well, you don't know everything about me. So, if I'm going to be a dentist, I'm going to need some decent qualifications. And I am going to work hard, I've decided. No getting sidetracked, especially by boys.'

'Tilly, you have never shown any interest in boys, so it's hardly going to be a sacrifice, is it?'

'Well, from what you told me, I don't actually think I'm missing much.'

'What I told you was secret, so don't you go blabbing ...'

'As if I would. But I wish I'd been there, if only to see that teddy on his bed.'

'Well, I only saw it for a few seconds before he knocked it onto the floor, but I think it might have been wearing a football shirt.'

'That figures. More of a mascot thing than something to cuddle. Boys and their football ...'

'There were actually a couple of other balls in the room, you know. Ones I was paying more attention to.'

Tilly didn't get it at first, and then she laughed out loud, jiggling her cup as she sloshed gin into her lemon squash and accidentally splashed some onto her hand. 'Yuck!' she said. 'That's something I do not want to think about. Looking at pictures in Biology was bad enough. All those wrinkles and hair and stuff. How you let them anywhere near you I don't know.'

'I don't think I will again.' I stared out into the gloom, my foot tapping to the music, hoping I might see him come in but also hoping just as much that I might not.

'What? Not ever?'

'Maybe, one day. But not him. Not Paul Jacobs. It was sort of necessary, you know, the losing my virginity thing, but I think next time I'd like it to be with someone who actually knows what they're doing.'

Chapter 9

EVE

Waking up in my old bed at home still felt comforting, as if I had never really left. The narrow cracks in the ceiling which I was sure had grown wider, and the swirly pattern in the curtains where I had imagined I had seen pictures that were never really there. The gurgling sounds of the pipes coming from the bathroom next door. My dressing gown on the back of the door, my posters still above the bed, Buster snuffling at my hand asking to be walked, or cuddled, or fed. But beneath the familiarity I knew things had changed and would never be quite the same again.

I didn't live here anymore. My life – my real life – was in Wales now, in that small room in Block P that I had asked to hang onto for a second year, and with my new friends and my English course. Oh, how I was loving that course. I was already living and breathing those wonderful novels and poems, absorbing the language and the imagery, spending hours reading and discussing and analysing. And being away from all that for the whole of the summer felt a bit like a bereavement, as if the better part of me had been left behind, and what I had brought home was just a shell. I was going to miss it all so much. And then, of course, there was Josh …

During the last few weeks at university Josh had slowly crept his way into my head and he was still there. I thought about him a lot. Well, most of the time, if I was being honest about it. I didn't want to. I had gone away to study and to take the first steps towards an independent future, to push away bad memories and start again. And it was not as if Josh was ideal partner material, after all. His family lived too far away – somewhere near Leeds – so hopping on a train (or more likely, several trains) from Wales to see each other now he had left uni was not going to be easy, and certainly not frequent. He was destined to a future in a suit, a numbers man more at home with a calculator than a book. Someone who wouldn't know a sonnet if it jumped up and bit him! And yet, despite our differences, or maybe because of them, we seemed to be drawn together. I liked being in his company, liked the feel of my hand in his, found myself wanting to rush and tell him everything that happened, as soon as it happened, no matter how silly or small. I still did it now, by phone, saving up all my news for our twice-weekly calls.

But something wasn't right. Even as we'd parted at the station, I had pulled back as soon as I felt his arms close too tightly around my waist, his pelvis push against mine as we said our goodbyes. Was I being fair, expecting him to under-stand? And to wait? Or was I just being a coward? Because, even after all the months that had passed, I knew without doubt that it still all came down to Arnie. What Arnie had done to me, the panic he had planted in me, about boys, about men, knowing that he had taken away my curiosity and the wonder of discovery, and replaced them with a wariness bordering on fear.

I still woke up sometimes, sweating, panicking, with it all running through my head, second by second, like a film in slow motion, the sensation of him pressed into my skin, the smell and the taste of him rising up through my nostrils, making me want to cry, to run, to scream.

But Josh wasn't Arnie. When I closed my eyes as Josh kissed me, I didn't see Arnie, not anymore. I didn't imagine myself in danger, didn't want to run. It felt nice, right, as if I belonged there, and all I wanted was for it to stay that way, moving slowly, safely, at a pace I could deal with.

I had the long summer break now, to think about things, to work out what I wanted. We were young, I still had my degree course to get on with and he had a job to get started on, whether that turned out to be based in his own home town or somewhere further afield. There was no rush to plunge into serious territory. No rush to make declarations of undying love, to fall naked into whatever bed beckoned. Somehow I had managed to put all of that off, to postpone any drastic decisions, to keep Josh in the limbo-land of maybe-one-day. But I couldn't push him away forever, or I would risk losing him. As if distance didn't already pose a big enough threat. There had to be a way to make it work, because I couldn't let Arnie win. We had to be the winners: Josh and me.

I felt a thump as Buster hauled himself up, his back legs

scrabbling about in mid-air for a few seconds, onto the bed. The old dog seemed pleased to have me home, my long absence already pushed aside as if I had never been gone.

'Come on, Boy. Let's get you walked, shall we?' I climbed out of bed and hunted for clean underwear, a T-shirt and jeans among the clothes, most of them dirty, that I had brought back with me and that now lay in a heap partly in and partly out of my suitcase in the middle of the carpet. Sarah was stirring in the other bed, mumbling something that sounded like 'Grow away', before sinking back down into a snuffly sleep.

It seemed only fair that I take over dog duties for a while. Buster was technically mine anyway, and Sarah had done more than her share while I had been away.

The house was quiet, Mum and Dad not yet having emerged from their room. When I got to the foot of the stairs, I saw that the newspaper hadn't even arrived on the mat yet, and I put that down to that paper-girl friend of Sarah's having a bit of a lie-in now the school holidays had begun. It was only when I went into the kitchen and looked at the clock that I realised it was still only half past six.

The streets were empty, just an occasional car and the rattle of the milk float disturbing the silence. We took our time, with nothing much to hurry back for, and Buster seemed to relish the chance to investigate every clump of earth, every piece of litter, and sniff to his heart's content at all the exciting smelly evidence that other dogs had been there before him.

I didn't see him at first, the man coming towards me along the pavement on the other side of the street. He was dressed for work in an office somewhere, by the look of him. Suit slightly too tight, a plain white shirt and a not-quite-straight blue tie, a tatty brown leather briefcase dangling from his hand as he hurried along, head down. But once I had spotted him, even at a distance, even without a full view of his face, I knew who he was. Arnie O'Connor.

It was not cold that morning but I felt a shiver run through me. I didn't want to look at him, and definitely didn't want him to see me or run the risk of him coming over to talk to me. I should have turned my back towards him, walked off in the other direction or hidden behind a tree, but I found I couldn't move. I just stood there, rooted to the spot, and I couldn't look away.

He didn't look up at all. He drew level with me, just yards away across an empty street, and then walked right past, probably off to catch an early train, his feet pounding the pavement, the wires and earpieces of a Walkman visible above his collar, utterly oblivious to my presence. I wondered where he was going, what job he did, what music he might be listening to, and then wondered why I should care. Because I didn't. He looked ordinary, just some unremarkable man on his way to work. He didn't look frightening or threatening at all, and I had the sudden feeling that even if he had looked at me he probably wouldn't have recognised me or remembered who I was. I meant nothing to him and, in that moment, I couldn't understand why I had allowed him, or the memory of him, to still mean so much to me.

***

Lucy and I sat side by side on the swings in the playground. She was my oldest friend and it had been far too long since we'd had the chance to spend time together and catch up on what was happening in our lives. In many ways we were entirely different. Lucy had no wish to go to university. She never had. Life through her eyes was a very simple and straightforward affair. You finished school, you found a job and you got married. Two babies, maybe three if the first two had not produced the required one-of-each, a little house with a garden, and life was pretty much complete. By the sound of it, she was well on her way. She was working at a florist's now, a job that surrounded her with beautiful things, paid a decent enough wage and would, in time, mean that she could design and make her own bespoke wedding bouquet, and all the table decorations and buttonholes too. And Robert had done the expected thing on her nineteenth birthday, going down on one knee and spending the regulation one month's salary on a ring. The wedding itself remained a hazy vision of rose petals and satin and yards of frothy white fluff, and was apparently unlikely to take place for at least three or four years, but that didn't seem to matter at all. The dream was everything.

If only my own life could be so easily plotted and planned. But for me, there was so much more to cram in. I wanted to get my degree, develop a fulfilling career, hopefully in teaching, and perhaps travel a bit. And somehow I needed to include Josh in all of that. Not as the be-all-and-end-all of my life, the hub that everything else revolved around, as Robert so clearly was to Lucy, but as equals. I liked to imagine our lives being like the swings Lucy and I were sitting on now, swaying around, soaring up and away from each other every now and then, each on its own path, but always within reach of each other, the long stretchy chains keeping us close and making sure that when we touched back down we were still side by side. I shook my head to clear such fanciful thoughts.

Lucy was talking about her job, about a customer who had come into the shop and ordered six dozen red roses for his girlfriend, and another who had sent just a single rosebud, and which she thought was the more romantic of the two. I wasn't sure there was a right or a wrong answer to that. Love, romance, sex, they were different things to different people. And none of it, none of the important stuff, was about roses, was it?

'I saw Arnie yesterday,' I said, right out of the blue. Lucy was still the only person I had ever told about that night at the party, the only one I could say my thoughts out loud to, and seeing him so unexpectedly was still very much in my thoughts that day.

'Really?' She pulled her swing to a stop, digging her heels into the tarmac, and turned to face me. 'To speak to?'

'No. Oh, no. I don't think I would ever want to speak to him. No, he didn't even see me, but I saw him. Watched him walk by ...'

'And?'

'And what?'

'Well, how did it make you feel? Didn't you want to just rush up and smack him one? Or shout out and tell the world what he did? I mean, now you've had time to calm down about it all, you must want to ... I don't know, get some kind of revenge, or something?'

'God, no. I don't want to drag it all up again. I just want to forget about it, make it all go away.'

'And has it? Gone away?'

I shook my head, closed my eyes and fought back the tears. 'No.'

'Oh, Eve. It's been ages. It must be a year ago now, or more. You can't let it upset you after all this time. Arnie's just a scumbag who means nothing. Ignore him. Avoid him. Forget about him! You've got your Josh now, haven't you? Who I am dying to meet, by the way.'

'I'm not sure he is *my* Josh exactly.'

'But he's your boyfriend, isn't he? You said you'd been going out. Meals, drinks ...'

'Oh, yes, all of that.' I felt a smile force its way, unbidden, onto my face.

'And you're not seeing anyone else? And he's not either?'

'Well, I'm not, and I don't think he is. Well, I bloody well hope not.'

'Then of course he's *your* Josh! So, tell me what he's like. Do you have a picture?'

'No, I don't. I should have got one, shouldn't I? To put in a frame by my bed and swoon over before I go to sleep every night.' I laughed, but I could see she thought I meant it. She probably had one just like that of her Robert. 'But he's ... well, tall, I suppose. Taller than me, anyway. And he's got dark hair, and brown eyes, and he was studying Maths and Business, would you believe! How I ever got mixed up with someone who's into Maths I do not know!'

'Prospects?'

'What do you mean, prospects? Can he keep me in the manner to which I've become accustomed? A man of good fortune? Lucy, honestly, you sound exactly like Mrs Bennet, trying to marry me off!'

'Who's Mrs Bennet?' She looked bemused for a moment and I couldn't really be bothered to start explaining. You've either read Jane Austen or you haven't.

'Oh, never mind. He's finished his degree and he's going onto a graduate-entry scheme at a bank, starting in a couple of weeks. Just waiting for the details to be finalised. So, yes, he has prospects as you call them. The chance of a good steady career ahead of him. But that has nothing to do with why I like him.'

'*Like* him? Not *love* him?' She stood up and pulled me along with her, making way for some children who were hovering nearby, waiting to use the swings, but luckily also giving me enough time to think before I answered her.

'Well?' she said, as we moved to a bench beneath the trees. 'Do you love him?'

'It's more complicated than that, Lucy. To me love means some really huge all-encompassing thing. You know, being prepared to do anything for that person, not being able to imagine a life without them in it, giving myself body and soul ...'

'Aha!' She lifted her fingers to my chin and slowly turned my face back towards her. 'That's the problem, isn't it? The body bit of that sentence? You haven't, have you? Given yourself ...'

I shook my head. 'Arnie O'Connor has a lot to answer for.'

'Arnie O'Connor is a nobody. A loser whose brain is in his trousers. Only you can decide what to do, and when, and who with, and if you're not ready, for any reason at all, then you don't do it. Okay? Nothing to do with Arnie Knobhead O'Connor.'

'And is that how it is with you and Robert? Not ready yet, despite all the years you've known him and the wedding plans and saving up for a life together?'

'Not ready? Don't be daft. We've been at it like rabbits for months now!'

'Lucy!' I was shocked. 'After all you said about taking things slowly and saving yourself? When did this happen? And why didn't you tell me?'

'I don't tell you everything. Well, maybe I do, actually, but you weren't here and it's not the sort of thing I'm going to talk about in a letter or blurt out down the phone while you're standing there in your hall surrounded by people I don't know, now, is it?' She held out her left hand, and let the small diamond catch the glint of sunlight, tilting her finger one way and then the other. 'Yes, I was hesitant for a while, especially when we first got together. We were only fourteen then, can you believe! It's a big step. But then, suddenly, just recently, I knew the time was right.' She gave me a jokey wink and nudged me gently in the ribs. 'It's amazing what having a ring on your finger can do.'

***

Josh's voice down the phone sent a warm glow through me. 'Sorry I didn't ring yesterday,' he said. 'Mum and Dad were celebrating their anniversary, and we all went out for a meal in the evening. Aunts and uncles, neighbours, Uncle Tom Cobley and all. It was their silver, and I'd completely forgotten about it, so I had to do a quick rush out to the shops and get a card and a present and everything. Took me all afternoon.'

'Fifty pence.'

'Um, no, I managed to get them something a bit more expensive than that.'

'For saying sorry, you dumbo! Fifty pence, remember?'

'Oh, right. Wondered what you meant then for a minute.' He laughed, then paused. 'But if I owe you money, Eve, I'm afraid I'm going to have to come down there and pay it. Can't have debts building up, can we? And fifty pence is not a trifling sum ...'

'Says the future banker,' I giggled. 'You couldn't even buy a cup of tea or an ice cream for that these days. Do you mean it though? About coming down here?'

'Of course. If you'll have me. Not that I have anywhere to stay ...'

'We've got a sofa. Well, we've got a spare room too, but it's stuffed full of Mum's knitting and sewing stuff, so the sofa's probably a better bet.'

'And do you think your parents will be okay about a strange man turning up and moving in for a while?'

I really wasn't sure how they might react as I had never presented them with such a question, or even asked them to meet a boyfriend, before. 'How long is a while?'

'I thought maybe a couple of weeks? Ten days, at least. It's a bit far to come just for the day, so I'd like to make the most of it while I can, before work starts in earnest. Thought we could maybe go out and about, and you can show me some of the sights, Big Ben, Buck House, take a boat trip on the Thames, that sort of thing.'

'I would love that.'

'So, you'll ask them? Only, if I have to pay for a hostel or a B&B or something, I probably won't be able to stay more than a night or two.'

'Yes, I'll ask them. Beg them. Convince them. Persuade them. Bribe them. Lock them in the attic. Whatever it takes!'

'That keen to see me, eh?'

'Yes. Yes, I am. It feels like forever since ...'

'Yeah, I know.' His voice had gone quiet, serious. 'It's actually only been nine days, you know, but I've missed you. A lot.'

'Me too.'

'Maybe, when I'm in London, we could, you know ...'

'What?'

'Maybe try taking things a step further? Only if you're ready, of course.'

'Sex, you mean?'

'Well, I wouldn't have put it quite so bluntly, but yes. It's time, Eve. We've waited long enough, don't you think? And now we know each other better. Trust each other.'

I took a big breath and closed my eyes, glad he couldn't see me. 'Yeah, maybe.' I didn't want to say that if we hadn't got that far with two uni rooms at our disposal and twenty-four-hour privacy on our side, then there wasn't much chance of us doing it with my parents breathing down our necks and me sharing a room with my sister.

There was an awkward silence, as though he was waiting for me to say something else, but eventually he just said, 'Right. See you soon then, I hope.'

'Yes.'

'I love you, Eve.'

And that was when I put the phone down, because I had no idea what to say in return.

Chapter 10

SARAH

I remember looking up from a magazine when he first came into the room and just thinking, *Wow!*

Josh Cavendish was probably the best-looking man ever to walk through the door of our house – not that many usually did – and he was Eve's. My boring bookish sister Eve had managed to bag herself a boyfriend to die for!

'This is my little sister, Sarah,' Eve was saying, throwing her bag down on an armchair and bending to pat Buster as he bounded towards her, almost knocking her over. 'And this is Buster.'

Josh held out a hand and beamed a smile at me, and all I could do was grin like an idiot, squirm at the fact Eve had called me little, and hope my face hadn't gone red.

'Hi, Sarah.' He gripped my hand and pulled it up to his lips for an elaborate kiss, his eyes twinkling with amusement. 'Nice to meet you. I've heard so much about you.'

'Have you? You shouldn't believe it, whatever it is she's said.'

'Oh, no, it's all good, honest. Eve talks about you a lot.

About when you were kids and everything, sharing a room, decorating the Christmas tree. All the fun stuff. I wish I had a sister I could show off about. Or a brother, but it's just me. Anyway, I hope you don't mind me staying, crowding your space and all that. I'll try not to get in the way, I promise.'

The thought of coming down in the mornings to find this gorgeous man asleep, and quite possibly only partially dressed, on the sofa where I was now sitting, was something I was sure I wouldn't mind at all. I put the magazine down and budged along, hoping Josh might sit down next to me.

'Ooh, Josh, someone seems to have taken a liking to you,' Eve said, and for a moment I thought she meant me, that my face had given away what I was thinking, but of course she was talking about Buster who, as soon as Josh sat down – not next to me but in Dad's armchair – was struggling to haul himself up on to his lap.

'Animals always know who their friends are,' Josh said, helping the old dog up and rubbing his head. 'And it looks like we're going to get along just fine.'

'Do you want a cup of tea, or something cold?' Eve sat on the arm of the chair and patted Buster too, her fingers joining Josh's as they worked their way over the wiry hair behind the dog's pointy ears. 'Mum'll be home soon, and I know she's planning a big welcome meal, so we'd better stick to drinks only. I won't offer you a biscuit.'

'Tea's fine, thanks. And I'm not hungry. I had a sandwich on the train.'

'Well, I'd like a biscuit,' I said, trying to make sure I wasn't going to be ignored. Now, or for the next ten days.

Eve looked at me and shook her head. 'I'm not your slave, Sarah. You know where the tin is.'

And from that moment on, I knew exactly how it was going to be. Josh this, and Josh that, and me expected to just disappear into the background.

I stomped my way out to the kitchen and grabbed three of the best and most crumbly biscuits from the tin and took them upstairs, where I sat down on Eve's bed and made sure I dropped as many crumbs as I possibly could all over her covers.

***

Tilly found herself a job that summer. It was only mornings, in a little bakery, helping out at the back of the shop with all the mixing and baking that went on at the crack of dawn and then serving in the shop when it was busy, but suddenly she was acting as if she was so grown-up, earning her own money, mixing with her new friends, and leaving me behind. The last thing I wanted to do was work unless I really had to, but I have to admit I was feeling a bit left out and more than a bit sorry for myself.

'Are you not going out anywhere today, Love?' Mum said, one morning over breakfast. 'It's looking like a lovely day out there. A shame to be stuck indoors. And, once you get your GCSE results, you may not get the chance quite so often.'

I knew what she meant, of course. While they'd allowed me a few weeks off to enjoy the summer, it was only a matter of time until she and Dad expected me to plan my life, make the big decision, face up to my choices. Basically, either to go back to school for another two excruciating years, or find a job. But, having looked at my diary that morning and counted back, I had a terrible feeling there could be another option looming, and it wasn't one any of us would have chosen.

'Why don't you see if Tilly's free?' she went on, absent-mindedly buttering too many slices of toast, even though everyone else had already left the table. 'There must be something you girls would like to do together.'

'Tilly's working mornings, Mum. Remember?'

'Oh, yes, I think you did say. Well, later then, when she finishes.'

'Yeah, maybe. But I think I'll just sit in the garden. Read a magazine on the sun lounger, maybe try getting a tan.'

'Up to you.' Mum put the knife down and started digging a teaspoon into the depths of the jam pot, trying to hook the last strawberry. 'Make sure you don't burn though. There's a bottle of sun cream in the bathroom.'

'Yes, Mum.' I raised my eyebrows and sighed. What did she think I was? Five? I think I knew how to look after myself by now. 'Shouldn't you be getting off to work? It's nearly ten to nine.'

'Oh, my! Is it really? Okay, Love.' She stood up abruptly, still chewing on her toast, and picked up her bag. 'I'd best be going then. Pop the plates in the sink for me, won't you? See you later. Be good!'

If by popping the plates in the sink, Mum actually meant I should be washing them up, then I supposed I'd better get it over with straight away, before the jammy traces stuck fast.

I let the water run hot and dipped my hands into the bubbles. Washing up and reading trashy magazines, my insides fluttering about with a fear I was nowhere near ready to face, while my goody-two-shoes sister, with her brains and her perfect life and her oh-so-perfect boyfriend, was out having all the fun. Why did life have to be so unfair?

Josh had settled in quickly, as though he'd been around forever. Mum liked him instantly, and Dad wasn't far behind once they discovered a shared love of chess, a game neither Eve nor I had ever really got to grips with. He had that sort of mathematical, logical mind, I supposed, as opposed to Eve's ridiculous passion for English and my total disinterest in just about any school subject you could choose to mention. Still, I almost wished I had some Maths homework to do, just so I could ask Josh to help me with it. How Eve had managed to attract someone like Josh I would never know. What I wouldn't give ...

I shook my head and got on with the dishes. What was the point of drooling over someone who had probably hardly noticed I existed? I only really saw him in the evenings anyway, when he was poised over the chess board with Dad, or Eve was either squashed up to him on the sofa or sitting with him at the table poring over their maps and plans. Dad made sure we girls were both upstairs in bed before Josh unfurled his blankets on the sofa every night, with a look that hinted of 'no hanky-panky under my roof' and Josh was always up and dressed by the time we came down again for breakfast, so I never even got a glimpse of him with his top off.

They were out early most days, Eve and Josh, off on a bus

somewhere, or to visit a museum or a park, making the most of the time they had together, rucksacks piled high with Mum's door-step sandwiches and Dad usually slipping them a few pounds to treat themselves to a drink or an ice cream. Of course, Josh would be gone soon enough, back to somewhere miles away and, once he was working nine to five, who knew when we would ever see him again? Eve would be unbearable then. I dreaded it already. But then all the attention would be on her – as usual – and not on me. I would have some time to think about what to do, at least.

***

I had forgotten just how boring sitting doing nothing could be, especially when thoughts I really didn't want to deal with kept trying to force their way into my head. By half past one I had had enough sun and celebrity gossip and decided I might walk down to the shops and meet Tilly after all. Sometimes they let her take a few bits home. Bread rolls that had got a bit too burnt on top, doughnuts not quite round enough to put in the window. And I was hungry. Perhaps, if she emerged without the tell-tale paper bag in her hand, we could go for chips. With plenty of salt and vinegar, and the warm grease soaking through the bag. And then, maybe I would tell her ...

I saw her before she saw me. She was coming out of the shop, arm in arm with Lauren James, and I stopped, a few yards along the road, and watched them. Lauren was a year older than us and not someone we had ever hung around with before, but they'd both found part-time jobs in the same shop on the same day and I had tried not to let myself get jealous as the two of them had quickly grown closer. I hadn't realised at first just how close, but I certainly realised it now.

I had always known Tilly wasn't particularly interested in boys, but *girls*? They didn't know I'd seen them, of course. The giggling, their hips bumping along together as they walked, the smiles ... and the brush of their lips, a kiss so quick I could have blinked and missed it, when they thought nobody was looking. No wonder she'd pulled a face when I'd told her about my fumbles in Paul's bedroom.

I didn't go after them. I just stood and waited until they disappeared around the next corner, and then I turned back. I wouldn't say I was shocked exactly. More surprised. That she hadn't said anything to me, when we had always shared our most secret of secrets. That she had cut me out, chosen not to tell me. Why? She didn't trust me, I guessed. Or thought I wouldn't understand. Or approve.

Well, whatever happened now, this would probably be the end of the kind of conversations we'd always had before. About boys, and who we fancied, and who we didn't. Come to think of it, they always had been quite one-sided conversations. And how was I meant to tell her that I'd seen them, and that I knew? Unless I pretended I didn't, and waited for her to say something herself. If she ever did.

My tummy rumbled noisily, and I headed for the chip shop. I fancied chips and my sister's boyfriend, and Tilly fancied girls. Well, one particular girl, anyway. I had lost her. My best friend, and my confidante. First Eve had left me, and now Tilly. Just when I really needed someone I could talk to.

***

I could tell they'd had a row as soon as they came in through the door. Eve went straight upstairs to get changed, and after a while I could hear the bath water running, so she was clearly in no rush to come back down. Josh was polite enough when Mum asked about his day, but he had that strained look on his face that made it pretty obvious he preferred not to talk.

Dinner was awkward, although Mum and Dad seemed totally oblivious to the atmosphere, her running back and forth to the kitchen stirring things, and him just chattering on about the cricket and where the two 'young things' were planning on going the next day.

Eve pushed her food around her plate at dinner, and muttered something about having promised to spend the next day with Lucy, who didn't work on Wednesdays in lieu of having to do all day on Saturdays. In lieu? What sort of talk was that? Eve was starting to sound like she had a Latin dictionary stuffed inside her head, or up her backside, since she'd gone to uni. In lieu? The only loo we usually ever talked about being in was the toilet!

'So Josh will just have to amuse himself for once,' she said, sounding all haughty, not looking at him at all.

'I think I can manage that,' he replied. 'I'd quite like to visit the Science Museum actually, which I'm sure is not your kind of place at all.'

'Fine,' she said, although everything sounded far from fine to me.

'Maybe Sarah could go with you, Josh,' Dad said, and I was just about to protest that science was absolutely not my thing when I realised it could mean spending time alone with Josh – maybe even a whole day – and the idea suddenly seemed far more appealing. 'I hear she's been at a bit of a loose end these last few days, mooching about the garden doing nothing.'

'I have not!'

'Yeah, come on, Sarah.' Josh gave me a dazzling smile. 'You never know, you might enjoy it. It's not all engines and mole-cules, you know. They've got a spaceship and aeroplanes and stuff about the human body ... and besides, I could do with the company.'

I knew he was probably only doing it to wind Eve up, but he had asked me, publicly, to go with him, so why not?

We sat side by side on the sofa after dinner. Dad had gone out to play chess at the pub and Mum was in her sewing room, busy making some elaborate quilt blanket she'd prom-ised for a friend's grandson's christening. Eve had disappeared upstairs again, looking sulky and annoyed, but Josh didn't seem all that bothered.

I found out a lot more about him that evening as we chatted while watching TV. He talked about Leeds and his mum and dad and how sorry he was not to have any brothers or sisters of his own. 'You can be my honorary sister,' he joked, but the last thing I wanted was to be his sister. We sat so closely together that I could feel the warmth and solidity of his leg against mine, right through his jeans.

'Is everything all right?' I finally found the courage to ask. 'With you and Eve? Only, she doesn't seem very happy today.'

'I don't know.' He sighed, turning to look at me. 'She can be a bit ... complicated, can your sister.'

'Can she?'

'Well, maybe that's not the right word. More confusing. Contradictory. I don't know, but it's probably not something I should be talking to you about anyway. It's ... private stuff. Personal.'

'Oh. You mean sex, don't you?'

For a moment he looked shocked, but then he threw his head back and laughed, long and loud.

'Sarah! You surprise me. You're not quite the little girl I was led to believe you are. To listen to Eve, anyone would think you're still in pigtails and playing with dolls. What can you possibly know about sex? You're only fifteen.'

'Sixteen! And a half.' Things between him and Eve were not as perfect as Eve had led me to believe. Maybe I had a chance after all. 'Not so much younger than Eve. And I haven't had a doll for years.'

'Sorry. My mistake. Or Eve's. Do you know, I think we might just have lots of fun tomorrow, you and me.'

He had that look in his eyes then. Like fun could mean much more than just spending a day at a museum.

'I'm sure we will.'

'Time you went up to bed, I think.' He pulled away from me, quite abruptly, his hand brushing against my arm as he stood up. 'It's late, and we don't want your old man to come home and catch us alone, do we?'

'Don't we?' I put on my best innocent face and held his gaze for just a second too long.

'Night, Sarah,' he said, and then he did something he hadn't done before. He leaned forward as if to kiss me on the cheek, but I moved my head just at that exact moment and managed to catch the last of it, just at the edge of my mouth, in a delicious kiss-that-missed sort of a way.

'Oops!' I said, the taste of him sending a sudden thrill through me. I took a reluctant step back and looked up at him, wanting so much more.

He lifted his finger to his own lips and then across to mine, leaving it there for a few seconds. 'Tomorrow, Sarah,' he said, and pushed me gently towards the stairs.

Eve never did say what had happened between them, why they had rowed. She was already in bed when I went up, and had turned her back, a clear sign she wasn't going to confide in me. I lay there in the dark for ages, my hand lying against my still flat stomach, wondering if I could be wrong about my dates, and hoping so hard that I was. This wasn't the time to have to deal with an unwanted pregnancy, or to have to think about Paul Jacobs, when I had already consigned him to the past, with a big 'mistake' label over his head. Not when all I really wanted to do was work out what I was going to wear the next day that could lift me, once and for all, out of little-sister territory and get the gorgeous Josh to see me as the grown-up potential girlfriend I knew I could be. Because if Eve didn't want him, I certainly did.

Chapter 11

EVE

Five years later

'Your sister's had the baby.' Mum sounded excited down the phone, but all I felt was a cold hard lump that suddenly appeared somewhere at the back of my throat, making it hard for me to swallow, let alone breathe. And a ridiculous urge to cry. 'A little girl,' Mum went on, utterly oblivious to my discomfort. 'Seven pounds on the dot, and pretty as a picture. They're calling her Janine Caroline. Caroline, after me! Ooh, I'm that pleased! But it'll be Janey, for short. Just think, only hours old and she has a nickname already!'

'Right.'

'Right? Is that all you can say? You're an auntie now, Eve. And after all they went through the last time ... Oh, you will come down, won't you? To see her, I mean. And us. It's been so long.'

'I'm busy, Mum. The start of a new school term. I can hardly just up and go.'

'Of course not. But at the weekend? We're only a couple of hours away on the train, Love. And isn't it time this silly feud ended? She's your sister. The only one you're ever going to have.'

'Well, I wish she wasn't.'

'You don't mean that! Surely, by now, you could let bygones be bygones. It's been five years, and it's not as if you and Josh were engaged or anything ...'

'As if that would have stopped her, even if we had been. He was my boyfriend, Mum. *Mine*. And she took him. It's not what sisters do.'

'Oh dear. Look, I know it was you who first brought him home, Love, but there didn't really seem to be anything that serious between you. He was your friend, yes. Boyfriend, if that's what you like to call him, but boyfriends come and go, don't they? And he was your first. You certainly weren't showing any signs of wanting to settle down. Your course, your career ... and, well, it's not as if I approve of the way they went about it. Under our own roof, and your sister getting pregnant so quickly, but you have to admit they've made a go of it. He's Sarah's husband now, Eve, and the father of her child. After all they went through, losing that first baby, can't you at least try to be happy for them now?'

'Give my congratulations to Sarah. Well, to both of them, and I'll send a card, but—'

'I really think it would be nice if you spoke to your sister yourself, Love. Maybe a phone call, if you can't come down just yet ...'

Nice? Surely we were beyond being nice?

I made an excuse about someone knocking on the door and hung up. Mum didn't understand. Well, I don't suppose anyone did really. I had loved Josh. No, I hadn't run around telling the world how I felt, chucking myself at him, snogging his face off in public. I wasn't that sort of a person. Not then, and not now either. I had my reservations, my inhibitions. I knew that, and so did Josh. And we had been dealing with them. I had never said the magic words. Never told him I loved him. But he'd known how I felt. Hadn't he? And we'd been getting there, or I'd thought we were. Taking our time, getting to know each other slowly. Not ripping our clothes off and jumping on each other the way so many other couples seemed to do without a moment's thought. I had believed he would wait, until I was ready, until I was absolutely sure, but all it had taken was a few hours away from me, an offer of sex he clearly couldn't refuse, and there he was, in bed with somebody else. And not just any old bed, or any old body. *My* bed. And *my* sister ...

How was I supposed to forget that? Or to forgive? It was hard to know who I felt angrier with, who had betrayed me the most. Her? Or him?

I moved the papers around on my crowded dining table. It was half past nine on a Sunday evening and I was alone, as usual, in my tiny rented ground-floor flat in the back streets of Cardiff, and I still had a pile of marking to do for the morning. A class full of fifteen-year-olds reading the First World War poets, and all most of them had managed to write were a few words about how boring it must have been in the trenches or a paragraph clearly copied from a text book. What

127

about the language? The imagery? The emotion? To me, it leapt from the page and grabbed me by the throat. But they weren't all like me. In fact, very few of them were. Most of them, I had to concede, were probably a lot more like Sarah. Heads filled with boys, and bodies filled with the rush of hormones, desperate for school to end and what they saw as their real lives to begin. I sometimes wondered why I bothered.

I pushed the homework aside and closed my eyes. I couldn't stop the images and the emotions that were flooding into my head, and they had nothing to do with the war poets. That awful day, when I came home early from seeing Lucy, was still so clear in my memory. The silence of what I thought was an empty house. Mum and Dad still at work. Every step I took up the stairs, Buster pressing at my heels. Opening the bedroom door and seeing them there, a tangle of naked limbs and crumpled sheets. *My* sheets. Somehow, that meant more, hurt more, than I could ever explain. Not only had my sister stolen my boyfriend, and so casually taken the one thing he was meant to be saving for me, but she had chosen to do it in my bed. When her own, untouched and perfectly made, was just feet away.

Josh sat up instantly, surprise, shock – and was that shame? – written all over his pale face as he saw me standing in the doorway. But Sarah just lay there, flat on her back, a big purple-red suck mark on her neck, her small breasts horribly exposed, and gazed up at me, her expression totally unreadable.

'Eve. I'm so sorry.' Josh was tugging at the bedclothes, trying to hide himself, and her ...

I heard Buster jump up onto the bed, tail thumping, as I turned away, but Sarah pushed him off, his paws sliding as he landed awkwardly on the floor.

Sorry? Was that it? What was he thinking? That this was another of those fifty-pence moments, when I would laugh it off and say that saying sorry wasn't necessary, that everything was going to be all right?

Sorry. Sorry. Sorry.

The word had run around and around inside my head as I charged blindly down the stairs, Buster knocking against my ankles, almost tripping me up, and straight into Dad, coming in through the front door, with a badly folded newspaper under one arm, his keys still dangling in his hand.

'Eve? What's happened? Whatever is the matter?'

I pointed up the stairs, wordlessly, leaning on the banister for support, and he dropped the paper on the hall table and walked up past me, slowly, cautiously, as if he expected to find a burglar or a giant spider, or maybe even a dead body, when he reached the top.

I couldn't stay, after that. The idea of sharing a room with Sarah, or of sleeping there, in that house, that bed, after what they had done ...

I spent that first night at Lucy's. I wailed and raged and cried, and she listened, like the true friend she had always been, as I spilled out all my hurt and disbelief and heartbreak, until we both fell asleep, buoyed up with vodka, exhausted, my pillow damp with tears. And then, the next day, Lucy went round to the house and packed me a bag of essentials, refusing to divulge my plans to my parents who, she assured me, were clearly as outraged as I was, and I got on a train to Beth's. I didn't ask Lucy about Sarah, if she had been there, what she had said. I really didn't want to know. And with a bit of luck, I had thought, since Dad had apparently thrown him out onto the street and chucked his bags out after him, I would never have to set eyes on Josh Cavendish ever again. How wrong I was.

I spent what was left of that summer shuffling about between my uni friends, from one town and one sofa to another, calling my parents from time to time to let them know I was okay, that I was surviving, but knowing the last place I wanted to be right then, despite their pleas, was home.

It was only when I moved back into my room at Bryden and immersed myself in the second year of my English literature course that I was finally able to feel anywhere like normal again. From then on, I was determined to lead the only life that mattered.

Sarah's pregnancy had shocked us all. I couldn't believe she had been so careless. Or that Josh had. We all knew about being careful. There had been lessons at school, embarrassing though they were, and Durex machines in the toilets in just about every pub we ever sneaked into. Magazines packed with agony-aunt pages and advice columns. I knew Josh carried a condom in his wallet. I'd seen it and been impressed by his good sense, even if I had checked a few times over the months we had known each other, to make sure it was still there.

How had they let it happen? I couldn't help dreaming up scenarios in my head. And blaming myself. Because we'd had such a nice day, hadn't we? And I'd been the one to spoil it.

Hyde Park. Lying side by side in the grass, me on my back, twisting the long dry stems together, trying to make a bracelet, him propped up on his elbows, holding one thick blade of grass and tickling me with it until I begged him to stop. Sharing a paper bag of grapes, a bottle of lemonade, a kiss ... I know I probably reacted too strongly, pushed him too hard, spoke loudly enough for a couple on the path behind us to turn around and stare, but his hands had been moving too quickly, finding their way into my clothes, and it had been broad daylight ...

We didn't speak on the way home. He had finally lost patience with me; he'd waited long enough, he'd said, and nothing had changed. Nothing ever would. He'd called me frigid, said he was going to leave, pack up and go the next morning. I made some excuse about having to see Lucy, hoping he would just leave while I was out, but then I think it was Dad who suggested Sarah go out with him, to some museum or other, so he wouldn't have to go alone. And before I could do anything, say anything, she was agreeing to it. Smiling up at him the way she always did, like some kid with a crush.

I could imagine it all. Rightly or wrongly, I could see it unfurling in my mind. Sarah getting bored with the exhibits at the museum, as I had known she would. Them going for food instead, and drinks. Cans of cider on some bench some-where, as she was too young for the pub. Sarah giggling, talking, spilling out confidences, tilting her face at him, throwing back her hair, flirting, letting him know she was interested, willing, available ... His arm going around her on the train, their bodies squashed together, close, too close, and then stumbling into a quiet, empty house, her dragging him upstairs, or perhaps him dragging her, the raw passion taking over, or maybe just the need for revenge, pushing all thoughts, all common sense, aside. Had it been like that? I would never know. But she had him then, didn't she? Trapped, like a fly in a web, bound together by what they had done, and by what they had made. A baby, who didn't even survive long enough to make any of it worthwhile.

I looked up at the clock. It was getting late. I quickly finished the last of the marking, giving it the same level of inattention the students so obviously had, and pushed it aside. I wondered, briefly, as I boiled the kettle for a final cup of tea, what they would be doing now. Sarah and Josh. She would probably be propped up in her hospital bed, her new daughter pressed – I hoped painfully – to her nipple, her hair all messy, and wearing one of those hideous open-fronted cotton nighties. Or maybe she'd be trying to sleep in a noisy ward, lying there wide awake, finding it hard to believe what had just happened but seeing her baby in its little transparent cot beside the bed and knowing it was true. And Josh? He would have been out wetting the baby's head with his banker mates in some pub somewhere, or more than likely crashed out by now in their little flat above the dry cleaner's, still in the clothes he'd worn all day, shattered after hours of hand holding and brow mopping, his camera bursting with photos of little Janine that he couldn't wait to share with everyone he knew.

It was hard and, after five years, it still hurt. If only Josh had waited. If only he had cared about me in the same way I'd cared about him. He'd told me he loved me, just days before, and I had believed him. But he hadn't meant it. Hadn't meant any of it. He couldn't have done. It had just been a way to try to get me into bed. And, when it hadn't worked on me, he'd simply transferred his words, his attention, his body, to *her*.

Oh, yes, I still had my books, my teaching career, a little boxy home of my own, miles away from the life I once knew, a few friends from uni who I still met up with from time to time, but that was all. I hardly ever saw my family. I had lost my sister, and I had lost Josh, irretrievably and forever, and had never felt the urge to replace him. I didn't know who to trust anymore, or if I ever could, and the idea of meeting another man, embarking on some sordid, loveless sex life with anyone else, sent shudders through me. I was alone, and I was lonely. Sarah had stolen my life.

***

'Miss?' Laura Wilson, one of my Year Eights, was standing in front of my desk, with an open poetry book in her hand and a puzzled look on her freckly face.

'Shouldn't you be outside with the others?' It was break time and I had been hoping for a few minutes of peace, a cup of coffee and a doughnut, with my feet up, in the staff room.

'I suppose. But I wanted to ask you something, Miss.'

'Can't it wait?' I started gathering up my paperwork and bundling it into my bag, ready for the next lesson down the hall.

'I suppose,' she said again, but she didn't move away.

'Go on then, but make it quick.' Oh, God, I sounded prickly. This really wasn't the sort of teacher I wanted to be. 'Sorry, Laura. Don't mind me. I must have got out of bed on the wrong side this morning!' I plastered on a smile, dragging myself away from the memory of the restless, sleepless night I had endured thanks to Sarah and her baby, whose tiny face I could already picture as a miniature version of Josh's. 'Go on, ask away.'

'Well, it's what Keats wrote about the clouds, and the stubble, and the gnats.' She held out her book, and I could see the poem we had been studying, 'To Autumn', and the light pencil marks she had made all over it. 'Don't worry, Miss. I will rub those out again when I've finished, I promise. But the last verse of the poem's not just about what happens to the crops and stuff in autumn, is it? Not just about night time coming, or winter?'

'What do you think it's really about, Laura?'

'I think it's about dying, Miss. You know, the changes, moving on, being ready to give up ...'

I took the book from her hand and motioned for her to sit down beside me. 'And does that make it a sad poem, do you think?'

'Oh, no. I think it's beautiful, and such a nice way of saying things that aren't nice at all.'

'I agree. The language makes it very special, doesn't it? And the image of the fruits all bursting into life and then not being there anymore, and the spring lambs now grown up and bleating on the hillside. It's a lovely portrayal of nature, and its cycles.'

'My granddad's dying, Miss,' she said, suddenly. She looked up at me, her face betraying nothing of what she must be feeling. No tears.

I put the book down on the desk. 'I'm very sorry to hear that.'

'It's okay, Miss. I'm sad, but he's not in any pain or anything. He's just old, and it's his time. That's what my dad says, anyway. But Keats says it even better, doesn't he, Miss? I think the swallows are gathering now, like at the end of the poem, and he'll be gone soon. And then, before we know it, it will be spring, and my mum will have her new baby, and everything will start again.'

'That's a lovely way to think about it, Laura. I didn't know your mum was having a baby, but I'm so glad the poem has meant something to you. Something personal. Helps bring it all to life, doesn't it? Gives the words real feeling and depth.'

'It's the way you explain things, Miss. It sort of makes sense of the words that are hiding behind the words. Do you know what I mean?'

'Yes, I do. And thank you for coming to talk to me. I know it's not always easy to talk individually in class. If you like Keats, there are other poems I could show you. Other poets too.'

'Oh, yes, please. I'd like that. I'd much rather sit on a bench with a book to read than go out there playing with a ball or doing each other's hair or something. Such a waste of time.'

She stood up to go and I could see myself at that age, my own yearning for knowledge and understanding reflected in her earnest little face.

'Laura?' Remembering that time, and how I had felt, I had a sudden fear that maybe there was more to this meeting than she had let on. That maybe she was seeking me out, avoiding the other kids, because they were taunting her for spending her breaktimes alone with her head bent over a poetry book. 'They don't bully you, do they? The other girls? Because it's okay to be different, you know.'

'Oh, yes, I know.' She smiled at me and tucked the book under her arm. 'Don't worry, Miss. They leave me alone. I've got a big brother, you see. And nobody messes with me, or they have him to answer to.' She laughed. 'He's big and I'm small. He likes football and I like books. It's what makes the world work, isn't it? Us all being different. And who wants to be like everybody else anyway? Although I wouldn't mind being like you ... when I grow up, that is.' She looked up at me and pondered for a moment. 'I don't mean now ...'

I made it to the staff room with five minutes to spare, guzzled the doughnut quickly, wiped the line of sugar from my lips as I drank the last of my too-hot coffee, and dashed off to my next class. I had been asking myself why I bothered teaching and Laura had shown me the answer. I had to forget about my sister and concentrate on myself and my career, my future, my life. My passion for English, and for poetry, was important. Not only to me, but to the children, even if it turned out to be only one in every hundred who felt the way I did.

***

Little Janey was almost three months old by the time I finally met her. I had decided to bite the bullet and go home for Christmas, to see Mum and Dad, and to catch up with Lucy and Robert, who I hadn't seen since their wedding day. Poor old Buster was sick too, struggling along at the grand old age of thirteen, and not expected to live for much longer, and I couldn't let him slip away without a final hold of his paw and a slobbery kiss goodbye. It was inevitable I would have to see Sarah and Josh, but I also knew it was time I learned to deal with it.

Our old bedroom didn't look a lot different, despite having nobody living in it anymore. Mum had made new curtains and there were new duvet covers on the beds, and quite possibly new sheets as well, but the wallpaper and carpets hadn't changed and the beds themselves still stood as they always had, just feet apart, against opposite walls. I paused in the doorway, pushing back the memories of seeing the two of them lying there, and forced myself to step into the room and lay my case down on top of my old bed. I would sleep in Sarah's. It wasn't as if she would care, or have any say in the matter, now she had a home of her own. And Mum would just tell me I was being silly, or over-dramatic, if I refused to use the room at all.

'Come down for a cuppa,' she called up the stairs, 'once you've unpacked.'

Buster waddled towards me as soon as I'd settled on the sofa with a mug in my hand. He was looking really old and slow, his once black coat now dull and almost totally grey, his eyes cloudy. 'Hello, Boy.' I let him rest his muzzle in my open hand as he sniffed at me. 'Are you pleased to see me?'

'I don't think he can see you very well at all, Love,' Mum said, offering the biscuit tin. I saw she'd got my favourite garibaldis in specially. 'He gets by pretty much on smell these days.'

I picked out two biscuits and gave one of them to Buster and he chewed at it, dropping soggy crumbs on the carpet and not bothering to seek them out.

'We don't try to make him walk anymore. Just take him out into the back garden to do his business. He sleeps most of the time. Won't be long now, I think. I just hope he goes peacefully and we don't have to take him to the vet for ... well, you know.'

I could feel the tears coming, but what good would they do? They couldn't save him. Nothing could. 'I'm just glad I'm here,' I said, pulling myself together. 'And that we can have this last Christmas with him.'

'Your sister said she'd be round with Janey at about four,' Mum said, taking the conversation away from the inevitable. 'And Josh will join them as soon as he's back from work. I'm cooking a roast chicken.'

'Right.'

'I know you find it difficult, Love, but it's nearly Christmas, so do your best, eh? We've missed having everyone here together these last few Christmases. First you staying away, spending time with your friends, and then Sarah off to Josh's parents every other year. I thought maybe the two of you could put the decorations on the tree, the way you always used to. It might help break the ice a bit, help bring you closer again. I've even bought a new fairy. That old one was falling apart.'

To be honest, I hadn't even noticed that the tree was standing bare in the corner or that the cardboard box of decorations was waiting at its foot. 'But she was my fairy,' I said, feeling ridiculously indignant all of a sudden. 'I made her at school.'

'Yes, I know, and I'm not throwing her away, don't worry. I never would. She'll go in my box of keepsakes, along with all the Mother's Day cards and little drawings I've hung on to all these years. Or you can take her home with you. Whatever you like, Love. But I thought, now we have Janey, it was time to get a few new bits, you know. I bought one of those Baby's-First-Christmas baubles too, with a teddy on it. She'll like that.'

It was only when I heard the front door slam that I realised Sarah had arrived and, there having been no ring of the bell, she must still have her own key.

'We're here, Mum,' she called out, quite unnecessarily, as she bumped several hefty carrier bags and a baby car carrier along the hall and into the room. 'Oh ... Eve.' She stopped dead still and just looked at me, as if she wasn't sure what I might do.

As it was, I did nothing. I didn't stand, didn't rush to hug her or help her with her bags, didn't say anything at all. I just sat and looked at her, waiting for her to make the first move.

'Long time, no see,' she said at last, a coldness in her voice that didn't quite match the look of indecision and hesitance on her face. 'Would you ... um ... like to meet your niece?'

She turned the baby carrier around on the carpet and eased the blanket away from her baby's face, bending to unstrap her and lift her free. And then she handed her to me, laid her gently in my open arms, and I looked at her little chubby face, so like Josh's, and fell instantly in love.

Chapter 12

SARAH

I watched them very closely that evening. The embarrassed, almost shy hello, the awkward shaking of hands, two pairs of eyes that couldn't quite look straight into each other's for more than a second or two.

'Josh.'

'Eve. It's good to see you. How's life?'

'Oh. Okay, you know ...'

Janey was still on Eve's shoulder, asleep but dribbling frothy beads of milky spit onto her jumper.

'Here. Let me take her. So you can drink your tea.' Josh leaned forward and eased the baby away from her, and Eve wriggled her shoulders, as if they had been locked in position and she was finally free to move. She took her cup from the coffee table in front of her and sipped at it. I could tell by her expression that the tea had gone cold.

'It's been a long time.'

I glared at Josh, urging him to stop, to leave it. Why open up old wounds? Cans of worms, best left undisturbed? We all knew there was an almost tangible feeling of frustrated held-back anger hovering in the room, and that there was a very fine line between being mature adults and all three of us yelling what we really felt and tearing each other's eyes out. But he took no notice and just kept ploughing on.

'A shame you live so far away. Now that Janey's here ...' It all just sounded so false, so trite, as he gazed adoringly into Janey's eyes and rocked her gently in his arms and I wished that he had just once looked at me in the same way. 'Well, it could be the time to let bygones be bygones, don't you think?'

'I can't just up and move because you've had a baby, Josh.' Her voice was spiky and her eyes glinted with the iciest of stares. 'My home is in Wales now, and my job ...'

'I know that, but perhaps we could see more of you, even so? It's been a long time since you've been back. Holidays and Christmases spent with friends, or on your own.'

'I've been okay. Last Christmas with Beth and Lenny, down on his dad's farm. And I went to Portugal, with Fran. You remember Fran, one of my flatmates from uni?'

'Of course. But still, it doesn't seem right, Eve. Christmas is about family.'

He just kept on, as if her going was nothing to do with him. Or us. As if it had never happened. I didn't know how Eve must be feeling but I was feeling decidedly uncomfortable. There was only so much playing at civilised either she or I could stand. She had her reasons for staying away, and we all knew what they were. We hadn't felt like family for a long time.

I heard a key then, fumbling in the lock of the front door,

followed by a mumbled swear word as the whole key ring fell onto the carpet, and the jangling of metal on metal as it was hastily retrieved. Mum half stood but soon sat down again as the living room door burst open, bringing a gust of cool air in from the hall.

'Ah. Well, this is nice!' Dad had finally arrived home from the office, his face displaying the usual last-day-before-the-break ruddiness, the tell-tale whiff of whisky hanging around him as he bent to kiss us all, in turn. 'All my girls here together.'

Eve, last in line as she was sitting furthest from the door, put her arms around his neck and hung on tightly. 'Good to see you, Dad.' Her eyes glistened with tears I could see she was fighting to control.

'You too, my dear girl. Now I want to hear all the latest about that school you're at, and how the flat's coming along too, of course. Have you decorated that kitchen of yours yet? Those yellow walls gave me the heebie-jeebies!'

So, he'd been down there then? To visit? And Mum too, probably. It was the first I'd heard about it. But of course they had. Eve was still the blue-eyed favourite, the one who had been wronged, and we all knew it.

'Next on the list, Dad.'

'Glad to hear it. I'm not too bad with a paintbrush, you know. Only too happy to pop down for a day or two and help out, while I'm off work for Christmas. Make a change from sitting around here stuffing my face with turkey left-overs.'

'You're always welcome, Dad, but I haven't really decided yet when I'm going back. I have things to do here, people to visit. And a new niece to get to know ...'

143

She looked at me as she said that, and I was glad that whatever had gone on between the adults, it was not going to affect how she felt about Janey. Janey mattered now, more than anything or anyone. None of it was her fault, after all.

'Shall we eat now?' Mum said, a little too eagerly, wiping her hands on her apron and heading for the kitchen as if the decision had already been made. 'Don't want the chicken to get dry.'

If it had been up to me, I would have put Janey down in her car seat while we ate, but Josh was having none of it. 'She'll be fine here with me,' he said, juggling cutlery in one hand and the baby in the other. I watched him struggling to cut his meat but I was too far away from him, at the opposite end of the table, to offer much help and I already knew he wouldn't thank me for it if I did. I did wonder, briefly, if he was using our baby as some sort of shield, a barrier to hide behind, giving him the perfect excuse to back away from the conversation around the table, to focus all his attention on the one person who was not going to judge him or ask difficult questions. He was good at that, was Josh. Dodging the important stuff.

'Tilly's coming home for the holidays too, Sarah,' Mum said, pouring extra gravy onto her plate. 'Her mum says she's bringing a friend with her. A girl she got friendly with at college. That'll be nice, won't it?'

I couldn't help but wonder if Tilly's so-called friend was more than that, but I had never broached the topic of her apparent liking for girls with Mum. Or with Tilly, for that matter, although I knew the thing with Lauren James at the bakery hadn't lasted. Lauren was now living quite openly with an older woman and they were adopting a child together, according to Eve's friend Lucy, who'd heard rumours she was only too happy to pass on. No, despite our childhood friendship, Tilly and I didn't really have a lot in common anymore, with her away, still studying, and me a stay-at-home wife and mother. I thought perhaps we had outgrown each other now we'd taken such different paths.

'You could pop next door and see them both sometime before they go back.'

I nodded, if only to keep Mum happy. 'Maybe, yeah.'

'Fancy a game of chess after dinner, Josh?' Dad said, chasing the last Brussels sprout around his plate. 'Try as I might, I've never managed to get anyone else around here in the least bit interested. Something to keep us busy, while the girls do the tree.'

'Bit tired to tell you the truth, George.' Josh yawned, theatrically, and tilted his wrist, peering past Janey to look at his watch. 'I think I could do with an early night. I still have a half day at the bank tomorrow, before we close up at lunchtime.' He peered down the table at me as if looking for approval, although I knew it wasn't needed. 'You stay longer though, Sarah. I know how much you've always enjoyed rummaging through that old box of decs. Janey can come back with me.'

It was typical of Josh. I could tell that having Eve there was getting to him, especially as she was so clearly not about to play his game of pretending none of it had ever happened, or even to meet him halfway. Now he was looking for a way out, an escape route, coward that he was. Leaving me behind to deal with it, the mess we had made together. And I knew I would have to, one way or another, or let the stupid feud go on forever. The battle over Josh had been fought and won long ago, but now we had to live with the fallout and get through Christmas, and I hoped Janey's presence might turn out to be the way to do that. It was obvious Eve was smitten with her.

'No, it's okay. You get off if you need to. Leave Janey here with us. She'll be needing a feed soon and I'm not sure there's any expressed in the fridge. You know she prefers the real thing anyway!' I looked down at my swollen boobs, pushing against my shiny top, and wobbled them around a bit, trying to make him laugh. Breasts always had been Josh's thing, although his interest level had certainly dropped off since they'd turned into milking machines. The sooner I got Janey onto formula the better, if I had any hope of a decent sex life again.

He didn't react, not even a smile, just stood up and passed her to me diagonally across the table before draining the last of his single I'm-driving-tonight glass of wine and setting off for home. Oh, God, Josh was only twenty-six. We'd only been together five years and we had a whole lot of married life ahead of us. How had he got so staid and middle-aged, and so lacking in any kind of sparkle?

I closed my eyes for a while and leaned back in my chair. I could so easily have nodded off, but Janey was starting to wriggle and make little distressed noises, signs that she needed her milk. I wasn't usually shy about feeding in front of my own family, as long as I had a shawl or something to drape over us, but Eve was here and something held me back. I made an excuse and took Janey upstairs. I thought twice about using our old bedroom, where I could see Eve's case still lay half unpacked, and went to sit on Mum and Dad's bed instead.

When I came back down twenty minutes later and put Janey, now full up and fast asleep, back into her car seat, Mum was busying herself in the kitchen, piling far too many plates into a sink full of suds. Dad had retired to his usual armchair, where he had already dozed off and was gently snoring, so I didn't think chess would ever have been a real contender. And that left us sisters, Eve and me, sitting on the floor, one on each side of the decorations box, as we'd done so many times before, only this time we were a lot more subdued.

'The fairy's gone,' Eve said, eventually. 'Before you start looking for it. Mum's bought a new one.'

'Oh.'

'Time for a change, apparently. Now Janey's here.'

I stopped running my fingers along the tangled string that held the lights, and pulled my hand away from the box, putting it gently on her arm. Well, someone had to make the first move. 'And does that apply to other things too, Eve? Now that Janey's here, can we ...? Change things between us? Start again, maybe?' I was holding my breath, with no idea how she might react.

When she turned her face towards me, I saw for the first time how much older she looked, and how sad.

'I don't know. I want to. I really do. You're my sister and

you've always meant so much to me, but ... I'm just not sure that I can ever trust you again. Either of you. I was let down, cheated on, betrayed ... by the two people who meant more to me than anyone else on earth – even more than Mum and Dad, terrible though that sounds. I loved you, both of you; didn't you know that? And I thought you both felt the same way about me. But ... Oh, Sarah, you shouldn't have done it. That's all. You should have stopped and thought about what you were doing. To me. Your own sister. It was thoughtless, unnecessary. Cruel ...'

'I know that now. I can see how hurt you've been. But not then. It was just a bit of fun back then. To start with, anyway. Harmless fun. Or it would have been, if you and Dad hadn't both come home early. You need never have known. And if I hadn't ended up pregnant, of course. But how was I to know you loved him? You never said.'

'And why would I? I hadn't even said it to Josh, so I was hardly going to tell you first, was I?

'I guess not. But we just clicked, you know? Really quickly. Yes, I fancied him like mad – and I still do. But it's more than that now. We're really making a go of it, and we have a daughter. Doesn't that count for anything?'

She didn't answer.

'And I love him too, Eve. Just as much as you did.'

'You can't really know that, can you? What I felt?'

'No. You're right. I can't. And we were wrong to do that to you, but it's been years, and things change. I've had to grow up fast. And we're together now, Josh and me. Parents, and I – *we* – want to put things right.'

I saw her swallow, her gaze cast down towards the carpet as her fingers fiddled with a shiny gold bauble which she then dropped back into the box. Not one had yet made it onto the tree.

'Don't you think we've already been punished enough for what we did? First, losing you. And then losing the baby ...'

'Punished?' She lifted her face and glared at me. 'You must be joking! Look at you. He married you, didn't he? Yes, we all know he was pushed into it. By his parents. And ours. All that guilt, and bringing-shame-on-the-family stuff. Anyone would think we were still living in the dark ages. And all because you wouldn't even consider doing the only truly sensible thing.'

'Get rid of it? That may have been the sensible answer in your mind, but not in mine.'

'No, so you just went right on with it all, didn't you? Did the *right* thing! Rushed into being the blushing bride, knocked up but still doing the whole white dress and big bouquet routine, even though it was just a handful of people at the registry office – and you still only sixteen! And for what? To lose the baby just weeks later. What a waste ... If you'd just waited, talked it through, looked at all the options. I mean, did you even stop to consider if any of it was what Josh actually wanted?'

'We talked. Of course we did. All of us. Both families. Except you, because you'd run away, like a spoilt brat who'd had her favourite toy taken away. What do you think happened, Eve? That Dad turned up with a shotgun? No, it was a joint decision. To stick together. To have the baby. It wasn't just me. Josh didn't want me to get rid of it either. He takes his responsibilities seriously. You just have to look at him with Janey ... and you talk about options. What options? Adoption? I couldn't give my baby to someone else. Never see it again. And I'm sure Mum and Dad couldn't have faced that either. Their first grandchild. And as for abortion, that was never going to happen. Never! Josh is a Catholic, remember? He's been brought up to value life. *All* life.'

'Well, I can't say I remember ever seeing him go to church, or pray, or cross himself, or any of those things they're meant to do. He never looked like much of a Catholic to me. And do practising Catholics carry condoms around in their wallets? Not that he used it, in your case, obviously.'

I didn't reply. I couldn't. Of course he had used a condom. How was he to know I was already—

'But of course getting pregnant gave you the easy way out, didn't it?' Eve carried on, almost spitting with fury. 'I wouldn't be surprised if you did it deliberately.' She was staring at me like some kind of mad woman, her voice raised to the point where I expected Dad to wake up or Mum to burst back in to see what on earth was going on. 'Because then you could drag your good Catholic boy back down here from Leeds and guilt-trip him into standing by you, moving in together, marrying you. It's crazy, all of it. You hardly knew each other! But you knew you wouldn't have to go back to school if you were married, didn't you? Let's face it, you've hardly had to lift a finger as far as work goes. What? A few shifts in the dry cleaner's downstairs? Your exam results were crap, so what else were you qualified to do except lie on your back? But you've got a home of your own now, Sarah, and a clever, handsome, hardworking husband, even if you did have to steal him from your own sister. It's what you always wanted, isn't it? Your dream life. One that could have been mine one day. *Should* have been! And now he's given you another baby. A living, breathing baby this time, and one who looks so much like him it makes me want to scream. And you say you've been punished? None of it sounds much like punishment to me.'

She hauled herself to her feet and started draping lumps of tinsel rapidly and haphazardly onto the branches of the tree and, for now anyway, as I sat there shocked and shaking, it was pretty obvious the conversation was over.

***

As Christmas Days go, it wasn't so bad. Not as awkward as I'd expected it to be. We sat around the table, and then around the TV, ate, drank, dozed. Eve made a point of helping Mum, constantly going in and out of the kitchen, bringing more beer and snacks and cups of tea. It gave her something useful to do, I suppose, and kept her away from having to talk to me. I could have counted the words we spoke to each other on the fingers of one hand, although Mum and Dad didn't seem to notice, or chose not to as it was Christmas. At around eight o'clock, Eve took her turkey sandwich and her slice of cake, said goodnight and went upstairs to read. On Christmas Day!

Josh took that as our cue to leave too, bundling Janey up

in her new snowsuit and packing her many presents into the same giant-sized paper Santa sack we had used to carry our presents to the family that morning. I had given Eve a book token and she had presented me – *us* – with Mothercare vouchers for Janey. Token gestures. Nothing too personal, nothing that required any thought.

Josh had already had far too much to drink and I watched him stagger a bit as he lifted the car seat containing our daughter in one hand and the sack of presents in the other.

'Here. Let me ...'

'I can manage, Sarah. You just get the car started and warmed up a bit before I bring her out into the cold.'

He bent over Mum and kissed her on the cheek. 'Thanks, Caroline. For the hospitality. And the jumper.' He was making his way over towards Dad as I went outside with the car keys in my hand and tried to clear the layer of frost from the windscreen.

'Well, that was a bit of a nightmare, wasn't it?' he said, when he had clipped Janey's seat into the back and climbed into the car beside me, rubbing his cold hands together.

'Was it?' I was concentrating on reversing out of the drive with only narrow stripes of clear glass to peer through as the heated rear window had not yet fully done its job. 'I didn't think it was that bad.'

'Oh, come on! You could have cut the atmosphere at that dining table with your dad's old carving knife. Which was pretty blunt, did you notice? I don't know about yours, but my turkey looked like it had been hacked off the bone with a pair of nail clippers.'

'Tasted good though.' I tried to steer the conversation in a safer direction, but Josh was having none of it.

'And as for Eve. What's wrong with her? So bloody sourfaced. Still holding a grudge after all this time? It's not rational, not ... sane.'

'What we did must have come as a shock to her, and we've never really talked about it, have we? Not in years. Never apologised, even.'

'Well, how could we, when she buggered straight off back to Wales and never came back?'

'That's true, but ... just mind your language in front of Janey, okay?'

'Oh, for God's sake, she's what? Twelve weeks old? Thirteen? She's not going to take any notice of what I say, is she? She can't even manage to say Dada yet, let alone start to copy swear words.'

'Maybe, but I think we should be careful. It won't be long ...'

'Whatever.' Josh sank down in his seat and closed his eyes, a sure sign he didn't want to pursue that particular line of conversation any further.

'And as for the jumper your parents gave me ...' So, he wasn't asleep then.

'What about it?'

'Did you look at it? Really look at it? It's bloody massive, for a start. How big do they think I am? And green! I'll look like an overgrown leprechaun if I wear that thing,'

'They mean well Josh, and Mum knitted it herself. Their tastes may not be quite the same as ours but—'

'They aren't. You're right there. That whisky your dad bought tasted like gnat's pee. I bet he got it in one of those cheap supermarkets. A tenner a bottle!'

'You do know you can come across as a total snob sometimes, don't you?'

'And you do know that you'll say anything for a quiet life? You never want to upset anybody. It's all Yes, Dad, No, Dad. And you should have told Eve to stop being such a drama queen. She's not Lady Macbeth or Ophelia or whoever she teaches those kids about in her lessons. And it's time she realised life is not one long bloody tragedy!'

'Me? Why's it up to me to tell her?' I pulled the car into the kerb outside the dry cleaner's and looked up to the darkened windows of our first-floor flat, realising I'd forgotten to close the curtains and set the dial on the thermostat before we set off and the place would probably be freezing.

'Because she's your sister.'

'Is she? It doesn't feel that way anymore.'

'Oh, let's forget it, shall we? She's not our problem.' He opened the car door and hesitated before getting out. 'And the last thing I want on Christmas Day is an argument.'

'Me too.'

'Let Eve have her little strop and go off to bed with her book. She's turning into one of those boring career women, forever a bloody spinster. She'll probably be getting a tweed suit and a couple of cats next!'

'A bit unfair,' I said, but I laughed anyway, undoing my seatbelt.

'Right! We'll get this little one inside and tucked up for the night, and then we can break open the real stuff. I've got a bottle of single malt up there that a client gave me. You won't find that in the bargain bucket. Oh, no, I forgot, you can't, can you? Breastfeeding, and all that. Never mind. I can drink your share! Then maybe we can snuggle up and have an early night of our own, eh?' He leaned over and ran his fingers over my breasts and I could feel the old familiar tingle, right through my coat. 'Without the book, obviously!'

And it would have been a good night. I'm sure it would. Half an hour later and Josh had that old hungry look in his eyes that I'd missed so much. A large glass of whisky, downed quickly, was already working its sexy magic as he pushed me onto the bed and pulled my top off over my head, his mouth nuzzling my neck and sending all kinds of long-lost sensations rushing through my body, from my head to my toes and all places in between. It would have been the best Christmas present of the day, if only the phone hadn't rung and spoiled the moment. Eve's was the last voice I had expected to hear. Eve in tears, begging me to come. Now ...

Poor old Buster couldn't have chosen a worse time to die.

Chapter 13

EVE

It's not easy trying to find a vet that opens on Christmas Day, but in the end we didn't need to. Just as Sarah came crashing through the door and up the stairs, the poor little thing slipped quietly away in front of us on the hall carpet, pressed up close to the radiator, his old grey head resting on his outstretched paws. It was as if he'd been waiting for her to get there, so he could say his goodbyes to all of us together. No pain, just his eyes closing, a few little twitches, and a final breath that sent him into eternal sleep.

I had never seen anyone, or anything, die before. Never seen my dad cry either, but he did that day. I watched Mum clutch his hand as we all sat in a circle on our knees around Buster, stroking him, talking to him, hugging each other, not quite believing he had gone. It was Mum who broke away first, grabbing the banisters to pull herself up and bustling off to put the kettle on, while Dad started talking about finding the spade and whether the ground would be too hard for digging. Both being as practical as possible, trying to hide their grief.

Sarah and I just sat there, numb, saying nothing. It felt, to me anyway, like his loss marked the end of an era, the end of our childhood, which was pretty stupid, considering we were both already grown-up and not even living in the house anymore. But Buster had been my dog, my companion through my teenaged years, until I went to uni, and then I had drifted away from him, left him to the care of the rest of the family, and he had become theirs too. We had all loved him, unconditionally. Mum and Dad had brought him to visit me in Wales a few times, and he had sniffed his way around my flat and the tiny patch of garden at the back, his tail thumping against my leg at each reunion, but there had never been any question of him coming to join me there full-time. Buster lived here, in this house, and now he had died here.

I waited until Sarah had planted her goodbye kisses, burying her wet face in the fur at his neck, and then, when Dad came back with an old blanket to wrap him in, I lifted up his little body and carried him slowly down the stairs.

Mum made mugs of tea and over-sugared them (for the shock), and we sat around for a while, the TV off and the room in darkness except for the lights twinkling on the Christmas tree in the corner.

'I could ring and ask Josh to come round and help dig,' Sarah said, lifting an arm up over her eyes and sniffing into her sleeve. 'Oh, but he's been drinking ...'

'It's okay, Love. I can manage.' Dad opened the curtains and gazed out into the utter blackness of a back garden it was impossible to see. 'You need to get back to that little daughter of yours.'

'I wonder if we should leave it until the morning, George?' Mum was gripping her mug so tightly I could see her knuckles turning white, but she hadn't drunk a drop.

'Yes, I think you're probably right.'

'Then we can do it properly. Choose the right spot. See what we're doing. Have time to think of what to say ...'

'I'll be going then.' Sarah stood, taking a last look at the wrapped bundle on the armchair that had been Buster, and bent to kiss Mum, and then Dad, goodbye. She hesitated in front of me. Should she? Shouldn't she? I could tell she was waiting to take her cue from me. And, right then, what had happened between us in the past didn't seem to matter quite so much. I didn't stand up but I put my hands on her shoulders and she bent down, her face next to mine, and hugged my neck. There was a faint smell of baby milk and what might have been whisky in her hair and, through her open coat, I realised for the first time that her top was on back to front.

'Happy Christmas, Love,' Mum said, absentmindedly, as Sarah left. But we all knew that it wasn't.

***

Work took over my life again as soon as I returned to Cardiff. There was something about that first term back after Christmas that seemed to re-energise me. Most people hated winter but I liked it, had a certain respect for it. All those cold starts, reluctantly stepping out of my pyjamas, then standing too long under the shower before eating a big bowl of porridge and going out to brave the weather; waiting for crowded early-morning buses: a new woolly hat and gloves, courtesy of Mum's regular pre-Christmas knitting marathon; frost forming on the windows in the staff room on a Monday morning until the heating kicked in and the steam from the kettle did its job.

I liked the thought of the playground becoming a makeshift football pitch again, instead of a place for idle bench gossip, the girls who loved to push the boundaries with their ever-shorter skirts and open toes happily retreating back into their uniform trousers and warm, sensible shoes. The classroom was a haven against the cold world outside where the bare trees waited to send out their tiny specks of fresh new greenery in the weeks to come, standing, as I hoped I might be too, on the verge of new beginnings.

'Good break?' Our PE teacher, Simon Barratt, warmed his big freckly rugby-player hands on his coffee mug, then put it down so he could take a biscuit from the tin. He was new to the school, only having been there a term, but I had already come to like him.

'Not bad. Nothing special. You?'

'Oh, the usual. Home to see the family. Too many games of Scrabble. Too many trips to the pub. I did manage to get to a match though.'

'Match?'

'Football. Just local, but there's nothing like a chilly afternoon on the terraces. Except actually being out there on the pitch, of course. Football, rugby, hockey. I'll give anything a go! Do you ...?'

'No! Not me. Never been into sport, I'm afraid.'

'Well, that doesn't leave us much to talk about then, does it? I'm afraid it's more or less the only thing I know anything about. A simple man, me!'

'I'm sure that's not true.' I dipped into the biscuit tin. Two broken custard creams and one very hard fig roll, left over from before Christmas. Time someone went out to buy more.

There didn't seem any need to hunt for something else to say, so we soon fell into an easy, companionable silence, each sipping at our drinks and nibbling at our stale biscuits until the rest of the staff came dribbling in, one at a time, hanging up coats and scarves, shaking their hair free from their hats and flopping into armchairs to take a quick look at the paperwork for their first lessons of the day.

Sarah and I, although we hadn't exactly parted as friends, had managed to clear the air somehow over Christmas. We'd both said what we'd felt, painful though it had been, and I knew nothing could ever change what had happened between us, so maybe the only way to go now was forward. Standing side by side, lost in our own thoughts and memories as Buster was buried beneath Dad's old apple tree on Boxing Day had brought a strange sense of closure. Now it was time to put the past away and concentrate on what mattered.

English was still my passion, and teaching it was my calling, the one thing that gave me a reason to get up every morning, that made me feel truly alive, as though I had a purpose. I had spent the last couple of days writing new and, I hoped, more exciting lesson plans, thinking more deeply about ways to bring my subject alive in the minds of the children in my classes.

Dad had helped, without even knowing he was doing it. He had insisted on coming back with me, driving me all the way home so I needn't get the train, and had soon set to work on the kitchen which was now painted a muted shade of pale grey with a pure-white ceiling. It was something he'd said, as he'd wobbled at the top of the stepladder, paint dripping down his sleeve, that had made sense to me, acted as some kind of lightbulb moment. 'Looking at paint charts is nothing like standing here and seeing the real thing, you know, Love,' he'd said, leaning back and admiring his handiwork. 'Somehow, just seeing that little coloured oblong on a sheet of paper, side by side with all the other little oblongs, doesn't give you the full picture, does it? A sense of what it will really be like. Every time I tried to picture this *smoky dove* on your wall, the *misty haze* and the *ecru explosion* just kept edging into view, making me doubt my choice. Sorry, *our* choice.' He laughed. 'Oh, don't mind me. I'm sure you have no idea what I'm talking about!'

But I did. For some of these kids, a poem was just too packed, too full-on. There was just too much to concentrate on. They couldn't take it all in at once. Image after image clambering for attention, fancy words taking the place of the vocabulary they were familiar with. And Dad was right. Grey wasn't just grey, was it? Not if you were looking at a poem, where every word mattered and every picture formed just a little differently in the mind of every person who imagined it.

I pulled the paint charts out of my bag now, piles of them, sneakily pocketed in the DIY store at the weekend, and set off for my first class of the day. The line-by-line examination of First World War poetry, with all its pain and hopelessness, could wait for now. It was time to get back to basics.

The noise coming from the classroom hit me before I opened the door. Loud, bored, restless teenagers on their first day back after a long break. I was pleased to see their reaction as I came into the room though – the sudden muting of their chattering, the settling back into chairs. They may not be great English lovers but they were willing to sit still and listen. They respected me, which mattered more than I could say.

'What colour is the sky?' I threw the question out at them while still arranging my pile of papers on my desk, before I had even sat down.

Of course I was met with puzzled faces. What was this? A lesson for four-year-olds? There were a few mumbles before the answers started.

'Blue. Sky is blue.'

'No. Look out there. It's more like white, with all that cloud.'

'I don't think the sky really has any colour, does it? It's just air, and the colour's a reflection. Or something like that. Like water.'

'That's why it's black at night.'

'Is it? What about red sky at night, shepherds' delight?'

'Sky is not red! It's blue.'

I laughed. Such a lively debate in progress, so quickly, and about something so simple.

'Okay.' I started walking down the aisles between the desks, handing out my paint charts. 'If the sky really is blue – not today, obviously, but on a clear, sunny day – what sort of blue is it?'

'Sky blue!' one boy called out from the back of the room, and everybody laughed.

'Bit of a cliché, Jake. Now, why don't you all take a look at these? See some of the different names the paint manufacturers have used for their blues, each one a slightly different shade.'

Their heads went down, their interest captured.

'How about this one? *Crushed cornflower.*'

'Yes, I can imagine a sky being just that colour,' I said, peering over Jake's shoulder.

'But cornflour's white, Miss. My mum uses it making gravy.'

Now it was my turn to laugh. 'Not that sort of cornflour, Jess. In this case, it's an actual flower. Does anyone know what a cornflower looks like?'

'No, but it must be blue.'

'So, what do you all think about using flowers to help us name colours? Bluebell, rose, lily, poppy ... What kind of images do they bring to your mind?'

'Soft, pretty, delicate. Pale, maybe.'

'And is that the sort of sky the soldiers in our poetry would have seen, looking up from the trenches?'

'No, Miss. That would have been a much darker, scary sky. More like navy blue.'

'They were in the army, not the navy!' one of the boys chipped in.

'So you wouldn't use navy to describe your sky, if you were writing a war poem?'

'No, Miss. It gives the wrong image. Makes you think of the wrong kind of navy. Ships and sea, not trenches. Or it does me anyway. It mixes up words that don't belong together.'

'It does, doesn't it?'

'And the sky would only be dark at night. In the day it could easily be pale blue or pretty, like a cornflower, couldn't it? It's not like the sky knows there's a war on.'

Some of them giggled, but I was impressed. This last comment had come from Robert, a boy who had never shown the slightest interest in poetry, and rarely spoke up in class.

'But if we were choosing a way to describe the sky that adds to the atmosphere of the poem? Does cornflower send out the right message? Help to form the right image?'

'No, Miss,' Robert replied. 'But *crushed* cornflower does, doesn't it?'

They were getting it! Robert was getting it!

'Can you explain what you mean?'

'Well, it must have felt like the sky was crushing them, pushing them down, especially when they were lying there, being shot at, or there were bombs falling, Miss, all trapped lying down in the mud in that trench. Their spirits crushed, even while they were looking up at a clear blue sky. And their hopes, and their confidence, maybe even their actual bones, all crushed, Miss.'

Was it ridiculous to feel a lump in my throat, a tear trying to ease its way out and down my cheek? I turned away and walked slowly back to my desk, giving myself time to recover.

'And that,' I said, waving my paint chart in the air, 'is what imagery is! Using words to make pictures in readers' minds.

To make associations. Think how we've come from crushed cornflowers to crushed spirits, crushed men. The magic of words. And choosing the *right* words.'

'And blue means sad too, doesn't it, Miss? Like those men would have been.'

'It certainly does.'

'And it means rude, like in blue movies!'

I couldn't help laughing. The conversation was veering away from poetry, but these kids were interested, engaged, thinking about words and how to use them. Thinking for themselves. There were times when I wouldn't swap being a teacher for any other job in the world, and this was one of them.

***

When Simon Barratt asked me out for dinner, I was dumbstruck. Not just surprised, but actually speechless, his invitation coming so completely out of the blue. I must have looked like some kind of confused goldfish, standing there opening my mouth with no words coming out.

'Sorry,' he said, slipping into his anorak and picking up his kit bag. 'I didn't mean to put you on the spot like that. If you're already spoken for ...'

'Spoken for?' I hadn't heard that expression in years.

'I just meant that I'd understand, you know, if you already have a boyfriend. Oh, not that I'm asking you out on a date,' he spluttered, his usually pale face going almost as red as his hair. 'Look, let's start again, shall we?' He grinned and busied himself fiddling with the zip on his bag which, as far as I could see, needed no fiddling at all. 'Ms Peters, I wondered if you might like to accompany me – as friends, colleagues, whatever you like to call it – to a restaurant. It would save me having to eat alone, I am perfectly prepared to pay, and you might actually enjoy it!'

His grin was infectious and I found myself grinning right back, my face probably turning just as red as his. 'Well, now that you've explained it so clearly, I would be happy to accept. Except for the paying bit. I must warn you that I am absolutely starving and might very well eat more than you can reasonably afford, so we will split the bill. Deal?'

He stuck out a hand and I took it. 'Deal!'

'Shall we go now, or would you like time to go home and do whatever it is you girls do before going out? Change out of your work clothes? Put on a bit of lippy? I am quite prepared to wait, and to pick you up at your door later. Not too much later though, 'cos I'm pretty starving myself. After all that running around the sports field this afternoon, I am in serious need of replacement calories.'

'Now would be fine, actually. There's nothing I need to go home for. Maybe a drink first though, as it's only half past four. Not quite dinner time!'

'Sounds like a good plan. The Red Lion's not far. Then what do you fancy after? Italian? Indian? Steak and chips?'

We left the staff room together, and I was sure I saw at least two or three pairs of eyebrows raised in interest. The gossip would be all round the school by the morning.

'Let's skip the Red Lion and try somewhere a bit further out, shall we?' Simon said, looking back over his shoulder. 'I have a feeling, with it being so close by, we might end up not being entirely alone in there.'

'You read my mind!'

As it turned out, Simon, despite his earlier protestations that he could talk about nothing but sport, was surprisingly good company. The absence of a Welsh accent had made it clear he was not a local, but I had never tried to work out where he might come from.

'Buckinghamshire,' he told me, taking a long swig of his pint, then wiping the back of his hand across his mouth in search of misplaced froth. 'I'm one of the Bucks young bucks! Or that's what my dad always called my brother and me. Still, we were off like a couple of stags the moment the door was left open, so he wasn't far wrong. Running wild, having a lark, getting into trouble! Oh, not the breaking the law type of trouble. Just high spirits, you know. And the occasional drink-sodden party. How about you? Miss prim-and-proper convent girl?'

'No!' I said, indignantly, before realising he was pulling my leg.

'Londoner though, right?'

'I didn't know it was that obvious. I don't have an accent, do I?'

'Eve, everyone has an accent. Just some are a bit easier to recognise. No, I grew up on the outskirts, remember? Even the Underground comes out as far as Amersham. You're no Eastender, but you have that London sound to you. Somewhere west, right?'

'Ealing.'

'I knew it! Used to play there with my brother sometimes. On the common. A picnic, a cheap ball, a pile of jumpers for a goal, while Mum and Dad went into the pub for a sneaky half!'

'Do you have any memories that don't revolve around a ball or a beer?'

'I did warn you I'm a simple man. Best things in life, sport and booze. Oh, and a touch of romance of course, but I've had slightly less luck in that department.'

'No Mrs Barratt then?'

'Only my mum! How about you? Any boyfriends, fiancés, husbands, ex-husbands lurking in the background?'

'No. Always been single. Work takes up so much of my life, I haven't really had the time.'

'Now, there's an excuse I've heard plenty of times before. Probably coming out of my own mouth! But in your case, it's a shame. Pretty girl like you ...'

'Simon,' I was blushing again, and I wasn't sure where all this was leading.

'Sorry.'

'You know, you remind me of someone. He used to say sorry a lot too.'

'Ah, but did he mean it?'

'I thought he did. At the time. But no, I don't think he did, not in the end.'

'Meant a lot to you, did he? Sorry, you don't have to tell me if you don't want to.'

'He did, yes. Too much, probably.'

'Yeah, I had one of those. Anthony, his name was.'

'Oh! You're gay?'

'Don't sound so shocked. Yes, I know I'm not the stereo-typical gay man, what with my beer habit and my rugby-playing and all. But we come in all shapes and sizes, you know.' He didn't say any more, just sat and gazed into his beer, and for some inexplicable reason I leant across and put my hand over his. He looked up and smiled. 'So, now you know why this isn't exactly a date that we're on! Still, Anthony's history. And history's not our specialist subject, is it? Let's stick to what we're good at, eh? And what we care about. And right now that's food! Come on, Eve Peters, put your woolly hat back on. Let's go and eat.'

Chapter 14

SARAH

Josh was in one of his moods. Janey had been awake half the night and, although it was me who'd got up and seen to her, his sleep had been disturbed, and now the toaster had set the smoke alarm off, he couldn't find an ironed shirt and he was in danger of missing his train.

'I've got a meeting. I might be late back.' Still buttoning the same shirt he'd worn yesterday, he grabbed his briefcase and offered a half-hearted peck that missed my cheek by a good couple of inches. 'Don't do me any dinner. And, for God's sake, get the bloody iron out today. I can't keep turning up looking all creased and crumpled. This job is important. It's what keeps food on the table and the rent paid, remember?'

I stared after him as the front door banged so loudly I expected it to shake the walls. Silence fell. I went over to the window and lifted the edge of the nets, if only to check he really had gone. And there he was, rushing off in the direction of the Underground, his case bashing against his thigh, tie flapping loosely at his neck. I waited until he'd rounded the corner and had disappeared from sight before I turned back to the mess that had once, pre-Janey, been an ordered and tidy flat.

It was one of those lucky mornings when, having guzzled an early bottle – I had long since given up on breastfeeding – Janey had fallen back to sleep and, still in my pyjamas and with my hair in desperate need of a wash, I had a little time to myself. I knew I had to use it to make a start on the chores. And that's what they felt like these days. What had once been the exciting grown-up experience of looking after our home, keeping it clean, arranging flowers in a vase, buying little ornaments to make things look nice, had become nothing but a series of never-ending chores. And, sad though it was, I had to admit that even our sex life had dropped into that category too. A chore.

Back in the bedroom, with Janey snuffling in her cot against the wall, and the window open to let in some air, I lay down on our dishevelled double bed and stretched my arms and legs out wide, relishing the space, the freedom. Eve and I had called it 'making stars' when we were small, our single beds just about wide enough to accommodate our little arms and legs when they were thrust outwards as far as they would go, shaping ourselves into big pointy stars, as we reached out and found each other's fingertips across the divide. We even did it lying outside in the snow once or twice, a few feet apart, flat on our backs and giggling, looking up into a black, pre-bedtime sky, imitating the beautiful, twinkly stars that we could wonder at but never touch, never count. Mysterious, magical stars, each one separate but all linked together into little clusters, like families. The Plough. The Bear. Gemini, the twins. It's how we had imagined our future. All shiny and perfect, with the two of us spreading our wings, following our own dreams (even if I had never fully worked out what mine were), yet still staying close enough for our lives to touch when we needed them to. Where had that dream gone?

And now I had a bigger bed, longer limbs ... but that wasn't all that had changed. I still loved the feeling of space, of taking up all of the bed, knowing it was all mine, even if only for a very short while. Nobody to bump into, nobody tugging at the covers in the middle of the night, a pillow I could thump and mould to my head's shape and my heart's content. I still dreamed of some vague, magical, glittering future, but Eve wasn't in it. And Josh? I wasn't sure about Josh anymore either.

Josh had been distracted lately. I could tell there were things on his mind, but he didn't share them. He'd been promoted at the bank and there was talk of moving him to a bigger branch or even Head Office, of a higher salary, more responsibility, us moving to a house, with the help of a mortgage at special staff rates. I don't know how he felt about any of it, if he found it as scary as I did, because he didn't talk to me about things like that. About things he obviously thought I wouldn't understand. Career, money, home ownership, long-term debt. I wondered sometimes how different it would have been if he had married Eve instead of me. Clever, competent Eve, who would have been a credit to him as he moved up the career ladder, when the client meetings and managerial dinner parties began. But now all that was up to me. I would have to learn to be the corporate wife.

Who was I trying to kid? He didn't need me to help his career. He didn't love me either. Oh, he said he did, when it was required. Just the basic three words. Written in birthday cards, said in front of his parents, murmured in the middle of our infrequent sexual encounters. But it never felt real. Not that intense, passionate kind of love that was supposed to pour itself out in a thousand different laughing, touching, spontaneous ways. Never that.

I could still hear Eve in my head during the argument we'd had the previous Christmas, telling me that Josh had made a mistake tying himself to me, that we shouldn't have rushed into being together just because I was pregnant, that we hardly knew each other. And she was right. Six years on, and she was the one with a bed all to herself, a life of her own making, a bright future ahead. Eve was still busy making stars, while Josh and I ... well, sometimes we still didn't know each other at all. Or even like each other all that much. But at least we had Janey ...

Our daughter was ten months old now. Crawling around, clinging to our ankles, or the furniture, pulling herself up, not far off the walking stage. Dropping food all over the floor, tipping toys out of boxes, making mess everywhere she went. But she had those eyes, that smile, that giggle that melted hearts. Janey was the glue that held us together. Josh may not love me in quite the way I'd hoped for, but he loved her. Unconditionally. No doubt about it.

I stood up and smoothed the covers straight. The room needed hoovering but the noise would wake Janey and I couldn't risk it, so I headed back to the kitchen and made a start on the dishes. If Eve really believed this was my dream life, a life I had cheated her out of, she was wrong. Sometimes it felt much more like being trapped in a nightmare.

***

It took a while to happen, but we did move to a house. It was small, a lot smaller than Mum and Dad's, and a few miles – and tube stops – further out of town, but the advantages were obvious. No more hunting for a parking space in the street, no more putting coins in the electricity meter, no more chemical smells wafting up from the dry cleaner's downstairs or the owner phoning to see if I could pop down and do a few hours whenever he was short staffed. We had three bedrooms, one of them admittedly more like a cupboard with a cot in it, and a small gravelled driveway at the front, and a long thin back garden made of nothing but weed-filled grass and wonky fence panels, but it was ours.

Eve came to the house-warming party, just as she had turned up seven months earlier, for a few hours on a Saturday, for Janey's first birthday, despite the distance she'd had to travel and it being so early in the new school term, and then again at Mum and Dad's for a few days at Christmas. We saw very little of each other nowadays but we seemed to have arrived at a kind of uneasy peace, and I think she wanted to stay in touch, for Janey's sake. I hadn't been sure she would make the journey again, despite it being April and the Easter holidays, with no work for her to rush back to, but clearly the lure of another afternoon in Janey's company had worked its

usual magic and there she was. This time with a man in tow
as well!

We had just about managed to get all the cardboard boxes
unpacked and everything more or less in its place, with a
lot of help from Mum, and Dad had whizzed round the lawn
that morning with his hover mower before stowing it back
in the boot of his car and driving it home again, so the place
looked respectable enough, if a little in need of redecoration.
Josh lit a barbecue and I had spent most of the day before,
in between Janey times, making and icing a cake in the shape
of a house, marzipan chimney and all. We'd bought wine,
and nibbles were laid out in bowls at intervals around the
house and garden; I'd put fresh flowers and a brand-new
hand towel in the bathroom to detract from the old cracked
tiles and pampas-green bath we couldn't yet do anything
about.

It was the first time Josh had ever invited any of his work
colleagues home, I supposed because our previous home
hadn't been up to the job, and I was feeling anxious about
meeting them, but Mum and Dad had arrived first, their
presence settling my nerves a little, and they were quickly
followed by Eve, who introduced her tall, good-looking friend
as Simon but told us nothing else about him. I could tell that
Mum was curious, as we all were, and itching for information,
and I felt pretty sure that by the end of the evening she would
have wheedled a few useful snippets out of Eve, if not the
poor man's entire life history.

Eve looked poised and perfect that day, her nails varnished
silver, her hair cut and coloured, and wearing a short and

shimmery pale-grey dress so new I could see she had forgotten to remove the price label at the back and discreetly did it for her with a pair of scissors from the kitchen drawer. Her perfume, one I recognised straightaway as Calvin Klein, wafted subtly around her, clinging to the neck of the dress, and made me only too aware that the only scent coming off me was likely to be a mixture of soap, cheap shampoo and Janey's strawberry milk.

It wasn't like Eve to dress up like that. Her job, her new life, were changing her and I guessed this man of hers just might be important too, someone worth making the effort for. As the afternoon wore on, I noticed how he placed his arm across her back to guide her through the crowds in the kitchen, how he bent to whisper in her ear before pouring her another drink, how totally at ease they were with each other, and I felt a small pang of jealousy as my own husband flipped burgers and chatted animatedly to his banking buddies and barely looked in my direction at all. He did look at Eve though, as did every other man at the party. I couldn't help noticing that.

Of course, Janey was the real star of the show. I'd bought her a red dress and shoes, and her hair had finally grown long enough to be pulled up into a tiny pony tail, topped off with a matching red bow. She looked cute, toddling about with half a burger bun in her hand, grass stains on her tights, ketchup smeared around her mouth, being picked up and chuckled at by just about everyone in turn.

'Time for bed now, Janey.' The heat of the barbecue had died down to a glow, and there were no buns left, just the wilted remains of the salad, a plate of burnt sausages that most people seemed keen to avoid, and numerous discarded paper plates and empty glasses dotted about. Josh was wiping his hands on a tea towel and play-chasing Janey around the garden, dodging legs and chairs, but she was having none of it. What child wants to be shuttled off to bed while there are still people to give her attention and all kinds of potential fun and games to look forward to? When he caught her she screamed, at first with excitement, but that soon turned to distress as she realised she had been tricked, it wasn't a game, and it really was bedtime.

'Can I?' It was Eve, holding out her arms. 'Maybe she'd let me get her into her pyjamas? You know, the novelty factor of someone new doing it, and then a story once she's all tucked up?'

Josh hesitated, already halfway into the kitchen. 'Why not?' he said, handing the wriggling Janey over. 'You are her auntie, after all, and it means I can get back to the party and concentrate on my guests. Thanks, Eve.'

'I'll come with you,' I said, following them to the stairs. 'You don't know her routine, or where anything is.'

'I'm sure I'd manage, but yes, come.'

'So, how are things?' she asked, when we had Janey changed and lying in her cot, her little eyelids already closing before we had even chosen a book to look at. 'The house is nice, by the way.'

'Fine. And, yes, I like it. I think we can make something of it, with a bit of paint and a few garden plants. More room for Janey too, now she's walking.'

'More like running, I'd say. She's grown so much since I last saw her.' She leant over the cot and kissed her own fingers, gently placing them on Janey's forehead.

I laughed, pleased that Eve was talking to me, actually talking to me, as if we were on the way to being close again. 'Yeah, she never stops. Come on, she's exhausted. Let's leave her. Fancy a glass of wine, or are you keen to get back outside to your Simon?'

'He's not *my* Simon, Sarah. He's a work colleague. We enjoy each other's company. We go to the cinema together, or out to eat sometimes, and he's teaching me to drive. He's a friend. Probably my best friend, to be honest, but that's all.'

'If you say so.'

'I do! His parents live not that far from here, so it made sense to travel up together. He even let me drive some of the easy non-motorway bits. We're heading over there when we leave here, actually. Only fair to spend some time with his family, seeing as he's had you lot inflicted on him all after-noon.'

We got to the bottom of the stairs and I led her into the now deserted kitchen and hunted around for an unopened bottle of wine. There wasn't one.

'Will lager do?' I opened the fridge and took out two cans. 'Looks like the wine's all gone.'

'Yeah, sure, Anything. Simon's driving, not me this time, so booze is allowed!'

'So ... Simon? You'll be spending the night at his parents' place?'

'Oh, give it a rest! They have a spare room. I will be sleeping in it. Not everybody jumps straight into bed together, you know. And he's not that kind of a bloke ...'

'They're all that kind of bloke, Eve, given half the chance.'

'You've got really cynical, haven't you? What's going on? Is Josh playing away or something?'

'I don't know. I hope not. But when he works late, I can never really know where he is, can I? Or where he spends his lunch breaks? Oh, he knows where I am all right, stuck here with Janey, but it's different for men, isn't it?'

'Not necessarily. Sounds to me like you're having trouble trusting him.'

'Is it any wonder? Look how quickly he cheated on you.'

'It took two, Sarah.' She was glaring at me now, and I realised I had stepped over a line. This was not the best direction to take the conversation in.

'I know. And I'm sorry. Nothing we can do to turn back the clock though, is there? And now my garden is full of young intelligent career women I don't know anything about, and any one of them could be ...'

'What? Next on his list? God, you really have got it bad, haven't you?' She took a swig of her beer, straight from the can, and leaned forward to lay her cold hand on mine. 'If you're that worried, you'd better do something about it. Yes, you're a stay-at-home mum, but you can still make the effort.'

I looked down at myself. I'd dressed for comfort, in cotton trousers and a floppy blue-and-white striped blouse, and there was a mark on the front, probably from Janey's mucky fingers. 'I try.'

'Then try harder. Get your hair done. A good cut. Highlights, maybe. And look at your nails, all bitten down. Looking good is so important, if only for your own self-confidence. I soon discovered that, once I started teaching. Dressing like the kids, in baggy clothes and trainers, doesn't work. Look the part, and they respect you more. I think that works with men too. Give 'em a bit of razzle dazzle, if you want to keep them interested. Not that I'm any sort of expert in that department! But you're only twenty-three, Sarah. You used to be so into fashion. You shouldn't be dressing like Mum! Especially at a party, even if it is only in your own back garden. I don't mean to sound harsh, but you did ask. Maybe you should—'

'Ah! Here you are.' Eve stopped abruptly as Simon came in through the open back door, peering at his watch. 'I don't want to rush you, but should we be making a move soon, do you think? Oh, not interrupting anything, am I?'

'Of course not,' I said, putting my drink down. 'Just catching up. You know, sister stuff.'

'Yeah, we haven't done a lot of that lately, have we?' Eve came closer and gave me a loose hug. It was the first time she had shown any sign of affection in years. Maybe now she had a new man of her own she had finally decided to let the past go. 'But think about it, Sarah. What I said. Don't leave it to chance. Don't leave it too late.' She laughed. 'You don't want to end up like me!'

Like her? I had no idea what she meant. She was dressed beautifully, had a good job that she loved, and a handsome man eager to drag her away. What would be so bad about ending up like that?

And then they were back outside saying their goodbyes,

Eve pulling Mum, and then Dad, into hugs much tighter than the one she had given me, and neither of them, despite their best efforts, still any the wiser about Simon or his place in her life. I watched as Eve approached Josh, holding out her hand to him, but he threw his arms around her, planting a kiss on the top of her head. Did he hold her for just a moment too long? Or was I looking for things that just weren't there? He'd been drinking, he was having a good time, and they were old friends. Still, his gaze followed her, all the way to the door.

I walked through the house with Eve and Simon and waved them off from the step. The evening was getting chilly and darkness was falling. I watched the lights of Simon's car until they disappeared around the corner, then I closed the door and stood for a moment in the empty hall, stifling a yawn. I felt ridiculously tired all of a sudden and hoped it wouldn't be long until the other guests decided to call it a night too. With no food left, and no wine, I didn't think there would be much reason for them to stay.

I spent a few minutes clearing things away in the kitchen, pouring the remains of Eve's can of lager down the sink before finishing my own. I could hear Josh laughing at something outside, and knew he would be expecting me to go back out there and join his friends. But first I went up to check on Janey. She was sleeping soundly, making little contented snuffles, one thumb placed loosely in her mouth. As I leaned over the side of the cot to kiss her goodnight, all I could smell was Eve's perfume, as if she had left a little of herself behind in my house, imprinted on my daughter's skin.

Chapter 15

EVE

It was one of those lazy Sunday mornings, early in August, and I'd spent ages being unusually domesticated, making real lemonade and a fat, squidgy ginger cake. Simon was stretched out on my one and only sun lounger, engrossed in the sports pages of his newspaper as he munched on a thick slice of the cake, flicking crumbs across the lawn for the birds and wiping his sticky hands down his jeans.

'What do you fancy for lunch?' he said, looking up and peering at me above the sunglasses that had slipped, sweatily, down his nose.

'Lunch?' I rested my elbows on the small patio table and sipped my drink, trying not to pull a face at its unexpected sourness, making a mental note that more sugar was needed next time. 'It's just gone eleven, and we've only just had ... well, elevenses! You can't be hungry again already.'

'No, no, thinking ahead, that's all. Wondered if you'd like to take a walk to the pub later and grab a roast maybe. I could ring and book us a table.'

'Thanks, Si, but it's such a nice day, I'd rather stay here, and I'm not sure I could eat anything heavy. I could do us a salad?'

'Salad? I'm a growing lad!'

'You grow much more and you won't fit through the door. Now, stop thinking about food and help me with the crossword.'

'Me, help you? Now I know you're having a laugh. Give me *A Question of Sport* and I'm your man, but show me an anagram or one of those cryptic thingies and I don't have a clue.' He laughed, loudly. 'Ha! Just made a joke there, I think. Clue! Get it?'

'Fine. You get back to your sports pages and leave the intellectual stuff to me.' I adjusted the flimsy parasol that was fluttering above my head and moved my plastic chair round a bit, to keep the sun off my face.

'Don't knock it, Eve. It's what makes us such good friends, you know. Our differences. Chalk and cheese, that's us. I mean, we wouldn't want both of us battling over that puzzle, trying to outdo each other, would we? You see it on trains. A couple of businessmen huddled over their own copies of *The Times* crossword, desperate to be the first to finish it, probably filling in any old rubbish in the boxes just so it looks like they've cracked it. All that rivalry. It'd be the same if we were both runners, or tennis players. Always vying to be the fastest, or the best, trying to beat each other. No, I like it this way.'

'Me too, actually.' I put my pen down and looked at him. 'We complement each other, don't we?'

'What? Like me telling you how clever you are and you telling me I'm the best hooker you've ever seen?'

'Not that sort of compliment, you dummy.' I rolled up my paper and flicked it at his arm. 'And, you may have the morals of an alley cat, but why would I call you a hooker?'

Simon roared with laughter. 'Oh dear, you really don't know anything about rugby, do you? I'll explain it all to you one of these days.'

'Is it anything like the rules of cricket? All that being in when you're out and out when you're in stuff?'

'Not exactly.'

'Let's not bother then, eh? Sport's not my thing.'

'And messing around with words isn't mine. But I love you anyway. Best buddies?'

'Always.'

We sat in silence for a while, enjoying the sunshine and the last of the lemonade. When I looked up to swat a persistent wasp away from the sugary rim of the empty jug, I saw that Simon had nodded off to sleep, his face, usually so pale and freckly, already turning redder than it should. I had a wide-brimmed straw hat in the flat somewhere and I went in to find it, although I was not entirely sure it would fit Simon's head, which was considerably bigger than mine. Failing that, I'd just have to wake him up and get him to move into the shade.

I had the contents of the hall cupboard out all over the carpet when the intercom buzzed, and still no hat. I was expecting the caller to be some sort of door-to-door salesman or a neighbour asking if Simon could please move his car. A nuisance, but easy enough to get rid of. I picked up the handset by the front door, and there was the hat, which had clearly been hiding all along, right there beside me, wedged between two winter jackets and a mac on the coat stand.

'Hello?' I tugged at the hat and managed to free it, knocking the mac onto the floor in the process.

'Eve? Is that you?'

It couldn't be! But it definitely was. I would have known that voice anywhere.

'Josh? What are you doing here?' My heart was thumping nineteen to the dozen. 'Is everything all right? With Sarah? Janey? Mum and Dad?'

'Everything's fine.'

I was aware that I was just standing there, shocked into silence, rolling the battered old hat around in my hand, the contents of a cupboard scattered at my feet.

'Eve? Are you still there? Can I come in, do you think? Or are you going to leave me out here on the step?'

I pushed the button that opened the main door, pulled my own door open, and watched him walk across the communal hallway towards me. He was smartly dressed – too smartly really, for a summer Sunday – and he was carrying a bunch of roses. White roses, wrapped in cellophane, with a yellow bow.

'For you,' he said, thrusting them forward and leaning in to peck my cheek. 'A sort of peace offering, as I've turned up uninvited.'

'Thank you.'

'It is all right, isn't it? Me coming here? You're not ... well, busy, or entertaining or anything?'

'Entertaining?' I had visions of me doing a twirl while

singing into a microphone. 'Oh, you mean do I have a man here? Did you interrupt me having passionate daytime sex? Afraid not. Just my friend Simon. He's out in the garden, having a nap. But, of course, you've met Simon, haven't you? At your party.'

'Oh, then maybe I should go?'

'Don't be daft. Not when you've come all this way.' I stood aside and ushered him in, nudging the pile of cupboard stuff away with my foot and closing the door behind him. 'Why have you come all this way anyway?'

'I had to come to Cardiff for a conference. Starts properly tomorrow, but there's a meet-and-greet and a dinner this evening. I had a few hours to kill, it's too early to check in at the hotel, and I knew you were nearby. I've parked outside on a yellow line. I assume that's okay on a Sunday? Not likely to get a fine? Look, you really are sure about me being here? This Simon bloke isn't going to mind?'

'Mind what?' Simon had come in from the garden and was standing in the open doorway that led from the kitchen to the hall, rubbing his eyes, one half of his face decidedly redder than the other. 'Ah, it's Josh, isn't it? The errant ex.'

I laughed, or tried to, and popped the straw hat on top of Simon's head, where it wobbled a bit before tipping over one eye. 'And now my brother-in-law!' I gave him a warning scowl.

I could see Simon give a slight shake of his head. He removed the hat and tucked it under his arm, still staring at the two of us as if he wasn't sure what he was expected to do next.

'Sorry, Si, but do you mind going back outside? With your

face shaded this time! And I'll bring us all out a coffee in a minute. I just want a few words with Josh first, okay?'

'If you're sure. Call if you need me, okay?' He went, I could tell a bit reluctantly, although he didn't make it too obvious, and I led Josh through to my small living room and pointed to an armchair.

'I'll just put the kettle on and do something with the flowers. Coffee all right? Or would you prefer tea? I expect I have a bottle of wine somewhere.'

'It's a bit early, and I'm driving, remember?' He sank back into the cushions and smiled up at me. 'No need to fuss. Coffee's fine. White. No sugar.'

'Yes, I remember.'

In the kitchen I leaned on the counter and took a big, deep breath, waiting for the water to boil and my heart to stop pumping out a rhythm like some old over-heated steam train. I hadn't seen him on his own, away from my sister, for years. I wasn't sure how that made me feel, or even if I had ever truly forgiven him for what he had done. But now Josh Cavendish was here, in my home, and I had no idea why.

I could see Simon through the kitchen window. He had moved into the chair I had been using, under the parasol, and was leafing through my newspaper, his own abandoned on the sun lounger, alongside the hat. His jaw was moving up and down, very slightly, as if he was grinding his teeth, and I knew he was probably holding back a lot of what he would really like to say. I had told him enough about my relationship with Josh, and how it had ended, for him to have formed a pretty strong opinion of him – and it wasn't a good one.

'So?' I handed Josh his coffee and sat down on the chair opposite.

'Oh, don't look at me like that, Eve. There is no *so*. No hidden agenda. I was in the area, I had time on my hands, and I've never seen where you live. Call it curiosity if you like.' He blew over the surface of his coffee, took the smallest of sips, then put it down on the table in front of him. 'Bit too hot.'

'Does Sarah know you're here?'

'In Cardiff, yes, if she was even listening when I told her where I was going. I'm sure she just tunes out most of the time when I talk about work. But here in your flat, no. I didn't know myself until an hour or so ago. It was a spur of the moment decision.'

'Yet you just happened to have my address with you?'

'Okay, so I looked it up in her little address book thing before I left home. Just in case, that's all ...'

'Well, it's nice to see you.' Was it? But then, what else was I meant to say? Bugger off, you bastard? All I felt at that moment was confused. I wasn't sure whether I was supposed to love him, hate him, treat him with indifference, or just accept him now for what he had become. My sister's husband.

'Nice?' His eyes twinkled. 'Is that the best you can do? Do you remember that conversation we had once, about that word? Whether it was poetic enough for you?'

'No, I don't.'

'Come on, Eve, you must do. It was the evening you whacked me round the head like you were fending off Jack the Ripper and ran off into the night! I never did really understand what that was all about.'

'I have never whacked you round the head. And I honestly can't see any point in dredging all that up again. Now, why don't you pick up your mug and we'll go out into the garden and you can meet Simon properly. You were far too busy with your own friends to pay him any attention at your party, and I don't see why I should neglect my invited guest for the sake of my uninvited one, do you?'

'Sometimes, Eve, I have no idea whether you're joking or you're actually telling me off.'

'Good,' I said, not knowing the answer myself. 'I like to be an enigma. Keep you on your toes.' I stood up and led the way back to the kitchen, where I'd left Simon's coffee waiting on the side. 'But if you behave yourself,' I added, as I picked up the mug in my free hand and we stepped out into my small garden, 'and act like a brother-in-law is supposed to, I might even let you stay for lunch.'

I did try to keep the conversation flowing, but it wasn't easy. Josh and Simon glared at each other across the garden table like a pair of stags squaring up for a fight, and although they both spoke easily enough to me, I don't think they said more than a few words to each other.

'I think I'll be making a move now,' Simon said eventually, stretching as he pulled himself up to his full height and rescued his paper from the lounger.

'You sure? What about lunch?' I stood, took a couple of steps around to the other side of the table and tugged him into a hug.

'Think I might head off to the pub for one of those roasts you didn't fancy. Watch the Formula One on their big-screen TV. Leave you two to talk ...'

'Well, if you're sure. You're welcome to stay, you know. My little telly can't compete with theirs, but there's plenty of food here.'

'Not really in a salad mood. See you soon, eh?' He kissed the top of my head and held out a hand, stiffly, towards Josh. 'Don't bother coming to the door, Eve. I can see myself out.'

'Well, that was a bit awkward, wasn't it?' Josh said as soon as Simon had gone. 'The man is so obviously jealous.'

I laughed. 'Jealous? What of? You?'

'Well, I did come crashing in and wreck his plans, didn't I?'

'Plans?'

'Oh, you know what I mean. A sit in the sun, a pub lunch, just the two of you. Very cosy. And he's just a friend, you say? Looked more than that to me. Looked like he was settled in for the rest of the day, until I turned up. The night too, I shouldn't wonder.'

'Josh! It's not what you think. Not that it's any of your business. Now, tell me why you're really here. I don't buy all the "just passing" nonsense.'

'Don't you?' He reached across the small gap between our chairs and laid his hand on my bare arm. 'I still think about you, Eve. What we used to have. I still care about you.'

I knew I shouldn't, knew I really didn't want to, but I felt it anyway, as soon as he touched me. The same spark I had felt all those years ago, when we were young and free and single. I pulled my arm away from him, quickly. 'No, Josh. Whatever it is you're thinking, the answer is no. You're not allowed to care about me anymore. Not in *that* way. You're married. To my sister.'

'I don't need you to remind me of that, Eve. But it doesn't stop what I feel, does it? Or what I remember? We had some good times, didn't we? At uni. And then, when you came to the house that day, to the party, in that little shiny dress, and with him – that Simon – hanging on your arm, and on your every word ...'

'It wasn't like that. Not like that at all. Simon and I ... oh, never mind. No, it strikes me that you're the one who's jealous, not him.'

'You could be right.' He grabbed my hand and trapped it between his own. 'I made a mistake, Eve. A big, bloody awful mistake, that I'm still paying for. Every day of my life. And I've never had the chance to tell you that. I thought that now, here, miles away from everybody, while it's just us, I might be able to say a proper sorry, and maybe even ...'

'Maybe even what?'

'I told you once that I loved you. Only once. Do you remember?'

I nodded, the warmth of his hands seeping into my skin.

'But you didn't say it back. Not then. Not ever. I suppose I just need to know whether you did. Love me, I mean.'

'And what possible good would it do, to either of us, for me to tell you that now? It's been seven years. Seven years too late. And it wouldn't matter how many times you said it to me back then, would it? Not if it was just words. You clearly didn't love me for real. Not enough, anyway, because you made your choice, and it wasn't me. We can't go back. No matter how much ...'

'What? No matter how much you might want to?'

I didn't answer.

'I'd go back in a heartbeat if I could,' he said, his voice little more than a whisper. 'To be with you, stay with you, have you still in my life.'

'But aren't you forgetting something, Josh? Like why you cheated on me in the first place. I wouldn't sleep with you, remember? Is that why you're here? Unfinished business? Hurt pride?'

'Don't be ridiculous. And we were working on all of that, weren't we? I knew you had your reservations, your anxieties. Inhibitions, even. I can't say I understood them, but I always thought we'd get there, that things would change. We were taking it slowly, taking our time ...'

'But time ran out, didn't it? You couldn't wait any longer. And along came Sarah.'

He closed his eyes and tightened his hold on my fingers. 'I know. Bloody stupid of me. And I'm sorry. I wish I could go back, start again, but I suppose it's too late now, isn't it? There's Sarah to think about, and Janey. And now you've got Simon. Lucky sod's got the one thing I never had.' There was a bitterness in his voice I had never heard there before. He opened his eyes again and stared into mine. 'Good, is he? In bed?'

I pulled away from him. 'You can't ask me that!'

'I just did. Do you love him, Eve? The way you loved me? *More* than you loved me?'

'I never said I loved you.'

'You may not have said it, but you did. I know you did. Why else would you have been so hurt, so angry, that you'd leave home, move right down here and not come back? You loved me and you couldn't bear to see me and Sarah together. You still can't!'

'God, you are so arrogant, so bloody sure of yourself. And, no, I don't love Simon. Not in that way. I've told you, he's a friend. My best friend. But I have no idea what he's like in bed. What *anyone's* like in bed—' I shouldn't have said it, blurted it out like that, but now I had I couldn't take it back.

'Anyone? What do you mean? That you still haven't ...?'

'I don't want to talk about it. I'm going to make us some lunch.' I stood up and headed for the kitchen, but he was up immediately and right behind me, reaching for my waist, stopping me in my tracks, turning me round to face him.

'Yes, I'm still a virgin, okay?' I could feel my face flaming. 'Is that what you wanted to hear?'

'But you're almost twenty-six, Eve.' He looked confused, his brow furrowing. 'A beautiful, sexy, grown woman. Why on earth ...?'

There were tears now, rushing up into my eyes, and nothing I could do to stop them. 'Why do you think?'

'Tell me.' His face was close now, his eyes searching mine for answers.

'Okay, have it your way. Make me say it. It's because of you, okay? You. I didn't want to be – couldn't be – with anyone else. It's only ever been you.'

He pulled me into him, my wet face pressed against his

shirt, his fingers moving up from my waist and curling into my hair. 'Oh, Eve.'

My arms went around him as if a magnet had pulled them in, and I clung to him as I cried.

'And what about Simon?'

'Simon's gay, you numpty.' And that was when I lifted my head away from him and laughed, and suddenly Josh was laughing with me.

'Got that wrong then, didn't I?'

'Totally.'

'But not the rest of it? Because you did love me? And you still do? I didn't imagine that bit?'

'Of course I love you. I was angry with you, so angry, and I couldn't forgive you, but that didn't stop me loving you.'

'So, what are we going to do about it?'

'Well, I'm going to make lunch, and you're going to sit here in the sun and wait for me to come back. You can read my newspaper, watch the bees, even wear the hat if you want to. And after that ... I don't know, Josh. I really don't know.'

I took my time in the kitchen, letting my breathing slow and my thoughts start to clear. When I came back, we picked at our food, leaving as much as we managed to eat.

'It's because I'm only hungry for you,' Josh said, taking my hand in his, and we both laughed at what a corny line that was, but I knew what he meant because I felt it too. Somehow I wasn't afraid anymore. Maybe it was the passage of time, or the heat of the moment, or just knowing that this was it, finally, my chance to take back what I had lost, and that I couldn't let it pass by, couldn't waste it.

We left the plates, the flapping parasol, the solitary straw hat, and walked back into the flat, my hand still cradled inside his as I led him through the hall and into my bedroom. The bed creaked as we sat on it, and I felt myself shiver as Josh very gently removed my clothes, his fingers lingering on my skin, taking his time, making sure I was with him, willing, wanting this as much as he did. No rush, no panic, no fear, just a warmth that crept over me and a feeling of coming home, of being where I had always belonged.

If only I had allowed this to happen the first time around. If only I hadn't let thoughts of that scumbag Arnie hold me back, colour my judgement, ruin my life ...

But none of that mattered now. I was older. Wiser, perhaps. No, not wiser. This was far from wise. But I was certainly more confident, and more accepting. The past couldn't be undone, but this was now, and Josh was here, where I had so badly wanted him to be. I didn't stop to think, to question, to let common sense in. I went with my heart, and we made love, slowly, tenderly, his hands guiding me, showing me where to go, what to do, while he took me to places, sensations, heights I had had no idea existed. And not for one moment did I think of Arnie, or of Sarah. Or even Janey, and what this could do to her. Just Josh. Only Josh.

Later, when I woke from a warm, wet, wonderful sleep to find Josh gone, there was one of those small plastic bags that the banks use, full of fifty pence pieces – maybe twenty or thirty of them – lying next to my face on the pillow, with a scribbled note beside it. I held it up to the fading evening light coming in from the window, and read the words:

More sorry than I can say.

I had almost forgotten our rule about not saying sorry and having to pay up if we did. I held the note against my chest and smiled, all the old memories flooding back. I just wished I knew, this time, what it was he was so sorry about. Was it the afternoon we had just spent together? Oh, God, I hoped not. I didn't regret a single moment of it. Or did he just mean he was sorry for the mistakes of the past? For abandoning me for my conniving, back-stabbing, teenaged sister?

It was only as I reluctantly got out of bed and headed for the shower that I realised he must have brought the coins with him, that the apology had already been planned before he even arrived. I might never know whether what had just happened between us had been planned too, but that wasn't what he was saying sorry for. And, rapidly pushing aside the image of Sarah that had suddenly popped into my head, I knew I wasn't sorry about it either. After all, she was the one who had stolen him from me. All I was doing, in some small secret way, was reclaiming what was rightfully mine.

Chapter 16

SARAH

There was no doubt that Janey was the invisible glue that held our little family together. We had wanted a baby so badly. Not to replace the one we had lost exactly, but to give some sort of meaning to our situation, to justify our marriage, not only to everybody else but to ourselves too. We had married so young, and so quickly, and for one reason only, yet the baby we lost had left an emptiness I had never expected to feel. Trying again seemed like the only way to make things right.

It had taken us so long to make baby number two that I had started to worry there was something wrong. I knew I was okay. I must be. I had already been pregnant, and without even trying, but what if it was Josh? What if he wasn't producing good enough sperm, or any sperm at all? If he was ever to be told something like that by some well-meaning doctor he would inevitably start asking questions about my first pregnancy. How it had happened so easily then, when now it wasn't happening at all. But, in the end, we were lucky and Janey came along before we had reached the dreaded infertility investigations stage, and before we decided to give up and go our separate ways, which I had started to believe was a real possibility.

I often wondered why he had stayed with me so long, when it was obvious he didn't love me. Not deep-down love me, anyway, the way I had come to love him. But Josh took his responsibilities seriously. It must have been his Catholic upbringing, or perhaps just that he had no real reason to rock the boat, but it was his career that so clearly mattered the most. Not me. His job at the bank gave him status, fulfilment, ambition, and if he looked to his own parents for a role model marriage, then that was the kind of marriage we ended up with too. Practical, comfortable, functional. He worked and earned. I cooked and cleaned and lay on my back a couple of times a week, enjoying what he gave me but always desperately hoping for a level of passion that never quite materialised. The cracks had definitely started to form, like those tiny hairlines that appear on a ceiling and gradually get wider, while you're not even looking, until one day the whole lot comes falling down. But Janey turned up just in time, and changed things.

Janey became the reason Josh came home at night. He doted on her, right from day one. It didn't hurt that she looked so much like him either. Two peas in a pod, the absolute image, apples not falling far from the tree, and all those other silly phrases people kept coming up with as soon as they saw them together. For the first time, I saw true love in his eyes, but it wasn't directed at me.

As his career progressed, Josh worked harder and longer, often going away on business trips. Up north, Birmingham, Wales, the south coast ... I lost track after a while. To be honest, I never really understood why an assistant bank manager, or loans adviser, or whatever it was he called himself, would need to go to quite so many courses and conferences, but I felt it best not to question him too much and, if I had, I knew he would just have told me it was too dull and boring to explain. In truth, although I still worried that he might be seeing other women, getting close to one – or maybe more – of his young glamorous colleagues behind my back, on the whole I enjoyed the times when he was away. Janey was turning into a real daddy's girl, always sitting on his knee or clinging to his legs, always wanting Josh to take her up to bed or fetch her a drink or play with her in the bath. I knew it was wrong to be jealous. She was his child just as much as she was mine, but sometimes I just didn't get a look in, and it was only when he was not there that I got the chance to have her all to myself.

One Sunday afternoon, once Josh had put his case into the boot and driven off to some place in the Midlands that I had never heard of and couldn't be bothered to look for on a map, I decided to take advantage of what was left of the sunshine and wheel Janey out in her pushchair. Not that she really needed it anymore, unless she was in a lazy mood or got tired on the way back, but it was always handy for carrying stuff. She looked so cute that day, in her little T-shirt and shorts, with a white sunhat falling over her eyes, clutching a cuddly toy rabbit. In the bag hanging on the handles I had packed a ball, a couple of books, a picnic blanket, and all her favourite snacks, with no intention of going home until dinner time.

Halfway round the park we ran straight into a man. Quite literally ran into him or, more accurately, he ran into us, as he came tearing round a bend in the path, tinny music seeping out of headphones attached to a small player clipped to his T-shirt, and almost knocked me over.

'Sorry. Wasn't looking.' He pulled the headphones down around his neck, quickly switched the loud music off and stopped to catch his breath. 'Sarah? Sarah Peters. Well, I never. It *is* you!'

It took me a few moments to recognise the once chubby, shy boy I remembered from that day I'd tripped over on the bus as this now rather slim and handsome man out jogging in the park. Colin Grant!

'Oh, Colin. Fancy seeing you after all these years. How are you?'

'Good, thanks. And I obviously don't need to ask what's been happening in your life!' He bent down to take a closer look at Janey, who beamed up at him as if he was a long-lost and much-loved uncle and made a sneaky grab for his headphones. 'So, who is this gorgeous little lady? And who's the lucky man? Don't tell me you ended up with that jerk, Jacobs?'

'This is Janey. She's nearly four. And, no, I did not!'

'Glad to hear it. He was never good enough for you. And he's a used-car salesman now, you know. I bumped into him when I was looking for my latest. Needless to say I didn't buy it from his place! Anyway, enough about him. I don't suppose you fancy a coffee or an ice cream or something? If you're not in a hurry to be anywhere, that is. It's thirsty work, this keeping fit lark. We'll sit in the sun and you can tell all.'

'Nothing much to tell. Marriage. Motherhood. Busy, but boring. And I'm a Cavendish now, by the way, not a Peters. I married a banker. Josh. Not much else to say really. But I'm dying to know what you're up to these days. So, yes, please. I'd love a coffee, and Janey adores ice cream. Assuming she's included in the invitation?'

'Of course she is. Come on. The kiosk by the playground should be open. We might even be able to have a go on the swings, if nobody's looking!'

We walked side by side, Janey kicking her legs and singing to herself in her buggy all the way to the kiosk. Colin waved away my offer to pay, pulled out a ten-pound note that had been tucked inside his sock and bought us coffees in polystyrene cups and a couple of Penguins, with a small cornet for Janey that gradually dripped its way down her arm as we sat opposite each other on wooden benches in the sun.

'So?' he said, putting his cup down on the table in front of us. 'You want to know what I've been up to? Everything since we last met? It could take a while.'

'Okay, maybe just the edited highlights then.' I laughed. 'I would like to get home before dark!'

'Well, I suppose the biggest thing – the most important thing – is that I'm a doctor now. Well, almost!'

'Wow! Really?'

'Not quite consultant yet, mind. Very much a junior. Still in training, so to speak.'

'But I'm impressed, even so. Beats my one and only part-time job, behind the counter at the dry cleaners', that's for sure.'

'Ah, but look what you've done. Brought a little life into the world. That outranks any achievement of mine. Something I'll never be able to do.'

'Oh, come on, Colin. So men don't have wombs. That's just biology. That's not to say you can't have kids of your own one day. Assuming there's a Mrs Grant in the picture, obviously.'

'There isn't. No wife, no girlfriend. Or boyfriend, before you ask! No, I've just been too busy, too focused on my studies, and too damn knackered to be honest.' He picked up his cup and took a sip. 'Was that Mrs Grant thing your way of finding out if I'm available, by the way?' His eyes danced with merriment.

'No! I am a respectable married woman, I'll have you know.'

'Shame. But you can't blame a man for trying. I may be one-hundred-per-cent single, but for you I would definitely make an exception.'

It was just banter, I knew that, but I could feel myself blushing just the same. 'Come on, get that drink down you. You promised us swings, remember?'

The next hour passed by in a flurry of fun, Colin chasing Janey up the slide steps and then running back round to catch her at the bottom, pushing her higher than I could ever have managed on the swings, and whizzing the roundabout, with all of us on board, so fast I thought I might be sick.

Back in her buggy, Janey's eyelids were drooping. Colin walked with us as far as the park gates and leant forward to kiss me on the cheek. 'It's been lovely seeing you again, Sarah. We must do it again. Soon.' He took my hand in his, his fingers warm, his thumb pressing against my rings. 'A walk, lunch, coffee, or maybe something a tad stronger ... whatever suits. I'm sorry I don't have a card or a pen or anything to give you my number, or to take yours. I don't even have my phone with me. When you go out running, you don't normally carry a lot of stuff. Well, I don't. Just money, for emergencies.'

'Like having to buy ice cream!' I pulled my new mobile phone out from the bottom of my bag. 'Here. Tap your number in for me. But call yourself ... oh, I don't know. let's say Carol, shall we? I wouldn't want Josh to see I'm collecting men friends in my contact list!'

'Jealous type, is he?'

'I wouldn't say that. It's just easier somehow. No questions asked.'

Colin handed the phone back. 'There! Now you have my number – or Carol's anyway – but I don't have yours. So whether we ever speak, or meet, again will be entirely up to you. Our future is in your hands.'

I laughed. 'Such power!'

'You will though, won't you?' He was still holding my hand. 'Call?'

I nodded, slipping my hand out from his. 'Yes. I can't promise when, and I have no idea of your shifts, so you'll probably be in the middle of an operation or something, but yes, I will call.'

'Bye then. And bye to you, little Janey.' He laid his fingers gently on the top of her sleeping head and stroked her hair. And then he was gone, jogging away from us along the path, pulling his headphones back over his ears. I stood at the gate and watched until he went around the corner and disappeared from view. He didn't look back.

***

Josh was very quiet. He sat sideways on our second-hand sofa with his feet up and stared at the TV. There was a quiz show on, but I could see he wasn't watching it.

I worked around him, picking up discarded newspapers, running a duster over the coffee table, steering the hoover around the room. Normally he would have complained that he couldn't hear the questions, insisted that the room was clean enough already, and couldn't I find a better time to do all this stuff? Today he just sat there and said nothing at all.

It was a Friday evening in November, already dark outside, and we had eaten early, Janey perched between us at the dining table, smearing ketchup over everything, herself included. Now, face and fingers wiped, she was settled in an armchair, playing with her dolls, waiting for Josh to put her in the bath and tuck her up in bed.

'Do you ever wonder where we would be now, if we hadn't got married?'

Where had that come from all of a sudden? I was in the kitchen, putting the cleaning things away in the cupboard under the sink, but there was a small open hatch in the wall linking the two rooms and I could hear him through it, even though, at this angle, I couldn't see him. Did he even realise I wasn't there in the room with him anymore?

I closed the cupboard door and went back into the living room. Josh was still staring sightlessly at the TV. The quiz had finished and there was a wildlife programme on in its place. A pack of wolves roamed across the screen, in search of prey.

'Sorry. What did you say?'

He turned towards me. 'You heard. If we hadn't got married, if you hadn't been pregnant, what would have happened to us, do you think?'

'*Us?* Us, as in us together, do you mean?'

'Well, no. I don't think we would have been together, would we?'

I sat down at the other end of the sofa. 'No, I guess not.'

'I mean us, separately, Sarah. What would you be doing now? What would I be doing? With no pregnancy, no wedding, would you have gone back to school, do you think? Got a proper job? Or would you have latched on to some other bloke by now, got married anyway?'

'Latched on?'

'Okay, that was a bad choice of word. But, being married, staying at home, doing all this domestic stuff, it's what you would probably have chosen, isn't it? With or without me?'

'Look, whatever this is all about, let's not talk in front of Janey, okay?' I picked her up and made for the stairs. 'Time for bed, sweetheart.'

'Want Daddy to take me.' Janey squirmed in my grasp and

stretched out her arms towards Josh, almost knocking me off balance.

'You sit down. I'll do it.'

He was gone a long time, probably dreading the conversation to come, but he had started it and I knew it had to be finished. When he came downstairs, he sat back in the same place on the sofa and gazed straight ahead at the TV again, even though I had turned it off.

'What's this all about, Josh?' I had made us both a cup of tea and put a couple of biscuits on the saucers. 'Are you trying to tell me you regret our marriage? Our life? Because it's a bit late now. We made a mistake, yes, but we made our choice, and, like it or not, we *are* married. And we have Janey ... There's no going back.'

'I know that. It's just that sometimes ... sometimes it's hard not to feel trapped, you know. Hemmed in. I'm going to be thirty next week. Thirty! Can you believe it? Where did the years go? Don't you feel that we should be out there, doing other things, exciting things? Thirty's still young, isn't it? But it feels like we've been married forever. Short of money, sitting on someone else's castoff furniture, tied down by a mortgage, eating bloody custard creams like a pair of pensioners. Never going anywhere ...'

'Going anywhere? Where do you want to go? Out for dinner? A day at the seaside? We can do those things. If we're careful with our money we might be able to manage a week away next summer. Spain or—'

'Spain? Crammed around some noisy, smelly pool, surrounded by other families with screaming kids, necking pints of cheap lager and eating the same crap we get at home?'

'What then? What is it you want? Where is it you want to go? Tell me, and we'll try to do it. Because don't you think I need a break too? A change from all this? It's not always easy for me either you know, stuck here every day, washing and shopping, with nobody to talk to, and dealing with Janey's mess and her tantrums.'

'Tantrums? Janey doesn't have tantrums. She's a good kid.'

'She is for you, yes. Not always so good for me. Not when I'm trying to hurry her up so we're not late for nursery, or trying to get her to eat her carrots, or to tidy up her toys. You come home in the evenings and you get the good bit, the fun stuff. And you only have to cope with any of it for ... what? An hour at the most. And then there are your trips away, the late meetings. I feel like a single parent sometimes. Like you can do what you like, when you like, and I'm the one who doesn't have any choice, any time, any life of my own.'

'I came home early tonight, didn't I?'

'Yes, you did.'

'And as for work, I do it for us, Sarah. For the family. To earn us the money we need to survive. Not for fun. God, when did we last have any bloody fun?'

We sat in silence. Josh rested his elbows on his knees, his head in his hands. He looked like one of those old white thinking statues, as if he was pondering something hugely important, carrying the weight of the world. 'I'm sorry,' he said, eventually.

'What for?'

'For not being what you want. What you need. I've tried

to make a family here. To be what you wanted me to be, but I'm not sure it's really worked, has it? It's just so hard.'

'It doesn't have to be.'

'Really? You don't think so? We're ticking along, Sarah. And that's not what either of us wanted, is it? Not what we deserve, just to tick along. I thought having Janey would fix things, but it hasn't. It's changed things, in lots of ways. Given us a purpose. And I love her. You know I do, but …'

'But you don't love me.'

'Don't put words into my mouth. Of course I love you. I love you like a sister, like a best friend, like the good, kind person you are, but let's face it, Sarah, we're not love's young dream, are we? We don't set the world alight. Truth is we've made a real mess of things, haven't we? A lot of the time I know we'd be better off apart, and I'm sure you do too, but we can't … Look, we're stuck with it, aren't we? This life. For better or worse, we're stuck with it.'

'So, you're not leaving me?' My hands were shaking now, the thing I had feared the most suddenly voiced out loud, out in the open. 'That's not what this whole conversation has been about? You asking for a divorce?'

He lifted his head and looked into my eyes, took both my hands and held them tightly until the shaking stopped. 'No. I don't really know what this conversation is about. Some sort of mid-life crisis, I suppose, even if thirty's not quite the middle. A "what-if" kind of a question. Life passing us by. Oh, I'm just trying to put what I feel into words that make some sort of sense, trying to be honest with you, so we know where we stand, so neither of us has to live with a lie. But, no, I'm not leaving. How can I? The thought of our little Janey growing up without me, or how my life would be without seeing her every day. No, that's never going to happen. Unless you want me to leave ...?'

'No!' I moved closer, felt his arms close around me. 'And we can try, can't we? To make things better? We'll go somewhere nice next week, live it up a bit, for your special birthday. And then we'll make more effort to do some of those other things you want to do – travel, go zip-wiring, learn to ski. Whatever. You're right, we are still young, and we mustn't waste that. No more ticking along. And no more custard creams, I promise.'

And no Colin, I thought. I hadn't called him, and I wouldn't. Not now. It just wouldn't be fair. Not if I meant it about trying. From now on, hanging on to my marriage had to come first. But I didn't delete his number. He stayed right where he was, hiding behind the fictional Carol in my contacts list. Just in case.

Chapter 17

EVE

I think having a lover suited me. Not for me the washing of smelly socks or the humdrum day-to-day existence so many marriages seemed to slip into. We relished all the good bits and never had to deal with the bad. Josh and I didn't see each other often enough, admittedly, but when we did it always felt new and exciting and electric.

The miles that separated our life together, such as it was, and Josh's other life with Sarah meant it was unlikely we would get spotted by a neighbour or one of Sarah's school-gate mum friends when we ate in a restaurant or sat in a pub somewhere. There was something liberating, yet comfortingly safe, about the time we spent together, openly pretending to be a couple. Nobody knew, nobody cared, nobody disapproved. Except Simon.

'Just don't get pregnant,' Josh had said, soon after we started out. As if the whole onus was on me. As if, like my sister, I might have some devious plan to trap him and lure him away

213

from her, our whole lives led by what happened, or didn't happen, inside my uterus.

'I wasn't planning to.' I took my newly acquired packet of pills out of the bedside drawer and waved them at him in evidence.

'Good. One child is enough. Believe me, if it wasn't for Janey, I'd be here, with you. All the time. But bringing another baby into the mix ... well, I have no idea what I'd do then. I can't be in two places at once, don't want to have to deal with all the broken-home stuff and how it would affect our Janey, having to split her time between us and see me playing dad to some other child. And then there'd be the finances to get to grips with. And as for the fallout in the family, can you imagine it? What our parents would say? I think I'd probably be excommunicated!' He'd laughed, although it wasn't remotely funny. Especially the bit about playing dad. As if he couldn't possibly imagine feeling proper fatherly love for any accidental child we might produce together.

Sarah had his home, his name, his beloved daughter. We both knew that, and none of those things were going to change. They'd talked about their problems, about the possibility of breaking up, but the crisis moment had passed. Decisions had been made, even though Sarah had not been given all the facts. So she had her marriage intact, on the face of it anyway, and I had what was left. The real unshackled Josh, the passionate Josh, who arrived out of the blue, bringing flowers and laughter, and threw me onto the bed within minutes, every single time.

I knew it wasn't ideal. I should have wanted more, should

have been angry that he couldn't commit to me, but strangely it worked. For far longer than we could ever have imagined, our part-time love affair actually worked. When he was there, for that one afternoon, that one night, that one weekend, nothing else mattered. And when he wasn't, I had a job I adored, a home of my own, and Simon.

Simon had met someone. A tall, dark-haired vet called Gregory. Gregory had a thin pointed face, and a nose so beak-like that somehow we had started to make 'Gregory Peck, peck, peck' jokes, which we both found hilarious, behind the poor man's back. I liked Gregory though. Not that it would have made much difference to anything if I hadn't. Simon no longer talked nostalgically about Anthony, his lost love. He had regained a certain sparkle that I had always known was missing, and I was happy for him. I just wished he could have felt the same way about Josh and me. 'You're better than this, Eve,' he would say, shaking his head. 'You shouldn't be the mistress, the bit on the side. Married men who cheat are ... well, they're bad news. You deserve a man of your own. A chance to have children.'

As far as I was concerned, I *had* a man of my own and, as for children, I had classloads of them all day, every day, to satisfy any little lurking shreds of maternal instinct. I could live without having any of my own. For now, anyway. But one day, when Janey was older, maybe Josh and I would be together, properly, openly, and both of us still young enough for a baby. It was me he loved, after all. It's what he told me and what I chose to believe. Without that it would have felt wrong, sordid, but I didn't let it. The life he had at home was a sham, a front,

215

and if he still had any kind of sex life with my sister at all, I would rather not know. As the years passed by so frighteningly quickly, I chose not to think about that, not to torture myself with it, and certainly never to ask.

***

It was one evening early in September when I got a call from Dad, just as I was coming in through the front door after work. There was no preamble, no 'How are you?', no warning. He just came right out with it. 'Your mum's not too good, Eve.' There was a short silence and then, his voice cracking, he went on, 'We've had a bit of bad news.'

I felt a chill run through me. 'What kind of bad news?'

'She found a ... Oh, God, Eve, there's no easy way to say this. She found a lump. Only small, so small she was convinced it was nothing, so she didn't do anything about it for a while. A few weeks, you know. She didn't even mention it to me at first.'

'Dad, you're scaring me now. Are you talking about a lump in her breast?'

'Yes. Like a pea. So small. You'd never think it could ... Anyway, we've been up to the hospital a couple of times now. You know, for tests and scans. One of those biopsy things.'

'And ...? What are you telling me? That she has cancer?'

'I'm sorry, Love, but yes. They say they've caught it early, but yes. It's cancer.'

I sat down on the bottom step in the hall and dropped my bag down beside me, waiting for my blood to stop pumping so violently through me, waiting for the sudden panic to die down. 'And? What happens next? Does she need drugs? An operation? Please tell me she isn't going to have to have a breast removed ...'

'Slow down, Love. It's early days. They're still hoping to remove just the lump part without taking the whole breast, but they can never be sure about these things. It depends if it spreads. Lymph nodes, and all that. She's going in next Tuesday.'

I wanted to be there, to get on a train or borrow a car and go straight home, but the new term had only just started and asking for time off and getting it agreed was going to be almost impossible.

'Oh, Dad. I don't know what to say. Is she there? Mum? Can I speak to her?'

'She's having a bit of a rest, Love. A little lie down. It's been very stressful. It's taken it out of her, put her off food, made her tired, a bit weepy, you know ...?'

'Of course it has!'

'So I thought this might be a good time to call you, to tell you what's been happening, get you up to speed, you know, while she's not sitting here listening. Not that there's ever a good time exactly, but you know what I mean.'

'Thanks, Dad. For telling me. Does Sarah know?' I usually tried not to think too much about Sarah, and on the odd occasions when we met we managed to rub along the best we could, but suddenly I felt worried for her. For what this news might do to her. She was still my little sister.

'Not yet, Love. I thought you first, being the oldest and the more ... well, capable, I suppose. Our Sarah's more likely to take it badly, I think, and you know I don't find it easy when there are tears. It's hard enough stopping myself from crying at the moment, soft old bugger that I am, but I'm determined to stay strong for your mum. Last thing she needs is me falling to pieces.'

'I'd like to talk to Mum though. When she's awake, feeling up to it.'

'Of course, Love. I'll get her to ring you. But we'll be all right, don't you worry. No need for you to rush down here or anything like that. We both know how busy you are. I'll keep you posted. Chin up, eh? For your mum's sake.' He gave a little laugh, one that wasn't fooling either of us. 'I'm going to leave ringing your sister until a bit later. After she's put our Janey to bed. Not looking forward to it though, I can tell you. Wish me luck!'

I didn't feel like doing much after a call like that. The thought of cooking, and even eating, had suddenly lost its appeal. A pile of homework in need of marking lurked in my bag. Would it really be the end of the world if I took an evening off, left it for another time? No, the end of the world would be if something happened to my mum. Cancer was a big thing, a frightening thing. And despite my dad's bravado, I knew this was serious.

I wanted Josh. I wanted to talk to him, to have his arms around me, to spill out all my worries and my fears. Mum was sick, she had who knew what treatments ahead of her, she might even die. But Josh was miles away, living his other life, and no doubt soon to provide Sarah with the comfort and strength I so badly needed myself. No, I couldn't have Josh, so I did the next best thing. I rang Simon.

I was still sitting on the stairs when he arrived, his regular school outfit of tracksuit and trainers making it obvious he hadn't yet been home. Although it had barely been half an hour since I'd spoken to him, he had already managed to grab a bottle of wine, two kebabs and a giant box of tissues.

'I'm covering all eventualities,' he said, budging me up and squeezing down beside me. 'You might want to drown your sorrows, eat yourself stupid, or cry your eyes out. Whichever way it goes, I'm ready. Now come here and give me a hug.'

I loved the big solid feel of Simon. I always had. He was like a huge, gentle bear, his arms encircling me as his chin came down to rest on the top of my head. The smell of the food, an inviting mix of warm meat and grease and spice, wafted from the carrier bag at his feet and my stomach rumbled.

'Let's eat.'

'Comfort food, eh? And a little something to wash it down with.' He hauled me to my feet and towards the kitchen. 'Nothing like a full tummy to chase the blues away.'

'Oh, Si, you really are the perfect man. Why did you have to be gay?'

'Good job I am. Gay men make the best friends, you know. Caring, sensitive, and without all the messy sex and heartache stuff. No blurred boundaries when you're with me!'

I let him sit me down at the table and watched as he opened cupboards and found plates and glasses, pushed and twisted the corkscrew into the top of the bottle and poured the wine.

'Better?' he asked as I took a long sip and he sat down, placing two kebab-laden plates in front of us.

'A bit. I just feel kind of numb to be honest. Like it's not real.'

'That'll be the shock. It's not easy dealing with news like that, when you were least expecting it too. It takes time to sink in. Did your dad say what her chances are?'

'Good, I hope, because they caught it early. But even so, you hear such terrible stories, don't you? It's just that word. Cancer. It sends shivers through me, knowing what it can do, how devastating it can be. But being defeatist isn't going to help her, is it? I have to be strong, and positive, or pretend to be when I'm talking to her anyway. And to my dad. He's not as tough as he likes to make out.'

'That's my girl.' He stroked my hand, neither of us having made any move yet towards eating the food in front of us. 'And this weekend I am going to drive you down there. Oh, don't argue. I'm due a visit home, so we can kill two birds with one stone. Oh, sorry. Bad choice of words.'

'Don't be daft. But, thank you, Si. I'd love to go and see them before the op, no matter what Dad says about it not being necessary. If you're sure.'

'Of course. I wouldn't have offered otherwise. Now eat up. We can't have you going all weak and fainting away, can we? Not when you've just promised to be strong.'

Once I'd started, I was surprised just how hungry I had been. We even raided the back of the freezer for ice lollies and ate them in front of the TV, although I couldn't say, afterwards, what it was we had watched.

'Thanks,' I said, showing Simon out later. 'That was exactly what I needed. To be fed and watered, and listened to.'

'My specialities, Eve. A shoulder to lean on, or to cry on if you should feel the need.'

'Oh, God, I haven't actually cried yet, have I? Is that normal?'

'Normal is whatever works for you. Crying will come, I'm sure. Probably when you get down there and it all becomes a lot more real. But for now, get yourself off to bed. A good sleep works wonders. I'll see you at work tomorrow. I might even bring you a breaktime doughnut.'

'Cure-all for everything?'

'I wish it was, but it can't do any harm, can it? And the perfect excuse to have one myself!'

I felt the shake of his laughter as I pulled him into a hug, then gave a final wave from the step as he walked away.

The phone was ringing behind me before I had closed the door. I was pretty sure it was either going to be Sarah or Josh. They would have heard the news by now. My hand hovered over the receiver, reluctant to pick it up. The last thing I wanted to deal with now was Sarah's tears, and the last thing Josh would want would be to have to deal with mine.

***

Mum looked pale, but otherwise her usual self. 'So nice to see you again, Simon,' she said, clasping his hands in hers as soon as she'd stopped crushing me half to death in the hall. 'And so good of you to drive Eve here.'

'No problem, Mrs Peters.'

'Caroline, please. Now, I know you can't stay long, but you've driven straight from work, so you won't have eaten. Do please come in and sit for a while. Have some tea, and I've made a cake.'

'Then how could I possibly say no? Just for half an hour, mind, or you'll have my mum after you. She's probably got food lined up too!'

Within minutes of our arrival she was fussing about hanging up coats, putting the kettle on to boil and generally keeping herself busy, something it was obvious she needed to do, while Dad hovered nervously in her wake and was quickly ushered away towards the living room with the promise of an extra-large slice of Victoria sponge.

'So, how are you really?' I said, following Mum into the kitchen. 'And don't just tell me you're fine.'

'But I am fine. Honestly, Eve, what's the point in fretting? I'm not in any pain. I'm in the doctors' hands now. Decisions will be made by those far more in the know about these things than I am, so there's nothing more I can do, is there? And if the worst comes to the worst and they tell me they have to ... well, you know, remove it, all of it, then that's what they'll have to do. I'm no spring chicken these days. Living is my number-one priority, not hanging on to bits of my body I can just as easily do without. How I look isn't all that important anymore. It's not as if I'm going to be parading around in a bikini now, is it? And my breastfeeding days are long gone.'

'Oh, Mum.'

'Now, don't you start blubbing. It'll make no difference. It will be what it will be. No long faces. No tears. Just cross your fingers, and maybe say a little prayer, okay? Now, tell me, does your young man take sugar in his tea?'

'One. And I've told you a hundred times, he's not my young man.'

'If you say so.' She turned away to pour the water into the pot, her shoulders tense and rigid beneath her hand-knitted cardigan. 'Sarah's coming over in a bit, with our Janey,' she added. 'I knew you'd want to see her. Janey, that is. Well, no, both of them, I hope. It's at times like this that families need to stick together, support each other. And, if anything should happen to me ...'

'Mum, nothing's going to happen to you. You're as strong as an ox. You're going to outlive the lot of us.'

'That's as may be, but we can never be sure about these things, can we? And if things don't ... well, then I need to know that you've got each other. No more silly fights. Your sister is your flesh and blood, and she'll need you.'

'She has Josh. And Janey.'

'Of course she does. And you have that lovely man in there.' She pointed towards the living room where we could hear Simon in mid-conversation with Dad, talking about football and the weather and how bad the traffic had been on our way down. 'But Sarah's your sister. She's been at your side all your life, and nobody can quite replace that, can they?'

All my life? We both knew that was far from true. I'd hardly seen her for years. And I didn't really want to. Despite my feelings for Josh and constantly telling myself he had been mine first, and what she didn't know couldn't hurt her, there was still a little sliver of guilt I couldn't quite shake off.

I helped Mum carry the tea through and we all sat and ate cake and avoided any further mention of our reason for coming.

'Auntie Eve!' Janey, now seven years old and so much bigger than I remembered her, broke the silence as she came bouncing in, like a mini whirlwind, as if from nowhere. I heard the front door close, loudly. Sarah clearly still had her key.

With Janey flinging herself at my neck and landing, laughing, in my lap, my first glimpse of my sister was through the tangled strands of Janey's hair as it flopped across my face.

'Hello, Eve.'

'Sarah.'

'Off your auntie now, Janey, please.' She sounded stern but I could see from her puffy eyes and flushed cheeks that she had been crying again. As if she hadn't cried enough down the phone the other night, almost starting me off too, just when I'd hoped for a good night's sleep and a chance to get my head around things. 'We have grown-up things we need to talk about. Go and get yourself a glass of squash from the kitchen.'

'And can I have cake?' Janey's gaze had latched on to what was left of the sponge.

'Take that last slice with you. If that's all right with Granny. And see if you can find Smoky, okay? Maybe you can play with him upstairs. I'll call you when we're finished.'

'Smoky?' I said, puzzled.

'He's Granny and Granddad's new kitten, Auntie Eve. He's grey and white, and he's ... how old is he now, Mum?'

'Ten weeks. Go on, off you go. There's a good girl.'

'I didn't know you'd got a cat.'

'Your mother could never face having another dog,' Dad said. 'Not after losing Buster. What with us both still working. And all the walking they need, of course, and the scooping up piles of poo. But a woman at the baker's was looking for homes. Her cat had had a litter – is that the right word? Five of the little scraps, and once your mum'd seen them it was all I could do to stop her wanting the lot! He's a dear little thing though.'

'But don't kittens make piles of poo as well?'

'Only little piles,' Mum said, seriously. 'And even then it's only while he's training, with a tray of cat litter and some newspaper in the kitchen. Once he can go outside by himself, we'll give him a cat flap and we won't have to worry about all of that.'

'Until he digs up your best plants!'

'Oh, don't be such a spoilsport. You'll love him when you see him.' Mum's face had gone all soppy. 'Now, Sarah, Love, I have no idea why you've sent Janey out of the room. There's nothing to talk about that we can't say in front of her.'

'I just don't want to worry her. Illness, hospitals, cancer … well, it can all be a bit frightening, can't it? It's bad enough for us adults to cope with, but she's just a kid. I've not told her anything about it so far.'

'Kids pick up on things, Sarah. Me suddenly turning up out of the blue. Your puffy face. Being sent out of the room. She'll know something's up. She's not stupid.'

'I know she's not stupid, Eve.' Sarah glared at me. 'That's

not what I'm talking about. I just feel I want to protect her, that's all.'

'Okay, girls,' Dad cut in. 'Enough, all right? There's no need to tell Janey anything now, is there? Nothing much to tell at this stage, anyway. And, Eve, I know you wanted to come down and see your mum before she has the op, and we both really appreciate that, but there's nothing to be achieved by any of us sinking into doom and gloom by talking about it. The plan is to get the op done on Tuesday and take it from there. None of us can be sure what they'll find or what might happen next. That could be the end of it, God willing. All sorted, job done, and no need to tell the little one anything at all. We can show you the leaflets they gave us, and I'll be taking some time off work afterwards to take care of your mum at home, but that's it. Nothing more to say. So, while you're both here, let's talk about happier things, take all our minds off it, eh? Now, what do you say to going out to eat? A nice steak dinner somewhere. My treat. No hospital talk, just all of us together again, having some fun.'

'Okay.' Sarah forced a smile.

'Simon. Won't you come too? You'd be very welcome.'

'Thanks, Mr Peters, but no, really. I should be getting going now. I promised my own family a proper visit.'

'And Josh? Will he be back from work yet? Wanting to join us, do you think?'

I held my breath. Oh, I would have loved to see Josh. I hadn't spoken to him since Mum's news and I missed him. But not here, not like this, having to hide my feelings and put up a front.

Sarah checked her watch. 'I could ring him and find out. He stops off at the pub sometimes on a Friday, on his way home.' She pulled her mobile out from her bag and tapped in a number.

'No answer. Shall I leave a message?' She looked up as if expecting the rest of us to tell her what to do, but then seemed to make a rapid decision of her own. 'No. Let's go without him. Everywhere will be filling up if we wait, and I would like to get Janey home to bed at a decent time. I'll text him so he can sort out his own dinner. Two more pints and a bag of crisps, probably!'

Simon got up to go. 'Well, have a nice evening, everyone. I'll be back for you on Sunday, Eve. Around four-ish, okay?'

I nodded, feeling his hand resting on my shoulder, giving it a reassuring squeeze.

'Right then. Just let me get changed. Can't be seen out in this old thing.' Mum stood up, gave Simon a goodbye hug in the hall, and disappeared up the stairs.

'Is she all right, Dad? Really?'

'Coping in her own way, Love. As must we all.'

I followed Simon out to the front door and waved him off as Sarah headed for the kitchen in search of Janey. Only Dad remained in the living room, and when I peered round the door I saw he had his eyes closed and was resting his head in his hands. I decided to give him a few minutes to himself.

'Okay, where's this little kitten then?' I called, putting on my jolly voice. 'Come out, come out, wherever you are. Time Auntie Eve had a cuddle.'

Chapter 18

SARAH

D ad wasn't coping very well. Mum having to have a full mastectomy had come as a shock, and now that she had been back at home for three weeks and we were all learning to come to terms with things, the reality of it all seemed suddenly to have hit him hard, in some ways even harder than it had hit her.

She'd always been the one in charge at home, much as she would have denied it and pretended otherwise. While Dad earned the bulk of the money and dished out smiles and treats and pats on the head, the real day-to-day nitty-gritty things, like the housework, the finances, the decisions about where to go on holiday, what colour to paint the hall, what to have for dinner, had always rested with her. But now she was bruised and battered, and, for now anyway, her zest for life seemed to have gone.

She spent a lot of time in bed, feeling weak and sick after her first chemo session and dreading the ones yet to come. Even when she did get up and about, there were still so many

229

things she could not do, partly because of the after-effects of the surgery to her chest and under her arms, partly because the chemo had taken it out of her so all she wanted to do was sleep. No hoovering, no heavy lifting, no driving, no going to work. Her appetite went up and down like a yoyo and she was a lot more careful about what she ate. She had decided too that in the interests of as healthy a lifestyle as possible, they would both give up alcohol altogether, just when Dad could have used a stiff drink, but he did what she asked. It was obvious he felt helpless and useless and hopelessly ill-informed, but he wanted to please her, to support her in any way he could, so the whisky bottle remained resolutely unopened. I wasn't sure if he had even seen her scars yet.

Josh was working longer hours than ever, and I did wonder if it was his way of avoiding me, Mum, the illness, all of it. I'd seen it before, when Janey had caught a nasty bug, and that time she'd come home from school to tell us she had nits, and when I had a particularly bad period and there was blood on the sheets. He backed away from it, kept his distance, made sure he didn't have to deal with any of the mucky unpleasant stuff, waited until whatever it was had passed before easing himself back in as if he'd never been gone.

Sometimes I felt about a hundred years old, as if the weight of the world and all its sorrows was on my shoulders. Eve was miles away in Wales, Dad was crumbling and Josh was distant. And that just left me.

I went down to the park once, around the same time of day I had bumped into Colin Grant that time. I suppose I was half hoping to see him again, run into him as if by accident, but he wasn't there. Of course he wasn't. And, if he had been, what then? Pick his medical brain about Mum's illness? Stop for a coffee? Arrange to meet again? No, I couldn't, and shouldn't, go down that route, much as I needed someone to talk to, to take my mind off all the bad stuff, to make me laugh again. But Colin wasn't the answer. I had to concentrate on the family now, and on myself for a change.

With Janey settled at school and Josh moaning about me doing nothing all day, I had only recently found myself a job. Only part-time in a solicitor's office, working four mornings a week and one whole day every Friday when the place was at its busiest, with so many people choosing that day to complete their house moves. I did filing, photocopying, answering the phone, but I was so grateful to have even been considered for the job, let alone offered it, that I loved every minute of it. It had given me a reason to buy some smart new clothes to replace my sad old mumsy uniform of jogging trousers and baggy T-shirts, so often over the years stained with baby sick, the whites faded to dingy grey.

Josh had never wanted me to dress up. He said it would just attract other men, that I should only look nice for him. And there had never been any need to because we rarely went anywhere that called for posh outfits. But the new job, and the new clothes, had given me a sense of pride and self-worth, something that had been sadly lacking in my life while I was just a stay-at-home mum. It didn't matter what Josh thought. I was doing this for me. Only, now, just as I was starting to find myself, I was being swallowed up in domestic chores and family stresses all over again. Not that I blamed anyone. It wasn't as if Mum had got ill on purpose, and I felt angry with myself for the little shivers of resentment that ran through me. It wasn't fair. But then, life wasn't fair either, was it?

'You can leave that, Love. I can do it later.' Dad had come into the room behind me as I ran the hoover round the carpet and I jumped as I felt his hand fall unexpectedly on my shoulder.

'It's okay. I've started now, so I might as well finish.'

'You sound like that Magnus Magnusson!'

'Who?' I leaned down and flicked the switch to off.

'You know. *Mastermind*. It's what he used to say.'

'Right.' I had no idea what he was talking about. 'I'll just put this away and then I'll be off to pick up Janey from school. Tell Mum I'll come back tomorrow some time to put the washing on and get that ironing pile sorted.'

'Sarah, you do too much. I'm not totally inept, you know. I'm sure I can manage a few basic chores.'

'And there's a casserole in the oven. Should be ready in an hour or so. I've peeled you a few potatoes and carrots. They're in water, in saucepans, so you just have to—'

'Slow down, Love. It's not that I'm not grateful. I am. And I know your mum is too, but we will get by. We won't starve, or die of dust poisoning if the cleaning falls a bit behind. Go and enjoy your own life, your own family.'

'You *are* my family.'

'Of course we are. But you know what I mean. Go home and put your feet up. Watch a bit of telly. Open a bottle of wine. Have a drink for me, as I'm not allowed one anymore! Or go out for a meal. Take that husband of yours that we see so little of. I'm more than happy to have Janey for a couple of hours. Here, take this.' He reached into his pocket, opened his wallet and handed me a couple of twenty-pound notes. 'Treat yourself.'

I tried to say no, but he was having none of it. Sometimes it's just easier to give in. And he was right. I was doing too much, trying to keep two households afloat. I did need some time out. And Dad wasn't the only one who saw so little of Josh. I had hardly seen him for days myself. We needed to spend more time together, to try to get some of the normality – maybe even the fun – back, to go out for an evening that didn't involve me being up to my eyes in pots and pans and Janey's homework, Josh dozing on the sofa, and no conversation whatsoever.

'Thanks, Dad. Give Mum a kiss goodbye from me, won't you?'

'Of course. And don't you dare give my washing another thought. If a man can't rinse out his own underpants, well, what's the world coming to, eh?'

***

'I'm sorry, Sarah.' Josh's hand reached out across the pub table and rested on mine.

'What for?'

'This business with your mum. I can see how much it's hurting you. Coming out like this for a quick drink and a scampi and chips is all well and good, and probably one of your dad's better ideas, but I just wish there was more I could do.'

'Like?'

'Oh, God, I don't know. I'm not good in these situations, you know that. Hardly one for holding the sick bowl or knowing the right things to say, am I? And it's not me your mum needs, is it? It's your dad, and you two girls. I know I can't do much for her, but I should be doing more for you. Shall I take some time off work? Spend more time with Janey? You look worn out.'

'That's because I *am* worn out.' He was happy to spend more time with our daughter, I noticed, but there was no talk of spending more time with me. I couldn't help but wonder how an offer like that was actually going to help lighten my load at all. Give me more time to go round with the hoover, I supposed. Still, I did my best to explain. 'If Eve was nearer, we might be able to share things somehow, but I just feel it's all falling on me. I know Dad says I needn't do so much, but how can I not? How can I leave him to struggle on his own? He's got enough to worry about. But I feel so stressed out, so bloody tired, and then when I get into bed I can't sleep for all the thoughts rushing round my head. Not much you can do about that, is there? Unless you can get hold of some knock-out tablets or something.'

'Tablets?' He looked shocked. 'Are things that bad?'

'Oh, take no notice. It's the tiredness talking. Things will get better, but yeah, if you could be at home a bit more, maybe help out a bit more, so I don't feel like I'm dealing with everything on my own ...'

'I'll talk to the boss. Ask for some compassionate leave, or just use up some of the standard holiday leave I'm due. Maybe we could go away for a few days? Yes, I know you want to be here for your parents, but you do need some time off. For good behaviour!' He smiled, that old sexy look in his eyes that still had the power to persuade me into anything. His fingers tightened over mine, his thumb drawing little invisible circles on my wrist. 'So we can get up to a bit of *bad* behaviour! We never did take that skiing trip we talked about, did we? Do you remember?'

'Skiing? Now?' Did he have any idea of what I really needed? A husband by my side, supporting me, not some ridiculous escape route where we got to play silly buggers in the snow. A holiday was obviously what Josh wanted. I wasn't sure it had a lot to do with helping me.

'Well, no, of course not. Stupid idea! I just meant that we always said we'd do more, you know, together, as a family, and we haven't really done it, have we? Not often enough anyway. But no long flights, no dangerous sports, no snow, I promise. Something closer to home, so we can get back if—'

'If what? She takes a turn for the worse?'

'That's not going to happen, Sarah. But, just in case, you know, we're needed. Somewhere by the sea maybe? South coast? Buckets and spades. Donkey rides. Ice creams. Janey will love that.'

'Do they still do donkey rides?'

'No idea. Who knows? Let's find out.'

'But, what about school?'

'We'll tell them she's sick. They're hardly going to come

round and check, are they? So long as she can tell a good lie when she goes back in.'

'I don't want to encourage Janey to tell lies, Josh.'

'No, of course not, but circumstances sometimes make it necessary, don't you think?' He picked up his glass and drained what was left of his beer. 'Everyone does it.'

***

We went to Bournemouth. A family room in a small hotel a short walk from the front. For October, the weather wasn't too bad. A bit windy, and not a lot of sun to soak up when we did venture down to the beach, but Janey loved the whole experience, insisting that, at seven, she was too old for building sandcastles but doing it anyway, her little yellow bucket gradually filling up with a collection of pebbles and shells that she spent ages finding and then arranging around the walls and turrets of her castle.

Worn out from all the excitement and exercise on that first afternoon, she was asleep within half an hour of dinner, curled up in a tight little ball in her single bed under the window, the fluffy teddy she had carefully chosen to bring with her clasped snugly in her arms. I called Dad from the bathroom, making sure I didn't disturb her, and was relieved to be told that everything at home was fine. No change. Nothing to worry about.

'Well, Mrs Cavendish,' Josh said, quietly pulling the curtains shut above Janey's head as I came back into the room. 'What shall we do now? We can hardly go out anywhere, or even just back down to the bar and leave her on her own, can we?'

'Watch TV, I suppose, if we keep the volume down.'

'Is that the best you can come up with? Away from home, after a nice meal where we haven't had to do our own cooking or washing up, an evening to ourselves in a posh room with a king-size bed, all buoyed up with sea air and wine and ... oh, come here, for God's sake, and take your clothes off.'

It wasn't that I was unwilling. Far from it! It had just been so long since Josh had shown any real interest in me that I felt almost shy as I pulled my T-shirt up and over my head. He stood behind me and undid my bra, his fingers finding their way round to cup my breasts as he nuzzled into the back of my neck. And then we were on the bed, my bottom lifting as he wriggled my jeans and knickers down, his body crushing me as he tugged his own clothes off and threw them on the floor.

I glanced across at Janey, still fast asleep. We had never made love in the same room as her before, never taken that risk of her waking up, seeing us, hearing us, not even when she was a tiny baby. 'Sssh. We mustn't wake her,' I whispered, anxiously trying to suppress the groan that threatened to come from my own throat as Josh's mouth moved ever lower down my body and his tongue flicked against all the right places.

'It's not me making the noise ...'

I could feel him breathe, hard and fast, his mouth and fingers moving expertly, his erection pressing itself against my bent-up knees as he crouched over me. It only took me seconds. The shudders ran through me, my eyes closed, my hands, which had been pinned beneath him, suddenly free to move but too tingly to do it, as he slipped back upwards, his face sticky and wet as it met mine. He pushed himself inside me then, not kissing, not speaking, just intent on his purpose, the sweat forming in a slimy layer between us. And then, in what felt like less than a minute, he was emptied, done. He lay for a moment, panting, then rolled away and sat up on the edge of the bed, his back towards me.

'Phew. It's been a while,' he said, taking a big breath and letting his shoulders slump.

I could hear Janey mumbling, stirring, saw a leg flop out from under her covers and her teddy drop to the floor.

'Just managed that in time, by the look of it. I'm gonna grab a shower. Then maybe pop downstairs for a quick one.'

'Isn't that what we just had?'

'Oh, ha ha. Not complaining, are you?' He glanced over at Janey, snuffling gently in her sleep, and headed for the bathroom. 'Marathon sessions and kids in the room don't really go together, do they? Keep it short and sweet! But don't you get up yet, Love. Lie there and have that rest you came down here for. You can relax in a long hot bath once I've finished in the shower. I bet they don't run out of hot water here, no matter how much of it we use. And I won't be gone too long. Just a couple of drinks in the bar. I am on holiday, after all.'

And so am I, I thought. But somehow I'm the one left with

the childcare again. And, for once, despite the orgasm I had so badly needed, and our daughter lying there all innocent and unaware, I wondered just what it was that still held us together. Because there had been no love in what we had just done. None at all.

Chapter 19

EVE

Four years later

I had to come back to London. What choice did I have? If Mum had only told me sooner how bad things were. Or if Dad had ...

We had all believed she'd beaten it. After a horrifying few months of chemo-induced baldness, her hair had grown back, greyer but surprisingly thicker than it had been before, and she had had it cut into a new shorter bob that took years off her. She had shooed away any idea of reconstructive surgery and had learned to live with special bras and the jelly-like inserts that fitted inside them, even daring to wear a swimsuit again when they headed off for their usual summer week in Bognor. As the years passed, she seemed to have accepted what life had chucked at her and found a new lease of life, dragging Dad off to ballroom-dancing classes and taking up yoga. But now, right out of the blue, the cancer was back, and this time it had spread, and quickly. Into her liver, and her bones.

We all knew it was probably only a matter of time, and it was time I couldn't afford to waste, cut off from my family, miles away in Wales, and unable to help them, or perhaps risk not being there to say the final goodbye. I handed in my notice, gave up the flat, packed up the bits of my life I needed to hang on to, which weren't all that many, and went home.

'Things won't be so easy,' Josh said on his last weekend visit to Wales before I left. 'For us, I mean. Living so close to each other. We can't afford to take risks.'

'What are you saying, Josh? That once I'm back home we're finished?'

'I hope not, Eve. I just mean that we can't be, you know, seen together, can we? Going out together won't be easy. And staying in together, like this ...' He waved his hand around to indicate the bedroom we were lying in, naked, with piles of moving boxes stacked up in the corner. 'Well, while you're staying at your parents' it will be damn near impossible.'

'I do know that, Josh. But it's not as if I see you often now, is it? What is it? Four or five times a year, if I'm lucky. Much as I wish things could have been different. But we could still meet up sometimes. A hotel somewhere, maybe? Out of town. And I'll be nearer so, without all the travelling, there should actually be *more* opportunities. And where there's a will, there's a way, as they say. If you still want to, of course.'

'You know I do.' If I didn't know him better I would have said he was sulking. Like a kid whose favourite toy was being taken away.

'But I do have to be there, for Mum and Dad, and sleeping back in my old room makes sense, to start with anyway. At least until I can find a job. And a flat of my own. And I won't pick one round the corner from you, I promise.'

For the first time I could remember, I actually felt glad when he drove away and I could get back to what mattered most. Taking those last few steps towards getting out of there and back to where, for now at least, I knew I belonged.

***

I felt guilty leaving work before the end of term, but everyone said they understood. They gave me a wonderful send-off. The staff room was decked with balloons and banners, and there was a huge cake, iced to look like a blackboard, and piles of good luck cards. Every class I taught had made me a big communal card of their own, some with quotes from the poems we had been studying or little rhymes they had written themselves, and some of the children brought me gifts, everything from flowers to pens to far too many 'Best Teacher' mugs for me ever to use them all. I had been at that school for more than twelve years, slowly moving up from newly qualified teacher to Head of English. But it was time to move on.

'Hello, Miss. Or should I say goodbye?' It was nearly five o'clock and I was starting to pack my hoard into a hopelessly inadequate carrier bag, wiping away an unexpected tear or two, and I didn't recognise the voice at first. Not even the face, until I looked hard into it and saw that earnest little girl still peering out at me with now much more confident grown-up eyes.

'Laura? Laura Wilson? It is you, isn't it?'

'Yep, it's me all right. I hope it's okay me coming in here. Reception was empty, so I took a chance. Never been in the staff room before! But I couldn't let you leave without coming to speak to you.'

'Oh, I'm so glad you did. How are you? What are you doing these days?'

She stood there, leaning against the sink, until I beckoned her towards a chair and sat down opposite her.

'You'll never guess, Miss.'

'I think we can dispense with the formalities now, Laura. I'm not your teacher anymore, so forget the Miss and just call me Eve. And I can hardly believe you're so grown-up. You must be, what? Twenty-two now?'

'Twenty-three. And I'm a teacher too. English, obviously!'

'That's fantastic. You always had that special spark about you. My star pupil, if I'm honest – and there's no reason for me not to be, now that I'm leaving.'

'Thank you. But it was all down to you, you know. No other teacher ever brought it all to life the way you did. Remember the paint charts?'

'I do indeed!'

'So, I just wanted to come and tell you what an influence you were on me. And that ... well, I hope you don't mind, but now you're leaving I hear there might be a teaching job going here and I ...'

'You're going to apply?'

'I think so, yes. Come back to where it started, tackle the council-estate apathy head-on, try to give something back.'

'That's fantastic. And mind? Why should I mind? I can't think of a more enthusiastic and suitable candidate. You're pretty much the same age I was when I first came here. It will be like leaving a little piece of me behind to carry on the good work.'

She grinned, her face lighting up with pride. 'I hope it's all right to ask but ...'

'Yes?'

'You're still called Miss Peters. So, you never got married?'

'No. Well, not yet. I guess I'm married to my job in many ways.' My thoughts flashed involuntarily to Josh, and to the ring my sister still wore, and the real reason marriage had never come to claim me. The wasted years. I forced a laugh. 'Maybe I'm waiting for the right man. Or the right time.'

'I wondered about you and Mr Barratt, that's all. I'm sorry. Being nosey, I know, but were you a couple? Did you ever get together? You were the talk of the playground for years!'

'Were we?' I had always prided myself on knowing what went on at the school, keeping ahead of any gossip, but this nugget of information had thrown me. Simon and me? The secret office romance? I laughed. 'No, Laura. You were all very wide of the mark there. Best friends, yes, for a long time. Still are, I suppose. But Simon's married now. To someone else. A lovely man called Gregory! And they've moved away, back to Buckinghamshire, where both their families come from.'

'Oh! I didn't see that one coming!'

'Good! As you'll find out now you're in the profession too, we teachers do need our private lives. Got to keep a few little secrets back!'

She giggled. 'Oh, yes, I intend to. Well, I won't keep you. I had to dash here to catch you before you left, and I'm sure we both have things to do. The dreaded marking, in my case. But I wanted you to have this.' She reached into her bag and withdrew a small rectangular parcel, beautifully wrapped in silver paper. 'A leaving present. And a thank you. Eve ...' She hesitated, as if finding it hard to call me by that name. 'You were the best and most patient teacher I could have wished for, and exactly what I needed back then.' She leaned forward and gave me a swift and gentle kiss on the cheek before a final wave of her hand in the doorway as she left the room.

I sat for a moment, gazing down at the present, drinking in the unfamiliar but welcome silence of the staffroom now everyone else had gone. A hoover started up out in the corridor, breaking the spell, as I pulled at the edges of the paper.

It was a book. A book of poetry. Keats, of course. What else could it have been? And with a little silver bookmark tucked inside. I eased the pages open, my gaze resting on the poem she had marked for me. 'To Autumn'.

And, as I read about the missing songs of spring and the mourning gnats and the soft-dying day, I remembered the conversation Laura and I had shared when she was just a little girl about to watch her granddad die and, not caring who might come in and find me, I sat and sobbed my heart out.

***

I still felt uneasy being back in our old room, seeing those two single beds standing there, Sarah's and mine, side by side. This was where it had all begun, the betrayal, the family rift, the whole ridiculous chain of events that had led us – Sarah, Josh and me – to where we were now, trapped in a stupid love triangle that only two of the three sides knew existed.

The June sunshine streamed in through the open curtains as I dragged my cases in and, even though I hadn't brought a lot, it was going to be hard to find space for everything. The rest of my stuff had been stashed away in a small lock-up storage unit on a nearby industrial estate until the day I found a place of my own. Leaving Wales had felt rushed but necessary, yet now I was back I wasn't at all sure what to do with myself. I hadn't been jobless or homeless before, and camping out in my parents' spare room felt horribly studenty and decidedly wrong for a woman my age.

I could see Mum was in constant pain, but she was trying to keep her spirits up. According to Dad, she was getting herself up to sit in an armchair for a short while every morning but by midday had usually retreated back to her bed. There was no question of her making it down the stairs or to sit in the garden in the sun. A nurse called every day, often more than once, and there was talk of one staying overnight. The medication, I noticed, was lined up on the bedside cabinet in military fashion, which I was sure was Dad's doing. His way of making sure everything needed was immediately to hand and that nothing could ever get forgotten. I have to admit that he looked after her, and waited on her, and ran about after her every need, in a way that very few men would find easy. Just seeing the word morphine on a label sent shivers through me. I tried to imagine Josh in a similar situation, having to cope with Sarah, or even me, lying there so sick and helpless, having to watch a nurse administer something like that, in stronger and stronger doses every day, and I just couldn't conjure it up.

I decided to take over the cooking and cleaning, starting with a big shop the morning after I got back. Sarah had enough to do, with work and Janey and her own home to look after, and whatever else I may have felt about her, I couldn't deny that she had done a great job keeping an eye on things at Mum and Dad's, pretty much single-handedly. I hadn't seen her for a couple of months and, when I did, it was clear that the stress was taking its toll. She was thinner in the face, her hair straggly and in need of a decent cut, and she was looking much older than her thirty-two years.

'How bad is Mum really? How long has she got?' I asked, the first night I was home, when Dad and Sarah and I sat in a silent circle around the kitchen table, picking at a super-market shepherd's pie. I didn't really want to hear the answer but burying my head in the sand was not an option now.

'No one can tell us that for sure, Love.' Dad put his cutlery down and wiped the back of his hand over his closed eyelids. 'Could be a few months if we're lucky ...'

'And if we're not?'

'Weeks, I guess. There was talk of a hospice, but I couldn't do that. She belongs here, at home. And, much as I want her to live forever, I don't want to see her suffer any longer than she has to. Or to be so dosed up on pain relief she doesn't know we're here.'

'Does she know? That it's just a matter of time? That there's no cure?'

He paused, gazing up towards her room, and answered in little more than a whisper, as if she might hear us. 'Yes, Love. She knows.'

None of us had much of an appetite. I think more of the meal went in the bin than actually got eaten that night.

'Let me help you sort out the bedroom,' Sarah said afterwards, when Dad had gone upstairs with two cups of tea to sit by Mum's bedside. 'There's still some of my old junk in the cupboard that I can shift to make you more room. Most of it hasn't been touched since I left home.'

I tried to put up a protest but she was so keen to help I just followed her up and let her get on with it, watching as she tipped old school books and bits of plastic jewellery and outdated music tapes into a couple of rubbish bags, and removed a few of her old long-forgotten clothes from their wooden hangers.

'You were right about the junk, weren't you? Why didn't Mum ever sort this stuff out?'

'Didn't like to touch what was mine, I suppose. And no need, while the room wasn't being used. Do you remember how you used to hide the vodka at the back of the wardrobe? Never found it, did she? Remember how she'd do a big hoovering blitz every now and then, then just leave us to get on with it? This was our personal space and she never did like to invade it.'

An image of a teenaged Sarah, and Josh, sprawled across my bed and most definitely invading my space, in the worst and most personal way possible, flashed into my head, as it had so many times before. But what was the point of dwelling on any of that now? Life had moved on and I had more than repaid her, many times over, for what she had done.

As drawer and shelf space slowly became available, I filled it, pulling underwear and toiletries and assorted bits and pieces out of my cases and finding somewhere to put each of them, gradually making the bedroom – and this time all of it, not just half – mine again.

'I see you still use the same face cream you always did,' Sarah said, picking up my bottle of Oil of Olay and waving it at me. 'And still the same Calvin Klein perfume. I remember the smell of that hanging over Janey's cot when you put her to bed the day we had that housewarming party. "Essence of Eve", Janey still calls it if we get a whiff of it when we're walking through the perfume department in Debenhams! A real creature of habit, aren't you?'

'I guess I am. Why change something if you love it? Why get rid of something if it works?'

'Like that school you've been working at for ever! It can't have been an easy decision to give that up. Any luck finding a new job?'

'There are a couple of possibilities I've seen. One's just English, one's deputy head ...'

'Wow. You are moving up in the world, aren't you? We'll have to curtsey to you soon!' She did a little bob, almost tripping over her own feet and we both laughed.

If only things had been different, I thought. Despite everything, sometimes I still really missed my sister.

***

Dad had wanted to leave work, try to retire a couple of years earlier than planned, to look after her, but Mum had insisted he just asked for extended leave. Six months. A year maybe, although they both knew that was optimistic. He would need something to go back to, she'd said, something to occupy his mind and keep him busy after she'd gone. And she was right, of course. He knew it, but just couldn't quite face the idea, shaking off her suggestion as if it was all a load of nonsense and she was going to live forever.

I sat there beside him on the sofa after Sarah had gone, and he told me what she'd said. I didn't know what to say, just held his hand. It was warm and solid, like the rock he had always been, but there was nothing he could do to hide the tears in his eyes. From me, anyway. Upstairs was different. He may have been breaking inside, but no way was he going to let Mum see it. Dad was a diamond, that was for sure. We were all so lucky to have him.

'And how about you, Love? No boyfriend on the scene? There's nothing your mum and I would like more than to see you settled and happy before ... well, you know. She's never going to see you wed, but it would have been nice to know you had someone to look after you. We did think that Simon—'

'Dad! I've told you so many times. Simon was never going to be the one. He's very happy with Gregory, and I am very happy for him. And you don't have to worry about me.'

'I don't? So there is someone then? Someone special?'

'Maybe. But it's complicated.'

'Love often is, Eve. Just as long as he's a nice chap, and not married or anything like that. I'd hate to see you hurt again.'

'I won't be.' I let go of his hand and stood up, not sure I liked the way the conversation was heading or the lie I had been hiding from him, from all of them, for so long. 'Now, what do you say to a nice cup of tea and a biscuit?'

'I say yes please. And maybe a drop of whisky in it, eh?'

'I thought you were teetotal these days.'

'What your mother doesn't know won't hurt her,' he said, giving me a wink. And, with that thought in mind, I went to boil the kettle.

I hated keeping secrets, especially ones that could hurt so many people. But he was right. As long as they knew nothing about it, nobody would get hurt, would they? But this wasn't the me I wanted to be. The deceitful daughter, who had spent far too long putting herself first, when there were so many more important things to think about, so many innocent loving people who didn't deserve what I was doing to them, even if they didn't know a thing about it. Being here, at home, made everything feel real all of a sudden. The guilt hung over me like a cloud. Family mattered. Life and death mattered. Not sex. Not revenge. Not this soul-destroying game Josh and I had been playing, hidden away from the world, pretending to be something we weren't and would never be.

Josh was never going to leave Sarah or Janey, never going to choose me, not after all this time. I knew that only too well. I had always known it. And now I was here, thrown back into having to face my sister day after day, watching my father suffering and my mother dying. Perhaps it was finally time to put an end to it, swallow my pride and my tears and do what I should have done years ago. Let Josh go. What on earth was I doing anyway, hanging on to a life that would never give me a husband or a child of my own? Pinning my future to a man who had no intention of sharing it with me. He'd cheated on me before, and now he was cheating on Sarah. What was I thinking, wasting my time, my life, on a man like that, a man neither of us could ever fully trust? I should have listened to Simon right back at the start when he'd told me I deserved better. He was right. If I wasn't careful I was heading for a lonely old age, one where I would look back when it was too late and realise what I had missed. I needed to give myself – and maybe Sarah too – a chance to be happy.

It didn't take long to track down the whisky bottle, stashed away in Dad's usual hidey-hole behind the chess set in the sideboard, and I poured a large slug into both mugs. Dad wasn't the only one in need of a stiff drink.

Chapter 20

SARAH

Josh went missing the night Mum died. He had called from work that afternoon to say he might be late home, which wasn't that unusual. I think the stress of Mum's illness, of watching her decline into what was little more than a prolonged drugged-up sleep, was having an effect on all of us, Josh included, and there were times when he needed to bury his head in work or just sit in a pub somewhere and forget about it all. I knew there was something horribly selfish about that, but it was just Josh being Josh, the way he had always been. Head-in-the-sand, run-away-from-trouble Josh.

When Dad rang, choking back tears, to tell me that her pain was finally over and she had slipped away in her sleep, all I wanted was Josh, his arms wrapped around me, his strength to hold me up, some words of comfort, but I couldn't find him. He wasn't at the office, where my call went straight to an answerphone machine. He wasn't answering his mobile. I sat and sobbed, unable to go to Dad, to leave the house because Janey was fast asleep upstairs, and watched the clock as I waited for the key in the door that didn't come.

I should have spoken to Eve, but something held me back. Besides, she knew where I was. Why couldn't she come to me? Call me? I pictured her in my head, holding Mum's lifeless hand, making Dad a cup of tea, taking over all the things that needed to be done. Doctors, the death certificate, calling various relatives and friends, being all super-efficient, while I quietly fell to pieces. It was a good job one of us was up to the job because I knew I wasn't. My mum, my lovely, happy, beautiful mum was gone, and I had no idea how I was going to carry on without her. Or how I was going to tell Janey.

I woke up at one in the morning, curled awkwardly into a corner of the sofa, and for just a few seconds I didn't remember. Mum was still sick, but she was alive. There had been no call. No news. But then I saw Josh, standing over me, his face pale and drawn, and the terrifying truth came flooding back. Slowly, he knelt down on the carpet beside me and pulled me towards him. 'I'm so sorry, Sarah,' he said, lifting his fingers and wiping the tears from my face.

'Sorry she's dead? Or sorry you weren't here?' Even as I said it I knew I was being unfair. How was Josh to know that she would die, that I would need him, on this one night out of so many?

'Shhh,' he was saying, trying to soothe me. 'I'm here now, okay?'

I let myself fall against him, the thick wool of his coat and the scarf still twisted around his neck taking the full force of my sobs, deadening the sound, like shock absorbers.

'How did you know?' I pulled back and looked at his face. 'About Mum? I tried to call you but you didn't answer.'

'It was Eve,' he said, hugging me tighter, throwing off the scarf and pressing my face against his shoulder. 'I had a text. Missed it in the noise of the pub. Only saw it later, when we were having a coffee back at Bob's place, and then I came straight home.'

'Eve?' Why had Eve contacted Josh, and not me? And by text? Who tells someone about a death by text? The questions came flooding in, none of the answers quite making sense. Why had he responded to her text and not to the missed call from me? And who the hell was Bob?

And then I smelt it. Her perfume. That distinctive Calvin Klein perfume I knew so well. It was there, on his neck, in his hair, lingering on his clothes. Eve's perfume, on *my* husband. And that was when I knew why he was so late home. He had been with her, comforting her, when he should have been with me. My husband was a liar, but in that moment I didn't have the strength to tell him so, or the will even to begin to understand.

All I knew for certain right then was just how much I wanted my mum. And that I was never going to see her again.

***

Eve said most of her more formal clothes were still in storage and she had nothing to wear to the funeral. I offered her something of mine, if only because it seemed the right thing to do, for Mum, but we weren't the same shape these days,

Eve being a couple of inches taller and at least two dress sizes slimmer than me, so we took a walk into town. I don't think either of our minds was really on fashion right then, so when she found a plain black dress on the charity shop rails and it fitted, she didn't bother looking any further.

Eve's eyes were as red-rimmed as mine, but she was putting on a brave face, sorting out all the funeral arrangements so Dad didn't have to. I hadn't tackled her, or Josh, about what had happened that night. I knew, from what Dad had told me, that he had been at home alone with Mum when she had passed away, so Eve had been out somewhere. He had called her, before he'd called me, but she hadn't answered. Still, he had got hold of her eventually and she'd returned at some point, but I didn't check on times or ask for details. A part of me didn't really want to know, didn't want to start putting the pieces of the jigsaw together. I couldn't be sure, not without asking her. Or him. And I could have been wrong. Eve can't have been the only woman in the world to wear that perfume. But there had been a woman. A woman with my husband, close enough to leave her calling card. A woman who wasn't me. It was impossible to know for sure but I was half-convinced it was her – my sister – and that they had been together that night. As to where and when, for how long, and perhaps most importantly why, I had no idea.

I watched them, at the crematorium and afterwards at home, but there was no sign of anything suspicious. In fact, I'm not sure I saw them say more than a few words to each other. Eve gave a short speech, standing behind the coffin, her voice wobbling a bit as she read one of those old-fashioned poems she had probably taught to classloads of kids over the years, and Josh sat quietly beside me in the front row, holding my hand. Back at the house, he took over the pouring of drinks while I kept a constant supply of food moving from kitchen to lounge, and Eve kept a close eye on Dad. We were, to anyone observing, a family looking out for each other and united in mourning.

The house was packed with people. Work colleagues, friends, distant cousins, many apparent strangers who I'd never clapped eyes on before, but Dad gave the impression he knew who they all were, even though I was fairly sure he didn't. I spotted Eve talking to her old friend Lucy and her husband Robert, Lucy nursing an obviously pregnant belly and refusing the sherry. And Simon had turned up too, Eve's best teacher friend, although he hadn't been able to stay for long, it being a school day. Such a shame he was gay. Mum had really taken to him, and he and Eve would have made a great couple. Maybe then I wouldn't have had to worry about what was going on between Eve and Josh which, when I thought about it now, was probably nothing more than the product of my overactive imagination.

Tilly was there, of course, with her parents who had been Mum and Dad's neighbours for what seemed like forever, and with her latest girlfriend, a pale, thin girl probably a good five or six years younger, who she introduced as Emma. We managed to find time for a quick catch-up but I had too many other people to look after, too many other things to think about, to spend as much time with Tilly as I would have liked. We swapped numbers and promised to meet up again soon, but her girlfriend scowled at me, sulkily, when Tilly wasn't looking. I really didn't have the time for petty jealousies, so I already knew it was a friendship I was unlikely to revive. Perhaps there are times when it's best to let the past slip away. Old times are rarely as wonderful as memory makes them, and Tilly's and mine were mostly based on dressing up, sneaking out to places we shouldn't and seeing what we could get away with.

Still, a crowded house all helped to show how much Mum was loved, which should have helped but somehow didn't. No matter how many people sat around chatting, eating and drinking, filling the space, there would always be one person missing. It should have been Mum boiling the kettle and piling plates with food, just as it had always been.

Despite the mess of crockery and crumbs and half-empty glasses left behind, I was glad when they had all finally gone and silence fell.

'I'm worried about Janey,' Josh said, as he helped me to clean up in the kitchen. Dad had headed off upstairs for a much-needed nap and Eve had gone out for a walk to clear her head.

'Where is she?' I realised, with a jolt, that I hadn't seen our daughter for quite a while.

'Outside, playing with the cat. She's very quiet, withdrawn. She's really not taken it well.'

'I'm not sure any of us has.' I looked up at him and saw the redness around his eyes, the tiredness in his face.

'No, but she's just a kid, and she's never had anyone close to her die before. What with just having moved to big school, and having to adapt to a new set of friends, it's not come at the best time for her, has it?'

'Is there ever a best time?'

'No, of course not. But I think we should do something, that's all ...'

'Like what?'

'I'm not sure. Take her away for a few days? Buy her something special?'

I was grateful that Josh cared so deeply for Janey but I couldn't help thinking that she wasn't the only one in need of help, that I was suffering too, but a few days away or a new necklace were never going to make any difference.

Josh picked up on my silence and changed tack. 'Okay, maybe not. Taking her out of school while she's still settling in isn't such a great idea. But she could put one of those memory box things together, couldn't she? Like parents do when a baby dies. You know, pick out a few things to keep, to remind her of her gran. I'm sure your dad wouldn't mind if she took a photo or two, a headscarf, a bit of jewellery maybe. Do we still have the card your mum and dad sent her for her last birthday? Something with a few words in her gran's own handwriting?'

'That's not a bad idea, actually. I'll have a think about it, how to broach it with her.' I carried on washing up the last few plates while Josh mainly just hovered behind me, getting in the way. 'She could use some of the photos of Mum, or of all the family together, to decorate the box, and maybe even spray the contents with Mum's favourite scent. There's nothing quite like a smell to bring back a memory, is there?'

261

'I suppose so. Newly cut grass always makes me think of playing cricket at school. Green stains on my knees! And one whiff of syrup pudding takes me right back to my granny Ivy's kitchen and my hands all covered in flour ...'

'I was thinking more of a dab of her usual perfume, not a clump of grass or a spoonful of syrup!'

'Yeah, of course. So, what was your mum's favourite, do you know?'

'Ha! Of course I do. Not something you men have a clue about though, is it? I bet you don't even know mine.'

'Yes, I do. It's that stuff you keep on the dressing table. In a blue bottle. Or is it green?'

'You really have no idea, do you?

'I'm afraid not, Love. They all smell the same to me.'

But not to me, I thought, as the back door banged open and Eve came back in, her arm draped around Janey's hunched shoulders. Definitely not to me.

***

Janey's memory box was a work of art. Taking her time over it, carefully filling and decorating it, had given her something to focus on, although there were still tears, especially at bedtime, and for a while she refused to sleep without a light on.

Josh was different too. More subdued. Death does that, I suppose. Brings a cloud that hangs over everyone it touches. We moved around each other, doing all the day-to-day practical stuff, but there were no more hugs. No sex. I knew I was putting up barriers, but they were necessary to protect me from feeling too much, hurting too much. If I let anyone in, even Josh, the floodgates would open. If I let myself think too deeply, cry too openly or for too long, I wasn't sure I would be able to stop.

Dad was still off work but he didn't seem able to cope with making any sort of decisions or facing up to sorting through Mum's possessions. He had allowed Janey to take whatever she wanted for her box, which in the end was very little, and Eve had gone into overdrive, up to her eyes in paperwork as she dealt with Mum's bank accounts and insurance policies and made a start on sorting out her clothes for the charity shop.

'I've found a bundle of letters,' she said one afternoon, when Dad had gone out for one of his aimless walks. We were working together, mostly in silence, bagging up Mum's underwear and nighties and old pairs of tights, all the things no one else could have any use for and Dad didn't need to make decisions about. I'd just come back upstairs from cramming a second load into the dustbin outside and making myself a sandwich. 'Love letters, with a faded red ribbon tied round them, like something from an old romantic movie. I only read a few lines from the top one, and looked at the signature at the end. I didn't want to intrude on something so personal, in case I read something I'd rather not see, but they're addressed to Carrie, so they're definitely hers, and they're from someone called Pussy Cat.'

'*Who?*'

'I know. That's what I thought! And they were hidden away,

wrapped in paper, inside a box, inside another box, under a pile of shoes at the back of her wardrobe, as if she didn't want anyone to find them. You don't think ... that they're from some other man, do you?'

'What? Our mum? Carrying on with someone else? Never! Do they have dates on them? Postmarks or anything?'

'No. She didn't keep the envelopes, but they look old. Probably written years ago.'

'So, not an extra-marital fling then. Or not a recent one for us to worry about anyway.' I took a bite of my sandwich and thought for a second or two. 'Previous boyfriend maybe?'

'Could be.' She grinned. 'Unless Pussy Cat *is* Dad!'

'Well, I've never heard her call him that.'

'Me neither. Could have been their little secret. You know, pet names ... Come on, I'll show you.'

'Is that them?' We had gone into our old bedroom where Eve had pulled the door closed and reached for a small pile of papers from under her bed.

She nodded, laying them out on top of the quilt. 'I hid them here in case Dad came back. Shall we just throw them away? Who knows what can of worms we might be opening up if we read them?'

I didn't sit beside her, preferring to stay leaning against the door, if only to make sure Dad didn't make an unexpected appearance. 'We can't say anything to Dad, just in case he's not ...'

'I know. But I'm kind of curious, aren't you? It can't hurt to read one or two, can it? And then we can chuck them out, or shred them or burn them, and nobody else need ever know.'

Mum had only been gone a matter of weeks and I wasn't sure I was ready to confront anything that might taint my memories of her, but the letters were lying there, right in front of us, and it really was a case of now or never. I nodded, slowly, reluctantly, and watched as Eve pulled the top letter from the pile and unfolded it. She began to read, her voice barely more than a whisper.

My dearest darling Carrie,

You can never know how much I have missed you these last few days. Not being able to touch you, or hear your voice.

I looked down at Eve and wondered, in that moment, if she was feeling what I was feeling. The letter was saying exactly what I felt about Mum now that she was gone, about not being able to see her anymore, or touch her or talk to her. I missed her so much. I could almost have written those words myself. I felt the prickle of tears beginning at the corners of my eyes, but Eve kept on reading, her head down, her voice steady.

I know your parents think we are too young to know our own hearts, and I cannot blame them for forcing this separation upon us, but we will show them, won't we, my love? That being apart will never break us. I go to sleep every night thinking of you and missing you, and wake up every morning wishing you were here beside me. I love you more than I can ever say. These six months will

fly by, I promise you, and then we will be together again
and forever. I purr at the very thought of you! I love you.
Yes, I do!
Your very own Pussy Cat.
xxx

'Oh my God!' There was a big fat lump in my throat just from listening to the words. Nobody had ever written, or said, anything like that to me. 'It's heart-breaking stuff, isn't it? All a bit corny, but he really did love her, didn't he?'

'Sounds that way. But who was he? And did he ever come back for her?'

'I have to admit, it doesn't sound like Dad, does it? He's never really been the hearts and flowers kind, and I've never heard anything about them being forced apart for months, have you?'

'Nope. All very mysterious, isn't it?' Eve gazed up at me. 'Shall we read the next letter? Find out what happens next?'

I swallowed the last of the sandwich, wiping my mouth and showering tiny breadcrumbs onto the carpet . 'Or shall we jump straight to the last one, and find out how it ends?'

'Sarah, that is so typical of you. I bet you turn to the back and read the last page of a novel when you're only halfway through the story too, don't you? Have you no patience at all? Obviously not, as you couldn't even wait until we'd finished up here to start stuffing your face! No, if we're going to read this love story, we have to read all the letters in order. It's the only way it's going to make any sense.'

'If you say so. Go on then, let's hear letter number two.

Although we're not going to see any of Mum's replies, are we? So we're only getting half the story, whatever we do.'

Half the story. Was that what I was getting too? I had been right beside her for a couple of hours now, squashed together in an airless room, but today there was no perfume, not on her skin, not on her clothes, and I could see now that there was no bottle of it on her dressing table either, no telltale scent to drag my thoughts in directions I didn't want them to go. Perhaps it had all just been in my imagination, the mad workings of a mind twisted by grief. Eve and Josh? Together, when Mum lay dying? Or rushing to each other as soon as they heard the news? No, surely not. But it was possible. They had history after all. They had been a couple once – just like Carrie and her Pussy Cat – before I had torn them apart.

'*Being apart from you is tearing me in two,*' Eve read, as if the words were echoing what was in my head. And there was something there, in her face, in her voice, that told me it was true. My sister had known love and lost it. She had lost it, lost *him*, to me. She knew the pain of being parted, and of being alone. And suddenly I didn't really care who Pussy Cat might have been, why he and my mother had been separated or how their story ended. What did it matter, now that Mum was gone? All that mattered was the truth. The truth of what was happening right now. Why Eve had never married, never found a forever man of her own, why Josh had come home smelling of her, why he had lied to me, and just how many times he – they – might have done this before. Made a fool of me behind my back.

And in that moment I hated her. Hated my own sister for

trying to take what was mine. Just as, for so many years, she had hated me. But she wasn't going to have him. I couldn't let her win. And for as long as she had no idea that I knew, no idea that we were now at war, it was me who held the upper hand.

Chapter 21

EVE

It was the hardest decision I had ever had to make. Running away to uni to escape the memories Arnie had implanted in my mind, leaving home so abruptly after I had caught Josh in bed with my sister, giving up a job I loved at a school where I had felt so settled and comfortable to come back here for Mum, and for Dad, all paled in comparison.

Josh and I were over. We had to be. I couldn't carry on seeing him, loving him, and still find a way to look my dad, or Sarah, in the eyes, day after day. Being back at home made everything real. Our seemingly impenetrable bubble had finally burst, just as I had always known it one day must. There was to be no happy-ever-after for us. How could there be?

He had booked a hotel room that evening. One of those cheap ones, with just a bed, a TV and a kettle. The sheet had a cigarette burn in it, the window didn't open properly, there was a faded abstract picture on the wall and a plan of the fire exits on the back of the door. In the tiny bathroom the plain white tiles in the shower were old and tired, a thin crack running diagonally up the wall from taps to ceiling, and as we lay on the bed after what I had already decided would be the last time we would ever make love, both of us staring at the ceiling, that was how I felt too. Plain and old and tired, like the tiles, the cracks in our relationship definitely starting to show. We were set in a pattern, a rut, and nothing ever changed. There was no joy anymore, no sense of wonder, no hope. Only a barely suppressed feeling of panic and fear. This was all too close to home, too ... sordid. We had been doing this for too long. It was leading us nowhere. This was no longer the sort of woman I wanted to be.

It wasn't an easy conversation, and not one I wanted to have naked, so I'd pulled my underwear back on, and my T-shirt, and sat up, cross-legged on the bed while Josh just lay there listening and slowly shaking his head.

'But why, Eve? After all these years, I thought ... well, that we would always be together somehow.'

'Somehow? What does that even mean? Because we're not together, are we? Not really. A few hours here and there. A bed, a bottle of wine, a kiss goodbye, and we're back to our own lives again. Our *separate* lives.'

'I thought that suited you. Fitted in. You had your career, your own place, your independence. I thought you under-stood ...'

'What? That you're married? That you have a child you can't bear to hurt, or to leave? Of course I understand all of that. How could I not, when they're my own family? But can't you see that things have changed now? I'm not hundreds of miles away anymore, I don't have a job to keep me occupied, I've given up my home, and I don't even have Simon around to talk to. I'm right here on your doorstep, under your wife's nose, and that is never going to work. It feels ... dangerous. Wrong.'

'But you'll get a job, a home, new friends. And I still want you, Eve. I still love you.'

'I wonder if you do. Really love me, I mean. And, even if you do, it's not enough. Look at me, Josh. I'm thirty-five. I can't go on like this. I need a life of my own. A real life. Maybe even kids ... before it's too late.'

He stared at me, as if I was some kind of alien, talking in tongues. 'Kids? But I can't give you kids, Eve. How could we ever get away with—'

'Get away with it?' I cut in, yelling at him now. 'That's exactly my point. I don't want to have children with someone who's trying to get away with it! Someone looking for excuses, trying to keep me hidden away like a dirty secret. I want someone I can be seen with, openly, in the streets, someone I can take home to meet Mum and Dad, someone who's proud to be with me, who *wants* to have children with me, live with me, bring up a family together, like a real couple. And that someone's not you, Josh, is it? It can never be you.'

The ring of his mobile from the bedside table stopped me in my tracks. Life outside these walls, intruding again. Couldn't he have put it on silent as I had with mine? Didn't I deserve even an hour or two of uninterrupted attention once in a while? Josh reached over and picked it up, glanced at it, then quickly switched it off.

271

'Sarah,' he muttered.

'She'll always be there, Josh.' I felt around on the floor for my jeans and tugged them on. 'But I won't be. Not anymore.'

'Come on. Just lie back down, let me hold you. You're upset, with your mum being so ill, and everything in your life changing. But this doesn't have to change. *We* don't have to change. Come on, we've got the room for the night. I can make some excuse, stay until morning.' His hand was working its way up under my T-shirt.

'And lie to Sarah again? What would you say? That you got drunk? Crashed on a mate's settee? We're not teenagers anymore, Josh. And I, for one, am going home now. You stay if you like. Make the most of the room. Don't want to waste it, do you? Not having paid for it.' I grabbed my bag. 'Don't bother getting dressed. I don't need you to drive me back, or risk being seen. I can call a cab.'

'Eve, you're being ridiculous.' He sat up, running his hand through his messy hair. 'Come back to bed. Please.'

I had my phone out, ready to look up a cab firm, when I saw it. A missed call. No, three missed calls. All from Dad.

'Something's wrong,' I said, flopping back down on the edge of the bed, my fingers fumbling as I dialled Dad's number.

Josh watched as I listened, tried to speak, nodded blindly, then crumpled down beside him. Mum was dead. While I had been here, letting her down, doing something I know would have made her so ashamed of me, she had slipped away, with only Dad beside her.

Josh pulled me into him, nuzzled my neck, let me cry. I knew I was shaking, and I think he was too. Then he got dressed quickly, tossed the room key onto the unmade bed and drove me back to the house, dropping me on the corner, away from the streetlights, where we wouldn't be seen, and drove himself home to Sarah. Neither of us stopped to look back.

***

The funeral had been tough. Keeping away from Josh, sticking to my resolve. But there were other things to think about, and to cry about, that day. I had got through it, holding it all in, trying to support Dad the best I could. But the letters were different. They tore into my heart. Other people's love, other people's pain, only served to drag my own back to the forefront of my thoughts. I shouldn't have read them. If Sarah had just said no, I probably wouldn't have done. But she didn't, so I did.

I knew we were stepping into Mum's secret life, one she had kept stashed away in a box, probably since before we were born, but the letters drew me in. It was a chance to get close to her again, to find out things about her that we didn't know. They must have been important, for her to have kept them for so long. Had she pulled them out from time to time, re-read them when she was alone? Had she remembered, reminisced, cried? Or had she simply forgotten they were there? We would never know. Yet, private though they were, there was something compelling about them. I should have stopped as soon as I realised what they were, but I didn't. I couldn't. The need to know more drove me on, turning page after page, even if Sarah was keen to get to the crux of the thing and then dump them in the nearest bin.

I suppose it was all tied up in how I was feeling about my own life, my own secrets. How would I feel if someone found them out and started picking over them after I was gone? But the sad thing was that Mum would never know, would she? That we had found them? It couldn't matter to her anymore what happened to them, who read them. But it did matter to me. I needed to know.

I was reading the third letter aloud when I heard the front door open and the clank of keys.

'Dad's back,' said Sarah, getting to her feet. 'I'll go and make him a cup of tea.'

She closed the bedroom door behind her and I got the distinct impression she was glad for an excuse to go. I knew Dad would never come poking about in my room, but I stashed the letters away again anyway, just in case. It was stupid, but somehow Mum's secret had started to become my secret, something I felt the need to hide just as much as she probably had. At least until I had read them all, and decided what to do with them.

I sat for a while, in the silence. Sarah had said nothing about Josh in days, but then why should she? I had done the right thing in ending it, I was sure of that, yet I longed to hear how he was, what he was doing, thinking, feeling. I needed him to be hurting as I was, if only to convince myself that he had loved me, that he still did. '*You can never know how much I have missed you these last few days. Not being able to touch you, or hear your voice.*' The words from Mum's first letter ran through my head. They felt so real, as if they were all about me. My life, my feelings. And they hurt. But, right then, only weeks after her death, we were all hurting. All quiet. All sad. Who was going to notice a little extra sadness amongst so much? In a way I had chosen the perfect time to break my own heart. Everything was masked and so easy to explain away because of my grief. I could cry and no one would question it. And, in my imagination, Josh would be crying too. But I didn't see him, dared not ask after him, and Sarah gave nothing away.

I went down to join the others. We sat in front of the TV and shared a pot of tea. Sarah was eating again, working her way through a packet of biscuits that no one else had any interest in. I suppose food is one of those things you either turn to for comfort or go off altogether. As in most things, Sarah and I fell into opposite camps. I don't think I had eaten anything since breakfast, and that had only been a slice of toast.

Dad looked better. The fresh air had done him some good, bringing a little colour back into his face, and the walking had tired him, making it easier for him to forget for a while and sleep. I watched him doze off in his favourite armchair, Smoky the cat curled up on his lap, and wondered what his life would be like from now on. Forty years with one woman, and then losing her, would be hard to recover from. And soon it would be Christmas. None of us would be looking forward to that. The first one without her. The cooking, the forced merriment, her presents not there under the tree. Christmas, the fearful word we had yet to say out loud.

'I think I'll be off now.' Sarah slipped into her coat. There was a paper poppy still pinned to it, a leftover from Remembrance Day a week or so before. 'Be there when Janey gets home from school.'

'She walks home by herself these days?'

'Oh, yes. Quite the Little Miss Independent, she is. And they do encourage it now she's at the big school. Well, you'll know that, won't you? From your teaching days.'

'You make it sound like I've retired! I am still a teacher, just one without a job at the moment.'

'Better get out there and find one then, hadn't you?' There was a chill in her voice that seemed to wipe away any imagined feelings I had of renewed closeness. There was still an invisible wall between us. We weren't close. Perhaps we never could be, not after so long.

'I'm trying. But Dad still needs me here.'

'Does he? I think what Dad needs is to get back to normal. Well, a new kind of normal, but a routine at least. And that's probably what you need too. Or the pair of you will sit here forever, moping about day after day, and that won't do anybody any good.'

'Well, as it happens, I have an interview next week. Not sure you'll like it though.'

'Why?'

'It's at Janey's school. English teacher, but deputy head as well.'

'Oh. I remember, you said there was one. Didn't realise where though. Janey's not been there long enough for me to get to know much about the teaching staff. I didn't even know there was a vacancy. And they've actually asked you in for an interview?'

'Yes, they have. No need to sound so surprised. You don't mind, do you?'

'Why should I mind? If it's good for your career ... and it's not as if you'd actually be teaching Janey, is it? Well, I assume not. I'm sure you can declare an interest and claim diplomatic immunity or whatever they call it. I mean, it'd be like having someone in your own family as your doctor. Imagine having to show Cousin Bill a boil on your bum! And Janey having to call you Miss Peters all the time, and you telling her off or giving her detention. Doesn't seem quite right. But it's a nice school, and local enough for you to get to while you're still living here with Dad. Go for it!'

'Thanks.' I held my arms out towards her, thinking we might manage a hug, but she sidestepped it.

Dad slept on after she'd gone, snoring gently. I turned the TV off. The clock ticked in the hall, the last of the tea went cold in the pot, and the light started to fade so I got up and closed the curtains. The room felt different without Mum in it. The whole house did.

When Dad woke up half an hour later, he opened his eyes and smiled at me, as if, just for a moment, he had forgotten she was gone. But then the cloud descended again and the lines sunk back into his face. 'Sarah gone home, has she?' His hand ran over the cat's fur, head to tail, and head to tail again, smoothing it until I could hear the gentle purring from right across the room. The cat had been Mum's really, and no doubt he missed her too, wondered where his number-one carer had gone. But Dad seemed to have taken over the role. They could be good for each other. Company. Something for Dad to care about, and to bring a bit of comfort.

'Let's have some music, Evie,' Dad said, pointing to the old stacking stereo system that had sat in the corner for as long as I could remember. The cat arched his back, stretched and jumped down. 'Pick out one of your mum's favourites.'

Mum and Dad had never really taken to CDs, and certainly not to any kind of new-fangled downloaded stuff as Dad called it. All of their records were just that. Actual vinyl records, the albums bearing outdated photos and psychedelic designs, the singles in small paper cases with a hole in the front to read their names through. 1960s and 70s originals, mostly, bought by one or the other before they had even met and now merged into one extremely diverse collection. Probably worth a fortune now that vinyl was said to be making a comeback. There were a few cassette tapes too, mainly for use in the car, and often recorded themselves from something on the radio or from their own records. Their preferences hadn't moved with the times either. Dad still liked his Status Quo and his Stones, which nobody would ever suspect from looking at him, and Mum had always been a little in love with Tom Jones and Engelbert, and hankered after bad-boy David Essex in his curly-haired days, having given up on Paul McCartney as soon as he married Linda and stopped eating meat.

I went to the sideboard and opened the double doors at the bottom. The records were lined up inside in cardboard boxes, the most played ones at the front, the ones they never touched but still couldn't bring themselves to part with tucked away at the back. I picked some out, one by one, and read the labels. All songs I had heard played so many times in this house.

'Eleanor Rigby'. No, not today. Too sad, especially with all that loneliness and churches where weddings had been.

'Yesterday'. Too many regrets and too many shadows. Why she had to go ... No, not this time, Sir Paul!

'Lily the Pink', by the Scaffold, with Paul's brother Mike, not quite so famous and not quite so handsome. '*Let's drink a drink ...*' I started to sing the words in my head, then put it aside as a possible for later, when I knew Dad would get the whisky out before bed.

And then I saw it. Tom Jones. 'What's New, Pussy Cat?' Yes, that had always been a favourite of Mum's. I could remember her playing it often and pulling Dad up to dance with her around the room, their hips rolling around just like slinky Tom's as they sang and laughed together.

I slipped the record from its paper cover and polished it gently with my sleeve, the way I had seen Mum do so many times, before placing it on the turntable and clicking the switch that brought the needle over. '*Pussy cat, pussy cat ...*'

I saw Dad's eyes light up with the memory, and then just as quickly mist over again. No, it couldn't be, could it? Yes! That was it. It was where they had got the nickname from. Suddenly it all came clear and I wondered why I hadn't seen it straightaway. Even some of the words he'd written had been lifted from the song. I looked up at the ceiling, towards the pile of old letters under my bed, towards Mum, somewhere up there in Heaven and hopefully looking back down. Everything was all right. She had led me to this cupboard, shown me a sign. Put my mind, and her own reputation, at rest. Dad – my serious, seemingly unromantic dad – really was the mysterious Pussy Cat after all!

And I liked that. That there had been a real love story between them, a secret past that neither Sarah nor I knew anything about. I must find the right time to ask Dad about it, I thought. To find out why they had been forced apart, and how they had resolved things and ended up back together again. A happy ever after, till death did them part. And I knew then that I wasn't going to read the rest of their private letters. I would slip them back in their box at the back of Mum's wardrobe and one day, when he was ready to face up to sorting through what was left of her things, he would find them, and hopefully they would make him smile. Or maybe cry, but either was good.

A story like that, a story of true love so close to home, gave me some sort of hope, that things would work out all right in the end, for the rest of us. For me. They usually do, after all. One way or another.

***

I got the job at Grange Heath School. The previous deputy head having left quite abruptly due to ill health, they needed someone to step in as soon as possible, and that suited me perfectly. With references and medicals to sort out, and me still feeling I should be around during the daytime to help

Dad for just a bit longer, we agreed on a start date straight after the Christmas break. New job, new term, new start ...

I was desperately looking forward to teaching again. It would have been just over six months since leaving Wales by the time the new job kicked in, but it had been a very long and harrowing six months. The absence of any real purpose now that Mum had gone was messing with my head, leaving too much time and space for my thoughts to wander back towards Josh and what I had thrown away.

I was in no hurry to move out. Dad had decided to go back to the office in the New Year too, but for now he still drifted about in a daze a lot of the time and, left to his own devices, would probably forget to buy food or iron a shirt for work, so I knew he still needed me, and I suppose I needed him too. The thought of being alone again and facing a new job, new people, was not an appealing one.

It was good to be back in touch with Lucy, who had somehow turned up at the funeral without me even thinking to invite her, and to have her living so near. My years away had taken a toll on our once close friendship, but we were both eager to put that right. 'You'll be a godmother, won't you?' she said, as we sat at a window table in her favourite coffee shop, watching the world go by. She was toying with the remains of an enormous almond croissant, licking her finger and dipping into the sprinklings of icing sugar on the edge of her plate, her other hand resting protectively across her tummy.

'Really? Me? I'm not very religious, you know. Well, not at all really.'

'That doesn't matter. The vicar's cool with it, as long as at least one of the other godparents is a God-fearing person who knows her christening from her confirmation and what to do with the candle! And Rob's sister fits that particular bill. So, why not you? You'd be perfect for the job. I've probably known you longer than anybody else, ever since primary school, and you're the right sort of person, you know, to guide him in the right direction, teach him to read, buy all the right presents ...'

'Ha! So, it's about presents, is it? I often wondered what a godmother's duties were, and now I know.'

'Of course it's not. But you're a teacher, you know a lot more about kids, and educating them, than I do. I don't want my son to have godparents who fill him up with sugar or offer to babysit and then just plonk him in front of the telly all day.'

'So I have to babysit as well? Is there no end to my duties?'

'Don't you want to do it then?'

'Of course I want to do it! I'd be honoured. But I don't know a lot about it. I've never been a godmother before.'

'Not for your sister's little girl?'

'Oh, no. We were still not speaking when Janey was born. I would have been the last choice, believe me. And Josh insisted on a Catholic ceremony apparently, which is hardly my forte.'

'Things better now though?'

'Between Sarah and me? Sort of. I'm not sure we'll ever be the way we were, but it's civilised these days.'

'And Josh? Is he behaving himself?'

I could feel the heat rising in my face. I lifted my coffee

and breathed it in, letting the effects of the steam act as my disguise. 'I suppose so. No idea. Why?'

'Oh, once a cheat, always a cheat. Calls himself a Catholic! What a hypocrite. And if he could do it you, he can do it to Sarah. I'd be watching him very closely if I was her. Thank God my Rob isn't like that.'

'How can you be so sure he isn't?'

'Honestly, Eve, do you think I'd be having this baby if I had any doubts at all? No, Rob's one of the good guys. A good husband, and definitely good father material. He has never so much as looked at another woman. And as for touching ... God, no! A wife knows these things. If Josh is still up to his old tricks, Sarah will have an inkling, believe me. I know I would, if it was Rob.'

'I wouldn't know.'

'I guess not. It really is time we got you married off, you know!' Lucy went on, oblivious to my discomfort. 'No man on the scene?'

'No. Been too caught up with life, work, Mum, just about everything else, to get mixed up with a man.'

'It might do you good if you did. If you want babies of your own, you can't leave it too long.'

'Ah, but I'll be a godmother soon, won't I? A baby I can spoil rotten but hand back come bedtime. Sounds like the perfect arrangement to me.'

'You don't mean that. I know you don't. And now you're more settled, with a new job on the horizon, it's the obvious next step, isn't it? I'll have to see who I can fix you up with. Maybe one of Rob's friends?'

283

'Lucy! Don't you dare! When – and if – I decide I want a man, I will find him for myself, thanks very much.'

'Well, don't be too long about it. This little one will want a playmate around his own age. And I quite fancy being a godmother myself. A fairy godmother,' she giggled, 'with a big dress and wings, and a wand and everything.'

'I hate to spoil things for you, but wands don't work. There's no such thing as magic.'

'Cynic!'

'Maybe, but men and babies and a life of domestic bliss are your dreams, not necessarily mine. And I might not even stick around long term, once Dad's back on his feet. I might go back to Wales. I like Wales.'

'Oh, come on, Eve. You can't run away forever. You only ever stayed there after university to get away from Josh and Sarah, and you only went there in the first place to get away from that scumbag Arnie.'

'Rubbish! I'd already applied and been accepted, before Arnie ...' I finished my coffee and pulled my coat back on. Arnie. I hadn't thought of him in ages, and I certainly didn't want to now. 'Look, I don't want to start some silly debate, or argue with you. We can't change the past, much as we might like to, but Wales was good for me. I enjoyed uni and I loved my job. Now come on, let's hit the shops. If I'm meant to buy suitably educational baby gifts for little Horace here, then I might as well start early.'

'Horace?'

'Well, if you've decided on a better name for him, you

haven't given me so much as a hint of it yet, so I'll be guessing until I get it right. Cyril? Arthur? Buzz?'

'Now you're just being silly.'

'Guilty as charged. Now, toys. How does a shape sorter sound?'

'Great. As long as you promise to stop trying to push a round peg into a square hole and stay here, where you belong.' She grinned at her own joke. 'Think seriously about your future, Eve, please. Accept that Wales is not for you. Not anymore. I need you here. And so does little Horace.' She linked her arm through mine as we headed out into the street. 'I've missed you.'

Chapter 22

SARAH

Josh wasn't happy. He never actually said it, but I could tell. Since we'd lost Mum the atmosphere in both homes had changed. We'd got through a low-key but quietly comfortable Christmas, based around a traditional turkey meal and lots of TV, keeping our gifts simple and raising a glass to Mum at what seemed the appropriate time, in the slow and satisfied gap after lunch where her home-made pudding would usually be trying to force its way in. Janey had cut up a lacy paper doily and made a new angel decoration in Mum's honour, but Dad had decided not to put up the tree, with all its memories, so the angel had taken pride of place on the mantelpiece. Josh had gone easy on the booze, and everyone had been in bed by eleven.

It had been our turn to go up to Josh's parents but Dad had needed us all to be together, and strong, so we had stayed, and they had come down on one of their rare but fleeting visits to us the day after Boxing Day. Josh had appeared pleased to see them, but the gloom soon descended again once they had gone. At first I thought maybe he was grieving for Mum the way I was, but the long silences, the gazing off into space, the valiant attempts to stick to his own side of the bed and the tossing and turning even when he'd managed it, all spoke of something more.

Call it intuition, but I had a feeling he was keeping something from me, and that it was something I really didn't want to hear. I wondered, not for the first time, if there was someone else, if he was about to leave me, or was thinking about it at least. A growing sense of unease began to eat away at me and, like a dog with a bone, I couldn't give it up.

It all came down to that day when Mum had died and I had sat at home alone and heartbroken, waiting for him to come back. There had been no evening out with the lads, no drunken falling asleep on some anonymous sofa, no Bob, I was sure of that. I had never challenged him about it though. If I had, he would only have lied to me anyway. So what was it? What did that whiff of telltale perfume mean? That it was Eve. It almost certainly had to be Eve. But was it just a one-off thing? An innocent drink together, for old times' sake? A renewed interest that had started now she was back home, and was in danger of igniting into something I still just might have time to stop? The more I convinced myself it was her he had been with, her on his mind now, keeping him awake at night, the more I knew I had to find out for sure. I needed the facts. I couldn't cope with my fears, or decide what to do about them, unless I knew what it was I was dealing with.

And so I started to snoop. Not a nice word, and not a very nice thing to have to do, but it was the only way. I must have been stupid, or at best naïve, not to have done it long before. Josh was always off out somewhere, disappearing for hours, days, weekends at a time, on business trips, courses, conferences. There had been so many opportunities for him to stray. A woman? Several women? A whole bloody harem, for all I knew. Yet I had pushed my doubts aside and never questioned too deeply. But now I wanted to know, and if there was something dodgy going on, there was sure to be evidence.

Josh worked in banking. He was methodical, analytical, sensible. He had bank cards and credit cards and he kept the statements. He hung onto his petrol receipts and his restaurant slips and hotel bills so he could make his expenses claims. He'd even done it when he'd been out with me in the pub that time, I remembered, when Mum had been ill and we'd gone for a scampi and chips that Dad had given us the cash for. No, I wasn't a client, but the bank wasn't to know that, and Josh wasn't so honest as to miss a trick like that. I'd seen him pocket the receipt and had no doubt about why.

It wasn't going to be hard to work out what he was up to, where he had been. The paper trail winding its way behind his every move would be like the crumbs on the path behind Hansel and Gretel. I just hoped it wasn't going to lead me to the wicked witch that otherwise went by the name of Eve.

He kept everything in a big blue document case in the corner of our little box room, tucked under the small desk he'd always used to sort out the household bills, a desk that had slowly been taken over by Janey and her homework. It was all just her dad's boring old stuff in that document case, as far as she was concerned, papers she had never been in the slightest bit interested in looking at, and neither had I. That was probably why Josh had never bothered to hide it, nor find a way to lock it. Dragging it out from its cobwebby corner was like taking candy from a baby. Almost too easy to be true.

They say you should keep important documents for six years, don't they? In case the bank needs to query anything. Or the taxman. Or, in this case, the wife. And there it all was, stuffed into orderly little pockets, carefully and helpfully labelled. *Electricity. Water. Council tax. TV licence. Insurance. Car. Household appliances. Travel. Work expenses. Wills.* His life, our life, past, present and future, pound for pound, recorded on paper, for all to see.

After a brief flick through the house stuff, I could see from the dates on the bills just how rigidly Josh had stuck to the six-year rule. There was nothing older, no doubt all fed through the shredder as soon as its usefulness was up. I moved on to *Travel*, and there were the photocopies of our passports. An itinerary for a school trip Janey had been on to Devon. Details of family holidays: a day trip on the ferry to Calais, a week in the Lakes, our long weekend in Bournemouth. We never had made it to the ski slopes. Nothing unusual, nothing incriminating. My hand hovered over the prime suspect, *Work expenses*. Would he have kept receipts once they had been submitted and claimed? Yes, of course he would. Well, photocopies anyway. I lifted them out, trying to keep them in order, and not to drop any, as I laid them out on top of the desk. It was the recent stuff I wanted. For the day Mum died, and definitely the months since. Where had he been, and who with? What was making him so distracted, and so restless? So sad?

The hotel, when I found it, was surprisingly local. The Garden Manor. Only ten miles away. It sounded grand but its cheapskate price didn't quite match up. Still, whether it was luxury or budget, what difference did it make? It was too near to home. He would have had no reason to stay there, when it was so easy to get home. Not for work anyway. Only for pleasure. The sort of pleasure he had chosen to keep secret. I felt the tears prickle at the back of my eyes as I tried to make sense of it all.

There was nothing since. Nothing that looked in any way out of the ordinary. No more hotels, no train tickets, no petrol for long journeys, no cosy meals for two. Nothing that screamed out at me that he was having an affair. Unless he had decided to be more careful, and destroy it all. But then, why not destroy the one vitally important hotel bill that gave the game away? And, if it was Eve, as I knew it must be, then of course he would have no need to travel far from home. She was living right here now, practically on our own doorstep. When was the last time he had been on a course, stayed away overnight? When had that all slowed down, stopped? Because it had.

I don't know what made me look back further, to earlier dates, to times before she came home, but I did. And there it all was. Mixed in among all the other places, the genuine trips, but easy enough to pick out when you know what you're looking for. Six years of it. Petrol receipts from garages in Wales, meals eaten in Wales, a florist's bill for roses bought the day before her birthday. He couldn't find a way to claim for those, surely? But it all added up. It all pointed to just one thing. Eve was still very much in Josh's life, and almost certainly still in his bed – or hers – and had been for a long time. God, maybe they had never stopped. Maybe it had been going on throughout our whole married life. And me ... well, I was probably the last to know, wasn't I? 'Mug' written right across my forehead, in big red letters for all to see.

I waited for him to come home, felt the rage burning inside me the moment I looked at him, but I said nothing. Did nothing. I dug my nails into my palms, fought back the urge to hit him, scream at him, but managed to hold it all in. I had to give myself time to think, to plan, not to dive in and do something instant and uncontrolled that I might live to regret. I was his wife, and that meant something. Or it did to me. Walking away, separating, divorcing, was a huge step, one I would not find easy, and who would it hurt the most? Me. Me and Janey. And wouldn't it be playing right into their hands? Like opening the door to Eve and inviting her in, to take my place, to take *him*. It would be giving him what he had probably wanted all along. Giving in. And so I bided my time, thinking, watching the pair of them, their every move. Hard though it was to carry on as if nothing had happened, that was exactly what I knew I had to do.

***

I'm not sure quite when I decided to play Josh at his own game. Oh, I wasn't about to leap into bed with anyone else.

That would simply give him the ammunition he needed to blame me, get rid of me, make me out to be the bad guy. But I was lonely, and in need of a sympathetic ear, someone who would listen and give me a hug and be on my side. I couldn't burden Dad, talking about it at work would look too much like I was asking for professional legal advice, and what did Tilly know about men and the trouble they cause? And so I did what I had wanted to do for so long. I opened the contacts list on my mobile and scrolled down to the fictional Carol.

He didn't answer the first time I tried and I was far too cowardly to leave any sort of message. *Hi, Colin. It's Sarah. Sarah Cavendish ...* What if he didn't want to talk to me, or didn't even remember who I was? How embarrassing would that be? I hung up quickly and tried to put the whole stupid idea out of my head. The man was a doctor, for heaven's sake. He was busy, important, and quite likely married by now. To some high-flying surgeon, or a sexy nurse. What would he want with me? Some girl from his past who he'd never really got to know properly the first time around, let alone the second. Come to think of it, what did I really want from him? That was the question I kept coming back to, but not knowing the answer didn't stop me from phoning again.

'Hello?'

'Colin?'

'Yep. Who is this?'

I held my breath, my thumb hovering over the *End call* button. If I was going to back out, now was the time. But I didn't.

'You might not remember me,' I said, hesitantly, 'but it's Sarah.'

'Sarah? As in Penguins-in-the-park Sarah? Of course I bloody remember you, you nit! How are you? And little Janey? Not so little now though, I guess. God, Sarah, I know you said you'd call, but it's been years! I thought you must have lost my number, or just decided you didn't want to talk to me ever again. Made me wonder what I did wrong!'

'I'm sorry. You did nothing wrong. I just ... well, life got in the way, you know, how it does.'

'Still married, I suppose?'

'Yes, still married.'

'Shame.'

I laughed. 'Colin Grant, you are such a flirt. Honestly!'

'Can't blame a man for trying. Now, come on, tell me why you've called after all this time. Couldn't resist me any longer, eh? Not that I'm complaining. It's great to hear your voice.'

'Yours too.' I stopped, not at all sure what to say next. 'I ... I don't suppose you're free to meet up, are you? For a coffee or something?'

'You bet I am. When? Now?'

'Wow, you're keen!'

'No time like the present. Let you slip away now and you might not call again for another God knows how many years. But at least, now you have, I've got your number at last!' He laughed. 'As luck would have it, I'm not working today, so name your place and I'll be there. Then you can tell me all about it. This life of yours, that's been getting in the way. I heard about your mum, by the way. Too late to send condolences or turn up at the funeral, but I am sorry.'

'Thanks. She'd been very ill and we all knew it was coming, but even so ...'

'Of course. Death is always hard to take, no matter how much you're expecting it. Believe me, I see it all the time at work and I never get used to it. Now, come on, where shall we meet?'

'Kiosk in the park?'

'Ah, you old romantic, you! Scene of our first date.' He did an exaggerated sigh. 'Half an hour, okay?'

I changed out of my floppy trousers and slippers and into a half-decent but not-too-dressy dress, my one and only winter coat and a pair of medium height heels, brushed my hair and peered into the hall mirror to add a flick of mascara and a touch of barely-there lipstick before grabbing my bag and rushing out to make sure I got there first.

The metal shutters were down over the kiosk window, badly spelt graffiti splattered across them in garish pink paint. The place was all in darkness and obviously not open for business. *Closed for refurbishments*, so the sign on the door said. I waited there anyway, on one of the old wooden benches that bordered the playground. There was a cold wind blowing and I started to wish I'd stayed in trousers, but from there I could get a good view along the path in both directions, so there was no danger I would be taken by surprise. I pushed my hands down deep into my pockets and pulled my collar up.

He looked just the way I remembered him, all confident smile and twinkly eyes, but so much smarter. I didn't know if he had rapidly raided his wardrobe for the best shirt and the cleanest jeans he owned, or if he dressed that way all the time, but topped off with a sleek black leather jacket, this tall, slim vision of the man bore no resemblance to the chubby kid I knew at school, nor to the sweaty T-shirted runner I had bumped into in the very same park all that time ago.

He ran the last few yards, sweeping me up into a hug as soon as he reached me, and my arms seemed to just fall naturally into place around his neck. His kiss on my cheek felt warm and welcoming. 'Well, Mrs Sarah Whatever-your-name-is-these-days ...' He held me out at arm's length and smiled, nodding towards the shuttered kiosk. 'I bet you knew this place was closed, didn't you? A clever ruse, to get me here under false pretences and then entice me away to somewhere a good deal posher. Come on.' He hooked my arm into his. 'Let's find a cosy corner in a pub somewhere, shall we? Life stories get told a lot better over a bottle of wine.'

'So, show me your little Janey, then,' he said, as soon as we were settled with a drink in front of us. 'She must be quite grown up by now.'

I pulled out my phone and flipped through the photos, looking for the best ones to show him.

'Oh, come on, let's see them all.' He took the phone from my hand and I watched his face soften, his smile light up his eyes as he gazed at my daughter. 'She's very like you, Sarah.'

'Do you think so? She has my hair, and maybe my nose, but she's a lot like her dad too.'

'Is this him?' Colin had come across some family pictures, the three of us squashed up side by side in some restaurant, and a couple I had taken of the two of them in the garden in the summer.

'Yes, that's Josh.'

He looked from me to the photo on the screen, and back again, as if he was trying to imagine us together, and shook his head. 'So, tell me. Tell me all of it.'

'There's nothing to tell.'

'Pull the other one! Tell me what he's done, why you're so clearly unhappy. And why there's not one single photo of just the two of you together. No smiley ones, no arms-linked ones, no ... well, no really happy together pictures. That says a lot, you know.'

'Oh ...'

What made me spill out all my problems, and my worst fears, to a man I hardly knew? I felt safe with him, for a start. He was on the edges of my life, not a close friend, not bound up in any way with my family or its troubles, yet not a total stranger either. And the way he looked at me, held my hand gently in his as we sat side by side on a long comfy corner seat in the pub, gave me the warmest, fuzziest feeling that he cared, really cared, and maybe even fancied me a little, which was exactly what I needed.

'Do you love him, Sarah?' he said, ten minutes later, when I'd been talking pretty much non-stop and had finally run out of steam and stopped to wipe my eyes and take a sip of my wine. 'Do you really love this rat of a husband of yours? And does he love you? Because, from what I can deduce here, he's not been very good to you, or very fair. Okay, you got off to a rocky start, pushed into things too quickly and much too young, before you knew each other well enough. I get that. But now?'

'About the getting-married-young thing ...'

'Yes?'

'I was pregnant.'

'Yes, you told me that.'

'He stood by me, Colin. He didn't have to. I have to give him credit for that. For doing what everyone said was the right thing, the honourable thing. But ...'

'Come on, spit it out. Whatever it is, you can tell me. I'm not about to spill your secrets all over town. We doctors know how to be discreet, you know.'

'Well ... I was never actually sure the baby was his. There, I've said it. In fact, it was highly likely it wasn't. There was someone else, just a few weeks before.'

'Not that wally Jacobs?'

'So what if it was? It didn't mean anything really, just teenage stuff that went too far, but then I missed a period. Just one, and I was trying to ignore it, hope I was wrong. I hadn't done a test. And later, by the time I was sure, it was just assumed the baby was Josh's. I mean, poor little Sarah, hardly out of nappies herself, surely couldn't have been with anyone else ...'

'Oh.'

'What does *oh* mean? It's not that I'm expecting you to approve. It was pretty bad of me, wasn't it? I do know that. Bad not to tell the truth, and to let him take the blame. And I have felt guilty about that, really I have. It's why I know it's not all Josh's fault. I led us into this disastrous marriage, without giving him all the facts. But when we lost the baby – a baby I never saw, although they told us it was a little boy – it didn't seem to matter anymore. It was all just so horrible, so sad, and I went to pieces for a while. He looked after me, cried with me, and I knew he must really care about me. *Me*, not just the baby, because there was no baby ...'

'And that's love, is it? Keeping quiet about something so important, tricking a man into marriage, basing your whole future together on grief? You had the chance to end it then, didn't you? After the baby died, you could have gone your separate ways.'

'Why would I? I loved him. We were married, and we decided to try again.'

'Replace the baby with another one? Don't you think that was just papering over the cracks? Trying to justify why you were together, give yourselves a reason to go on with the charade?'

'You don't know anything about it. About *us*.'

'I know that he doesn't talk to you, confide in you, treat you as if you're special. Which you are, by the way. And meeting up, quite likely sleeping, with another woman, who could very possibly be your own sister? Does that sound like a loving husband to you? Because it certainly doesn't to me. It doesn't matter why you got together in the first place, or even why you decided to stay together. None of that has to bind you together for ever. The man's clearly a shit, and I can't help wondering why you're hanging on so tightly to someone who might not actually be worth hanging on to. The only possible reason I can see why you would even contemplate staying is if, despite everything he's done, you still love him. Really love him.'

'I ...'

'It's not that hard a question. Love, or not love? It's something you should know instantly, isn't it?'

'There's more to it than that. I started out believing I was so lucky to have bagged him. He was gorgeous, so good looking, older than me but not treating me like a child. I fancied him rotten, and loved him right from the start. But love changes, doesn't it? I'm not some silly dewy-eyed teenager anymore. He has his faults. And so do I, I'm sure. But we have a daughter together. A home. He's all I know. We've been together all my adult life ...'

'And what sort of an answer is that? You stay because you know nothing else, have nothing else? Sarah, that's bullshit. You must know that. What about trust? Respect? Okay, what do I know? I've never been married, and luckily I haven't had my heart broken ... yet. But divorce isn't the shameful thing it once was, you know. You could walk away with your head held high, with money of your own, a chance to start again, build a happy life without him.'

'I know. But ...' But what? I didn't know what it was that held me back, so how on earth was I ever going to explain it to someone else?

'But you haven't even tackled him over it, have you? Now, listen to me. You needed a friend to talk to, and you chose me, and you asked for – well, sort of asked for – my advice, and my support. Why else are we here? So, that's what you're going to get, whether you like what I have to say or not.' He looked straight at me, his fingers under my chin, turning my face towards him, making sure he could hold my gaze. 'As I see it, you're hoping if you ignore it then it will all go away and everything will be rosy again. If it ever was. That's not the way the world works, Sarah. You tried to ignore that first pregnancy and look what happened. You have to face up to things, make positive choices, not rely on luck or fate or whatever magical force you think will come along and put things right. Men like Josh will get away with it time and time again if nobody challenges them or tries to stop them. It's time you stood up for yourself. Fight for him or throw him out. One way or the other, you can't just go on doing nothing. You have to know. And if it involves your sister ... well, you definitely have to know about that. You have to ask him. Ask *her*.'

I squeezed my eyes tight, nodded and looked up at the ceiling, down at the floor, anywhere but at Colin. I edged closer and laid my head against his big broad shoulder, trying hard not to cry. Of course he was right. My marriage had been as good as over for a long time and I hadn't been prepared to face it.

'I've always had a soft spot for you, Sarah. You must know that.' He rubbed his thumb backwards and forwards over the back of my hand, rested his chin lightly on the top of my head, and his voice dropped down almost to whisper levels. 'But none of this is about me, or what I feel. It has to be about you. What's best for *you*. I just want you to be happy, and being with Josh isn't making you happy, is it? So do something about it. Please. And when you need me, for anything, *as* anything, I'll be here. Okay?'

301

Chapter 23

EVE

Starting at a new school a term after everybody else made me feel I was constantly playing catch-up. Most members of staff already knew each other well, and even the two newest had had the months since September to get acclimatised and make sure they had found a favourite chair in the staff room and learned the others' names. The children moved around the building as if they were on wheels, whizzing round corners, dashing from class to class, creating a quiet but constant buzz that never quite reached deafening proportions. It was like a well-established ant colony, everyone knowing exactly where they were going and what their own place was in the hierarchy. Except me.

At home, life was settling down at last. Dad had gone back to work, which I felt sure would do him the world of good, and since Christmas Day I had seen very little of Sarah and absolutely nothing of Josh. A new kind of after-Mum normality was imprinting itself on our lives, and the start of a new year seemed to signal some sort of new beginning for all of us, one in which I had a sister and a brother-in-law, and a niece, and could finally live without the pangs of guilt that had been growing stronger and stronger ever since I had left my Welsh cocoon and come back into the family orbit. As New Year's resolutions go, I only had one. There would be no looking back, no more Josh and me, just the chance to build a life without him. And work was the ideal way to achieve it.

Grange Heath School was nothing like my old one. After only three weeks in the job, I could already see that the majority of pupils here actually wanted to learn, and had ambition and career plans and drive. Those in my A level English Literature classes were there because they had chosen to be, and really wanted to be, and there were a few potential Oxbridge candidates among them, if they worked hard enough to get there. The problems of apathetic kids and council-estate hopelessness were behind me and I was facing very different challenges now, trying to get the very best out of students who would be working with me and not against me.

'Thank you, Miss Peters.' Two girls who had stayed back after the last class of the day to ask questions – when had that ever happened before? – filed out and left me to gather up my books and papers. I was smiling, and actually humming quietly to myself, as I left the room, intending to head back along the now empty corridor towards the staff room. And that was when I saw him. Arnie O'Connor.

He was waiting on a chair outside the admin office, fiddling with a piece of paper, tapping his shoes nervously against the floor tiles, and staring out through the big glass doors at the front of the school. He didn't seem to be looking at anything in particular, just gazing into the distance, which meant, luckily, that he hadn't spotted me approaching from the side.

I stopped, trying not to let my shoes squeak, willing him not to turn round. My heart was racing, pounding in my chest, and for a moment I held my breath, not wanting any slight movement to catch his attention. It had been years since I'd last seen him, that morning he'd been hurrying to the station as I walked the dog, but I was sure it was him. People change, and he certainly had – shorter hair, a fatter face, definite signs of a paunch protruding from his open jacket – but not so much that they can't be recognised. It was him all right.

I suppose I'd expected, or hoped, that he'd be long gone by now, moved away somewhere, never to be seen again. No such luck.

'Mr O'Connor.' Cheryl, the school secretary, emerged from her office, smiling and holding out a hand to guide him. 'Would you like to come through now?'

I pressed myself flat against the wall, trying to make myself invisible, but I needn't have bothered. He didn't look my way, just stood and straightened his clothing before disappearing off through a door that quickly closed behind him.

The last thing I wanted was to hang around and risk coming face to face with the man who had single-handedly, and in one drunken violent encounter, ruined my life. If it wasn't for him I would have been more open, more loving, towards Josh when we'd first met. I would have discovered sex in the right way, slowly and warmly, with the man I loved, instead of fighting off a red-faced lech with octopus hands. I might even be married and happy and—

I shook the thoughts away. This wasn't the Arnie of the past. It was the Arnie of the present. The now Arnie. And, assuming he was here because he had connections to the school, quite possibly a child, or children, at the school, I was probably going to have to meet him, deal with him, even confront him, sooner or later. Not now though. For now, I would get out of the building and as far away from him as I could, until I had let my pulse slow down and decided what to do next. Because running away into the night and going into hiding miles away was not an option this time. I wasn't a scared teenager anymore. I was an adult, in a position of authority, maybe even of power. And I could not let him put me down again.

***

'Not expecting anyone, are we?' Dad said as we heard a car pull up outside. We had just finished our dinner and were enjoying our coffee in the living room, relishing the blissful silence created by not automatically switching on the TV as soon as we sat down, something Mum had always done, with a 'Let's just catch the News, shall we?' that usually led to at least an hour of soaps.

I went over to close the curtains and shut out the cold and gloom of a dark January evening, and peered out at the street.

'Oh, it's Sarah,' I said, watching her stride purposefully up the path, which was lit only by the small lanterns on the wall to each side of the front door, and use her key.

'That's nice.' Dad put his coffee down and started to get up from his armchair. 'I'll put the kettle back on and make her a cup.'

But he'd only taken one pace forward when she came bursting into the room like a whirlwind. 'Right, you,' she said, pointing a finger at me. She wasn't shouting, but somehow the controlled, determined way she spoke worried me a lot more than if she had been. 'I want answers. And none of your lies, because I am not stupid, much as you obviously think I am. I do have eyes, you know.'

For a moment, I had no idea what she was talking about, what it was I had done. Dad had sunk back into his chair, his mouth open in shock, and Sarah just stood and stared at me, as if she was waiting for me to speak.

'I don't know what—'

'Yes, you do. Of course you do. And don't you even think of skulking out of the room. What we have to say needs to be said. Right here, right now, so Dad can hear it too. Time he realised what sort of a nasty, cheating, conniving person his precious Eve really is.'

And then I knew. Of course I did. It was written all over her tear-stained face. Sarah had found us out. After we had kept our secret for so long, she had found out now, when it was over, when I had thought we were safe, that she was safe, from ever having to know. Oh, God!

'Sit down, Sarah.' Dad had found his voice. 'I'm sure whatever this is we can resolve it amicably. I don't want any unpleasantness. Your mother never—'

'Mum's not here, Dad. But if she was, I'd want her to hear this too. All the unpleasantness, as you call it. Every sordid little detail. Because your wonderful, caring daughter here –' She grabbed my wrist and clenched it so hard her fingernails made a mark, and pushed me, roughly, down onto the sofa, '– has been sleeping with my husband.'

I didn't deny it. I didn't say anything, just shook her off me and sat biting my lip, trying to breathe as normally as my inner panic allowed.

'Sarah …'

'Oh, don't you Sarah me. As if butter wouldn't melt. Good old Eve, giving up her job and her flat and coming home to save the day, to look after Mum, and you too, Dad, and being all responsible and capable, taking care of all the paperwork, nosing around sorting out Mum's things. Give her a bloody medal! But that's not really why you came back, is it, Eve? You came back for Josh. *My* Josh. So you could be near enough to carry on your grubby little affair right under my nose. The same affair that you've been having for years. Well, at least six years, to my knowledge, and probably a whole lot longer. Ask her, Dad. Go on, ask her if it's true.'

'Sarah, I'm sure you're wrong. There must be some mistake. Eve wouldn't—'

'Oh really? Wouldn't she? Ask her then. And while you're at it, ask her where she was the night Mum died.'

We all fell silent. The thoughts churned through my mind so rapidly I hardly knew where to begin. Was she guessing?

Bluffing? Or had she got proof? And how about Josh? Had she come to me first, desperate to get to the truth, or had she spoken to him already? Shoved him down onto a chair with the scratches from her nails all over him too? Had he denied it all? Confessed? Shouted, consoled, begged for forgiveness? I didn't know what he had already said, and I didn't want to be the one to tell her everything, break her heart, bring her marriage to its knees. Not if I didn't have to, and not in front of Dad.

'Well? What have you got to say for yourself?' Dad had that voice on now, the one he had used when we were little, when one of us had broken a vase or been cheeky to Mum, or come home with a bad school report. There was no anger in it, just disappointment, which was a whole lot worse. 'Is there something you want to tell me?'

'You can't deny it, Eve.' Sarah was digging away at me again, her face just inches from mine. 'Josh has told me everything. How you chased after him, got your claws in and wouldn't let go.'

I rubbed my wrist, where she had drawn blood. If anyone had claws in this family, it wasn't me. Chased after him? Would he really have said that? Tried to blame it all on me? Or was that just Sarah's version, the only version she could allow herself to accept?

'I know all about the hotel room you were shacked up in as Mum lay here dying. I didn't think you could ever sink so low, but then you always did get what you wanted, didn't you?'

'Okay, yes.' I spoke slowly, letting the truth – or a watered-down take on it – drip out of me, word by painful word. 'Yes, I have seen Josh, from time to time. We're old friends. We have a history. He came to visit me, in Wales, and I was pleased to see him. Surprised, but pleased. He was at a conference somewhere nearby, or so he said, but I had no idea he was going to turn up like that, on my doorstep. I didn't invite him.'

'You didn't turn him away either though, did you? From your flat, or from your bed? How long, Eve? How long has this been going on?'

'It's not going on. I didn't see him often. It was never meant to be a ... well, whatever it was, it's over. Finished. I finished it. Not Josh, but me. And I haven't seen him at all since he was here with you at Christmas.'

'Oh, bully for you. Did the honourable thing, did you? A shame you didn't think of that, or of me and Janey, a bit sooner, eh? Because you may think you're calling the shots here, but you're not. Not anymore. He's mine, and I am not letting him go, okay? Not to anyone, and certainly not to you.'

'I'm not asking you to.'

'Good. And don't pretend it was some great love affair. He would have left me long ago if it was. No, it was just sex. Easy, on-a-plate sex. I know why you did it though. Revenge. That's why. Because of what we did to you, all those years ago. I took him from you and you just couldn't wait to pay me back, could you? Well, you've had your fun, and it's over. And don't you even think of contacting him. He doesn't want to see you, or talk to you. And don't you for one minute think he loves you, because he doesn't, okay? We're going to make a go of our marriage, despite you and your bloody games. So stay away. From Josh, and from me. And from Janey. Because from now on, you have no sister and you definitely have no niece. You may teach at her school, but you make damn sure she's never in one of your classes. If I hear that she is, or that you're trying to talk to her about anything not strictly school-related, I will come up to that school and tell the whole damn staffroom exactly what you've done. See how that goes down with all your new colleagues. What that does to your precious career, which – let's be honest – is all you've ever cared about anyway.'

And then she was gone, the front door slamming hard behind her, and Dad and I sat staring at each other, a huge gulf of hurt hanging between us like a cloud just waiting to burst.

'Is it true, Eve?' The pain in his voice was almost too hard to take.

'I love him, Dad. I've always loved him.'

'And that's a good enough reason is it? Where's your self-restraint, your pride? She's your sister. Your own sister.' He stood up and fetched the whisky bottle, pouring himself a large glass before tilting the bottle in my direction, his hand shaking.

'No, thanks. I'm not going to find answers in booze, am I? Oblivion maybe, which is a pretty attractive option right now, but ...'

'But what, Eve? I thought this family had hit rock bottom when we lost your mum, but this is about as low as things can get. I'm just glad she's not here to hear any of it, and me wishing she wasn't around is not something I ever thought would happen. Is it over? Between you and him? Really? Or is that just what you told her?'

'It's been over for weeks, Dad. I had thought – hoped – nobody need ever know. And, no, I'm not proud of myself, you're right there. While I was so far away, I could tell myself I wasn't hurting anyone, but coming back here made it feel very real all of a sudden. And sordid. Not what I wanted anymore. Oh God, do you think she really has had it all out with him? Have they really decided to stick together? Or is she just saying that to keep me away?'

'So you're calling your sister a liar now, are you? That's a bit rich coming from you. And as for how they decide to go on from here, that's not your business, is it? Or mine, for that matter. I just hope, for our little Janey's sake, that they can mend this, one way or another. But I'm not going to find it easy to forgive the damage you've done, Eve. And I'm damn sure Sarah isn't either. I think perhaps the sooner you find yourself a place to live the better. The last thing I want is for Sarah to stay away from this house because you're here. Or to keep Janey away. I love that little girl, and right now I want to see her a damn sight more than I want to see you.'

Chapter 24

SARAH

Josh and I moved through our lives like fish swimming side by side, usually in the same general direction but separated by invisible water and rarely touching. Sadly I was not blessed with the three-second memory they say fish have, and thoughts of what they had done, and more importantly, what they might have felt, or continued to feel, for each other, kept me awake at night.

Josh had no idea what I had discovered, no idea I had confronted Eve, or that I knew all about their affair. Why hadn't I told him? Yelled at him? Insisted he tell me everything and promise it was over? Partly fear of where it would all lead, I suppose, but also partly, I had to admit now, because I no longer really cared enough about what he did to risk losing everything I had. This was not love, this was marriage, and the two did not necessarily go together like a horse and carriage, no matter what that old song might say. If what Eve had told me was true, that she had been the one to develop a conscience and end things between them, then perhaps he was still angry with her, or still hurting, or still hopeful of a reconciliation. I had no idea which way his thinking might go, no idea what he felt, but it was not the right time to rock the boat, in case it was me who fell overboard, so I was not going to ask.

I saw Eve as little as possible, and watched Josh like a hawk, checking his stories for lies, his document case for suspicious bills, his phone for any evidence of contact. It was no way to live.

***

When Eve moved out of Dad's, I was pleased. I would be able to visit him whenever I liked without the risk of bumping into her. Sticking to calling round in school hours, when I knew she would be at work, was all very well, but it meant Janey got to see so little of her granddad and trying to make up excuses for why she hadn't seen her auntie in ages was becoming difficult. I suppose she saw her at school, but I didn't want to know about any of that and I was hoping Eve had listened to me, for once, and was keeping any contact strictly professional and absolutely minimal. Miss Peters was acceptable. Auntie Eve was not.

Eve's speedy return to Wales would have suited me fine, but she was settling into the new school and once she'd got a mortgage and decided to buy her own place, I knew it wasn't going to happen. Still, it wasn't as if I would have to see her at all, if I chose not to, now she had moved. But then I realised she would once again have a private space, not a million miles away, where Josh could go, and where their meetings could remain unseen, undetected. And that bothered me.

As the months went by, my worries lessened and I started to believe everything would be okay. Eve had a career again, a purpose in life, and I had warned her off in a way that I didn't think she would try to fight against, especially now Dad knew and so clearly disapproved. She'd always been Daddy's girl, and would hate the thought that she had let him down. I finally felt I could breathe again.

For Janey's twelfth birthday, which was coming up in September, we booked a week in Spain. It would have been wrong to keep her out of school at the start of a new school year so we went early, with Josh moaning about the exorbitant cost of fights and hotels as we were going in the school holidays, and about how many other screaming brats were likely to be there spoiling the peace and quiet because of it, but the break was something I felt we all needed.

I loved watching the two of them splashing about in the hotel pool and throwing a ball and racing each other along the sand whenever we went down to the beach, Janey's skin turning a lovely golden colour as the days progressed and Josh's shoulders peeling in the places his haphazard sun cream spreading had not quite reached. We treated ourselves to ice creams every day, in at least a dozen flavours, tried some unfamiliar Spanish seafood dishes, and ate lots of oily salads and far too many chips, and Janey was allowed to sit with us in the bar in the evenings, something she had never done at home. She spent time curling her hair and choosing what to wear, took sneaky sips of our cocktails and laughed at the comedian's risqué jokes, even though I felt sure she didn't really understand most of them. We felt like a real family again and here, away from home, it was easier to push the spectre of my sister aside, much as they had probably pushed all thoughts of me aside when they were miles away in Wales. There's something about distance that muddies the waters, wobbles the edges a bit.

Although her periods had started a few months before, that holiday was the first time I fully realised how quickly Janey was growing up, small breasts starting to fill out her bikini, her eyes following one of the dishy waiters every time he passed our table and, worryingly, his following her too. She would be a teenager before we knew it and, if my own teenage antics were anything to go by, we would have our work cut out fretting over what she was doing, and who with, in the years to come. All I wanted right then was to hang on to her childhood as long as I possibly could, and to make sure it remained a happy and secure one. And that meant hanging on to Josh.

We had booked a suite, which meant that Janey's bed, although not in a separate room, was at least tucked away around a convenient L-shaped bend that gave both her and us some privacy. Worn out from all the swimming and the late nights, she slept deeply and well, and we took advantage of that. Josh, mellowed by too much cheap booze and the effects of the sun, pounced on me most nights as soon as our clothes were off. I can't say I was always in the mood, and it was hard to keep the thoughts of him doing the same thing to my sister away, but I closed my eyes and tried to live in the moment, letting his hands do their work. By the time the week was over I felt confident that some sort of bond had been reformed, and that, for now anyway, we were solid again. The danger had passed.

***

Another Christmas was coming, the first since I had confronted Eve about the affair, and I wasn't at all sure how I was going to deal with it. Thankfully, it was our turn to go up to Josh's parents, so at least Christmas Day itself would be okay, but there was still the problem of Janey wanting to see the family all together and to spend time with Eve, and what we should do about buying her a present. I did wonder if, now the air had been cleared and the skeletons were out of the cupboard, and with a bit of distance between us, we might find a way to get past it all. How hard could it be, after all, for us to be in the same room for a few hours, having a drink, watching TV, opening presents? It had to happen sometime and, for Janey's sake, I didn't want there to be a nasty atmosphere.

I went straight round to Dad's after work one afternoon and asked him what he thought.

'I think it's time, Love,' he said. 'I can't say I'm happy about what went on, but you're both my girls and I hate to see you falling out. I'm not saying you should forget about it, but a fair bit of water's passed under the bridge now and maybe a spot of forgiveness wouldn't go amiss? Or a truce. For Christmas, at least. I know your mum wouldn't have wanted—'

'Oh, Dad. Don't!'

'Well, I still think about her and what she would have said, even if you don't. Christmas is a time for families, and for being kind to each other. Eve's not a bad girl, you know. She made a mistake, and she's sorry for it. And, to be honest, Josh was just as much to blame, but he's still welcome in this house, as long as you want him to be.'

'Of course I do. He's my husband. And Janey's daddy.'

'Then all I can say is that you're a lot more forgiving than I could ever be. Sometimes it's been all I could do to hold my tongue when I've seen him.'

'Don't, Dad, please. No trouble. I don't want it all dragged up again. And as for forgiving him – *them* – well, I'm trying, but I'm still not sure I can trust him. Or her. He's got his work Christmas party tonight at some flash hotel. Tells me he'll be staying the night so he can drink and enjoy himself, that no wives are going, that it's just colleagues and clients, and that I'd hate it anyway. But ...'

'You're not sure he's telling the truth?'

'Dad, I'm not sure I will ever be sure he's telling the truth.'

'Then call his bluff. Turn up.'

'Without an invitation? He'd kill me.'

'Turn up incognito then. Hide behind the Christmas tree, disguise yourself as a waitress, peer through the window from the car park. Whatever you need to do to see what he's really up to.'

'Dad! I'm not a spy.'

'Maybe you should be. If you want to know what's going on, you need to see it with your own eyes, but I don't think even Eve would have the brass neck to go with him to some-thing like that, in front of all his work friends.'

'No, you're probably right. And I'm not going to go crawling around in the dark looking like the neurotic wife with her nose pressed against the window. But I think I might just call Eve this evening, to make sure she's at home.'

'That's my girl!' Dad laughed and put his arms around me. 'It will all be all right, you know. And as for Christmas Day, well, Eve will be here to keep me company and to pull a cracker or two, then she's off to her pal Lucy's on Boxing Day to coo over that new little baby of hers, so let's say the day after that, when you're back from Leeds, shall we? For a good old family get-together. I'll even put up the tree this year. I don't suppose you'd like to come here, with Eve, and decorate it, would you? Sometime in the next few days? Get the box out, untangle the lights, fight over who puts the angel on top, like you used to?'

'That might be a step too far, Dad, but if Eve's keen I'll send Janey round to help her. How's that? She does miss her auntie since she moved out, and none of this is Janey's fault. I don't want her to miss out, or to start asking too many questions. So far I've just palmed her off with stories about Eve being really busy at work and with settling into her own place. But she's always asking to see her.'

'Perfect.'

So that's what we did and, although calling any of it perfect would have been a big stretch of the imagination, another Christmas went by and we all survived it. Josh got plastered and stayed out all night at his swanky hotel do, but Eve answered her phone and I could hear her TV in the background as I made some excuse about checking on what she was buying for Dad, so I knew they weren't together. We all met up at Dad's after Christmas as planned, and Josh sat with a perpetually refilled drink in his hand at the opposite end of the room from Eve, who spent most of the afternoon producing food and the evening playing Monopoly with Dad and Janey. The tree twinkled, with its little angel balanced on top, and Smoky the cat enjoyed playing with the screwed-up balls of wrapping paper. The only thing missing was Mum, but there was nothing any of us could do about that, and her absence made everything else seem petty and unimportant.

***

I was at work, rummaging in my bag for a tissue, when I felt my phone vibrating from somewhere in its depths. The bosses didn't like us to use our phones in the office and it was expected that all personal calls would be dealt with in our own time. Still, I always kept it switched on, but on silent. I think probably all mothers do, just in case.

I peered down into my bag, dreading a call from Janey's school to say she was sick or in trouble which would mean having to ask for time off to go and fetch her, but when I pulled the phone out the name illuminated on the screen was Carol. Also known as Colin! I felt my stomach do an involuntary flip and dropped the phone back into the bag unanswered. I hadn't been in touch with Colin for months, ever since that afternoon in the pub. I wanted the chance to deal with my marriage in my own way. It was obvious that Colin disapproved of Josh, despite the fact he had never met him. But I was also ridiculously afraid of my own churned-up feelings. Colin was an attractive, single man who I really needed to stay away from for fear of letting myself get dragged – or, even worse, going too willingly – into something incredibly enticing but decidedly wrong.

After a while the vibrating stopped and I carried on typing up the contract I had been working on all morning. Why was it that every few minutes I made a mistake and had to double back and correct it? My mind refused to stay on the job, so I gave up and went to make myself a strong cup of coffee. I couldn't help thinking that I should have answered his call, and wondering why he had called at all. I looked at the screen again to check if he had left a text or a voicemail, but he hadn't.

I was beginning to think it was just a one-off, probably to wish me Happy New Year or something, until he called again, a few days later. This time he had clearly chosen a time of day – around half past two – when he knew I wouldn't be working, Janey would be at school and Josh safely ensconced at the bank, but even though I had been at home, I still missed the call. Only by a few minutes, while I'd been in the kitchen boiling a rather noisy kettle, but this time I didn't have a boss breathing down my neck, and therefore no excuse not to call him back.

'Sarah!' He sounded so glad to hear me. 'Thanks for calling back. I didn't know if you ... well, if you were deliberately avoiding me, or just busy. Anyway, I've got you now. Look, could we meet up, do you think? I'd love to hear about your Christmas and just how you're doing, really. I would have liked to send you a card or bought you a little something, but then I realised that was probably not such a great idea. Questions asked, and all that. But I wanted to talk to you. There's ... well, there's something I need to tell you.'

'Oh. Sounds serious. Can't you just tell me now, on the phone?'

'You're not keen to see me then?'

'I didn't say that. Of course I am! Oh, go on then. It will be good to catch up. When and where?'

'Same pub as last time? Tomorrow lunchtime? Around one thirty? My treat.'

I sat holding the phone for ages once he'd gone. I liked Colin Grant, probably a little too much, and the butterflies were already fluttering away inside me at the thought of seeing him again. I hoped he wasn't about to tell me he had landed some hot-shot job at a hospital miles away and that I was never going to see him again, or that he had met someone and was about to get engaged or, worse still, married. I knew I had no claim on him, no right to a say in his future, but I wasn't quite ready to lose him.

***

When I got to the pub he was already there at the bar, a bottle of wine and two glasses in front of him and a menu tucked under his arm as he tried to pick everything up and head for somewhere to sit.

'Here, let me help you with those.'

He turned and smiled at me, letting me slide the menu out from the grip of his arm and pick up the bottle as he leaned in for a kiss on the cheek.

I tilted the bottle and read the label, feeling myself blushing at his touch. 'Hmm, Merlot. A good choice.' I turned my back quickly, leading the way across the pub to a free table. 'How is it that you know me so well?'

'Lucky guess,' he said, putting the glasses down and ushering me into a corner seat. 'And a good memory. It's what you asked for last time.'

I laughed and we settled ourselves down, side by side.

'Good Christmas?' he said, staring at me as if he expected me to tell him it was dire.

'Okay, I suppose. The usual family stuff.'

'And the other-woman problem? Your sister? Did you resolve it?'

'Yes and no. I went to see her, told her what I knew, and she didn't deny any of it. We had a blazing row, in front of Dad, which wasn't ideal, but I don't think she'll go near Josh again. So, it was all a bit upsetting but I survived. Still here, still married ...'

'And your husband? What did he have to say about it all?'

'Nothing.'

'Nothing?'

'I haven't spoken to him about it.' I knew it sounded stupid, and Colin's face told me he thought so too. 'Didn't mention any of it. According to Eve, it's been over for a good while now, and I decided to let it lie. I didn't want to start a war I might not win, risk my marriage, upset Janey, put her in the firing line ...'

'So he got away with it? You let him off scot-free? What on earth is wrong with you, girl? Are you a glutton for punishment, or what?'

'I knew you'd have a go at me. That's why I've kept my distance. Look, Colin, it's my marriage, my life, and I know you mean well but ...'

'But it's all sorted, right? He's going to be a good boy for evermore, never do anything like it again? For God's sake, Sarah, you've as good as given him bloody permission. You blame it all on your sister, tear a strip off her, yet say absolutely nothing to him. The man can get away with anything and you don't just put up with it, you decide not to even tell him you know.'

'But—'

'There is no but, Sarah. No possible circumstance where this can be considered right, which is why I'm going to tell you something I've known for a couple of weeks. I wasn't sure if I should say anything, but honestly, your head-in-the-sand attitude gives me no bloody choice. You need to know what he's really like, what he's capable of.'

I could feel my face drain of colour, my hand start to shake. Whatever it was, I didn't want to hear it.

'I saw him, Sarah. I saw him, at a hotel, just before Christmas. One of those huge places where they have all the corporate parties. The Georgian. I was there for a hospital-staff do, sitting at the bar in the lobby, getting a bit of air away from the party, waiting to get served, and I saw him. I wasn't a hundred per cent sure at first. I've only ever seen him in a few photos on your phone, but I followed him – *them* – up the stairs. He had his arms around this woman, his hand resting on her bum. They were laughing, staggering a bit, probably tipsy, and he took out a key and led her into one of the bedrooms. Room 112, not that that's particularly relevant, but it does mean you could probably ring and check, if you needed to. I waited a while, but they didn't come back out. And when I went back downstairs I checked the board by the door, and there it was. The bank, *his* bank, booked into the Embassy Room, while my lot were in the Carlton Room on the other side of the hotel. So it was him, Sarah. No doubt. And I bet he didn't come home that night, did he?'

I shook my head and swallowed the lump forcing its way up my throat, threatening to escape in a sob. I didn't know what to say. Would he really do it again? Cheat on me? Lie to me?

'And the woman? What did she look like? Did you hear what he called her? Could it have been her? My sister? I called her that night and she was at home, but that was around nine. I assume this was later? Was it her, do you think?'

'I have no idea, Sarah. I didn't get a close look at her, and I wasn't looking at my watch either, but does it matter? When it was, or who it was? He was taking a woman to bed, and it wasn't you.' He took hold of my hand. 'I'm sorry. That sounded much harsher than I intended. But you needed to know. How can you decide what to do if you don't have the facts?'

'Do?'

'Yes. You have to do something. This time you really have to. If you don't, he's going to walk all over you forever. And you deserve so much better.'

And then he turned my face towards him, gazed at me for a few seconds, and kissed me. Very gently, very slowly, he kissed me on the lips, and his mouth was warm and tasted of everything that Josh's didn't. Of caring and comfort, and love.

Chapter 25

EVE

The Christening went like a dream. Lucy and Rob had called the baby Nathaniel, although he had very quickly become Nat to everyone but me as I somehow couldn't quite shake off thinking of him, as I had all through Lucy's pregnancy, as Horace.

Despite my lack of knowledge of church etiquette, I managed to stand in the right place, repeat the right words, and even hold the baby for a while without dropping him headfirst into the font. The set of Beatrix Potter books I had chosen as his gift were already in pride of place in the brand-new white bookcase in his nursery as I helped Lucy change him out of his posh and rather girly lacy gown and back into his more usual T-shirt and dungarees while Rob held the fort downstairs, refilling glasses and passing round the sausage rolls.

'So? What's happening with you? We haven't seen you since Boxing Day.'

'Not a lot really. New school term, so I'm pretty busy at

work. Did I tell you I saw Arnie O'Connor? Gave me a bit of a fright but I may have to get used to it. I looked up the files in the admin office and it looks like he's got two kids at the school, a girl called Rebecca in Janey's year, and a boy, Samuel, three years older. And he lives just a few streets away from my new place, which could be awkward. He's the last person I want to bump into at the corner shop.'

'Would he recognise you, do you think?

'Well I recognised him the moment I saw him, so yes, probably. I haven't changed that much since school, have I?'

'Nope. He may still live locally, but what happened is all in the past now, isn't it? Best forgotten. Just keep out of his way. And if he's got kids, and presumably a wife, we can assume he's mended his ways.'

'I'm not sure he has got a wife actually. She's down at a different address. Separated, or divorced, but definitely living apart. Shared custody, from what I can gather. And keeping out of his way might not be possible. He's a parent and I'm the deputy head. There's bound to come a time when our paths cross, officially I mean, and I won't be able to avoid it.'

'Meet him head-on then. Seek him out, talk to him, clear the air, then it won't be hanging over you, waiting to happen. Take control. Get this thing over with, on your terms, not his.'

'Do you think I should?'

'Of course I do. You're not some frightened teenager anymore, Eve. You're a strong independent woman, and he's no match for you, believe me. Stand up to him, like you'd tell any of the kids to if they were being bullied.'

'Bullied? I'm not sure that's—'

'That's exactly what it is. The man scared you half a bloody lifetime ago and he's still scaring you now. Don't let him!'

'You're right.'

'Of course I am. I'm always right. Just you ask my Rob! Who, by the way, we have left alone down there for long enough.' She wiggled Nathaniel's feet into a pair of Thomas slippers and hugged him to her. 'Let's get this young man back to his party, and get ourselves a slice of cake before it's all gone. They're like gannets, Rob's family. Not to mention the champers. We only bought three bottles and I've heard two corks go pop already.'

***

I was feeling all warm and fuzzy when I left. Not drunk. Far from it, as I was driving myself home. But there was something about being with friends and becoming a fairy godmother, as Lucy insisted on calling me, and being all fired up to tackle Arnie O'Connor, that had put me in a happy, mellow mood. I had a good job, a nice home of my own, and for once, the future was actually looking good. Hopeful. Full of promise.

It was quite mild for January, and I drove slowly, with the window half open and the radio turned up high, singing along with the songs, even when I only knew a handful of the words. I thought I might drop in to see Dad, see how he was, have a cuppa and tell him how the christening went. It was a Sunday and I knew it was possible that Sarah and Josh might be there, but we'd got through Christmas okay, so I felt the storm had passed now and being in the same room was possible again. If there was going to be fallout it would have happened by now. Besides, Janey might be there too, and I always loved seeing her.

The curtains were still open and, as I parked outside, I could see straight in. Dad, the back of his head just showing above the top of his armchair, the TV flickering away on the wall, Smoky the cat perched on the windowsill staring out at me, his big green eyes shining like beady little emeralds in the semi-darkness. No sign of anyone else, which was probably for the best when I really thought about it.

Dad took his time coming to the door. Although Sarah had no qualms about using her key, I still preferred to knock.

'Come in, Eve, my love. Such a nice surprise. I was just watching one of those old films you used to love. Do you remember? Sunday afternoons there'd always be something on when you were kids, and we'd all sit together and watch it with a bag of sweets or a nice cake to munch on. John Wayne or James Bond, or something romantic that would get you girls sobbing into your sleeves.' He headed for the remote control on the arm of his chair and was about to push the off button.

'Well, don't switch it off on my account. We can do that now, can't we? Watch it together with a cup of tea and something to eat. Look, I brought some christening cake back from Lucy's. I couldn't eat any after all the sandwiches and sausage rolls, so I sneaked a big chunk of it into a bit of tinfoil for later, but it's too much just for me, so we might as well share.'

'Sounds lovely. I'll put the kettle on.'

'No, no, you get back to your film. I'll do it.'

He settled back into his chair and I closed the curtains around the cat, who didn't look like budging from the window-sill, and went out into the kitchen.

It was funny, but everything was still exactly where it had always been. Since we'd lost Mum he hadn't changed anything. Even Mum's favourite cup still hung alongside the others on the old wooden mug tree and when I peered behind the door there was her apron, still hanging there as if she was going to slip it on over her head and start baking at any minute. The room was clean, but it could do with a lick of paint, maybe some new blinds, but I got the feeling Dad would be reluctant to change anything. This had been Mum's domain, and he wasn't yet at the stage where he thought of it, or the rest of the house, as his to do what he liked with. They had always made decisions together and, now they couldn't, it was easier to make no decisions at all.

'So, what's the film about, Dad?' I handed him his tea and pulled out the smallest of the coffee tables from their nest of three so we had a place to put the cake plates down. 'Tell me what's happened so far.'

'Well, this girl here – the one with the dark hair – she was engaged to this fella. Bill, his name was. But now she's met this other one – Anthony, he's called – and she's fallen for him, but she doesn't know how to tell Bill, or her parents, because they've already spent a fortune on the wedding and it's in three days' time.'

'Oh dear. Tricky!'

'Anthony hasn't actually declared himself, or asked her to call the whole thing off, but you can see he's mad about her, just trying to do the decent thing, not steal someone else's girl, you know ... but she can't go through with it, the whole big white wedding thing, whatever this Anthony says or doesn't say, because she's realised Bill's not the man for her.'

I bit into my cake, my gaze fixed to the screen. It all sounded familiar. In fact, I had a feeling I'd seen the film before but, even if I hadn't, it was a sure bet that the girl would dump the boring fiancé she had never really loved enough and run off with the man of her dreams. That's what romances were all about, providing the happy ending you already knew was coming before the film had hardly begun.

'Since when have you been into rom-coms, Dad? Isn't there a good Western on one of the other channels you'd rather see?'

'Nothing wrong with a bit of love from time to time, Eve. Beats people shooting each other and chasing Indians about. And I can get soppy, I'll have you know, when the occasion demands. Besides, I'm particularly enjoying this one. It reminds me of something, a long time ago, when your mother and I ...' He stopped and shook his head, then reached for his tea and took a long slurp.

'Go on. You can't stop there. I'm intrigued now. What are you saying? That you stole Mum from another man and ran off together into the sunset?'

I was about to laugh at my own joke when I saw him nod his head.

'Yes, actually. Oh, I know you'd find it hard to imagine, but we did fall head over heels, your mother and me, almost as soon as we met.'

'In the queue for a bus, right? Isn't that what you told us? A cold, wet night, and the bus was running late, and you offered to share your umbrella.'

'That's right. But there was a part of the story we didn't tell you about. Well, a person, actually. Someone we hurt, quite badly, but when you feel the way we did ...'

'What are you saying, Dad?' Somehow, neither of us was watching the film anymore. 'That she was already with someone else?'

'She was, yes. Not just with him, but engaged to be married to him. Sean Barker, his name was. Nice enough bloke, but not right for her.'

'And you were? Right for her, I mean.'

'I thought so. And so did she, because she broke off the engagement just a week later. Dumped him for me. And her parents were not pleased, I can tell you. They'd known Sean and his family for years, the venue was booked and the invitations had gone out and everything.'

'Oh my God! So, what did you do?'

'Bided my time. All I could do really. They were hardly going to give us their blessing, were they? Change the name of the groom and go ahead with it all as if nothing had happened! No, they made us promise to stay apart. Six months, which felt like a lifetime I can tell you, but that would be long enough to bring us to our senses, or so they thought. And, if we still felt the same way after that ...'

'And did you?'

'Well, obviously, or we wouldn't be here now, would we? Or you and your sister certainly wouldn't! No, we survived it all right, missed each other, wrote to each other secretly. I think, in a way, it made us stronger, made us more sure, you know. I wish sometimes I'd been more forceful about our Sarah, when she was in such a rush to marry Josh. We all knew it was too soon, but it was their choice, wasn't it? Some time apart might have helped make things clearer, but they had a baby on the way, which changed things. Not something your mother and I had to bring into the equation. Not in those days!'

'There have always been unplanned babies, Dad. They have a lot to answer for.'

'They do indeed. Do you know, I've still got her letters somewhere. There's something special about a real hand-written letter, isn't there? Not like all this emailing and texting people do today. Your mum would probably think I was daft for keeping them, but I told you I can be a soppy old sod when the occasion demands.' He lifted a hand and wiped it across his eyes. 'Oh, I do miss her, Eve. You've no idea.'

'The letters, Dad.'

'What about them?'

'Would it surprise you to know that she kept yours too? I found them, at the back of her wardrobe, when I was sorting through her stuff after the funeral. I should have said something but I didn't want to upset you, rake up old feelings so soon after ...'

'She kept them? All these years?'

'She did.'

He gulped. 'Where are they now? You didn't throw them out, did you?'

'No, Dad, of course I didn't.'

He leaned over and turned off the TV. 'Show me, Eve. I think I'd quite like to rake up old feelings now. Good feelings. And thank you.'

'What for?'

'For not throwing them away.'

***

I had to do it. Lucy was right. Sometimes the past does have to be dragged back up, confronted, put in its place. I had to talk to Arnie, in my own time, on my own terms. I needed to know what he remembered, whether he felt any remorse at all for what he had done to me, and that I could cope with knowing I might run across him at any moment.

It wasn't really a conversation I wanted to have on school property, but I was far too much of a coward to just go and knock on his door. As it turned out, I didn't have to do either. I was leaving work early one afternoon, with nothing but a check-up appointment with the dentist – Sarah's old friend Tilly – to look forward to, and was about to climb into my car in the car park when I saw Janey walking out through the school gates with two other kids from the school. A girl, and an older boy. They were ambling along slowly, the girls chatting and giggling, the boy fiddling with a phone, the weight of too many books crammed into bags pulling their shoulders down on one side, when a tatty black estate car pulled up alongside and they clambered in. As he turned his head towards me I saw immediately that the driver was Arnie

O'Connor. And, from the shocked look that flashed across his face as his eyes locked onto mine, I knew he had recognised me too.

The car drove away. I watched it, the two small heads through the back window, and the less distinct outline of the two bigger male heads in the front. So, that must have been Arnie's children, and it looked as if Janey was going home with them. For tea? A homework session? A sleepover? Something about that unnerved me. I decided, there and then, to seek him out and have it out with him, before another member of my family got sucked into his orbit.

I came out of Tilly's surgery an hour later, with a clean bill of oral health for another six months, a request to be remembered to my sister, and Arnie still on my mind. Usually, at five o'clock in the afternoon, I would still be at work, sorting out lesson plans or running an after-school club or getting into rehearsals for a school play, but my early finish had thrown my routine and I had a hankering for some sort of horribly unhealthy takeaway, a whole box of Maltesers to myself (because my well-behaved teeth deserved a sugary reward) and a marking-free evening in front of the TV.

The chip shop was already open and doing a good trade, mainly from kids still in school uniform whose parents were probably not home from work yet and had left them a fiver to feed themselves. A plate of ham salad and a bowl of fruit was no doubt the last thing on their minds, but who was I to talk, considering my own less than healthy food choices? I joined the queue, checking the prices on the board behind the counter and rummaging in my bag for my purse.

'Eve? Eve Peters? It is you, isn't it?'

I froze, my hand halfway back out of my bag, as his hand touched my arm. The voice was exactly the same as I remembered it and, when I turned around, so was the face. Arnie O'Connor. Had he followed me here? Or was it just one of life's horrible coincidences?

'Yes.' My voice came out so small I could hardy hear my own reply.

'I thought I saw you outside the school, in the teachers' car park. Working there now, are you? I didn't have you down as a teacher. Always thought you'd end up doing something, I don't know, earth-shattering. Write a bestseller or become Poet Laureate or something. English always was your thing, I remember.'

He was smiling down at me. Arnie O'Connor, wrapped up in a big overcoat and with a stripy scarf draped around his neck, was smiling down at me, as if we were old friends, as if he knew me well enough to have worked out my whole future.

'Arnie ...'

'That's me. As I live and breathe. Well, what a surprise, running into you again after all these years. What must it be? God, we were what? Eighteen, when we last met? Half a lifetime ago! I can hardly believe it. How time flies.'

'When you're having fun?' I couldn't help the sarcasm creeping into my voice as I finished his sentence for him.

'I suppose so, yes. Well, not all of it, obviously. Life's had its ups and downs. And you? What have you been up to? You went off to uni and just disappeared off the face of the earth.

I thought the old Welsh dragons must have gobbled you up.'
He laughed out loud, putting his hand on my arm again. I
promptly shook it off.

'I've wanted to talk to you for a while, actually.' Was my
voice shaking as much as my hands were?

'Have you? What about? School stuff? Not my Becky
playing up again, I hope? I've already been called up to see
the Head once. It's not always easy, being a single dad. To a
teenaged girl, anyway. My lad's not so bad. I understand him
better, I suppose. Give him a football and he's happy. Not the
same with girls ...'

'Yes, Love?' I had reached the front of the queue and the
man in the white overalls was waiting, his big red hands
splayed out on the counter that separated us. 'What can I get
you?' Suddenly I had lost my appetite, but I ordered anyway,
watching him select a piece of battered fish with his tongs,
scoop up a mountain of chips and wrap it all up tightly in
paper.

Arnie was ordering for four. No wife, so Janey must be
staying for tea then? I hovered for a moment after paying, not
quite ready to walk away on unfinished business, and soon
we were both back outside on the pavement.

'I don't suppose you fancy coming round to mine and eating
this lot together, do you? Sam'll eat up in his room as always,
and my Becky's got a mate round, hogging the kitchen table
with all their school work. We'd get the dining room to
ourselves. It would be good to catch up, and you did say you
wanted to talk to me about something.'

My thoughts were whirring and buzzing around my head

like bees. Arnie O'Connor was the last person on earth I wanted to spend time with, but I had made up my mind to have it out with him, and an opportunity had presented itself. Having Janey nearby would stop me from shouting at him or losing my temper, or maybe even hitting him, and somehow her being there made me feel safer. What was he going to do to me, after all, if Janey and his own kids were in the house? I bit down on my lip, closed my eyes for a second or two and then nodded. 'Okay,' I said and, with the Maltesers forgotten, we walked side by side past the corner shop, along the darkening street and up to Arnie's front door.

The house was small and untidy, a pile of discarded trainers in the narrow hallway, assorted coats hooked over the end of the banisters, a bald patch in the stair carpet that looked like a cat had been clawing at it.

'Food!' Arnie called out, apparently to nobody in particular, as I followed him through into a small beige-coloured kitchen at the front of the house.

'Auntie Eve!' Janey leapt up from her place at the table and threw her arms around me. 'What are you doing here?' She pulled back and gazed up at me.

'Just wanted to have a word with Rebecca's dad, that's all. And we happened to bump into each other.'

'Auntie?' Arnie looked at us curiously.

'Janey's my sister's girl.'

'Oh, Dad, you and Janey's auntie aren't ... you know?' Rebecca's face crumpled in disgust. 'Oh, you're not, are you? Please tell me you're not. That would be gross!'

Arnie leant into a cupboard for plates and grabbed a giant ketchup bottle from the fridge. 'Not what, exactly?'

'I think the girls are worried that we might be an item. You know, together, as in a couple.' I looked at Janey. 'Which, I hasten to add, Sweetheart, we most definitely are not!'

'Almost were once though, eh, Eve?' He gave a little laugh and nudged me on the arm, as if we were old friends, as if I would agree and laugh too. 'We certainly had our moment, back in the day.'

I felt my insides churn as the memories flooded in. 'I don't think so.'

'Really? How about that party we went to? Whose was it? Not sure I remember now, but we did have a bit of fun there, I do remember that. And on the way home too!' He winked at Janey and carried on unwrapping the food.

I heard Janey giggle, before her friend grabbed at the plates. 'Dad! Stop being so embarrassing. It's not funny, and I don't think Miss Peters thinks so either.'

'Oh, sorry, Eve. Should have kept my mouth shut, apparently. Honestly, kids act like they're the parents these days. Don't do this, don't say that. Always embarrassed by what their mums and dads get up to.' He laid his hand on his daughter's head and ruffled her hair, grinning at her. 'I bet nieces are pretty much the same. Anyone would think they were the only ones allowed to have any fun. Now, who wants vinegar?'

I felt the bile rise up in my throat, and it was all I could do not to be sick. Fun? Is that what he thought it had been? I already suspected his memories of that party were going to be nothing like mine. He had whitewashed them over, convinced himself it had all been just a lark, bigging it up into some kind of two-sided teenage romance.

'Come on, Eve, we'll take ours through into the other room. Wouldn't want to upset the fun police. Call your brother down and tell him his dinner's here, will you, Bex? Or run up and get him. It's not as if he'll hear you with the volume he has his music.'

I didn't like it when he closed the door behind us. The dining room was small and square and soulless, just a dark wooden table and chairs, with worn table mats on three sides, and a brown glass bowl in the middle with two wrinkled apples in it. He plonked his plate down on one of the mats and pulled a chair out for me to sit as I did the same.

'So, what did you want to talk to me about?' I watched him sprinkle salt from a white plastic shaker all over his meal and shook my head as he offered it to me. 'Becky's been playing up at school again?'

'Not as far as I'm aware. No, I wanted to talk about us.'

'Us? I didn't know there was an us. As you've just made one hundred per cent clear to your niece.' He pushed a lump of fish into his mouth and waited for me to reply.

'You. Me. All those years ago. The party ...'

'Ah, so you do remember? I was beginning to think I'd got my girls mixed up and it must have been someone else.'

'There were others then? Other girls you grabbed and mauled and—' I gathered all my strength to say the words, pushed back my chair and stood up, my face just inches away

341

from his as I bent down to look him in the eyes. 'And tried to rape?'

I don't know what I expected. Shock, denial, anger ... What I didn't expect was Arnie putting down his fork and spluttering little crumbs of golden batter across the table as he flung his head back and laughed.

'Raped? What on earth are you talking about? We had a bit of a fumble, that's all. And not a particularly enjoyable one as you suddenly ran off in the middle of it, as I recall. Talk about leading a bloke on! A prick tease, that's what they used to call girls like you.'

'How dare you? Have you never heard of consent? Of asking before you shove your tongue down a girl's throat or your hands down her knickers?'

'Oh, come on, Eve. We'd both had a few, we were having a bit of fun. A snog, a bit of a feel, seeing where it might lead. Everyone did it ...'

'Not to me, they didn't!'

'I'm not surprised, with an attitude like that. Frigid as the bloody North Pole, that's what you were. Probably still are, as you're evidently still a Miss after all these years. Typical spinster school teacher.' Another blob of food flew out of his mouth as he raised his voice and as good as spat the words at me. 'No man good enough or brave enough to take you on?'

The teasing, jokey father he had been just moments before disappeared before my eyes, and the real Arnie was back, taunting me, that same cold hard look in his eyes that I remembered so well. The two faces of Arnie O'Connor. All charm and bonhomie on the surface, but if Arnie didn't get his way, if Arnie was challenged, he didn't like it one bit. Never had.

I couldn't stay a moment longer. Lucy had been right. I had needed to confront him, but staying out of his way from now on was definitely the right policy. The man was an absolute bastard. No wonder his wife had left. I tugged at the door and, with as much dignity as I could muster, I stepped back into the hall, pleased that I was still wearing my coat and didn't have to stop to find it on my way out.

Janey and Rebecca looked up as I passed the kitchen door.

'You okay, Auntie Eve?' Janey said, standing up and about to come towards me, an open book still in her hand.

'Fine, Janey, Love. But I won't be staying for tea.' I looked at her worried face and shivered. I really didn't like the idea of leaving her here. 'Don't be too long now. Your mum will want you home.'

She looked at me strangely. 'I'm staying the night. Mum knows.'

'I see.'

'She'll be fine, Eve.' Arnie had followed me out into the tiny hall and he was so close I could feel his breath on the back of my neck. 'Leave her alone. Don't make her a part of this ... this nonsense.' His voice dropped so only I could hear him. 'What is it? Time of the month? Hormones playing up, turning you into some kind of drama queen? Just stop making ridiculous accusations, okay? I'm no rapist and never have been. Don't make a scene.'

'A scene?' I muttered under my breath, but I managed to

open the front door and escape to the step without saying what I would have liked to. 'You really are a piece of work, aren't you?'

'And you are quite clearly off your rocker. Now go off back to your sad, lonely, pathetic little life and take your wild fantasies with you. I have my tea to finish, and if you don't want yours I'm sure my Sam can polish it off for you. He's a growing lad. Goodnight, Eve.'

The door closed firmly and, as I looked back at the kitchen window hoping to check on Janey, the blinds came crashing down too. Suddenly all I wanted to do was scream, just as I should have done the night he attacked me. Things might have worked out very differently if only I'd had the courage back then. To tell someone, to talk about it, to fight back. But it was too late for any kind of justice now.

The lights were still on in the corner shop, so I went in and bought the Maltesers, and the biggest bottle of red wine I could find. If I was going back to my sad and lonely existence, as Arnie had called it, I might as well take my pleasures where I could.

Chapter 26

SARAH

I threw him out. Well, what else could I do? I'd let him off the hook the first time. Eve had assured me it was over, and I had reluctantly decided to believe her, so what good would it have done to start creating hell over something that was already in the past? Still, I had been tormenting myself for too long with mental images of them together, raging at Eve when she was just one half of the problem, yet refusing to confront my own husband. I had been weak and cowardly, and too scared of the unknown divorce-shaped void I could be chucking myself into to do anything about it. But now he was at it again ...

I knew he must be. Colin would have had no reason to make it up, to lie to me about something so important, so damning. And men didn't disappear into hotel bedrooms with strange women in the middle of late-night parties just to have a chat or play Scrabble, did they? This time I had to say something, do something. I didn't need Colin to tell me what I already knew.

Janey was staying at her friend Becky's, so I had the whole evening and the freedom to tell him that I knew and that I wasn't going to put up with it anymore, to shout and scream, pull the suitcases down onto the bed, rip his shirts to shreds and scratch his bloody eyes out if I felt like it, without her being there to see it. It was Janey who had held me back before. Her happiness, her security, her future had been at risk, just as much as my own. But how could she be truly happy if her parents continued to live this way? I would explain things the best I could, reassure her that we both still loved her but were finding it hard to love each other right now. I'd seen the articles in magazines, the problem page letters. I knew the score. Far better to have two calm and loving homes than live in the battlefield of a fragile, hostile one. And that was what our family life had become lately. Or more like a no-man's land, where we both knew we were at war but trod carefully around each other, pretending otherwise.

Would he admit to it? Argue? Shout back? Or leave quietly? Try to turn the tables and ask me to leave instead of him? I sat and nibbled my nails waiting for his key in the lock, the tread of his feet in the hall.

He was on time, for once, shrugging off his coat and shoes, going straight to the whisky bottle in the cabinet. There was no hello, no peck on the cheek, no 'How was your day?' Even those niceties had gradually died away.

'Josh.'

He turned towards me, took in the look on my face and plonked himself down in the armchair on the other side of the room.

'What's up?'

'If I said The Georgian Hotel to you, Room 112, what would you say?'

I watched him take a drink from his glass, staring into its amber depths, then gulping down far more than was necessary, before he looked back up at me.

'Wasn't that the place I went to for the staff Christmas party? And 112? That may have been my room number. I don't know. How am I supposed to remember something like that?' He shook his head. 'What about it anyway?'

'It wasn't your room number, actually. I found your receipt. You know, in that file you keep under the desk. I've found quite a lot of things in there lately. But no, you didn't stay in Room 112 the night of the party. You stayed in Room 245. Officially, anyway, as that's the room you booked and paid for. Whether you actually slept in it is another matter.'

He was looking decidedly uneasy. 'I have no idea what you're talking about. In fact, I've had a long day and I'm going for a bath, so can we leave this, whatever it is, for another time?' He started to stand up. 'Where's Janey?'

'She's at Becky's, so she won't be sleeping here tonight. And neither will you.'

'Pardon?'

'I know, Josh. About the other woman. The woman whose room you snuck into that night and probably didn't come out of again until morning. I'm not stupid. I know this isn't the first time, and it probably won't be the last. And it wouldn't surprise me at all if it was Eve. Oh, yes, I know all about Eve ...'

I saw him visibly flinch at the mention of her name.

'I have no idea what you're talking about. What about Eve?'

'Your affair, relationship, fling – whatever you choose to call it. I know. And I've known for a while, so don't even try to deny it. Eve's told me everything.'

He gripped the arm of the chair and sat back down. I don't think I had ever seen him thrown so quickly off balance, sitting there pale-faced, gazing straight ahead as if he had been robbed of the power of speech.

'Well, aren't you going to say something? Deny it, at least, like you usually do when I accuse you of anything, even if it's just not putting the sodding bins out? Knock me back with some rubbish about me being a nag or paranoid, or just plain wrong? Not that there'd be any point, because you know it's true this time. And you know that I know ... everything.'

'Sarah ...'

'Yes? Come on, Josh. Let's hear your version, shall we? How Eve's making it all up, how she's never forgiven you for leaving her all those years ago, how she's just being spiteful, out for revenge. Come on, tell me you haven't been near her, haven't slept with her, that you don't love her and never have. I'm ready for your lies.'

'Seems you've made up your mind already, so whatever I say you're not going to listen, are you?'

'Oh, I'll listen. I may not believe a word that comes out of your mouth but I will listen. I like a good fairy story.'

'Okay, so I did see Eve a few times, when she was living in Wales. It was hardly the love affair of the century. I shouldn't have, and I'm sorry. It was stupid of me, and wrong. Is that what you want? An admission, an apology?'

'It's a start, but no, what I actually want is for you to go. Leave. Get out of here. Out of this house, out of this family.'

'Look, let's not overreact here. The thing with Eve … it was over before it began really. A few meetings, meals out, a kiss and cuddle after we'd had a drink or two. I was away from home and she was … just there. It meant nothing. I haven't seen her, been alone with her, for months.'

'Oh, bully for you! I should be grateful, I suppose. And how about the woman at the hotel? Was that Eve too? Or is there some other poor soul you're stringing along nowadays?'

He couldn't look at me. 'What woman? Where are you getting this load of old rubbish from? I don't know about any woman, or what room I'm meant to have been in. I stayed over, like I said I was going to, so I wouldn't have to drive home, so I could have a few drinks.'

'Not all you had, by all accounts.'

'What bloody accounts? Who's been filling your head with all this stuff?'

'You deny it then?'

'Doesn't seem to matter what I say, you've made up your mind. Guilty, with bloody knobs on.'

'That's about it, yes. I can't do this, Josh. I can't put up with the way things are. I never really know where you are, what you're doing, or who with. I can't trust you anymore. If I ever could.'

'Oh, for fuck's sake.'

'Swear as much as you like, but this marriage isn't worth

the paper it's printed on. It isn't worth trying to save. You don't love me. I don't think you ever really have. If I hadn't got pregnant that first time ...'

'We would never have got together. Do you think I don't know that? That I haven't wondered how different things could have been, for both of us? But we made our decision, and we've made the best of it, haven't we? Made a life, a home, Janey ...'

'It's not enough. I want you gone.'

'And where exactly do you expect me to go? This is my house.'

'No, it's *our* house. You may be the main earner around here but that doesn't give you special rights. It's my house, my home too, and our daughter's. And we're not going anywhere. In fact, let's see what the divorce courts say, shall we?'

'Divorce? Let's not be so hasty here. We can sort this out. We don't need to get divorced. I can't get divorced. I'm a Catholic.'

'When it suits you.'

'What's that supposed to mean?'

'When did you last go to church? Confess? Pray? And why's there a condom in your wallet? Doesn't sound much like a good Catholic boy to me.'

'What have you been doing looking in my wallet?'

'Is that it? Is that all you can say? Because that condom's not there for me, is it? No, Josh, this is it. The end. We're over. Your suitcase is out on the bed. Pack a few things and go. We can decide about the finer details later, when we've got a bit of space between us. I want you out of here, or things will get a darn sight messier, believe me.'

'Meaning?'

'Meaning I'll fight you for every penny you've got, house, pensions, the lot. And tell your precious Catholic parents what you've been up to, not to mention your boss.'

'Oh, play dirty, why don't you? What do you want here, Sarah? Blood?'

'If I have to. Or you can give in to the inevitable. Get out of here, off to Eve's or a hotel, or a park bench for all I care. Wherever you can wriggle off to like the worm you are. And maybe then we can sort things out, amicably, from a distance, like civilised adults.'

'You bitch.'

'Really? I'm the bitch? I'm the one in the wrong here? I don't think so, Josh.'

'You've changed.' He looked at me, the hurt burning in his eyes.

'Yes, I think I probably have. I've grown up. I've realised no one's going to fight for me. I have to do it myself, look after myself, stand on my own two feet for once. And I can only do that without you here messing with my head. Because you've changed too, and I don't like what I see. Go and pack, Josh, please. It's the only way.'

He stood up, reluctantly, stopping in front of me as he crossed the room towards the stairs, and tried to take my hand. I tugged it away.

'No, don't touch me. I don't know where those hands have been.' I tried to hold back the sob that rose up in my throat as I shrank back into the sofa. 'I never want you to touch me again.'

'Sarah ...'

'No. No more. Just go.'

'But what about Janey? How will we ...?'

'I'll tell her. Oh, don't worry. Not the details. She doesn't need to know what a rat her father truly is. I wouldn't do that, hurt her, or try to come between you. You're still her dad and I wouldn't want to wreck how she feels about you. And of course you can still see her, whenever you like. Just not here, okay? No covering things up. No playing happy families. She needs to know the truth, or a version of it at least. That our marriage is over.'

'It'll cost. Me living somewhere else. A bed and breakfast, a bedsit. I won't be able to cover the bills for two places. Not for long. You do know that?'

'We'll worry about that side of things later. Or let the lawyers worry about it for us. For now, I just want us to take the first steps, to agree to separate, to accept that we can't stay together, live together, anymore. Please, Josh, don't make this any harder than it already is.'

He went quietly, in the end. Took his work clothes, his razor, his toothbrush, and went. I didn't know where he would go. I don't suppose he knew himself.

The house felt different, empty, silent, after the front door closed behind him. I still didn't know if it had been Eve that night at the hotel. Eve, or someone else. What difference did it make in the end? I wasn't sure I cared anymore.

***

Janey didn't take it well. Of course, she blamed me. Her precious father had gone, while she was out and without saying goodbye, and that had to be down to me. Something I had said or done. Dads didn't just leave home for no reason, did they? I did my best to explain, which wasn't easy without telling her about his relationship with her own auntie and God knows who else, but I was determined not to do that. Not to run him down, slag him off, burden her with my own feelings of hatred and betrayal. I didn't want to put her in the situation where she was expected to take sides, although she did anyway, and it wasn't my side she took.

Janey made it clear she no longer wanted to spend time with me. She took to going home with her friend Becky after school, eating there, coming home late with her homework already done so I couldn't even offer to help her with any of it, and hiding away in her room until bedtime.

After a few nights in a hotel, Josh had taken on a small rented flat not far away, above a florist's shop. Not dissimilar to the place we used to have over the dry cleaner's, I guessed, but smaller. Not that I went to see it, but he gave me the address in case of emergencies and, according to Janey, who was round there like a shot at the first opportunity, it was very plain and pretty much empty. Just a double bed, a small table with two wooden dining chairs, and a sofa too short and too tatty for her to sleep on with any degree of comfort. It didn't stop her asking to stay over, but Josh did at least have the sense to tell her that might not be such a good idea, not until he'd bought a few things to make it feel more like a home.

Dad was shocked when I told him what had happened, and yet I could sense a sort of virtual pat on the back, as if he felt I had finally done the right thing. 'Things will work out, Love,' he said, pouring me a second cup of tea. 'You've still got your job and a roof over your head, and Janey. And if paying the bills becomes a problem, please tell me. I have a little put by.'

'No, Dad. Josh got us into this, and it's Josh who's going to have to pay. And I don't just mean in money. He'll regret what he's done, now he's back in some pokey flat on his own.'

'And is he on his own? No woman on the scene?'

'I have no idea. I did wonder if Eve ...'

'Oh, no, Sarah. I don't think so. She told us that was over and done with. I don't think she would lie.'

'Wouldn't she? Well, we'll see, won't we?'

'Have you told her? That he's gone?'

'What? Give her the chance to go running right back to him? Oh, no. My marriage, or what's left of it, is none of her business. I can't stop him telling her, but I'm not doing it. It'd be like dropping a big fat present right in her lap.'

'Oh, Sarah.' He shook his head, sadly. 'I'm so sorry, Love, that it's come to this. This can't be easy for you. Or for our Janey. Must have hit her hard.'

'It has. But she'll get over it. I bet half the kids in her class live in some sort of fractured, patched-together family. Divorce, separation, step-parents. It's almost the norm these days. Not that that's what I would ever have chosen for her, but it is what it is. I can't go back now.'

'No, Love, you can't. Onwards and upwards, eh?'

I forced a smile and gave him a hug. 'Thanks, Dad.'

'What for?'

'Not judging me. Not saying you told me so, all those years ago. I gave it a go, Dad, my best shot, and I did love him. I really did. Shame he never felt quite the same way.'

'Well, here's to new beginnings,' he said, raising his cup and chinking it against mine as if we were drinking champagne instead of PG Tips.

'New beginnings,' I echoed, before grabbing my coat and heading back home to see if Janey was going to grace me with her presence after school.

***

It was Sunday morning and Janey had finally stopped over for the night at Josh's, in a brand-new sleeping bag on a blow-up bed which I'm sure she would later have great pleasure in telling me was so much better than her own bed and cosy duvet at home. She'd be wanting to move in with him soon, and I had no idea how I was going to deal with that. I just hoped Josh would be sensible enough, and fair enough, to tell her it wouldn't work. He was not the sort who would manage to look after himself particularly well, let alone a teenaged girl. Food shopping, cooking, laundry, the ironing, not to mention the moods, the periods ...

I lay in bed and stretched my arms and legs out, wriggling my fingers and pointing my toes, making one of those happy, good-to-be-alive star shapes that Eve and I had so loved making when we were kids, but there was no elation, no surge of hope, no wonderful feeling that anything was possible. Life had got in the way – real life – and the magic just didn't happen.

I had the house, and the double bed, to myself, and nothing to get up for. It should have been bliss, but a strange feeling of emptiness had descended and all I could think of was how alone I was. My mum dead, my husband gone, my daughter hardly speaking to me, a sister I could no longer trust. Dad did his best but there were only so many shoes he could fill.

I dragged myself up and into the shower, letting the water stream over my hair and face until it ran cold, then dressed in jeans and a floppy jumper and forced a bowl of cereal down. The scene from the window was one of bare trees, light mist, a layer of frost still carpeting the ground. I always found winter depressing. Perhaps everything would look better come spring. I gazed at my gaunt face in the hall mirror. Perhaps *I* would look better come spring. But I was on my own now and the sooner I got used to that the better.

Chapter 27

EVE

A date! At last, something to stop me obsessing over Arnie and pining over Josh. It had been years since I had been on a real live date, spent any real quality time with a man who wasn't either gay or Josh. In fact, I had *never* been on a date with a man who wasn't either gay or Josh!

Seb Barnes was a science teacher at the school, tall, dark and handsome, happily divorced, and a couple of years younger than me. My first thought when he asked me out for dinner was that he'd made a mistake, and my second was that I couldn't believe my luck. It was only when I got to thought number three that I started to worry. I was scared. I had no experience of dating, of what was the norm these days. Would he expect me to tell him all about myself, when I knew there were parts of my history I would much rather keep to myself? Should I offer to split the bill? And what happened at the end of the evening? Go our separate ways, or share a taxi, or would he be all chivalrous and want to see me to my door? And then what? A kiss on the cheek, or on the lips, an invitation to come in for coffee, or more? Should I avoid the garlic and not drink too much, and choose my underwear carefully, just in case? I felt like some silly teenaged virgin, frightened to do the wrong thing, and of the possible consequences if I did.

Of course there was no such thing as the wrong thing. Or the right thing. Every man, every date, every relationship, was different, and all I had to do was go with the flow, see what happened, what I felt. He might not even want to kiss me. He might spend an hour in my company and be desperate for an escape route for all I knew. And he was no Arnie O'Connor. I had to remember that. Any stupid lingering fears of being pressured or forced had to be pushed away now, or I would surely die an old maid!

I had changed my outfit four times, the discarded dresses and jackets and jewellery littering my bed, before I felt reasonably satisfied with how I looked in a simple white top and a pair of nicely shaped, soft blue trousers. I'd been to the hairdresser's after school, which wasn't strictly necessary but had given me a much-needed confidence boost, and I had the perfect pair of mid-heel shoes and a brand-new bag lined up in the hall and ready to go. Only the make-up to deal with now!

When the doorbell rang, the sudden unexpected sound sent my hand slithering away from my eyelashes, leaving a streak of mascara across my cheek. 'Oh, bugger!' I grabbed for a wipe and did my best to sort out my face before heading for the door.

The last person I had expected to see was Josh.

'Oh!'

'Is that all you can say?'

'Okay, then. What are you doing here?'

'Do I need a reason? Look, let's start again, shall we? Hello, Eve. I just wanted to see you. And to talk to you about something. Can I come in? Please?'

'Well, no, not really.' My heart had started to speed up. Josh had never been here, to my new flat, before, and a part of me just wanted to fling my arms around his neck, cover him in kisses and drag him inside. But we were past all that, weren't we? What did he want anyway? And why now? This was such bad timing I could scream. 'I'm about to go out. Look at me. New top and everything ...'

'I never saw anything wrong with the top you've already got.' He looked at the outline of my breasts and smiled, the old twinkle I knew so well appearing in his eyes. 'And as for the everything ...'

'Stop it! I don't have time for your nonsense. I told you, I'm going out.'

'I see.' He was pulling his disappointed, puppy-dog face. I looked down at my feet and tried to resist it.

'What do you see, Josh?'

'No time for me these days, eh? And out with who, I wonder?'

'With whom!'

'Oh, don't come the English teacher with me! Who the hell ever says whom?'

'Okay, sorry.' I tried not to laugh.

'Fifty pence, Eve. One for every sorry, remember?'

'Oh please, don't play the nostalgia card. We're older and wiser these days, and things are different now. Very different. We're finished, remember? You're talking to the wrong sister. The one who is allowed to go out with anyone she likes without needing permission from you. Go on, go home to your wife.'

'You haven't heard then?'

'Heard what?'

'That she's chucked me out. Because of you, I might add, so you do owe me a few minutes at least.'

'Because of me? Come on, Josh, she's known about us for ages, and I thought you'd talked about it and decided to put it all behind you. And you blamed it all on me, of course. You even told her I meant nothing to you. So I don't see why I owe you anything at all.'

'What? Whatever you may think, we have never talked about you. About *us*. She's never said a word to me, about any of it. I had no idea she knew. The first I heard about it was three weeks ago, when she as good as slung me out on my ear. Told me you'd confessed all, bloody ages ago. I just wish one of you had had the decency to tell me what was going on.'

'Decency? Oh, Josh, come off it! Looks like she's played us off against each other here. I thought you'd told her everything, and now you think I did.'

'Bitch!'

'Is she? I think she's probably just a woman who's been trying to save her marriage, any way she can.'

'Well, she's not doing that now.'

360

'She's really thrown you out?' I was very aware that we were still one each side of the door, and that he was expecting me to let him come in. I also knew I was wavering, already wondering if I should call Seb and cancel our date, or tell him I was going to be late. 'You mean permanently? As in you've split up?'

'Yes.'

'So, why now? What's changed?'

'I don't know. Some busybody's filled her head with lies.'

'About?'

'God knows. Me and you, in some hotel room, apparently. I wish! To be honest, I don't know what she's talking about, but will she listen? Anyway, I've got myself a little bedsit place for now. Pokey as hell. And she's talking divorce.' I saw his foot start to edge over the threshold. 'Oh, come on, Eve, let me come in. I need someone to talk to.'

'Well, it's not going to be me.' No, I couldn't do this. 'Not now. I'm going out, I told you, and I'm late.'

'When then?'

'I don't know, Josh. Things are okay between Sarah and me at the moment. Well, I rarely see her, and we'll never be as close as we once were, but we're not at loggerheads, and we're civil to each other. We're finally building bridges. She certainly hasn't told me anything about you splitting up, and neither has Dad but ... well, I'm not sure I want to rock the boat again. Since losing Mum I've realised how much I need my family. I actually want to make things up with my sister, even if it's only one tiny step at a time, and I'm sick of being the bad guy. So I think it's best we keep our distance, don't you?'

'No, I don't. We have a connection, you and me, and you know it. Always have, always will. Come and see me, Eve. Or we'll go out somewhere for a drink. Please. When you're not so ... busy. Here, let me leave you my new address.'

'I don't need it, Josh. I'm not getting into all this again.'

'Call me then. Same number.'

I looked up into his eyes and almost gave in. 'Maybe.'

He turned to walk away. 'Enjoy your evening,' he said. 'I hope he knows how lucky he is.'

Oh, God! Why did I have to still feel this way? I closed the door and leaned against it for a moment, waiting for my breathing and my pulse to fall back into their usual rhythm. How was I meant to go out with another man now, act as if nothing had happened, knowing that Josh wanted to see me, spend time with me, talk to me, knowing that the man I had loved all my adult life but couldn't have was finally free?

***

Seb did everything right. He didn't tut at me for being twenty minutes late, he helped me out of my coat and found somewhere to hang it, rested a hand on my back as we walked to our table, held out my chair as I sat. He was good company, filling my silences with chat and questions and laughter. I liked him. We seemed to have a lot in common, from our teaching backgrounds to our taste in films and books. We even ordered the same food and happily shared a bottle of chilled Chardonnay which we both declared to be so delicious that Seb ordered another.

We sat at the table long after we had eaten, finishing the wine, savouring our coffee. His fingertips brushed against mine across the table, perhaps on purpose, I wasn't sure, and it felt comfortable, non-threatening, friendly and warm. I didn't pull my hand away. But no sparks flew. Oh, I wanted them to. Wouldn't that be wonderful? To find what I needed in another man, a handsome, eligible, uncomplicated man who I could start all over again with, take home to meet Dad, build a new life with? But it wasn't going to happen. I knew it wasn't, because all I had been able to see whenever I'd looked tentatively into my future was a big Josh-shaped hole that now, suddenly, I felt I might be able to fill again. With Josh.

It was a mad thought, but I knew it was at least remotely possible, if I was prepared to wait. It wouldn't, couldn't happen overnight. I had meant what I'd said to Josh about the importance of family, about wanting to put things right between Sarah and me, but if I just let things settle for a bit, allowed Sarah time to grieve for her marriage, go ahead with her divorce, or maybe – because I couldn't rule it out – decide to change her mind and have him back ...

It wasn't my place to interfere, to dive in there and influence things, and I knew I mustn't. I had done that before and it had led to nothing but heartache. If their life together was really over, if Josh wanted to contact me, wanted me back, then it would happen, in its own time, and for now that was enough. I had no way of knowing how things might play out but if Josh and Sarah took that final step and went their separate ways forever, then everything would be different. We could start again if we wanted to, openly, without having to sneak around cheating or hurting anyone; perhaps we could even live together, have children together. I could be Janey's stepmum, as well as her auntie. How strange that would be!

But, of course, I was getting ahead of myself. I pushed the maelstrom of crazy thoughts aside and turned my attention back to Seb. Having paid the bill and flatly refused to allow me to contribute my share, he retrieved my coat and we walked outside together.

'Can I walk you home?' he said, linking his arm through mine. I had planned on getting a taxi and disappearing, enigmatically, into the night, but it wasn't all that far and the walk might help to clear my head.

'If you're sure.'

'Of course.'

We walked side by side but not so close as to feel anything other than comfortable, our feet falling into companionable step. Outside the flat, he turned me towards him and smiled, probably at my red nose as it was a lot colder out than I had realised. 'I've enjoyed this evening, Eve. Maybe we might do it again?'

I hesitated. The last thing I wanted was to lead him on, but I had enjoyed myself too.

'Only if you let me pay next time.'

'I could probably agree to that.' He pressed his cold lips to my cheek, gently, and watched as I fumbled for my key. No pressure, no expectation of more. 'See you at school.'

'Yes, see you. And thanks.'

'My pleasure,' he said and, once he'd seen me open up and step inside, he ambled away into the darkness.

Oh, how I wished he was gay. Another Simon Barratt in my life was exactly what I needed. A friend I could talk to, have fun with, feel safe with. But Seb wasn't gay, and I wasn't looking for the kind of relationship he'd probably want if we went on with this ... this thing. No, I'd have to tell him. Sooner, rather than later. But, for now I felt happy, and just a little bit tiddly.

I still remembered Josh's number. Of course I did. Like every line on his face, every inch of his skin, I knew it off by heart. But was I going to use it? That was the question.

***

Dad was sixty-five that spring. He had decided he wasn't quite ready to retire, and his manager at work had been persuaded to let him stay on for another year at least, but only if he agreed to go part-time. It seemed like the perfect solution. He still moped about a bit when left by himself at home for too long, but staying on in the office part-time would help to keep him busy and let him get used to a more gradual change.

Of course, we had a party. I took Dad down to the library on that Saturday afternoon, pretending I needed help researching a few bits to start a family tree, a project which he seemed eager to get involved in, and while we were out Janey threw herself into decorating his house with balloons and banners, and Sarah sneaked in a huge cake and laid out all the plates of food.

I knew now, officially, about the separation, and that Josh had not been invited to join us at Dad's.

'If I said 112 to you, would it mean anything?' she had said, staring at my face, the day she'd told me.

'No. Should it?'

'Or The Georgian Hotel?'

'Isn't that the posh place where Lucy's mum and dad had their ruby wedding?'

'No idea. Did they?'

'Sarah, what are you talking about?'

'Nothing. Just checking something, that's all.'

She turned away, seemingly satisfied, and the subject – not that I really knew what it was – was dropped. Since then we had managed to tiptoe around each other, not talking about Josh at all, carefully avoiding the elephant in the room, and I had resisted the urge to call him, biding my time just in case there was some long-term hope for us and for all this mess to finally end.

I had to admit I was a little disappointed he hadn't tried again to contact me, but that had always been Josh's way. Turn up, full of passion and promises, then disappear again for weeks at a time. I expected he was busy at work, and with learning to cope with his own place now there was no wife there to run a hoover round the carpet or an iron over his shirts. And looking after Janey every other weekend wouldn't be easy either. Teenaged girls could be tricky, as I knew only too well, having been one myself!

There weren't all that many guests at Dad's party. Far fewer than had come to Mum's funeral, but then many of them had been her friends, rather than his, and we'd not seen most of them since. This party was a more joyous occasion and we'd invited a few of Dad's colleagues from work, old friends of both sexes from a bowls club he used to go to but had slipped away from lately, some couples they'd met when Mum had dragged him off to ballroom dancing, and a few neighbours, including Tilly's parents from next door. Enough to fill the living room and to spill over into the kitchen, where most of the men seemed to gather, with one or two holding cigarettes and braving the garden.

I sat in an armchair, nursing a cup of tea and watching Janey. I hadn't seen much of her lately, except in passing at school, and hardly at all since that day in Arnie O'Connor's kitchen. It was lovely to see how much she was growing up. Although still my beloved niece who was happy to throw her arms around me excitedly when I'd arrived back with her unsuspecting grandad, she was now also a tall, pretty, confident teenager. When had that happened? Instead of hiding away upstairs or spending all her time playing with the cat, she stayed in the room with the adults, helping to pass food around and replenish cups and glasses. When we opened a bottle of champagne, with a loud pop that made everybody either squeal with delight or jump out of their skins, Sarah even offered Janey a small glass, which she sipped eagerly, giggling as the bubbles went up her nose.

'Shall we have some music?' Dad said, when the conversation started to flag and, for the first time since Mum's death, I saw him open the cupboard doors at the bottom of the sideboard, pull out the old boxes of records and flick through them, keen to keep the party going with a swing. He didn't pick out the Tom Jones he'd shed a tear over that day I'd worked out that he'd been the one to write the letters, but everybody swayed a little to some old Beatles favourites and joined in with the words of 'Lily the Pink'.

It was good to see him enjoying himself. And it gave me hope for myself, I suppose, a feeling that whatever pain came, there could be a recovery from it, and happiness again, given time.

By seven o'clock, they had all drifted away and Dad sat in his chair with a cake stain on his jumper and a contented look on his face as Janey finally went in search of the cat, who had been hiding from all the noise and bustle under Dad's bed, and Sarah and I set to work on clearing up.

'That went well, didn't it?'

I sloshed the plates around in a bowl of hot soapy water, noticing how shabby and cluttered everything was looking, and resolved to suggest Dad got himself a dishwasher, or even someone in to clean once a week, now he didn't have anyone to keep things in order in the kitchen. 'Yes, it did. Good to see Dad having fun again. And you, Sarah. I hadn't realised how long it's been since I've seen you smile.'

'Well, what do you expect when ...' She stopped and let the silence fall around us. 'I'm sorry, Eve. I've spent so long hating you, and blaming you, but what good did that do me? It's time to let it go, isn't it? What's happened is in the past. It's not as if we can change it. And Josh may not be my husband for much longer, but you ... well, you're still my sister.'

'I hope so. I really do.' I wiped my wet hands down the front of my trousers and held my arms out to her for a hug, not at all sure if she would accept it, but she did.

'You'll be okay without him, Sarah.'

'Like you are, you mean?'

'Maybe he wasn't right for either of us in the end.'

'He could have been though, couldn't he?' She pulled back from me, neither of us yet comfortable enough to stay pressed together for too long. 'If he'd just met one of us. If we hadn't both ended up falling for him the way we did. He wouldn't have had to choose then, would he?'

'I'm not sure he ever did choose, did he? The choosing was done for him, and even then he tried to hang on to us both.'

'For different reasons, though. I got the baby and the house and the respectability of a ring on my finger, and you got the sex. When, in all probability, it should have been the other way round! I just wanted the excitement really, not all the nappies and the domesticity. Don't get me wrong, I wouldn't be without Janey for the world. Not now she's here. But what I really wanted was what you had, of course, no matter what that might have been. I always was jealous of you, you know. Wonderful Eve, Mummy and Daddy's golden girl. The favourite. You had it all. The brains, uni, the glittering career ...'

'I would have swapped it all for the right man, marriage, babies.'

'I'm not sure that's totally true. You love your job, and it would have been such a waste. Like my life's been. Oh, Eve, what have we done? Thrown away the lives we should have had, chasing dreams.'

'Chasing Josh, you mean!'

'It's not too late though, is it? For you to meet someone,

get married, have babies. And for me to find a bit of self-respect, learn to live on my own, maybe get a better job?'

'Never too late. Life's what you make it really, isn't it? In fact, I have met someone. It's early days but ...'

'Oh, I'm glad. What's his name? What does he do? Is he nice?'

I thought about Seb. Yes, he was nice. Very nice. We'd been out a few times now, just as friends, me always cutting things short before they went too far, but I was warming to him. Maybe all those fireworks I had felt with Josh would never come again, but were they what I really needed? How about trust and security and the kind of cosy settled life Seb could give me? Although he wasn't pushing for it, I knew Seb wanted more from me. And I knew I could do a lot worse than to give it to him, but still something held me back.

If only Sarah weren't my sister ...

'I'm going to Becky's tonight, Mum.' Janey had appeared at the kitchen door, her voice cutting into our conversation and stopping it dead, which was probably just as well. 'Is that okay? Her brother's just passed his test so he said he can drop me home tomorrow.'

I saw Sarah sigh, her shoulders slump as she nodded her head. 'Yes, of course. Let me just finish off here and we'll go home and pack your bag, okay?'

'I'm not sure I believe her anymore,' she said quietly, as Janey went off to say goodbye to her grandad. 'I bet she's off to her dad's. That's why she's trying to stop me going over to her friend's place to collect her in the morning, because she won't be there. Just won't admit where she's really going in case I try to stop her. I swear she loves him a lot more than she's ever loved me.'

'Rubbish! She adores you.'

'If you say so. Now, let's find some tinfoil and wrap up a chunk of that cake. If I'm about to spend another Saturday night on my own, I might as well have something wicked to look forward to, even if it's just a bloody great pile of calories! And who cares if I get fat? It's not like anyone's going to see me naked, is it?'

Chapter 28

SARAH

They say kids can go off the rails a bit, don't they? If things change at home, if they feel their world is tilting and there's nothing they can do to right it. They start to stay out late, drink, hang about with the wrong crowd, tell lies. Pushing the boundaries, I suppose, trying to get some sort of revenge or control, asserting their own right to choose. When it happened to us – to Janey and me – I knew exactly why she was doing it. It was to punish me for throwing her precious dad out of the house, for not doing everything possible to keep our little family together. It would never occur to her to blame him, or to look beyond our separation for its reasons. Josh was living alone in a tiny flat while I kept the house. Josh didn't want any of this, Josh was happy to come home if only I would let him. Josh, in other words, could do no wrong.

I remembered only too well how Tilly and I had sneaked about, and Eve too probably, changing our clothes after we'd left the house, hiding alcohol in our rooms and our handbags, going to parties that Mum and Dad would never have wanted us to go to, experimenting with boys – or girls in Tilly's case. And look where that kind of behaviour had got me …

I didn't want that for Janey. Yes, she was growing up fast, but she was still my little girl. I wanted her to trust me, to talk to me, to love me enough to tell me what she was thinking, feeling, doing …

'No, Sarah. She's not here. Why would she be? It's not my turn.' Josh stood at the open door to his flat, his crumpled pyjamas and equally crumpled hair making it pretty obvious I had just got him out of bed. It was eleven o'clock on a Sunday morning and the little backstreet florist's shop that Josh lived above was closed, its blinds down, the peeling blue paint around its windows matching that on Josh's door.

I'd had a sudden urge to go clothes shopping at one of the big malls, and to take Janey with me, splash out on something to cheer ourselves up, have a nice lunch out. I didn't think Josh would mind. He'd had her all day Saturday, and had no doubt filled her up with takeaways and too many biscuits and let her stay up late. That's what dads did, and it was time I balanced things up a bit and showed her she could have a good time with me too. But she wasn't there.

'So where is she? You've surely not let her set off for home by herself this morning? Without even getting up to make her any breakfast?'

'Sarah, she's not here. She hasn't been here. I told you, it's not my turn.'

'I thought we'd given up on turns a long time ago. If she wants to come here, I let her.'

'Well, she didn't come here, okay? I've not seen her since last weekend.'

I felt a cold fear rush up and over me. 'But ... she said she was staying here last night. She took a bag, her night things, I gave her a fiver ...'

Josh turned and ran back up to the flat, coming back within seconds clutching his mobile. 'We'd better call her then, hadn't we? For fuck's sake, Sarah, how could you let her just disappear? And she's been out all night? She could be lying in a ditch somewhere for all we know.'

'But she said—'

'Call yourself a mother? No wonder she wants to spend so much time with me.'

'So where is she then, Mister Perfect Father? Because she doesn't seem to be spending time with you, does she?' I knew I was starting to shout. 'Looks to me more like you're providing a very convenient alibi for whatever she's really up to.'

'She's not answering.' He took the phone away from his ear and shook his head. 'Should we call the police? And what do you mean about an alibi? Where do you think she is?'

'I don't know. At a party, or with some boy? She's a teenaged girl, Josh. It's what teenaged girls do. Sneak about, cover their tracks, lie ... And no, I don't think she's in a ditch, or that this is something for the police to worry about. It's for *us* to worry about. Both of us. Because she's playing us, and if you hadn't split this family, she wouldn't be up to these sorts of tricks.'

'Oh, here we go again. Right, if you're so bloody clever, tell me what we're meant to do next. Send out a search party?'

'Well, we should look for her, if that's what you mean. And

I know exactly where we should start. At the O'Connors'. She spends half her time there these days, and if anyone will know where she is it's that Becky girl. In fact, I'd bet any money that wherever Janey is, she is too.'

'We'll start there then. I assume you know the address?'

'Yes, I do. I'm not in the habit of letting her go to strange houses. I always know where she is.'

'Not this time.' He stared at me, angrily, then shook his head again. 'Okay, a bit below the belt that. Give me a minute to get dressed and I'll come with you.'

'Too right you will.' I followed him inside. It was the first time I had seen beyond the doorway, which opened straight out onto the pavement. Janey was right. Upstairs was cramped and bare and incredibly lacking in homeliness. Her sleeping bag, the one we had chosen together, was rolled up in the corner of the sofa and there was one solitary photo, of her and Josh together, on the windowsill. He must have taken it from the house when he left, although all the others were still there, on my mantelpiece, where they had always been. The remains of a meal and two used cups sat on the table in the window, his work shoes lying on their sides underneath.

I didn't sit. I just stood in the centre of the room, listening to the crashing and banging coming from the bedroom as he dashed about getting himself dressed.

When I heard a key turn in the lock, I spun round. I don't know why, but my first thought was that it was Eve, that they were together again and she had her own key. That one of the cups on the table was hers.

Josh emerged from his room, hopping on one leg as he

pushed his feet into trainers, just as footsteps made their way up the stairs and in walked our daughter, her overnight bag over her shoulder and a half-eaten Danish pastry in her hand.

'Oh!' she said, seeing us together. 'Mum. What are you doing here?' There was no mistaking the look on her face. The look that said she'd been caught out, and it wasn't going to be easy to talk her way out of it.

***

I hadn't intended to see Colin again, but now I'd been inside Josh's flat, had a glimpse of his life plodding on as ever, without me in it, I decided it was time I started doing what I wanted to do, for a change. I didn't need Josh's permission to lead my own life, or Janey's to see whomever I chose to see. Neither of them had seemed particularly bothered about asking for mine, after all.

'I didn't know if you'd be seeing someone,' I said, squeezing in behind the only free table in Wetherspoon's and pushing my coat down in a bundle beside me. 'I don't want to tread on some other woman's toes.'

'You're not. And I'm not. Seeing anyone, that is. Oh, there have been women over the years. Of course there have, but nothing serious, nobody I'd walk over hot coals for. How could there be, when I only have eyes for you?' He put the two glasses of wine down in front of us, took the chair facing me and casually picked up the menu, his eyes dancing with merriment, trying to hold back a cheeky smile.

'You old flirt, you!'

'Not so much of the old, Ms Peters. I am younger than you, remember. Now, tell me everything.'

'The potted version?'

'That'll do for now.'

'Had enough. Told him I knew about the hotel, and the woman. Asked him to leave. He left.'

'Well, that's potted all right! But about time too. Good for you. I was beginning to think I'd pushed you too hard last time I saw you, and that you'd never go through with it. And now?'

'And now we're living separately. I'm going to divorce him, but I haven't got the ball rolling yet. I need to give Janey time to come to terms with things, and I'm a bit worried about the cost of it all, to tell you the truth, but it helps that I work at a solicitor's. I'm hoping they might give me mates' rates.'

'You didn't chuck paint all over his suits then? Maybe the dry cleaners where you worked before might have offered mates' rates too.'

'Ha. No, I did consider that, or cutting them up maybe, but no. I'm trying to be civilised about it all. For Janey's sake,'

'And how is Janey? How's she taking it? My parents split up when I was a kid, so I do know what it's like.'

'She's still living with me, but not taking it well. Playing the rebel daughter to perfection at the moment. She lied to both of us one weekend and spent the night at her friend's house, or more likely the two of them were out until all hours at some party somewhere, but she told me she was with Josh. She came back safe and sound, so no real harm done. Had some plan to turn up at his flat in the morning, let him think she'd come straight from mine, and let me think she'd been there all night. I think she was banking on us hardly speaking to each other so we'd never suss her out.'

'Cheeky little bugger! How old is she now?'

'Not quite fourteen. I suppose it's normal for teenagers to rebel a bit, but I'd hoped we might get another year or two before all that started. A rocky home life has a lot to answer for.'

'Don't you go blaming yourself, Sarah.'

'Oh, I don't. I blame Josh. One hundred per cent.'

'And your sister?'

'Her too, but I believe her when she says she's not been near him this time. Or I think I do. I can never be sure though, can I? Not when they've both lied to me before.'

'And you're not going to forgive him this time? Give in and take him back?' Colin sipped his drink and watched me, waiting to see if I was about to waver yet again.

'No way!'

'So if I was to ask you out, properly this time, on a – let's call it a date, shall we? – would you come? Let me treat you? Buy you a meal?' He took his hand off the stem of his glass and placed it over mine on the table.

I didn't have to think too hard about that one. I smiled, liking the feel of his fingers touching mine. 'I think I might, yes.'

'No time like the present then.' He passed me the menu. 'You can have anything you want, so long as it's under a tenner!'

I couldn't remember when I had last laughed like that, or

felt so comfortable in the company of a man. It had been a long time coming.

Without saying another word, I slipped my hand out from his and tugged off my wedding ring. It hadn't left my hand in more than eighteen years and needed a bit of encouragement to ease its way over the joint, but it soon came away, leaving a strange white indentation around the base of my finger. I expected to feel different, strange, perhaps even sad, my ring finger suddenly so exposed and bare, but all I felt was elation and a wonderful new sense of freedom. I slipped the ring into my coat pocket and wriggled my hand back inside Colin's, which was, I suddenly realised, exactly where it belonged.

***

I heard her being sick before I saw her, through the partially open door, on her knees in the bathroom, still in her nightie, hunched over the toilet bowl.

'What's up, Love? Got a bad tummy?' I stepped into the room and leant over her. There was only a thin watery yellow layer floating in the toilet so she hadn't brought much up, but her face was deathly pale. 'Come on, back to bed with you. No school today. I'll ring them. And I'll call the office too and say I can't come into work. I'm owed a bit of leave. Can't have you here by yourself if you're poorly.'

'I'll be okay, Mum. Must just be something I've eaten.'

'Well, we both had the same for dinner last night and I'm all right. Is it your period? I remember mine were pretty painful at your age. Come on. Up you get.'

She shook her head.

I helped her back into her bedroom and tucked her up, nipping downstairs for a glass of water and a bowl to leave by her bed in case she was sick again and couldn't make it to the bathroom.

It was a Friday and I had hoped Janey would be off to Josh's at some point over the weekend so I could see Colin without the awkwardness of having to try to explain myself. Still, a few hours curled up under the duvet and she'd probably be fine by the evening. I pulled her door to, closed the curtains and went down to make the necessary calls.

Over the last couple of months, since what I now thought of as the weekend of the big lie, Janey had definitely reined in her behaviour a bit. Whether it was guilt or the fact that she had finally resigned herself to the new way of things I wasn't sure, but she had knuckled down at school and was spending more time at home with me. She had even let me organise a small birthday party for her, just a few school friends at a pizza place, and not made a fuss about wanting some all-dancing, all-boozing kind of do that I'm sure she would have preferred given half a chance. I had started to let myself believe we might have turned a corner, and that the time was right to get going on the divorce.

The house was still just as it had been on the day Josh left. Apart from his own clothes and wash things, his folder of paperwork (evidence and all) and that one photo I'd seen at his flat, he hadn't taken anything else. His flat had come already furnished, with basic kitchenware included, and Janey had told me she'd helped him choose a portable TV. So I still had everything else. And Josh was still paying the bills. Well, not the food, which I could just about manage on my part-time wages, but he was keeping the roof over our heads, still paying the mortgage and the heating and the council tax. Divorce would change all that, I was sure. There was a limit to how far his salary could stretch and keeping two homes going indefinitely was never an option. I had to start thinking about the future. About how I was going to manage, and where I was going to live. About Josh one day wanting us to sell this house and divide the proceeds, paying me some sort of settlement or allowance, demanding half the furniture. I couldn't just sit and wait for the axe to fall.

The truth was that I liked the house. It was my home and had been for a long time now. I liked my comfy bed, the way I'd arranged the kitchen, the little tree in the garden that I sometimes sat under to read a magazine, and the shrubs I'd planted which were nicely settled now, just as I was. I didn't want to give it up. I sat in the quiet and let my thoughts run free. Maybe I could get a better-paid job, maybe I'd have a sympathetic judge who'd award me everything, or maybe Colin and I might—

'Mum?' Janey was calling me from the top of the stairs.

'What is it, Love?'

'Can I have something to eat? I missed breakfast and I'm starving.'

'Ah. Feeling better then, are we? What do you fancy? Coco Pops all right?'

'Could I have some ice cream?'

'For breakfast?'

'Why not? It might make my tummy feel better. And it's easy to swallow, isn't it?'

'If you've got tonsillitis it is, yes! Which I'm quite sure you haven't. But, go on then. Can't do any harm, if it's what you fancy. I've only got vanilla though.'

'With sprinkles?'

'Not much wrong with you now, is there? Carry on like this and you can go into school for the afternoon.'

'Oh, do I have to? It might be catching and I wouldn't want to give it to anyone else.'

'Very public spirited of you, I'm sure. Now get back into bed and I'll bring your ice cream up on a tray. But if it makes you sick again, you've only got yourself to blame!'

Chapter 29

EVE

I'd been teaching long enough to recognise when a pupil had a problem. Janey wasn't in any of my classes but I'd always tried to keep a watchful eye on her, if only from a distance, to make sure she was doing well in her lessons, wasn't being bullied or mixing with the troublemakers. The last couple of times I'd seen her in the corridors or sitting outside on a bench at breaktime, she had looked unhappy, a bit withdrawn, and if it was because of her parents' break-up then I couldn't help but feel at least partially to blame.

I was fairly sure Sarah had told her daughter nothing about Josh and me. She might well be aware that we had met at uni, and even that we had dated as teenagers, but the full details of our later connection had been kept from her, for which I was truly grateful. I loved Janey and the last thing I wanted was for our relationship to suffer or for her to think badly of me.

I was still debating with myself whether to try to catch her on her own and see if I could help in any way, when the dilemma was taken out of my hands. She came to see me.

'Auntie Eve – sorry, Miss Peters – can I talk to you, please?' I had found her hovering outside the staffroom door at the start of the lunch break one Friday, staring down at her own feet, and with no sign of her packed lunch. She was wearing her coat.

'You don't want to eat first?'

'No, I'm not hungry, and this can't wait. It's ... well, kind of personal.'

'What is it, Janey? Do you want to come into the Head's office? We can have some privacy there as he's out for the afternoon. Or would you rather go for a walk?'

'Yes, please. A walk, away from school. Is that allowed? We need permission to leave the building, don't we? But as you're ...'

'Yes, I think, in the circumstances, that will be okay. Let me just find my coat and we'll take a little stroll. I'll sign us both out.'

There was a small park just two streets away and we headed there, finding a wooden bench off the main pathway and sitting down side by side.

'Look, Janey, Love, I know it must be hard for you, the way things are at home. Your mum and dad have things to sort out and, whatever happens, they both love you, and none of this, none of it, is your fault, okay?'

'I know all of that. Mum's said it, in just about those exact same words, but it's what grown-ups always say, isn't it? When they've screwed up.'

'I suppose it is, yes. Well-meaning though, I'm sure. You do have to try not to let it worry you too much though, not to let it affect your school work, or make you unhappy. Things will work out all right in the end. They generally do.'

'I know.' She sat very quietly for a while, one hand finding its way into mine, as we watched a pigeon peck away at the remains of someone's discarded sandwich lying beside an overflowing bin. 'But that's not what's worrying me. Well, not just that. And it's so hard to talk to either of them while they're like this. All they really care about is their own problems.'

'Oh dear. I'm sure that's not true, and not how they want you to feel. But if there's something else bothering you and you really can't find a way to tell them, well, you've always got me. I'm a good listener.'

'But can you keep secrets?'

I smiled inwardly. Me, keeper of such a huge secret for so many years! Yes, I could keep secrets, but I wasn't at all sure that I should.

'That depends on the secret, Janey. Why not try me with it and we'll take it from there.'

She lifted her head and looked up at the sky as if gathering her courage and then just blurted it out.

'I think I'm pregnant.'

'What?' I could feel a sudden rush of panic flow over me, and my hands started to shake. This was the last thing I had been expecting.

'You heard. I'm pregnant, Auntie Eve. What shall I do? Mum and Dad will go mad, and there's school, and ...'

All I wanted to do was hug her, this sweet little girl I had loved all her life. I pulled her towards me and buried my face in her hair. Janey was only fourteen. Too young, too innocent, her whole life ahead of her. I could hardly take it in. Her shoulders shook and I could feel she was crumpling, struggling to cope. Oh my God, I was so close to crumpling too, but that wasn't why she had come to me. She needed help, advice, comfort, someone to take control ...

'Right. First of all, are you absolutely sure?' I tried to switch to sensible, capable, adult mode. 'Periods can be a bit hit and miss in young girls. It might be nothing. Have you done a test?'

'I was too scared to ask for one in the chemist's.' She looked up at me, her expression lost, her eyes pleading, and so like Josh's. 'What if someone sees me, or tells Mum? Even in the supermarket I didn't have the nerve to put one in my basket. You never know who's looking, and they cost so much.'

'Okay, Sweetheart. First thing we have to do is make sure, okay? Let's not start worrying before we have the facts. How late are you?'

'I haven't had a period for two months. And I keep being sick.'

'And – I'm sorry to have to ask you this, but you have actually slept with someone? Had full sex with him? Because this can't happen just from a kiss and a cuddle, you know.'

'I'm not five! I do know how it works.'

'I know, and I'm sorry, but I just needed to check, that's all. And this person – this boy – does he have a name?'

Janey shook her head.

'I'm sure he does, but you're not ready to tell me, eh?'

She shook her head again.

'Janey, you're underage. It's against the law.' I swallowed hard, trying not to picture my niece in the arms of some leering, lecherous boy. 'We will need to know who did this to you.'

'Did this to me? You make it sound like I was raped. I ... we ... wanted to do it. Together. I wasn't forced.'

'Okay. Look, we can come back to all that later. For now, let's get you tested, and decide what's best once we know for sure, okay?'

She nodded and snuggled closer into my side. 'Thank you, Auntie Eve.'

'What for?'

'For not shouting at me. Not giving me a lecture. For helping me.'

'I'm not sure I have helped you yet.' I closed my eyes for a moment, letting the awfulness of the situation wash over me, then took a deep breath and looked at my watch. I had to stay strong, for Janey, no matter how sick and helpless I suddenly felt. 'Half an hour left until we have to be back. Chemist's?'

'Okay.'

'Don't worry. You can wait outside. I'll buy it, let them think it's for me.'

'Do you wish it was?'

'Where did that come from?'

'You don't have any children and Mum said you'd like to. Maybe, if I have the baby, I can give it to you?'

I wanted to laugh at the sheer ridiculousness of the idea, but it was all just too tragic, too real, to do that. Instead I wrapped my arms tightly around my niece and held her close and wondered which one of us was going to cry first.

***

'We have to tell your parents, Janey.'

'No!' We were in my flat, after school, staring at the pregnancy testing stick that was showing an undeniably positive result.

'Come on. Your mum will be wondering where you are. Let me drive you home and we can tell her together. Putting it off won't make it go away, you know.'

'But not now, not today. I need to think about it first. Talk to someone about what I want to do.'

'An abortion clinic, do you mean? Or a counsellor? Because I can come with you. Or your mum will. You really are way too young to make this kind of decision on your own. You do know that, don't you?'

'That's not what I meant. I want to talk to the ... the father. He should know first, before Mum and Dad. He should have some say in what happens, shouldn't he? To the baby, and to me.'

'Maybe. That depends, Janey. On who he is. Is it someone from school? From your class? Because if he's your age, he'll probably be even more shocked and frightened than you are, I shouldn't wonder. And his parents will have to know. And quite possibly the police.'

'Police?'

'I told you, Love, it's against the law. You're only fourteen.'

'Then I won't tell anyone who he is. You can't make me. It's not his fault, and I don't want him to get into trouble.'

'Oh, Janey. You were grown up enough to get into this mess. Now you're going to have to be grown up about dealing with it too. Honesty is what we need now, and a clear head. Abortion is one option, and the one I would advise you to at least consider, but if you decide to go ahead and have the baby, and keep it, then you're going to need all the help you can get. With school, with money, being woken up in the middle of the night ... and while you're living at home, it will be a lot of work and disruption for your mum as well as for you. And how will you involve the baby's dad if you don't want anyone to know who he is? It won't work. It can't work.'

She looked at me with that stubborn expression I had seen before, when she didn't want to go to bed, didn't want to do her homework, thought she knew best. 'It's my baby.' She gulped and laid a hand over her stomach. 'Mine. Nobody else's.'

'Not his? The mysterious father?'

'Well, yes, his too.'

'Look, Janey, this is not the sort of secret I can keep. I'm sorry, but your parents have to know. I'll let you have tonight, to think, to talk to the dad if you must, but tomorrow I'm going to have to talk to your mum. Or your dad. Whether you want me to, whether you come with me, or not. Do you understand?'

She nodded, wiping the back of her hand across her cheek.

'Are you sure you don't want it?' she pleaded. 'You could adopt it so it stays as part of the family.'

'It doesn't work like that, Janey.'

She dropped her head and stared at her feet. 'Can we go now? I don't want Mum getting angry about not knowing where I am again.'

'Of course we can. But tomorrow ...'

'Yes, I know.' She stood up and turned her back on me. 'Tomorrow you're going to wreck my life.'

My heart went out to her. So young, so unworldly, so bloody scared. 'Okay, I'll give you until Sunday, so you can have a proper think, maybe even tell your mum yourself, but then I'll have to do it. You do know that?'

She nodded, reluctantly.

But as for wrecking your life, I think you've done that for yourself, I was itching to say, but I didn't.

I reached for my car keys and drove her home, neither of us speaking on the way. Come Sunday, unless Janey found the courage by then, I would have to go and see one of her parents, or both of them. I'd probably find it easier talking to Josh. Yes, I'd start with Josh, and just knowing that I was about to see him again made me feel almost as wobbly as knowing what it was I was going to have to say.

***

I should have known she would run away from it. She wasn't answering her mobile and, although as she'd got out of my car on Friday afternoon, she had promised to meet me outside her father's flat at eleven on Sunday, she didn't show up.

I sat in the car and waited, radio on, tapping my fingers against the steering wheel. Ten minutes, fifteen, twenty ... At half past eleven I climbed out, locked up and walked slowly towards Josh's door. At least, I hoped it was Josh's door and that she hadn't deliberately given me a false address. I wouldn't put it past her.

The florist's shop was closed. I looked up at its aged sign. *Petalicious*. Something about such a frivolous name plastered across such a weathered old wooden shop front made me smile. I peered past the half-closed blinds at the big vases of flowers and sprigs of foliage hovering there in the gloom. The place sounded vaguely familiar and I thought it might have been the shop Lucy had worked in for a while when she first left school.

I heard the click of a lock and the door to the side of the shop opened.

'Hello, Josh.'

He looked shocked to see me. 'Eve. Wow! I didn't expect this.' He ran his hand through his hair, which was probably the longest I'd seen it since we were in our twenties, and stood aside to let me in. 'Come in and go up. Excuse the mess. Bachelor pad, and all that. When Janey's not around, anyway. She does try to tidy things up when she's here.'

'She's not here now?' A sudden hope had welled up in me that she had arrived before me and had been here all the time.

'Nope. Not my turn this weekend.' He closed the door and followed me up the narrow staircase. The combination of plain scuffed walls, threadbare carpet and low-wattage light-bulb with no shade gave it a gloomy air. 'Which is good, because it means I get to see you by yourself. Now, I'm hoping you've come because you can't live another minute without me but I'm guessing that's not really why.'

We passed through a tiny square landing and into a cramped living area, his hand resting on my back now as if to steer me in the right direction.

'Josh, I ...' I hesitated. Now I was here I felt uncertain. Could I really tell him about Janey? Should I be the one to do it? Perhaps I needed to give her another chance to do it herself. Wherever she was hiding away, probably in her own bed, she couldn't stay there forever. And when she surfaced she'd have to face up to what was happening. A secret like that couldn't stay secret for long. What harm could another day or two do? She might even be confessing all to Sarah at that very moment.

'It's okay. I feel a bit tongue-tied too. It's been a long time. Too long.' He guided me to a small sofa, pushing a pile of papers aside so I could sit down. 'Let me get you a coffee. Or something stronger maybe? And then we can talk.'

'It's a bit early for something stronger. Coffee's fine.'

He went through an archway into a tiny kitchen with no door, and I watched as he poured water into a kettle and quickly rinsed a couple of mugs he'd fished out from a pile of washing up in the sink. I couldn't take my eyes off him, the shape of his head, the way he moved, the easy familiarity of those long fingers wrapped around the mugs, everything I remembered and cherished and still loved. When he came back and squeezed down into the seat beside me, it was all I could do not to spill my heart out. Instead I concentrated on not spilling the coffee.

'Is it really over between you and Sarah? No going back?'

'No going back, Eve. Why would I want to? There's nothing there worth saving.'

I put my coffee down on the tiny foldaway table beside me and turned towards him. 'You do know how I feel about you, don't you?'

'I thought I did, but the last few times ... well, you made it pretty clear we had no future. Family first, and all that.'

'Maybe I was wrong. If Sarah really doesn't want to put things right. If she really doesn't want you ...' What was I doing? This was not what I had come here for. The timing was all wrong. I needed to wait, until they were divorced, until he was free, until Janey had shared her news, had the baby ...

Before either of us could say anything else, he bent his head towards me and I felt his lips close over mine. The warm rush of remembered feelings flooded through me. This was what I had missed so much, what I still dreamed about, the one thing I had thought I could never have again. I had traded this man, this love, against keeping my family, and family had won, but now everything was different. Maybe, just maybe, I could have both.

'Whatever it was you came here to say,' he said, pulling back and nuzzling his face into my neck, 'I'm sure we could say it so much better without words.' His fingers were on my buttons now, slowly undoing them one by one, his touch sending little shivers across my skin, and then he reached for my hand and started to pull me to my feet. 'Come to bed, Eve.'

And I would have done it, would have let myself fall right back into that big warm glorious pit of coupledom I had been longing for, but as he pushed me down gently onto his bed my gaze fell on the bedside table, and the two wine glasses sitting there. Two glasses? By the bed? I shrugged him off me and sat up, trying to get a closer look. One of them had a mottled pink mark along the rim. Lipstick. It couldn't be anything else.

'What's this?'

He was right behind me now, kneeling with his hands on my shoulders, his face buried in my hair, so I wasn't able to see the guilt I knew would be written there. His hand shot out and scooped up both glasses. 'Just stuff I haven't got around to washing up yet. You know what we men are like!' He was trying to laugh it off, probably hoping I hadn't spotted the lipstick. Maybe he hadn't even spotted it himself, but the speed of his reaction said it all.

'Who is she, Josh?'

'Who?'

'The woman who was here, drinking wine? And very recently, I would assume, unless your washing up habits really are that bad. Oh, please tell me it wasn't last night, that you weren't about to have sex with me in a bed that's still warm from the previous occupant. When did she leave, Josh? This morning? Must have been early, because I'd been outside quite a while before I came in and I didn't see anyone go.'

396

'Eve. Don't.' He put the glasses down again and held on fast to both of my hands. 'She was nobody. Nobody, okay? Just someone I had a drink with. Someone from work. But she didn't stay the night. Honestly. And, even if she had, you surely couldn't blame me. You didn't expect me to live like a monk, did you? We were over. Me and Sarah. Me and you. I had nothing left. Nobody ...'

'What's her name?

'God, Eve, you're sounding like Sarah now. Like a bloody wife. It doesn't matter who she is, or what her name is. It's none of your business.'

'Yes, I get that now.' I was trying to do up my buttons so I could leave with a shred of dignity, but I'd got one in the wrong hole, and the water building up in my eyes wasn't helping. I couldn't see a thing through the mist. 'So, all this wanting to see me, to talk to me, what was that all about? I thought you wanted me back, Josh. Stupid fool that I am, I thought we might ...'

'We still can!'

He was still talking, pleading, but I didn't hear the rest. I picked up my bag and ran, out of the bedroom, down the stairs and out of the flat, into the street, slamming the door behind me. As I burst out, all dishevelled and with tears running down my face, I don't know who was more startled. Sarah and Janey, as I bumped right into them halfway up the path, or me.

Chapter 30

SARAH

I'd found Janey being sick again that Sunday morning, and something about her pale face, how quiet she had been lately, her rebellious sullen moods, started to ring a very worrying bell. Thoughts I really didn't want to have flew into my head. No, she couldn't be. Surely not? She was fourteen. Still at school. She had never been with a boy ... But how did I know that? How did I know what she had been doing? I couldn't watch her twenty-four hours a day. All the afternoons she was late back from school, that time she'd lied about being with her dad, staying overnight at her friend Becky's ... I should have taken more interest, made sure I knew where she was, talked to her about contraception. There were so many places kids could find to have sex if they really wanted to. In the park? In alleyways? Cars? God, I should know. I'd done it myself when I was not much older than she was.

I tried to quash all the questions and recriminations that were bouncing around in my brain. Facts first. I led Janey back to her bed and sat down, heavily, on the edge. 'Janey. Tell me if I'm wrong. Oh, please let me be wrong.' I grasped her hand and tried my best to adopt an understanding, caring face rather than that of the angry, spitting-feathers mother tiger that I could feel myself turning into. 'But you couldn't be pregnant, could you?'

She couldn't look me in the eyes. No words came out. She just nodded her head, very slightly, and burst into tears.

'Are you sure?' I suddenly felt like crying myself. This couldn't be happening. Not to my baby girl. 'You've done a test?'

She nodded again, leaning into me as if she was hoping I would cuddle her up, wave a magic wand and miraculously make everything all right.

'And does anyone else know?' I have no idea why that should matter, but it did. I wanted her to come to me first, to talk to me first, about anything, everything, especially something as big as this. 'Your dad?'

'No!' She sat bolt upright and shook her head. 'I don't want Dad to know. He'll hate me.'

'He could never hate you.' I pulled her back towards me, feeling her small body shaking against mine. 'But, as for the boy, whoever he is, I don't think Dad will be too pleased with him.'

'Don't tell him. Please. Can't we just ... not tell Dad at all?'

I couldn't think straight. 'Don't be ridiculous, Janey. He has to know.' We sat in silence as I waited for my thumping heart to return to some semblance of normal. I had been here before. Me a teenager. Me thinking I might be pregnant. Me being way too scared to tell anybody. And now it was happening all over again, but at least Janey had taken that first step and confided in me. Everything felt unreal, as if I was watching the scene play out in a film and not here in my own home. 'I'm sorry, but I don't know what to say or what to do right now. It will be okay though. We'll sort this out somehow, I promise. But just give me a few minutes to think, eh?'

I left her half sitting, half lying on her bed, and went downstairs. There was a half-empty bottle of gin in the cabinet. Not something I would ever normally drink, and left over from when Josh's parents had last been down, but I needed a drink and it was the only alcohol in the house, so it would have to do.

Two large glasses later, I went back upstairs. Facts. I needed facts. My feelings of panic and shock had to be pushed aside if I was to be of any real help to my daughter. 'Right. Tell me everything. How far gone do you think you are? Who was it that got you in this condition? And what do you want to do about it? In any order you like, but we're not leaving this room until you give me answers.' Oh my God, I sounded so heartless, so bloody practical, but it was either that or crumple in a heap, and how was that going to help?

She didn't tell me, of course. Well, the two months gone part was easy enough, as my quick mental calculations led me straight back to that night when she'd lied about being with her dad. Where had she really been? But the rest just drew a blank. She wasn't going to tell me who the father was, and as for any kind of plan, she clearly didn't have one. It was going to have to be up to me to decide what to do or at least to present her with options, none of which were going to be easy.

'This happened to you, didn't it?' she said. 'But you lost the baby. My big brother or sister. I heard Gran and Granddad once, talking about it. How being pregnant so young had ruined your chances, made you marry Dad.'

'Well, you shouldn't have been listening. It wasn't like that. I was older. Sixteen. I'm not sure I had any real chances to ruin back then. And I loved your dad. Nobody made me do anything I didn't want to.'

'And how do you know I don't love my baby's dad too?'

'Oh, Janey. You're fourteen. You don't know anything about life or being in love. You're hardly more than a baby yourself.'

'See? That's what grown-ups always say. That we're too young to know what we're doing, or what we're feeling. We're only kids, and kids know nothing. If you and dad hadn't split up ...'

'So, you're saying it's our fault? We sent you off the rails, did we? When all we've tried to do, both of us, is protect you, make the whole separation thing as easy for you as we could, show you how much we both love you ...'

'It wasn't enough, Mum.' She was crying again, letting slow tears roll down her face unchecked. 'Nothing's felt the same since Dad left. We don't feel like a proper family anymore.'

'And this boyfriend of yours, whoever he is, filled the gap your dad left in your life, did he? By pushing himself inside you and making a baby you're not ready, or able, or mature enough, to look after?'

'It wasn't like that. He ... he made me feel special. And he will help me and stand by me. I know he will.'

'Have you told him?'

'Not yet.'

'But you want to? You really think he'll want to be a father, do you? Clap his hands with joy and rush you down to Mothercare to choose a pram?'

'He might.'

'And he might just as likely turn his back on you, pretend it's not his, want nothing to do with it. And you're underage. The police might have to get involved, but they probably won't even prosecute him, if he's a kid himself, so what is that going to achieve? Just more upset. No, I am beginning to think the best thing you can do is not tell him. Not tell anyone. We can find a clinic, say you've got a tummy bug for a few days, then have you back at school in no time. All done, put behind you, forgotten. Nobody else need ever know.'

'No.'

'What do you mean, no?'

'I don't want to get rid of it. I want to keep it.'

'Oh, for heaven's sake, Janey, be realistic. Who do you think will end up looking after it? Getting up in the night, changing nappies, making up bottles, while you're at school? Me, that's who. And I don't want that. Not at this point in my life. I've only just found my freedom, got my own life back. It'll need eighteen years of time and attention. It's a baby, not a bloody doll!'

'Well, I'm not having an abortion, and you can't make me.'

'Then let's go and see what your precious father has to say, shall we? Because I can't cope with this. Not now. Not on my own.'

***

Eve flew out of the door like a bat out of hell. A bat in a hurry, with her blouse half undone. She didn't stop, didn't speak, just pushed past us and ran off down the road, climbing into her car which was parked a few yards away, not all that far from mine. I don't know why I hadn't spotted it when I'd parked. Having my mind on other more important things, I supposed. But suddenly this was important too. What was Eve doing at Josh's? And why was she leaving in such a hurry? There could only be one explanation. They were seeing each other again. Sleeping together again, despite all her worthless assurances, and she'd seen us through the window and was trying to get out unseen before we arrived. I couldn't imagine any other reason why she'd be in such a rush, so obviously upset, partially undressed, and so unwilling to stop and say hello once she'd been rumbled.

Josh opened the door before we'd rung the bell and looked, momentarily, surprised to see us.

'Expecting someone else, Josh?' I said, sarcastically. 'I think the person you're looking for may have just driven away.' I was aware of Janey, looking up at the two of us, clearly confused.

'Why was Auntie Eve in there? She was supposed to wait ... She's told you, hasn't she?'

404

'Told me what?' Josh was looking down the road at Eve's retreating car, not properly listening, but I was.

'Told him ...? Oh no, she knows, doesn't she?' It shouldn't really matter but suddenly it did. It really did. I grabbed Janey by the shoulders and turned her to face me. 'You told Eve before me?'

'What the hell's going on here?' Josh pulled us apart and beckoned us in. 'Come inside, both of you, before the neighbours come out and start taking bloody pictures.'

I'd had enough. Not only had Eve thrown herself at my husband – again – but my own daughter had decided to confide in her. This huge secret that was weighing me down like a lead block, wasn't a secret at all. Bloody Auntie Eve had got there before me. Was there nothing my sister wouldn't take from me?

I rushed in and went straight to the bedroom. The covers were rumpled, there were two wine glasses, and the undeniable smell of her perfume ...

'How could you?' He and Janey had followed me up the stairs and were standing right behind me. My hand flew up and swiped angrily across Josh's face. If he hadn't turned away as quickly as he did, I would have had his eye out.

'How could I what? You come in here, shouting like a mad woman, chucking your fists about. That's domestic violence, you know. I could have the law on you for that. In front of Janey too.' He turned his attention to his daughter then, standing stock still in the doorway, her face even paler than it had been earlier, and lowered his voice. 'Sorry, Janey. But what is it Eve's meant to have told me? And why are you raiding my bedroom? What are you here for anyway?' He had one hand on Janey's shoulder but he was still close enough for me to hit him again if I chose to. 'Hang on, Sarah, have you been drinking? I can smell it on you. You have! Did you drive here? With our daughter in the car? For fuck's sake, what were you thinking? You could have killed someone.'

'Well, I didn't, but I'm seriously considering it now. I just can't decide whether to kill you first, or my treacherous, lying sister.'

'Hang on! You think that Eve and me ... No, no, you've got it all wrong. We didn't—'

'As if I'm going to believe that. All the evidence is staring me right in the face. Which brings me to why we're here. Something else I should have spotted sooner, but didn't. What sort of a mother does that make me, eh? Well, it's your problem now, Josh. You're the perfect parent, the chosen one, so you sort it out. I'm going.'

'No, Mum. Don't!' Janey pleaded.

'I don't know what's going on here, but whatever it is I'm not letting you drive.' He snatched at my bag and pulled out my car keys, stuffing them in his trouser pocket.

'Suit yourself. I'll walk.' And I strode out, head high, making sure I slammed the front door even louder than Eve had. By the time I got to Dad's, half an hour later, and after dashing straight to his toilet to empty my gin-fuelled fit-to-burst bladder, I found I had just about calmed down enough to tell him everything without bursting into tears.

***

Josh came after me later. Of course he did. Janey had somehow found the words to tell him she was pregnant and there was no way he was going to let that lie without storming into Dad's and demanding answers.

'How did you know where I was?'

'Where else would you be? You weren't at home. I've dropped Janey off there, with strict instructions she's not to go out or to go anywhere near this boy, whoever he is, until we get back. And I was pretty damn sure you wouldn't have gone within a mile of Eve, unless you really do intend to kill her. So you had to be here. You can't hide away from this, Sarah. Our girl's in trouble and we need to talk about it. All three of us. Now!'

I could feel Dad hovering, knew how much he wanted to help, but that he couldn't. This wasn't something we could resolve over a pot of tea.

'Did you come in your car, or mine?'

'Yours. I figured you wouldn't be up to coming back to collect it from my place. Come on, let's go. I can get back home on the bus later or call a taxi, but I think we need to talk, don't you?'

I pecked Dad on the cheek, followed Josh out to my car and climbed in the passenger side. He was right, I had been drinking, and this wasn't the time to argue about that.

'Who is he? Do you know?' Josh turned on me as soon as we were out of sight of the house.

'I don't know. I did wonder if it might be that boy Samuel, her friend Becky's brother. She's spent a lot of time there lately, and he's been driving her home, but she's hardly mentioned him otherwise, so I might be way off the mark.'

'Well, she wouldn't, would she? Mention him. Not if she didn't want us to know about him, the little oik. I'll twist his bloody bollocks off if he's been anywhere near her.'

'Bit late for that. The deed's been done.'

'Too right it has. And where were you when this was going on? I thought when I left her with you that you'd look after her. Properly.'

'Left her with me? You make her sound like a package. She's my daughter. She belongs with me.'

'And some role model you were. Like mother, like daughter, that's what I say.'

'What do you mean by that?'

'You know exactly what I mean.'

'Pregnant in my teens? Well, that took two, Josh. I didn't do it by myself.'

'No, you didn't. But it should have taught you something, shouldn't it?' He was yelling again, his hands tight on the steering wheel. 'God, if I could go back, I wouldn't do the same again, I can tell you. I rue the day I ever looked at you, let alone got you up the duff. How different my life could have been.'

'You could have married Eve instead.' I almost spat the words at him. 'And lived happily ever after.'

'Yes. Yes, I could, and I wish I had.'

'Well, you didn't have to stay with me. Nobody forced you.'

'The baby, Sarah. I stayed for the baby we'd stupidly made together, the one you couldn't even hang onto, after every-thing—'

'The baby wasn't yours, Josh.' I don't know why I said it. Or spat it, more like. All I wanted right then was to hurt him.

He turned to face me, the whites of his eyes bulging. 'What?'

'Did you think you were the only one, Josh? My first? My one true love. Huh! Don't make me laugh!'

'Laugh? You tell me something like that and you think it's funny?'

'It wasn't yours. I was already pregnant when you came along. Oh, not by much, but—'

'No!'

'Yes! Did I ever actually tell you it was yours? Think about it, Josh. I was just a schoolgirl – an innocent young thing – caught in bed with her sister's boyfriend. Someone old enough to know what he was doing. Old enough to know better. Of course everyone assumed it was yours. Even you did. No question. No doubt. You were cast in the role of seducer and I didn't correct that. Why should I? Oh, I fancied you all right, like crazy, but you were also my very convenient way out.'

'How could you do that? Make me believe ... My God, you really are one cruel heartless bitch, aren't you?'

'If you say so.'

'So who was this other bloke then? The one who got away scot-free and left me to face the bloody music? No, don't tell me. I really don't think I want to know.'

There was a long silence before he said anything else. I could see his hands clenched white on the wheel, a little twitch in his neck, his jaw grinding as if he was trying to stay in control, biting back the words. 'And Janey? Please tell me that she's mine.'

'She might be.' I was enjoying watching him squirm.

'What do you mean, might be?' He was yelling now, his head turned towards me, his eyes all screwed up in anger. 'You know bloody well that I love that little girl with all my heart. So is she mine, or isn't she?'

I didn't see the lorry coming. Not until it hit us. Hard. Head-on, sending the car skidding across the carriageway and spinning onto its side. I don't think Josh saw it either. He was too busy shouting at me to concentrate on the road. Or to hear my answer.

Chapter 31

EVE

When Dad called me that Sunday evening, I couldn't take in what he was saying. He was crying, something he never did, or at least not like this. A terrible accident. Sarah injured, taken to hospital. He was going there now, not knowing quite what to expect, picking up Janey on the way. No, Janey hadn't been in the car. And Josh, he wasn't sure. Not next of kin, so they hadn't told him, wouldn't tell him, but he'd been there too, in the crash, and it didn't sound good.

I should have been worried about my sister, been scared for her and for Janey, but all I could focus on was Josh. I should go there, to the hospital, sit in one of those little relatives' rooms, wait for news, but Dad told me not to. 'She wouldn't want you there, Eve,' he said. 'Not after what you've done.' And I knew he meant it, and so did she. She had caught me at Josh's flat, running away, my clothes undone, and of course she had told Dad. She always did. What were they meant to believe? But how could I explain, how could I tell my sister I was not trying to steal her husband, when given half a chance I knew that was exactly what I would have done?

I hated Josh, yet I loved Josh. I was angry with him, yet I couldn't stop thinking about him.

Whatever he had done, or whoever he had done it with, didn't seem to matter anymore. I just wanted him to be all right. And Sarah to be all right too. Why had they been together in the car? Why had Janey not been with them? The questions flooded in, but there was no one to give me answers. I wished with all my heart that we could all just go back a day, a year, twenty years, and that everything could have been different. But that could never happen. Life didn't throw those kinds of second chances around. There was no magic wand, and this was all too frighteningly real.

When Dad rang back, hours later, his words sliced through me like a hot knife through butter. Josh was dead. Josh. *My* Josh was dead. Dad told me about Sarah too, although I was finding it hard to listen or to understand. My breathing was ragged, my heart pounding. I thought I might be about to faint. Josh was dead. 'She's ruptured her spleen, and she's covered in cuts and grazes,' Dad was saying. 'And she sprained her ankle, badly, crawling out from the wreckage, but the most worrying thing is her hands. The car burst into flames, Eve.'

Flames? Had Josh been burned too? Had he got out? Died there, or in the ambulance, or later on a hospital trolley? Had he known where he was? Had he been conscious? Afraid? In pain?

'They say she tried to wrestle with the driver's door, tried to get him out, but the heat was too much. It beat her back.'

Dad made her sound like a heroine, a brave woman desperate to save her husband. The husband she had already thrown out, didn't want anymore, didn't love ...

Dad didn't call again. This time he was definitely taking sides. I could hear it in the coldness of his voice, giving me the facts but no love, no comfort. His priority now was Sarah, he said. And Janey. Not me.

And so I was left alone, to think, to cry, to grieve. A big deep pit of darkness seemed to open out in front of me and drag me down inside it. There was no one to hold me, or to understand my pain, or to try to pull me out. Perhaps it was what I deserved.

***

I couldn't go to work, couldn't sleep, couldn't stop blaming myself, and Sarah, and the mystery woman he'd been seeing behind both our backs. Who was she, and what did he feel for her? Even now, I was jealous. Of a woman I couldn't put a face to and probably never would. If not for her, I would not have run, could have kept him with me, kept him safe ...

I kept reliving that morning in my mind, so sorry I'd flounced out, sorry I hadn't stayed to hear what Josh had to say, stayed to set the record straight with my sister, to support Janey as she told her dad her news, as I'd promised her I would. If only I had done that, perhaps none of them would have had to go out, the car might never have been on the road ...

413

But I hadn't, and now he was dead, and even in his last moments it had been Sarah there beside him, not me. The deadly game of bat and ball we had been playing all our adult lives was finally over, and Sarah had won. And come out of it as a heroine, selfless to the last. No, how could I think that way? How could anyone be a winner when the man in the centre of it all was gone forever? Wild, crazy, mixed-up thoughts, that lacked any sense of reality, kept creeping in. I felt dizzy, sick, exhausted, but if sleep was to keep evading me, then I needed a drink, some way of inducing oblivion, to stop the memories and the recriminations haunting me.

I poured myself a large whisky, took one gulp and threw the rest down the sink. It tasted vile, burning its way down my throat, reminding me of Sarah's burnt hands, of Josh's face, his body, engulfed in fire. I closed my eyes and tried to blot it out. Drinking wasn't going to help. Nothing was. Even if I went to sleep, I knew I would dream, and the dreams would be just as horrifying as reality. Probably worse. All I really needed was Josh, alive and well, his arms around me, laughing as he claimed a fifty-pence piece every time I said I was sorry. He'd be a rich man these last couple of days, the number of times I'd thought it. But none of that was going to happen. Not now. Or ever again.

I felt adrift, with no one there to turn to at the absolute lowest and most devastating point in my life. Lucy was still living in her new-motherhood happy bubble and I didn't want to be the one to burst it. Dad was distant, pouring all his sympathies in Sarah's direction, and she was still ignoring me.

But there was always Simon. Simon was the only person I could call who would listen, and care, and not even think to judge me.

I didn't invite him to come running, and certainly hadn't expected him to, but there he was, standing on my step, with a small overnight bag and a massive box of man-size tissues in his hands.

'Come here.' That was all he said, dropping his stuff on the mat, then opening his big arms wide and engulfing me inside them. 'I remember we did this once before, didn't we? When your mum was ill, and we ate curry – or was it kebabs? – and drank wine and ...'

'I'm not sure that would solve things. Not this time.' I emerged from the warmth of his jumper, wiping my runny nose on it as I moved, and looked up through the mist of my tears into his gentle, caring face.

'You really did love him, didn't you?'

I nodded. 'You know I did. Still do ...'

'Oh, Eve, what am I going to do with you? The man was a cheat, an adulterer, a chancer. Okay, I know, I know. That's not what you want to hear. Grief is a terrible thing, and it's taking you over right now. You're only going to remember what you want to. The good times, the person you wanted him to be. And you're going to be sad for a long time to come. But you will come through it, my lovely. And out the other side. It just might take a bit of time, that's all.'

We snuggled up on the sofa, with a cuddly blanket over our knees and a takeaway pizza I was sure I wouldn't be able to eat, but remarkably my long-lost appetite seemed to come flying back with a vengeance, and I ate almost as many slices as Simon did.

'I think you needed that.'

'Probably did. Thanks, Si. I'm so glad to see you. I presume it's just a flying visit? You must have work to get back to?'

'Feigned a shoulder injury. Well, it's easy enough to do when you teach PE. Told them I'd need at least until Monday before I'd be back.'

'Simon. You sneaky liar!'

'I wouldn't do it for just anyone, you know. So I can stay a while. Long enough for you to wash your snot off my jumper at least.'

I laughed for the first time in days. 'Thank you. I've missed you. So much.'

'You too, Kid.' And he kissed me on the nose, but not before giving it a good wipe with a tissue, to make sure it was clean.

***

Something drew me to the scene of the accident. It was easy enough to find out where it was. The local news had been there like a shot, cameras, reporters ...

It was Sunday afternoon and I was on my own again now that Simon had gone. I was due back at work the next day. There was only so much compassionate leave a boss was prepared to allow when the deceased was simply a brother-in-law, and trying to explain that he had been so much more than that wasn't an option.

Josh had been gone a week. I had called Dad, asked after

Sarah, who the nurses kept telling me on the phone was not willing to let me visit, tried to make peace, but she wasn't having any of it. And nor was he. The funeral was being delayed, he told me, until Sarah was well enough, but I would not be welcome anyway. I should do the decent thing and stay away. I wasn't sure I could. Not even for Dad.

I parked some distance away from the crash site and walked, wrapping myself up in a long coat, a scarf pulled up over my mouth and chin. The vehicles had been taken away but I could still see skid marks on the road, the remains of some sort of powdered stuff which I assumed they must have used to put out the flames, a thin strip of tape tied around a damaged tree, maybe to protect the evidence or to keep people away because the tree was in danger of falling down. It looked solid enough though, despite the split in its trunk. There were slivers of glass and a mangled wing mirror still lying in the earth at its base. Several people had left flowers, and I bent down and added my own bouquet to the pile. White roses, the first flowers he had ever bought me, that day he'd turned up in Cardiff and our affair had begun.

'Hello, Auntie Eve.'

I turned quickly, and there was Janey, just a few feet behind me. Her eyes were red and puffy and she too had chosen to envelop herself in the biggest and baggiest of coats. We stood and stared at each other. There were no words.

'Mum says she hates you. She says it was all your fault. Was it?'

'No, I don't think so, Janey. Accidents happen, and we don't know what caused this one, do we? It could have been anything. Brakes, a slippery road ... Maybe your dad just lost concentration for a moment.'

'Mum says they were arguing.'

'In the car? I don't know about that. I wasn't there, and nor were you, so maybe we'll never know for sure. Grown-ups fight all the time.'

'But you were all fighting about me, weren't you? Mum didn't like it that I told you first. Probably that's what they were fighting about in the car too. Me, and the baby. So if it's anyone's fault, it's mine.'

'Oh, no, Janey. None of this was your fault. The problems we had, your mum and dad and me, they went back years, Love. Long before your pregnancy.'

'I told him, Auntie Eve. The father. That afternoon, the day it happened, while Mum and Dad were out. I rang and told him.'

'Did you? And what did he say?'

She looked up at me, tears welling up in her eyes, and I felt her small hand slip into mine. 'He was angry. He said he didn't want it, that he'd pay to get rid of it.'

'Oh, dear.'

'I thought he cared about me. I thought he'd be pleased.'

'Boys aren't usually pleased when they make babies they hadn't planned to have, Janey. Look, you really do need to tell me who he is. How this happened. It's the only way I can help you. I know it's hard to talk to your mum right now, while she's so poorly. And your dad ... well, he ...'

'Go on, say it. He's dead. My daddy's dead.'

'Yes.'

'I don't want him to be dead,' she sobbed, pulling her hand away from mine and wrapping herself tightly around me, her arms finding their way inside my coat.

'Nor do I, Janey.' It was all I could do not to break down completely, but this child – Josh's child – needed me, and I needed her.

'And I don't know what to do. Whether I want to have a baby on my own.'

'You're not on your own, Sweetheart. You've got me.' I wiped the tears from her cheek and tried to force a smile. 'You've always got me.'

'I know, but I just need a bit more time. So I can decide ...'

***

The funeral finally took place three weeks after the crash. I had taken more roses – big white ones that smelt wonderful – but I couldn't do it, couldn't put them down on the wet ground with all the other tributes, as if I was just one in a long line of friends, acquaintances, colleagues, leaving little cards with their scribbled clichéd messages. They – he – deserved more. I left them in the car and took just one rose into the chapel, clutching it so tightly it more or less disintegrated in my hands.

I knew I wasn't welcome, that Sarah had decided this time she could not, or would not, forgive me. But it didn't matter. I was there for Josh, and for all that he had meant to me, and still did.

Janey looked so scared, so lost, and I wondered if she had

made any decision yet about the baby. If she'd spoken to a doctor, been to a clinic? Time was ticking by. Time she didn't have. Keeping it wouldn't be easy, but getting rid of it would be pretty hard too. She hadn't yet come back to school, so I'd had no chance to get her on her own to see how she was or what had been decided. My heart went out to her, but I knew better than to try to approach her, or any of them. Sarah would make damn sure she kept us apart. Making a scene in public, and in the midst of everyone's grief, was not my style, so I sloped away straight after the service. I knew it would probably be the last time I saw any of my family for a while. Dust would have to settle. Wounds would have to heal. But perhaps I was better on my own. I needed time to heal too.

I drove about for a while, aimlessly, windscreen wipers swishing out a regular rhythm, like a heartbeat, and with no destination in mind.

I pulled up in a gravelled car park surrounded by trees and closed my eyes, expecting to cry, but I didn't. Perhaps I was all cried out, like the rain, because that had finally stopped too. There was a burger van parked over by the gate that led into the woods, and I walked over and bought a coffee, with lots of sugar, and a Kit Kat. I hadn't eaten all day, but the smell of the greasy meat and the sight of all those slimy onions turned my stomach. I wondered what they would be eating at the wake. And if Josh's new woman, whichever one she was, would have had the cheek to turn up and eat sausage rolls and sip sherry with his widow.

I walked about for a bit, shivering in my black dress and the thin roll-up mac I always kept in the boot, wishing I'd

brought a proper coat, slowly drinking the coffee to warm
me, then tossing the empty cup and the chocolate wrapper
into a bin. The roses were still there, on the back seat. I could
smell them as soon as I got back into the car. I needed to give
them to Josh. Not the crash site again. That felt too morbid,
and too public. So I started the engine and headed back to
the last place I had seen him alive.

***

I was standing outside Josh's door, gazing into the florist's
shop window. There was a certain irony in bringing flowers
to a place like this that already had so many. I looked up to
the flat above, its windows in darkness, and tried to picture
him there, looking out, smiling, waving, but I couldn't
summon him up, no matter how hard I tried.

I heard footsteps and there was Janey, walking slowly
towards me. We seemed to have a habit of thinking the same
thing, arriving at the same place at the same time.

'Shouldn't you be at the wake?'

'I was, but it's all so serious and sad. I wanted to be with
Dad.'

'Me too.'

'Do you want to come in? I've got the key.'

'Yes, please.'

She opened the door. I pressed my lips to the roses and
laid them down outside, propped against the wall, and we
went inside together and up the stairs.

'I've been coming here, boxing up his things. He didn't have much here really, just clothes and soap and stuff, and a few files and papers. Mum says the landlord wants the keys back now so I probably can't come again.'

'That's a shame, but ...'

'Yeah, I know. It's just a flat. His real home was with me and Mum. That's where I'll remember him best. Do you think he would have come back? That Mum and Dad might have got back together one day?'

'I don't know, Janey. I don't think so.'

We stepped across the small landing and I could see she had been busy. No washing up in the sink, no clothes on chairs, no trace of him left. The heating wasn't on either and I felt a shiver run through me.

'You wanted to know how it happened,' she said, turning to face me.

I knew instantly what she was talking about. Not the accident. The pregnancy. It was as if our conversation from the last time we'd met had never been interrupted.

'It was at Becky's house.'

'Becky? Becky O'Connor?'

She nodded, but she couldn't look me in the eyes. She pulled out a dining chair and slumped into it, gazing out of the window into the street. 'Becky wasn't there. She'd been off sick and I went round after school, to see how she was, but she'd spent the day at her mum's. She did that. Kind of split her time between two homes, like I was starting to. He said she might be back later, that I could stay. Wait for her. He hung up my coat, gave me a drink. We watched some TV.'

'A drink?' I didn't sit down, just put a hand gently on her shoulder and hovered close enough for her to know I was there and that she could tell me anything, everything. 'Alcohol, do you mean?'

'I don't know. I thought it was just orange juice, but I think now maybe it wasn't. We sat next to each other on the sofa that first time. It felt nice, all warm and close, like it used to feel sitting with Dad, before he left. I felt sort of fuzzy, but happy, and safe.'

'But it didn't stop there? Things went further?'

'He kissed me. That was all. I hadn't expected it, but I liked it. I'd met him so many times, at the house, and he was always so nice to me, so friendly. He said I was looking very pretty. He held my hand, told me how soft it was. He made me feel ... special.'

'You said that was the first time? Were there other times, Janey?'

She nodded again. 'A few.'

'When Becky was out?'

'I started going round when I knew she wouldn't be there. Just for half an hour sometimes, to say hello. And once ... I stayed all night. I slept in his bed. I liked being with him, I liked it being our secret. I thought maybe he wanted me to be his girlfriend. He said he liked me. A lot.'

'And you slept together that night, in his bed? Had sex?'

She nodded. 'Yeah. And sometimes in the car, when he drove me home, and we stopped off somewhere on the way. It felt nice, natural. Like it was meant to be.'

'So natural he didn't even use a condom?'

'He asked me if I was, you know, on the pill. And I said I was. I didn't want him to think of me as some silly child.'

'Oh, Janey. That *was* silly though, wasn't it? You took a terrible risk. And he should have known better. You're only fourteen! And now he has the nerve to say he's angry with you?'

'He doesn't want another child, that's what he said.'

'*Another* child? You mean he's done this before? He's already a father?'

She nodded.

'And he's older than you by what? Only three years?'

I looked down at my hands. One on her shoulder, now gripping her so hard I was afraid I might hurt her. The other still clutching the roses.

She looked puzzled for a moment. 'Three years?'

'Well, I assume we're talking about Samuel, Becky's brother, and he's seventeen, isn't he?'

'No. It wasn't Becky's brother. Yuck! Why would you think that? It was her dad. Arnie.'

Chapter 32

SARAH

Janey disappeared for a while after the funeral. It had been a traumatic enough day already, and I couldn't see any point in coming down hard on her, laying down the law. If she wanted to get out of the house, escape the claustrophobia for a while, I wasn't going to stop her. It wasn't as if she could get into trouble, was it? She'd already managed that. And that was the next worry I had to confront. Recovering from my surgery, the skin on my palms still sore, the flashback nightmares still invading my sleep, it had been all I could do just to get through the funeral, but now I knew something had to be done about Janey's pregnancy, and the sooner the better. Every day that went by, every centimetre that baby grew, the decision would get harder. Or it would be too late for a decision to be an option at all.

We hadn't told Josh's parents anything. Not even about our separation. Divorce was not a word that had been allowed to enter their world, let alone adultery, and neither Josh nor I had figured out how to broach the subject. As far as they were

425

concerned, we had still lived together, happily married, in this house, until the end. The photos on the mantelpiece and his coat and shoes in the hall, retrieved from the flat just days ago, did nothing to dispel the myth.

If I were to tell them about Janey, I already knew what they would say. Their church, their conscience, their rigid views, had played a huge part in the decision Josh and I had made all those years ago, and I couldn't allow any of that to influence Janey's choices now. Abortion was a much more real option this time, probably the only workable and sensible option at Janey's age, but they wouldn't see things that way. I poured his mum another cup of tea, her hands trembling as she held the cup, her eyes red-rimmed and puffy, and watched his dad fiddling with his car keys. It was a long drive back. They wouldn't be staying much longer. And then, hopefully, Janey and I could deal with things, and they need never know.

Eve hadn't hung around after the service, hadn't approached us or tried to say anything. I couldn't decide if that was her being diplomatic and caring, not wanting to risk a scene, or if she was just being downright cowardly. Yet a part of me longed for her to be here, the big sister I could lean on, the wise one who would know just what to do, taking over the nitty-gritty stuff I couldn't cope with, as she had when Mum died, and injecting some of the strength I so badly needed but knew I lacked.

Janey loved her, and always had. Dad might be angry with her now, but he would come around. He had never been able to stay angry for long, not when it came to the precious daughters he had always insisted he loved in equal measure.

No, Eve would be forgiven and welcomed back into the fold. And I wanted that too, to be supported and protected and loved as part of that close little group we called family, but she had lied to me. Again. I missed her so much, especially now, but I just couldn't trust her.

I closed the door on the final guests soon after seven. Kisses, hugs, condolences, all over again. It was a cold November evening, starless dark, the skies still heavy with the threat of more rain, and all I wanted was to curl up on the sofa and be by myself. To let the events of the day sink in, to give in to the many conflicting feelings that came flooding in, and were in danger of overwhelming me. Pain, disbelief, anger, sorrow, fear, exhaustion and, much as I knew I could never admit to it now that it was all over, a growing sense of relief.

Colin had texted an hour or so before to see how I was, how the day had gone, but I hadn't replied. This was Josh's day and it wouldn't seem right to spend any part of it communicating with the man I hoped might one day be his replacement. God, how callous that made me sound.

When I heard the front door opening, I looked up, expecting it to be Janey. She'd been out for a while. She'd be hungry. What I hadn't expected was to see Eve standing there beside her. They were holding hands.

'Sarah ...' She hesitated, probably as unsure as I was about how I might react. 'Can I come in? Only, there's something we need to tell you.'

We? Since when had she and my daughter been a *we?* Talk about feeling excluded in my own home. But there was something about the look on Janey's face, and the way she clung to Eve's hand, that made me relent. I nodded and sat myself up, beckoning them both in.

'I'm sorry I didn't ... earlier. Well, you know how things are. I wasn't sure I would be welcome, and all I really needed to do was say goodbye in my own way. I didn't want to intrude.'

'But you're okay about intruding now?'

'It's not like that. This is about Janey, not you and me, not Josh.'

'What about Janey?'

Eve slid her car keys into her bag and perched herself on the edge of an armchair. 'Has Dad gone?'

'He was tired. We all were. There's just me.'

'Janey's told me something.' She pulled Janey closer, their knees touching, although Janey seemed to want to remain standing. 'About the baby.'

'Has she?' I turned towards my daughter who so far hadn't said a word. 'Janey?' I held my arms out to her and she stumbled into them, the big gulping breaths as she sobbed out loud pressing up and down against my chest. 'It's all right, Janey. You can tell me. I love you. We've still got each other and, whatever it is, it will be all right, I promise you.'

***

I so wish Eve had told me, all those years ago, about Arnie O'Connor. How had she gone through something like that, a sexual assault that had frightened the life out of her, and not told anyone except Lucy? Not Mum and Dad, not the police, not even me, her own sister. I tried to think back to that night, but nothing stood out. Nothing brought it to mind as any different from other nights. She must have come home from the party late, gone to bed as normal and just kept it all inside, all that hurt and confusion and shame, and I hadn't noticed a thing. Fast asleep, probably. And the next day, the next night, the next week, too busy with my own life, my petty jealousies, my hurt feelings because she was about to go off to uni and leave me behind, to see what was right in front of my face. What sort of a sister did that make me?

It explained a lot, of course. Her hiding away those last few weeks before she left, the absence of boyfriends, both then and now, the way she had kept even Josh, the so-called love of her life, at arm's length for so long he'd turned to me instead.

And now, here he was again. Arnie O'Connor, all grown up, but still that same evil self-centred man. Without a woman in his life – oh, how I would love to know why his wife left him – and no doubt needing to feed his ego, his appetites ... Not needing to resort to force this time, but putting on the charm, pretending to be kind, smarming his way into a young girl's affections, into her knickers, into his bed. And not just any young girl. His daughter's best friend. How sick and twisted is that? How could he do it? *Why* would he do it? Did it make him feel more of a man? The big comforting father figure he knew full well she was missing? Being what she needed, making her believe he cared? I shuddered to think how much worse it might have been if she had tried to resist him, the way Eve had ...

The police took it all very seriously. Took statements.

Brought in a specialist officer, a woman, who asked Janey questions, gently, sensitively. He denied it, of course. Put it all down to the wild imaginings of a silly young girl with a crush. What evidence did they have, after all? But the evidence was there, growing inside her, and with it the DNA that we knew would prove it was all true. So what if she was willing, what if she gave consent? He made out the whole thing had been her idea, that she had taken the lead. Would anyone really believe that? The lies and excuses poured out of him, but the facts were indisputable. He was thirty-eight. And she was fourteen. It was against the law, and the law was not going to let him get away with it.

Six months later

Becky didn't go back to school. We heard that, since Arnie's arrest, she and her brother had moved back permanently to live with their mother and had been enrolled elsewhere. Janey wrote her a long letter, telling her she missed her and didn't blame her at all, but it was never answered.

Eve's boss had a stroke and decided to retire, and she was offered the headship which, after a few anxious days of self-doubt, she agreed to accept. She's been seeing a lot of Lucy, I think mainly because she loves playing with her little godson so much. Simon and Gregory drive over regularly to visit now too, and Eve tells me they are thinking of trying to adopt, so hopefully she'll soon have another godchild to dote on. I do feel sorry that she never had children of her own, but she's not forty yet. It's not too late. Maybe, in time ...

With both her best friends back in her life and a new challenging job to really get her teeth into, I don't think I've ever seen her more settled and more positive about her life. The statement she gave to the police about what Arnie did to her when she was eighteen might all come to nothing. It's not easy to prove something from that long ago, but just doing it has made her feel better, freer, more in control, and he's going to prison anyway, no matter what.

There's still no love interest in her life, but I think it's going to take her a long time to get over Josh (longer than it will take me, that's for sure) and she's always been more than a little in love with her career. Janey is in her English class now, coming home waving paint charts and poetry books about, and loves every minute.

And Janey's baby? She couldn't go through with having it. Not once she knew the truth about its father and had had time to consider the effect it would have on her life, her education, her future. It was her decision, not mine, just as it had to be, although I admit I breathed a massive sigh of relief when she made it. It was probably the decision I should have been brave enough to make for myself when I'd been in her position all that time ago, if only the Catholic in-laws and the raging hormones and the stupid trying to get one up on my sister hadn't led me in the opposite direction.

The abortion was traumatic and emotional, as I'm sure any abortion must be, but we both went with her, Eve and me, and saw her through it, tears and all. And then we went home and put her to bed and sat up for hours drinking and reminiscing. About the good times we'd had as kids, walking old Buster the dog, the two of us decorating the Christmas tree, and how much we still missed Mum. Josh's name wasn't mentioned at all.

Slowly, we've slipped back into sisterhood. The only thing that had kept us apart, put us at loggerheads on so many occasions, made us into suspicious rivals and reluctant enemies, had been Josh, and now he's gone.

The evening I introduced her to Colin, I watched her every move. I couldn't let her swoop in on another man and take him from me. But of course, I was being ridiculous. Eve has no interest in Colin, other than as the man she can see is making me happy again. I didn't tell her, or Janey, that our relationship had begun longer ago than I let them assume. As far as they knew, we had met at the hospital, while I was recovering. A patient, already separated from her husband, meets a handsome single doctor and six months later starts to date him. It could have come straight from a Mills & Boon. Even Janey approves.

I still have nightmares though. I don't particularly like sleeping alone. The dark closes in, and the flames flare up again, and I feel the heat on my hands, where the scars still map out their story.

Tonight we drank too much Merlot, Eve and me, and she couldn't risk driving home. For the first time since we were teenagers, we are sharing a room, lying next to each other in my double bed with the curtains open, looking out at the inky black sky.

'Do you remember how we used to make stars?' I whisper, not sure if she's still awake.

She stretches out her legs in a V, bumping one into mine, and then does the same with her arms.

'Reaching out for our own dreams but always close enough to touch.' She links her fingers through mine.

'We're okay now, aren't we?' I say.

'Yes, Sprout. I think we are,' she mumbles as she drifts off to sleep.

There's no bond like it. Sisters. We had come so close to breaking it forever, but we're back. She's even calling me by my old childhood nickname again. Sprout! I like it. Now all I have to do is find a way to stop the nightmares, the memories, the horror, that still finds me, even on nights like this when all feels so right with the world. But I can't stop them. I never can.

I see it all happening again, as I always do, like a play being acted out on the inside of my eyelids. The lorry hurtling towards us, its horn blaring. The car rolling, out of control, crashing into the tree. The broken glass, the smell of petrol, the wisps of smoke. I look across at Josh, his head lolling forward, his eyes closed, and I am so scared. I manage to open the door, crawl out, hobble round to his side of the car. I hurt. There is a stabbing pain in my stomach, and in my leg. People are coming. Shouting. Telling me to get back, wait for the ambulance, the fire engines.

It's hot now. I push the duvet back to try to get some air. There are flames creeping, licking at the engine and I can see him, inside the car, my car, his eyes flickering open, his hand trying to lift itself, pushing at the steering wheel that's crushing against his chest. I have seconds, just seconds to open that door and pull him out. Seconds to save my husband. I grab the door handle. It feels stiff, hard, hot. It burns. He's looking out at me, frightened, his eyes pleading for help. But I don't do it. I can't do it. I can't help him, can't forgive him, can't save him. He has hurt me too badly. The fire is too fierce. If I stay, it's going to take me too.

I let go of the door as the flames leap higher and engulf the car. Someone grabs me from behind and pulls me away as everything explodes.

I wake up sweating, shaking, Eve still asleep beside me, blissfully unaware of what's happening in my head. Of what I have done. I lie there for a while, waiting for my breathing to slow, looking at the ceiling. *My* ceiling now. *My* bedroom. *My* house. All mine. I have the bank account, the life insurance money, the pension. I have my daughter, sad but whole again, with her life stretching out ahead of her, full of all the possibilities I so casually threw away. We hadn't started the divorce, nothing was official, so in the eyes of the law, and of his parents, we were married to the end. Surrounded by his things, I can almost pretend he never left. Those months we lived apart were simply a twist in time, a temporary hiccup, a bump in the road. He was still my husband. I was still his wife. But not anymore. I am a widow now.

Widow. I hate the word. It smacks of black cloaks and closed blinds and musty flowers and bereavement cards, but it's what I am. Not exactly a merry widow, but certainly a recovering one who has already thrown off the bleak black clothes and is wearing red again.

And, at last, I have my sister back. I close my eyes, pull the duvet up to my chin and try to sleep, feeling her warm toes lying next to my cold ones, her gentle breathing, tinged with the stale waft of wine, against my neck, her body still star-shaped beside me. It feels just like old times. Good times.

They say I'm a heroine, that I risked my own life to try to save Josh's, but it's not true. Maybe I could have – should have – tried harder, tugged harder at that handle, but I didn't. I let go. And I let him go too.

Because, sometimes, when everything else seems lost, the only thing you can do is save yourself.

THE END

Acknowledgements

First of all, I must thank Irving Berlin. Not that we ever met (I have never been to America and he has been dead for more than thirty years), but it was the lyrics of his song 'Sisters', written in 1954 for the movie 'White Christmas', that sparked the idea for this novel. When two sisters are close, there's usually only one thing that is likely to come between them – a man they both have their eye on! As the song says, 'God help the mister who comes between me and my sister ...' Copyright rules prevent me from quoting much more, but I'm sure you know the rest.

I come from a family of sisters. For the last four generations, my direct family line has not seen the birth of a single boy. My mum was one of two sisters and so was I. When my dad embarked on a second marriage late in life, what happened? Yes, another baby girl was born, adding a half-sister to the mix. Then I had twin girls, and now my younger daughter has two little girls of her own. So a big shout-out to all of them, and to sisters everywhere. It's a unique bond, based on the sharing of bedrooms, secrets and hand-me-down clothes, with love, friendship and usually a fair amount of rivalry thrown in. As sibling relationships go, I know no other.

As I emerge from my study, after months of scribbling and tapping away at my novel with just my characters, my goldfish, and a secret stash of chocolate for company, my thanks must go to my husband, Paul, who doesn't usually have a clue what it is I am writing about, rarely reads any of it, and is the first to admit he could never do it himself in a million years. His idea of a good read tends to be of the action thriller kind, involving air disasters or car chases, so when it comes to fiction we are not really on the same page, but he fully supports me just the same, I think in the vain hope that the proceeds of a future bestseller might just allow me one day to buy him a Lamborghini!

As always, I owe a huge debt to the various writers' groups and societies to which I belong, especially the Society of Women Writers and Journalists (SWWJ) which celebrated its 125th anniversary in 2019 and recently did me the honour of making me a Fellow. And love and thanks must also go to my many fiction-writing and romantic novelist friends, especially the ones I meet up with in real life rather than just on Facebook, who continue to encourage and support each other through the perilous ups and downs on the bumpy but always exciting journey to publication we all share. You all know who you are.

Thanks also to my editor and friend Kate Bradley – especially as, sadly, this is the last book we will be working on together – and to publisher Charlotte Ledger, assistant editor Bethan Morgan, copy editor Lydia Mason, and the whole team at One More Chapter for continuing to believe in me and to publish and promote my books.

I am eternally grateful too, to all the book bloggers, reviewers, and especially the readers, who say such lovely things about my novels. I don't mind whether you read on a screen, buy the paperback or borrow it from the library, as long as you keep turning the pages and enjoying the story inside. It's a scary, nail-biting moment when a new novel gets released into the world, and I do hope that this one has lived up to expectations. If you liked it, please take a moment to share your thoughts on Amazon or Goodreads. Even a very short review means so much. Authors and their work, and the sheer joy of reading and talking about books, could not continue to thrive and grow without you, the readers. Of all the hundreds of thousands of novels published every year, thank you so much for choosing to read mine.